A POISONING
at CASTLE GLOAMING

Also by Kay Blythe

Murder at Merry Beggars Hall

Writing as Natalie Meg Evans

The Dress Thief
The Milliner's Secret
The Wardrobe Mistress
A Gown of Thorns
The Secret Vow
The Paris Girl
Into the Burning Dawn
The Italian Girl's Secret
The Girl with the Yellow Star
The Locket
The Paris Inheritance

KAY BLYTHE

A POISONING at CASTLE GLOAMING

NO EXIT PRESS

First published in the UK in 2025 by No Exit Press,
an imprint of Bedford Square Publishers Ltd,
London, UK

noexit.co.uk
@noexitpress

ISBN
978-1-83501-214-7 (Paperback)
978-1-83501-215-4 (eBook)

2 4 6 8 10 9 7 5 3 1

Printed in Great Britain by CPI Group (UK) Ltd, Croydon CR0 4YY

The manufacturer's authorised representative in the EU for
product safety is Easy Access System Europe, Mustamäe tee 50, 10621
Tallinn, Estonia
gpsr.requests@easproject.com

This story is dedicated to my dear friend Jeremy Blackham, whose knowledge of seamanship was generously shared. I was again awed that one person can know so much. His patience with questions such as 'How fast is fifteen knots?' spared my blushes. Any factual errors in the story ahead are my own, attributed to my habit of writing notes in shorthand on scraps of paper.

From *The Weekend Sleuth*, available by subscription, price threepence.

The greatest barrier to solving a riddle is going to it with the answer already in your head.

You see a man cycling along with a bulging canvas bag over his shoulder and are told he is a thief. What has he stolen?

'Whatever is in the bag,' you say. 'Make the scoundrel empty it at once!'

He empties the bag, revealing nothing but sawdust.

'Ah, then he's stealing those sturdy canvas bags,' you declare.

'He is not,' says the woman who stands at her gate, watching the comings and goings on the road. 'He's stealing bicycles.'

Never assume, never presume.

Quote from a letter appearing in January 1923,
submitted by Mrs J. L. Flowerday

Chapter One

May 1922, The Royal Mail Ship
Llanstephan Castle
Off Cape Agulhas, Africa

At the rails of the boat deck, she pointed a half-bottle of champagne into the night and fired its cork at the brightest star. Holding the bottle to her lips as the ship steamed through the swell, she imagined herself on horseback, riding towards freedom. Here, at the most southerly tip of Africa, two oceans met, a warm and a cold current blinding each other with sound and fury. A pathway shone to the black-velvet horizon, made by the moon and the ship's lights, and her heart was crammed with possibility. A month from now she'd step into the life she had promised herself.

'Here's to the Union Castle Line.' She drank and let the bubbles dance down to her stomach, then laughed. Sirius, the dog star, shone brighter than all the others. Canopus gleamed above the horizon. What lay ahead was as mysterious as these celestial spheres, but when this ship docked at its home port of Southampton, England, she would get off and there'd be no going back.

She heard a bump a few yards away and peered towards it, seeing nothing but the moonlit rail. Maybe she'd heard the creak of the davits that secured the lifeboats, or the wind punching between the funnels. Only when she heard a door close, followed by a voice rasping, 'Portside,' did she realise she was no longer alone. She sank into a crouch behind a lifeboat, making herself small so her white collar and cuffs would not catch the moonlight and give her away. To be found in the early hours outside her cabin would bring trouble and nothing, *nothing*, must impede her now.

Was it passengers or crew out on deck? She could hear footsteps and a dragging sound, and bursts of muttered conversation. From the different vocal pitches, she gleaned it was a couple, a man and woman. Out for a kiss under the stars?

The man said, 'Take off my jacket.'

It was impossible to hear the response because the ship plunged into a trough and she grabbed a rope that hung from the lifeboat. She tumbled against the rail and only its robust bars stopped her from going overboard.

The motion had caught the couple unawares, by the sound of it. She heard the woman uttering, 'God, oh, God.' The man answering and the woman saying, 'Watch.'

Then silence, until she heard a slithering sound that reminded her of school dormitories, girls moving restlessly on canvas camp beds. That unbearable, raspy, fingernail sound...

A gasp, a grunt, and as the wind paused for breath, a hard, heavy splash.

She shut her eyes as feet stealthily re-crossed the boat deck. A door opened. It was the one to the second-class smoking lounge. It creaked, then gently shut.

Chapter Two

Jemima Flowerday followed a well-worn path to the canal. A friendly ticket inspector at the station had directed her to follow it westward, but not to venture onto the aqueduct.

'It is the tallest in the world, madam, and not for the fainthearted.'

When she saw its arches straddling the river valley, she must 'cross the water twice' and look for a tower above the trees. That would be Castle Gloaming.

'To cross the water twice' called up childhood fantasies of magical kingdoms whose doorways were hidden to all but the chosen. Whether she was chosen or not, it felt good to be moving after a two-day train journey. It was sometime past midday, and Jemima had sent her trunks ahead so she might walk unhindered. Bright sunshine pierced canopies of alder, willow and oak. She stepped carefully over their roots and hopscotched some puddles. It must have rained in the last few days and the air was as soft as muslin unpegged from the line.

Jack-by-the-hedge and cow parsley, edging past their peak, cast scents of garlic and warm milk. Spring seemed to be rushing away to make space for summer. On both banks, reeds and clumps of yellow-flowered flag sheltered nesting moorhens. Arrowheads of ducks moved serenely until a boat came around a bend of the canal and sent them to the sides. Pulled by a black-and-white horse with a bobbed tail and long mane, the boat's midsection was filled with coal. The man at the stern responded to Jemima's cheerful, 'Good afternoon,' with a cautious raise of the hand. She'd said it in Welsh, having learned several phrases on the train from London.

Her visitor's guide was a fund of information and, from reading it carefully, she knew that Castle Gloaming had been built seven hundred years ago by a Welsh prince as a stronghold against the English. It stood above the banks of the River Dee and the only way to it was by boat, on foot or by horse. 'Though a kindly rider will lead his mount the last part of the way', the guidebook advised. The fact that her trunks had been collected from the station by a lad from the castle, in a pony cart, bore this out. Jemima could have had the lad come back to pick her up, but walking was the surest way to get the lie of the land, and Castle Gloaming intrigued her... a Scottish-sounding name in a Welsh landscape? Her guide-book reported that its ruins had been restored in the last century by the first Earl of Muirhaven, who had renamed it to reflect his Scots heritage, though a stern note warned visitors not to ask for Castle Gloaming but for Castell Glan yr Afon. Anything else would earn a glowering look from a Welsh speaker.

Jemima hoped for a friendly welcome, despite the shortfall in her Welsh. She had been invited to the castle by Mrs Cornelia van Doorn, with an offer of a generous fee, to design a wardrobe of clothes for herself and her stepdaughter. A society dressmaker in London's Mayfair, Jemima wasn't averse to taking a short break somewhere new and fascinating. She was well ahead in her other commissions; her children, Tommy and Molly, were back at school; and a few days before she'd paid her monthly visit to the hospital where her husband was a permanent invalid. Her sister Vicky was minding the business so, all in all, this was as good a time as any for a holiday.

Striding along in a skirt of caramel jersey, a wrap-over coat with a fob button and pockets large enough to hide a rabbit – the last word in *now* – a tan cloche hat and kidskin gloves, she felt anonymous and wonderfully free... free to speculate on the character and identity of her client.

'Van Doorn is Dutch,' Vicky had surmised after reading the letter that had arrived from Castle Gloaming a few days before. 'I wonder how a "Mrs van Doorn" comes to be living in Wales.'

Jemima had suggested she might be an American of Dutch ancestry. 'And has bought a castle because it's what adventurous Americans do. Her letter mentions that she and her stepdaughter wish to launch themselves socially. Naturally, they need to be dressed. All in a fearful hurry... people do leave things very late. I'm being offered a week's stay to create my designs, after which I'll come home and swing into production. Mrs van Doorn intends to take a London house for the season.'

'The terms?' Vicky managed their household accounts.

'A hundred pounds plus my travel. I know. It's excessive.'

'Too good to be true! What if it goes wrong? You'll be stuck hundreds of miles from home,' Vicky had pointed out. 'Do castles have telephones?'

'Oh, I do hope not.' London life was so busy, Jemima secretly craved a spell of seclusion.

A flash of blue, and a kingfisher broke the canal's surface. Willow fronds shivered in its wake. A cormorant perched on a submerged branch, apparently staring at its own reflection, clattered into flight. A few paces on, a gap in the trees created a natural viewpoint, and Jemima gasped.

The aqueduct. She'd imagined arches and a parapet, like those she'd seen in France during her honeymoon before the war. But this structure, spanning the River Dee, had arches that, even at a distance, seemed to rise to mythical height. The sight of a lone narrowboat edging along it made her feel quite giddy. Thank goodness she'd been warned not to go that way. Imagine, being halfway to heaven and nothing to stop you rolling off the edge. She walked on, turning every few paces to look again at this eighth wonder... until she went flying and landed on her back on the grass.

Getting to her feet, she realised she'd tripped over the mooring line of a narrowboat drawn up against the bank. She brushed herself down. Had anyone seen her make a fool of herself? There was no sign of anybody inside the boat, not even when Jemima peered in at the cabin window.

It had an interesting name: *Miss Nettle*. On the cabin roof was a metal bucket filled with bunches of a plant Jemima identified as flat-leaf parsley.

'How delightfully herbal,' she murmured and continued on her way. She crossed a stone bridge and then a meadow to a second bridge. She had reached the river. On its far side, marooned in dense woodland, rose a tower.

Castell Glan yr Afon. Castle Gloaming.

'Take the stony path that goes uphill, then another and keep climbing.' The friendly ticket inspector had grimaced at this point and added, 'Good luck.'

Chapter Three

Jemima paused halfway across the river to watch a million gallons of the Dee race beneath the bridge. The current looked dangerous, the waters brown except where they exploded into surf against the stone piers. From here, she could see the aqueduct as a perfect straight line. After watching the toy-like narrowboat complete its journey into the haze, she went on her way.

She found an uphill path that cut through the wood and soon learned there had been no exaggeration of its steepness. Fortunately for her shoes and her appearance generally, it was a short climb and she emerged onto the castle mound. A turreted gatehouse rose up before her, a traditional barbican with turrets either side of a great door. She crossed a dry moat and stopped at the door which, with its iron rivets and reinforcements, looked far too heavy for her to open unaided. She yanked on a bellpull and waited.

Three times she clanged the bell before the door swung inwards. She had time to imagine a man-at-arms with a staff in his hand. What she got was a well-built man with black, curly hair receding slightly at the temples, and arresting eyes in a sunburned face. His clothing suggested the outdoor life; a waistcoat and a plaid shirt tucked into corduroy jodhpurs, which in turn were pushed into riding boots. His throat, what she could see under a blue neckerchief, bore the freckling of too much sun. She put his age at around forty.

His piercing grey gaze made her wonder if she ought to have gone to a different entrance. She was about to ask when he looked past her to the path she'd come up, as if he expected others to be following.

'Are you the one who wrote the letter?'

The abrupt question threw her. Jemima wrote a great many in the course of her work, and four had passed between her and Mrs van Doorn. Without knowing which one he meant, she could not satisfy him and so she answered simply, 'I'm Mrs Jemima Flowerday, the couturière from London.'

'That's what I meant. The famous J.L. Flowerday.' He shook his head, as if he believed she was being deliberately obtuse. 'I'll take you to Cornelia. Where's your luggage?'

'Delivered, I hope.'

'Good.'

His accent was unfamiliar to Jemima. Not English, not Welsh. No time to be curious as a sweep of the hand invited her to follow him down the passageway between the turrets. So far, her impression of Castle Gloaming was decidedly unfriendly. Glancing up, Jemima saw traces of an opening and an iron grille and wondered if it had been the chute through which molten lead was poured, in darker times, onto the heads of unwelcome visitors.

Her guide continued at a cracking pace across a flagged court-yard, giving her little time to appreciate the castle keep, except to note that the lower part was built of lichen-mottled stone while the upper floors were constructed from newer blocks. Square-bayed windows filled with tinted glass suggested that a substantial reno-vation had taken place; she wasn't about to enter a crumbling ruin. She wasn't sure if she was disappointed or not.

Six shallow steps led to an oak door whose mouldings looked

recently carved. The man – a steward, perhaps? – turned a hoop handle and walked inside. Jemima followed and stifled a gasp. How unexpected.

The entrance hall was vast, with a domed ceiling of sky blue. Within the blueness birds of paradise flew and soared. So cleverly painted, for a moment Jemima thought she'd stepped into an aviary. A mezzanine, supported by gilded columns and reached by a wide staircase, ran all the way around the great hall which had a marble mosaic floor. No time to admire, as her guide knocked at a door. Half opening it, he waited for her to catch up.

'This is where Cornelia likes to sit after lunch.' He gave her another of those piercing glances. 'You're fermenting a question.'

She smiled in apology. 'You're right. I can't place your voice. Something tells me you were not born here?'

'In Wales? No. Not in England either.' He gestured up at the birds of paradise. 'Like them, I was lured here and now I'm stuck.'

It seemed an odd thing to say to a stranger, but Jemima didn't have time to interrogate him further as he ushered her into a room that, like the great hall, was heavily gilded. Its focal point was an immense fireplace with a beaten-copper hood that shone in the sunlight streaming through richly tinted glass. Sofas and chairs were arranged as they often were in state rooms, facing each other and plentiful, but giving little impression of comfort. With so much to look at, it took Jemima a second to realise that a woman was seated on the sofa facing her – until she rose with a hand outstretched.

'Mrs Flowerday? I am Cornelia van Doorn and I am so, so happy to see you.'

'And I you,' said Jemima, returning the handshake. 'A pleasure to meet you at last.'

Cornelia van Doorn was small, around sixty years of age and still with claims to beauty. She wore a drop waist dress of lemon chiffon over an ivory silk base. Her hair was silvery white, gathered behind her head in a low bun. Diamonds glittered on her fingers, and one wrist was encircled by a bracelet of the same. Her style made a clear nod towards wealth, though not ostentation. The dress was Parisian, or a good copy, Jemima decided. Her accent, though… it was similar to the man's. He had retreated, closing the door behind him. Jemima felt emboldened to say, 'I've come a long way from London, but I suspect you've travelled further than I to reach Castell Glan yr Afon.'

'We call it Castle Gloaming, for ease.' Mrs van Doorn invited Jemima to sit on the sofa facing her. 'I cannot get my tongue around the Welsh language, though in Mrs Beddoe's hearing, we say, "the castle". Mrs Beddoe is the housekeeper,' Mrs van Doorn explained, adding seamlessly, 'yes, I have come all the way from Cape Town.'

That explained the Dutch-sounding name. Much of present South Africa had once been under Dutch colonial rule.

'The gentleman who showed me in?' Jemima asked.

'That was Lord Muirhaven.'

The present earl? Goodness. How looks deceived. 'I'm afraid I assumed he was some kind of paid retainer.'

To Jemima's relief, Mrs van Doorn smiled. 'That's his own fault. He dresses like a farmer. You see, he was exactly that most of his life, never brought up to expect the title. He was born and lived in the Cape, though on the other side from me. East coast, near Durban.'

Jemima rustled up a mental map of Africa. 'Cape Town is on the west?'

'Yes, on the Atlantic side.'

Jemima asked how Mrs van Doorn found herself so far from her native land.

'I came for the sake of my stepdaughter, Honor. Our intention was to reside in London, but then the offer came to take a lease on this place. A castle, who could resist?'

Anybody who has ever tried to live in one, was Jemima's private response, but it was too early to be flippant so she gave a social nod, adding, 'You are the earl's tenant and I presume he lives in the gatehouse?' She'd had time to notice, as she waited to be admitted, that the arrow-slit windows of the barbican were glazed, with the hint of curtains behind.

'He does,' the lady confirmed. 'The arrangement works well as he dines with us each day, but otherwise refrains from interfering. That isn't to say I'm confined here.'

'Which is where I come in,' Jemima suggested. She was conscious of her damp shoes on the cream-and-pink Chinese carpet and the grass stains on her hands from her tumble earlier, and suggested she freshen up before getting down to business. 'Your stepdaughter, Mrs van Doorn... when may I have the pleasure of meeting her?'

'We... she...' Mrs van Doorn sent an agonised glance up to the ceiling. 'She...'

Oh, good Lord, what was coming? To Jemima's dismay, Mrs van Doorn burst into tears.

Chapter Four

The storm did not last long. Mrs van Doorn dried her eyes and gave Jemima a wan smile. 'Forgive me.'

'Something has upset you, and I presume your stepdaughter is involved.'

The door opened and a woman entered, giving her opinion as she came in. 'Not only is Miss van Doorn involved, she's the cause of our current muddle. Hello. You must be our London guest.' The newcomer was a shade older than Jemima, in her mid-thirties, dressed in a navy jumper and slim skirt, a string of pearls at the neck and a silver watch on her left wrist. Fair curls were cut short in the *garçon* style. A little unevenness suggested that she'd wielded the scissors herself, and Jemima supposed it would be easier to find a sheep shearer round here than a hairdresser. They shook hands, but it was Mrs van Doorn who finished the introductions.

'This is Mrs Cleeve, my secretary. My helpmeet in all things. Elaine dear, I was breaking the news gently to Mrs Flowerday and you have rather jumped in the puddle.'

'Oh. Apologies.' Mrs Cleeve sat down next to Jemima and asked eagerly, 'You are going to help?'

Now Jemima was worried. Tears were not unknown in her line of work. The taking of measurements often required clients to stand for long periods, and seeing their head-to-toe reflection in underclothes for the perhaps first time in years brought out all kinds of emotions. But Mrs van Doorn's tears had come early and Mrs Cleeve's comment had muddied things further.

'I came here to design new clothes for two ladies with London ambitions,' she said. Her tone implied, 'That, and no more.'

'Exactly as I intended—' agreed Mrs van Doorn, in a way that suggested that something had occurred beyond her control. Something she couldn't bring herself to say.

Mrs Cleeve cut in. 'The bare fact is, she's gone.'

Mrs van Doorn leaned forward eagerly. 'Mrs Flowerday, we want you to find her.'

Jemima could almost hear Vicky saying, 'Now get out of this one.' Ha. Jemima had no intention of getting *into* it.

'If your stepdaughter has gone and you're worried, you must alert the police. Unless you've done so already.'

'No, no, no!' Lines appeared either side of Mrs van Doorn's eyes, wrecking the illusion of well-preserved beauty. 'No police. The moment they're involved fingers will point and gossip will start. From that, it's a short step to seeing our names in the newspaper.' She drew Jemima across to her own sofa to sit beside her. 'You know how it is, Mrs Flowerday. Let a girl get a reputation for being wayward, she never sheds it. Scandal will ruin Honor's future chances. We want her back, safe and sound, without setting rumours going.'

'Is your stepdaughter wayward?'

'Honor was always a good, quiet girl,' Mrs van Doorn assured her. 'But I'm afraid her head was turned.'

'By whom?' Jemima had seen four people since leaving the railway station, and three of them were residents of the castle.

Mrs van Doorn sighed deeply. 'We sailed to England just over a year ago. Honor's first time out of the country of her birth was the month-long voyage to Southampton. Before then, she'd been at a girls' day school. I wanted her to remember the voyage as a time of enjoyment.'

'Who exactly did your stepdaughter mix with?' Jemima could imagine Vicky rolling her eyes. *Don't get involved.* Trouble was, mysteries were addictive. It wouldn't hurt to know a little background.

'I permitted her to befriend other young people. Those in first class, naturally,' said Mrs van Doorn.

'Male and female?'

'Yes. A little set formed itself. We older ones looked on indulgently at first, but within the group were young women who, shall I say, displayed radical ideas.' Mrs van Doorn touched the silvery waves at her temple. 'New women. Hair cropped short like boys. Dresses that all but showed their knees. There was dancing of a sort I do not understand. I didn't want to disapprove, Mrs Flowerday, but a breath of sea air cannot change the scruples of a lifetime.'

Mrs Cleeve spoke up, sounding rather more pragmatic. 'They call themselves "bright young things" and, I daresay, they are.'

Jemima translated what she had heard: On the voyage from South Africa, Mrs van Doorn's old-world values had crashed head on with those of the post-war age. Young people had flocked to play deck quoits and laugh at each other's jokes. In the first-class ballroom, rather than waltz like their parents, they had the band strike up the Charleston or something syncopated. Young men in blazers with floppy hair had jigged about with girls with shingled curls and dresses that showed stockings rolled and fastened beneath the knee. For Honor van Doorn, fresh out of school, this freedom must have been, to misquote Charles Dickens, a glimpse of very heaven.

'You think she's run away to rejoin these friends?'

14

'We don't know,' answered Mrs Cleeve. 'That's what we want you to find out.'

Jemima took out one of her business cards and invited Mrs Cleeve to inspect it.

'Fleur du Jour,' the secretary read out loud. 'I'm afraid I don't speak French.'

'It is my business name,' Jemima explained. 'As the card states, I am a peripatetic couturière. A dressmaker who is prepared to travel.' She put emphasis on 'dressmaker'.

Mrs van Doorn, scrunching her handkerchief in her fingers, explained to her secretary that 'Fleur du Jour' was a play upon Jemima's name before adding, 'All this we know, Mrs Flowerday, but what your calling card does *not* say is that you have an interesting sideline.'

Jemima drew in a small breath. 'And that would be...?'

'Solving mysteries.'

How did this woman know? Not six months ago, Jemima had helped crack a particularly grisly case at Merry Beggars Hall in Suffolk. Yet she'd told nobody but her sister, and Vicky was discretion incarnate. Many years ago, Jemima had saved a young colleague from a charge of arson in the department store they worked in by painstakingly tracking every staff members' movements in the minutes before the fire began. More recently, she had exposed the milkman, who had been methodically charging every resident of her street for a phantom extra pint of milk per month. Jemima took pride in these triumphs, but could not imagine how her hostess knew of them.

For a moment, she teetered on the brink of walking out. However, fits of pique were not really an option when so far from home, so she sighed and asked, 'Who told you?'

Mrs Cleeve answered. 'You yourself, in a manner of speaking. We'd seen your advertisement in *The Queen* as a society dressmaker, and then we stumbled on this.' Leaving her seat, she fetched a tabloid magazine from a bookcase and brought it to Jemima.

It was *The Weekend Sleuth*, a true-crime journal Jemima read the way a schoolchild consumes adventure stories under the covers after lights-out. Privately, she admitted to being addicted to its torrid prose and scene-of-crime sketches. Vicky blamed it for stoking 'an unhealthy compulsion' for solving mysteries. Jemima stared at Mrs van Doorn and Elaine Cleeve in wonderment. Had she met two like-minded addicts?

Her hostess dispelled the idea. 'I picked this copy from a train seat when I was visiting Wrexham, where I bank. It passed the time on the journey and I might have left it for the next person to read, but for one particular section. Show her, Elaine.'

Mrs Cleeve found the place. 'The letters page,' she said, turning it around.

Jemima's eye fell on a familiar name. Her own. After her sojourn at Merry Beggars Hall and – if she were honest – a little puffed up by her success, she had written to the magazine's editor. Not to claim her laurels; a prosecution was underway, the matter sub judice. She had written simply to say that, in her opinion, the police should employ more female CID officers.

> I do not say women are better than men at detection, simply that our life-experience offers an alternate angle. People have two eyes, do they not? Two hands, a right and a left. Nobody would argue that having only one of each would make us more effective, but when it comes to criminal investigation, the perspective of half the population is excluded.

She had finished her letter on the apocryphal tale of the bicycling thief with the sack of sawdust.

The greatest enemy of detection is presumption. The presumption that there is only ever one truth, one angle, one answer.

The Weekend Sleuth had placed her letter in a prominent spot and it had attracted a strong response, some sympathetic, mostly not. One correspondent had suggested that 'Mrs J. L. Flowerday should confine herself to mending her husband's shirts and leave detection to those suited by nature to the role.' They being men, of course.

'Are you saying that this is what prompted you to invite me here?' Jemima asked.

Mrs Cleeve confirmed it. 'Mrs van Doorn knew of you from *The Queen* magazine. The coincidence of seeing your name again, but in a different context, convinced her that you would be able to help us find Honor.'

Jemima now understood Lord Muirhaven's gruff question: 'Are you the one who wrote the letter?'

'It seems you got me here on false pretences,' she said, not knowing whether to be angry or admire their audacity.

'It felt like a sign.' Mrs van Doorn stroked the diamonds at her wrist and met Jemima's eye in undisguised appeal. 'I genuinely need new clothes and so does Honor. Lovely as this place is' – she gestured towards the huge window – 'it is not London, Paris or even Cape Town. Llangollen, which is two stations away by train, is wonderful for tweed. Chirk, in the other direction, has a fine castle. Wrexham has...'

'Your bank.'

Mrs van Doorn looked discomfited. 'You understand, while we wish to be well dressed, Mrs Flowerday, until Honor is found, nothing can proceed.'

'We need her back home,' Mrs Cleeve supplemented.

'You are saying' – Jemima's thoughts broke ground ahead of her words – 'that I may create a new wardrobe for you both, so long as I find your stepdaughter first? What makes you think I can succeed where you have failed?'

'It's what you said in that letter, about the woman's angle, seeing what others fail to see. That, and your undoubted discretion makes you the perfect—'

Mrs Cleeve broke in. 'You won't flatter Mrs Flowerday into accepting. Plain-speaking will serve you better, Cornelia.'

'Very well. I offered you one hundred pounds, and I will double it to two hundred if you accept my terms. Oh.' Mrs van Doorn put a hand to the side of her head. 'My headache is back. I am not in robust health, I fear. Now, will you agree, Mrs Flowerday?'

Jemima felt she was being rushed into a decision. In four years of running a business, she had responded to some very odd requests. But this... what if she couldn't find the girl or, worse, found her in murky circumstances?

Her silence was misread, and Mrs van Doorn said forlornly, 'It was a foolish hope. Accept my heartfelt apology, Mrs Flowerday. Blame a loving stepmother who is out of her mind with worry.'

'I'm sure Mrs Flowerday won't blame you at all.' Mrs Cleeve leaned across from her seat to squeeze her employer's hand. Both women wore wedding bands, and Jemima wondered if they were widowed, or, as in her case, they were forcibly separated from their husbands. Mrs Cleeve wore only her wedding band, while Mrs van Doorn had so many rings, every hand movement left a glitter in the air.

Getting unsteadily to her feet, Mrs van Doorn said, 'Pray excuse me, Mrs Flowerday, but I always lie down at this hour as I sleep poorly at night. Ask Elaine for anything you wish. I will see you at dinner, I hope, at least?'

Jemima nodded. There was no walking back to the station today.

Her eye fell again on *The Weekend Sleuth*, open at her letter. She had written it with DCI Bullace's commendation ringing in her ear. Bullace had been the senior investigator at Merry Beggars Hall. An intelligent, attractive man, he had bid her goodbye with the following: 'What a pity you already have a profession, Mrs Flowerday, as I feel you would do rather well in mine.'

What would he say if he were here? 'Don't do it!' Or, 'Dive in, Mrs Flowerday. Show me again how a woman solves a mystery.'

No, he would say, 'What is the most important question that you have not yet posed?' It was Jemima's fateful decision to detain Mrs van Doorn and ask, 'Exactly how long has your stepdaughter been missing?'

Chapter Five

'Eleven days,' whispered Mrs van Doorn.

Jemima couldn't stop herself gasping. 'How old is the young lady?'

'Honor is seventeen.'

'Just seventeen, and you haven't been to the police?'

Her hostess was making her way to the door, using the backs of the sofas as support, and seemed not to hear the question. Her parting words were to Mrs Cleeve. 'Have Mrs Beddoe send up one of the girls to brew a pot of my special tea.'

Left alone while Mrs Cleeve went to fulfil the order, Jemima mulled over everything she'd heard. A girl missing for eleven days was potentially a girl in trouble. Or worse.

When the secretary returned a few minutes later, Jemima couldn't hold back. 'If my daughter, Molly, who is ten, went missing eleven *hours*, I would have all the police in London searching for her.'

'I'm sure,' Mrs Cleeve acknowledged. 'But dear Cornelia is absolutely set against involving the authorities. Will you consent to stay a few days longer, Mrs Flowerday?'

Jemima shook her head. It wasn't a 'no', more a reflection on what she had heard. 'I will think about it. Oh, and I should have asked, have my trunks arrived?'

They had, she was assured. 'Mrs Beddoe will have put your

things away. Of course, you'll want to change after your journey. There's oodles of hot water – and, good Lord, what will you think of us? Nobody's offered you tea.'

It was by now past two o'clock. And, yes, Jemima could do with something.

'Let's get you settled in.' Mrs Cleeve escorted her upstairs and took her around the gallery in an anticlockwise direction, into a different wing of the castle. 'I warn you, this is quite a maze,' she said, pausing before ushering Jemima into a large, light bedroom.

The centrepiece was a sumptuously dressed bed. The walls were hung with silk in muted colours, and the window was clear-glazed, promising a lovely view. A small table with two chairs suggested a place to write or read over a pot of tea.

'Your bathroom is there.' Mrs Cleeve pointed to a door.

'My own bathroom?'

'Oh, yes. Our modern Castle Gloaming was created from the ruins of the ancient one, designed by the present earl's grandfather for luxury entertaining. Not that we do much of that.' Mrs Cleeve went to the window. 'Come and admire. In winter, you would catch sight of the aqueduct, but not at this time of year.'

Jemima joined her to look out over the courtyard, the gatehouse turrets and the verdant treetops beyond. The river's course was inferred by the trees' snaking line. The sky above was full of chasing clouds.

'Shall I have tea brought up in, say, forty minutes?' Mrs Cleeve suggested. 'I'll join you, and we can make some headway in this awful business with Honor.'

Jemima heard herself say, 'Very well.'

When alone, she sank onto the bed, wondering if she was being cajoled into a corner. Like a farmhand of old, plied with drink until he foolishly takes the shilling, and wakes up to discover he's become a soldier.

There was time to take a bath in the enormous tub and change her clothes. With five minutes before Mrs Cleeve returned, she found notepaper and dashed off a message to Vicky.

Arrived safely, everyone friendly. Hope all well with you.

She put the note in an envelope, sealing it before she could be tempted to add anything that might unsettle her sister. Did this mean she was choosing to stay?

An unspeaking maid brought in a loaded tray and the sight of tea and Welsh cakes weakened Jemima's resistance further. One could hardly storm out after being treated so generously.

Chapter Six

Mrs Cleeve came back, bringing a framed photograph. It showed a girl in her late teens standing at a ship's rail. 'Honor in happier times. Shall I pour? Milk or lemon?'

Jemima said, 'Milk, please,' and studied the black-and-white photo. Honor van Doorn was smiling into the shot, and Jemima saw a girl with sun-bleached hair lifted by the breeze. Pretty. Young. She was squinting in a way that suggested the sun was glinting off the sea and dazzling her. One hand was clamped to the crown of a wide-brimmed sunhat with an exotic flower, almost certainly silk, attached to the band.

The photograph cut Honor off at the hip, and Jemima saw she was wearing a white top and what looked to be matching trousers. Were trousers a sign of the rebellion that so upset her stepmother, or simply reflecting the relaxed social rules on board a passenger ship? The girl's figure was good, as far as Jemima could tell. She seemed quite tall, her arms slender and well defined. The kind of girl who looked good in uncomplicated clothes.

'You say she's seventeen, but to me she looks younger.' Jemima accepted a cup of China tea.

'Honor celebrated her birthday in the New Year, so in a way you're right. She is just seventeen,' Mrs Cleeve informed her.

Jemima let this sink in. 'Making her sixteen on the voyage from

Cape Town. These plans of Mrs van Doorn's for a London debut...
while I know debutantes can be very young, it is fearfully early to
be tossed into the marriage mart. I take it a good marriage is Mrs
van Doorn's goal for her stepdaughter?'

Mrs Cleeve did not answer directly, but offered the Welsh cakes,
which were studded with currants and spread with melting butter,
saying that Mrs Beddoe made the best.

Fearing she'd been overly blunt, Jemima set aside the subject of
maternal ambitions. For now. 'Are you Welsh, Mrs Cleeve?'

'Please, call me Elaine. I'm not, I'm English. After I married, I
moved with my husband to South Africa. To Durban, in the Eastern
Cape. You could say I'm from everywhere and nowhere. Regarding
Honor and her marriage prospects, I agree with you. She is far too
young to settle down.'

Jemima bit into her Welsh cake, getting a delicious salty-buttery
sweetness and a hint of nutmeg. A suspicion was forming in her
head. 'Mrs van Doorn wishes to conquer London society and
Honor is the bait?'

Elaine Cleeve was emphatic. 'No. Mrs van Doorn wants Honor
to marry Hildebrand and remain here.'

Jemima, her mouth full, couldn't query 'Hildebrand?' so let her
face ask the question.

'Lord Muirhaven,' Elaine said, 'was known as Hildebrand
Woolton for the first thirty-nine years of his life. If you get to
know him, he'll likely ask you to call him that.'

'I'll stick with Lord Muirhaven,' Jemima replied. *Hildebrand* felt
a touch too theatrical.

Elaine continued: 'He never expected to inherit the title. I think
he assumed his uncle – the second earl – would eventually marry
and produce an heir.'

'But he didn't? How negligent. Hildebrand is the third earl?'

'That's right. The title passed to him very recently – he's still breaking it in, like new dress shoes. The earldom itself is a recent one.' Elaine offered a wry smile. 'Founded on money and ambition. The first earl was ennobled in 1860 by Queen Victoria.'

'Knighted for...?'

'According to contemporary newspapers, for financing the Crimean War. He was a fabulously wealthy industrialist. You don't need to spend much time here to realise that.' Elaine gestured around them. 'You'd have to have a king's ransom at your disposal to build a mansion like Castle Gloaming on top of a ruin. The first earl brought in materials by narrowboat from the Midlands – twenty horses were kept just to haul carts from the canal. It cost hundreds of thousands of pounds. He hosted the elite here in an attempt to embed himself more firmly into the aristocracy. Five years after the last stone was laid, he was dead – and broke.'

'I wonder if he thought it was worth the cost,' Jemima mused. 'And the current earl... is he content with his unexpected elevation?'

'Hard to say,' Elaine answered. 'It required a radical change in his life and nothing had prepared him for it. There was a family rift, you see. The first earl's two sons fell out many years ago. The younger, Hildebrand's father, left for Africa.'

'Still, I'm surprised Hildebrand wasn't educated here.' In Jemima's experience, ex-pat aristocrats sent their children home to be moulded and taught in British boarding schools.

'Not he. His father, Leopold Woolton, bought a hundred acres of orange grove in a place called Oosthoek. He married a local woman of dubious repute – you can imagine the ripples back home – and Hildebrand grew up thinking he'd inherit the farm and nothing more. He'll tell you if you ask. He was educated, such as he was, by his father and brought up by an African housekeeper after his mother died. He's not your average aristocrat.'

'Clearly not.' Jemima had mistaken him for the steward, after all. How must it feel, metaphorically at least, to have an earl's coronet plonked on your head and be expected to fill a position in a society you have no experience of? It might explain why Lord Muirhaven seemed to be hiding away in a remote castle gatehouse. She poured fresh tea and added hot water to the pot. 'I'm going to make a leap and assume that having a tenant helps with the upkeep of this place. He'll have to present himself at court sooner or later and take up his place in the Lords. Unless, of course, he's itching to go back to Africa.'

Elaine couldn't say what his long-term plans were. 'He succeeded to the title only eighteen months ago. As I've already mentioned, it came as a shock.'

'Has the engagement to Miss van Doorn been formally announced?' Jemima asked.

'There is no engagement.' Elaine Cleeve leaned forward, though nobody was within hearing distance. 'This is the thing. Honor doesn't want to marry Hildebrand and he feels much the same, calls her a cold fish. Mrs van Doorn cannot accept this and keeps on at her stepdaughter to be more appeasing. She threatened to keep Honor shut up here until she agreed to a marriage.'

'Then I am confused,' Jemima confessed. 'In her letter to me, Mrs van Doorn implied she was taking a house in London for the season with the intention of launching herself and Honor into society. Now you tell me the girl is to be shut away here until she agrees to wed her neighbour. Except of course, she's gone.'

Elaine's sigh conveyed a great deal. 'I understand your confusion. I don't think Cornelia knows what she wants other than to be allied to the Muirhaven title. It has become her obsession, and Honor's intransigence blocks it.'

'I can't blame a young girl for resisting an arranged marriage,' Jemima said with some heat. 'Has anyone actually asked Miss van Doorn what she desires?'

'She wants the London life,' Elaine said. 'She was so upset when they came here, instead of taking a house in Belgravia, which had been the original plan.'

'I can understand,' Jemima said gravely. North Wales and Belgravia were not interchangeable.

'In her own way, Honor has become as obsessed as her step-mother,' Elaine continued. 'At first Mrs van Doorn said no, no, no, then last month she agreed they would spend the summer in London, but on her terms. Honor would be presented at court and do the season, and then marry Hildebrand.'

Jemima put down her cup. 'Firstly, Mrs van Doorn has left it very late as the London season is already in full swing. Secondly – hasn't it occurred to anybody that Honor might have taken matters into her own hands?' What was to stop a healthy young woman walking the route Jemima had just walked, in reverse? A train from Trevor would take her to Shrewsbury and from there, on to London.

'We've thought of that,' Elaine said, a touch impatiently. 'I enquired at Trevor station. Honor didn't get on the train there, the staff were adamant. If you've finished your tea, I'd like to show you something.'

Chapter Seven

'Something' was Honor van Doorn's bedroom, requiring a walk along a gallery that curved around the side of the castle. Jemima felt she was moving like the slow hand around a clock face. Circular buildings were disorientating.

Honor's bedroom was light and feminine, with flowered prints and damasks. The view through her window was of a lawn sloping to a shrubbery. Absorbing the room's emptiness, Jemima felt sympathy for a girl who wanted London and, presumably, friends her own age.

Elaine flung open the doors of a wardrobe and invited Jemima to look inside. There was a modest collection of dresses, blouses, skirts and coats. Hats were on a shelf above. Two only, a fawn felt cloche and an oilskin cap for rainy days.

'Where's the sun hat she wore in that photograph, the one with the big, fake flower?'

Elaine had no idea.

Jemima studied the clothes individually. Almost everything bore the label 'Régal' which, despite the French spelling, Jemima knew to be a London wholesaler who shipped ready-to-wear to the colonies. Serving the wealthier end of the market, Régal was notorious for pirating the Paris collections and Jemima wasn't surprised to see a Patou-inspired sports ensemble, and a tunic and matching pleated skirt evoking Chanel, spring 1922. As Jemima was wearing a similar skirt, 'After Chanel', she made no judgement. Honor van Doorn had good taste, or her stepmother did.

'Are these all the clothes?' she asked.

'Pretty much,' Elaine answered. 'If you search the chest of drawers and look on the hook behind the door, you'll have seen everything Honor owns bar what she stood up in on the day she went.'

'She didn't pack a suitcase before leaving, as far as you know?'

Elaine pointed to the top of the wardrobe where three leather suitcases were stacked one on top of the other in diminishing size. 'That's her luggage. I've checked Mrs van Doorn's suitcases and the steamer trunks. They're all still here.'

'A small bag? If she travelled light...'

Elaine pointed to a holdall on the wardrobe floor. 'She might have found a laundry bag or a basket in the kitchen, I don't know. She didn't plan her departure, it seems to me. And before you ask, she has no money.'

'None at all?'

'Pin money. Her allowance is a few shillings a month.'

'Which she might have saved up. There won't be much to spend it on here.'

Without speaking, Elaine removed a handbag from a bedside cabinet and shook the contents onto the bed. A purse fell out, a comb and nail file, a silk headsquare and a pair of cream net gloves.

Jemima sorted through them, then searched the bag for evidence of a diary, or train or bus tickets. An address, a map – anything that might indicate a desire to break free. There was nothing of the kind.

'Shoes?' Wherever Honor van Doorn had fled, Jemima doubted she'd gone barefoot.

And yet, it appeared she had. In a cupboard were six pairs of shoes. Lace-up Oxfords like those Jemima wore next to black pumps suitable for church. There were gold leather evening sandals and a pair in pink-dyed snakeskin. There were tennis pumps and canvas deck shoes.

'So, what was she wearing on her feet?'

'That's the thing.' Elaine Cleeve was looking harassed. 'Her walking brogues are down in the boot room and that's the lot. Honor enjoyed going bare foot in the dawn and the day she went—'

Jemima interrupted. 'What day, exactly?'

'Sunday, May twentieth.'

A Sunday hereabouts would be quiet. Jemima wondered if that was relevant.

'When she didn't come down for breakfast,' Elaine continued, 'I got a little worried. I came up here and discovered her bed was empty.'

'What time was this?'

'About eight-thirty. I assumed she was taking a turn around the grounds. We don't go to church. It, er, got tedious, being stared at. The staff go to chapel however, and when they came back I asked if they'd seen her. They hadn't. By that time, I'd checked outside and found footprints in the dew, crossing the lawn.'

'Leading where?'

Elaine took Jemima to the window and pointed. 'To the shrubbery. It leads to the river.'

'Did the prints continue to the water?'

It had been impossible to tell. Elaine explained that once you were in the shrubbery, the ground was too rough to retain the imprint of feet.

Jemima couldn't imagine anyone leaving Castle Gloaming without their shoes, much less if their walk took them along rugged paths. Unless under compulsion. She chewed the thought for a moment, fearing this puzzle might take a dark turn. 'May I ask a blunt question?'

'Of course,' said Elaine. 'I'll try to answer.'

'You said Miss van Doorn has no money of her own. Her stepmother has wealth, however.'

'She's a millionairess,' Elaine said. 'And, before you ask, Miss van Doorn will inherit that fortune in due course. But that doesn't make her personally rich.'

Not yet, Jemima supplied silently. 'In the event of Honor's death, who's next in line to inherit?'

Elaine made a face. 'Not sure. Mrs van Doorn has a brother and some nieces in Cape Town. Them, I suppose, though they're not a close family.'

It felt unlikely that those relations would be in any way involved. Jemima took a stroll about the room, saying casually, 'Tell me about Honor's parents. Who were they?'

'They weren't rich, if that's what you're asking. Honor's mother died when she was young. Some sudden illness,' Elaine said. 'Her father passed away two years ago, of heart failure, out at sea. He was a mariner, and Mrs van Doorn's second husband. All the money derives from Mrs van Doorn's first marriage. Husband number one was in diamonds.'

That explained the brilliants. 'What did Mr van Doorn bring her, other than his name and a stepdaughter?'

'Looks,' said Elaine. 'He was dashing, but a man's man. From what I gather, he was happiest at the tiller of a boat.'

'Did he marry her for her money?'

Elaine hadn't been working for Mrs van Doorn long enough to know the ins and outs, but... 'From things she's said in passing, it was a happy marriage. I can attest that she's genuinely fond of Honor and considers it her duty to see the girl happy and well settled in life.'

It crossed Jemima's mind to point out that 'well settled' was not the same as 'happy'.

Her brain-cogs were whirring. Who would Honor's disappearance best serve? Honor herself, perhaps. Lord Muirhaven? Possibly, if it rid him of the irksome pressure to marry a girl he didn't like.

Jemima glanced covertly at Elaine and said, 'I presume Lord Muirhaven means to marry somebody, even if a raw seventeen-year-old isn't to his taste.'

A paint-water blush suffused Elaine's cheek. 'I suppose so, Mrs Flowerday.'

'Jemima, please. He'll have to produce a legitimate son, or the title will go extinct. Would that matter to him?'

'I can't say.' Elaine thought about it. 'It might.'

I should think so too. As the daughter of a moderately prosperous south London grocer, Jemima hadn't grown up with an ancient name to protect, but she had married the son of Lord and Lady Winterfold and knew better than most the claims of birthright. However, none of this took her nearer to understanding the present whereabouts of Miss Honor van Doorn. Barefoot, no money, no luggage. Jemima had to admit, it was an intriguing situation.

Striding back to the wardrobe, she inspected every garment from right to left. When she'd finished, she was left with a fragment of an idea. 'Elaine, show me the way back to my room and we can discuss terms.'

Chapter Eight

'So you'll take the commission?'

'You are Mrs van Doorn's right hand,' Jemima replied gravely. She had no intention of agreeing terms that were not firmly nailed down.

'Right and left, I often think,' Elaine said. 'I suppose you wish to discuss your fee.'

'I was offered one hundred pounds, which has since been doubled. I will accept two hundred, but I need to understand what is expected of me both as a dressmaker and a solver of riddles.'

'It's simple, really,' said Elaine. 'Unless Honor is found, dresses are redundant.'

'And even then, Mrs van Doorn still has to make up her mind whether she wants a London season or not.'

'Entirely correct.' Elaine was leading the way back to Jemima's room.

Jemima speeded up to put herself alongside her companion. She touched Elaine's arm to make her stop. 'Since you prefer plain-speaking, Mrs Cleeve, let me say it as it appears to me. I'm being offered a very large sum of money to act as a private detective and locate a missing girl. Dresses be damned.'

Elaine Cleeve extended her hand. 'Quite as you say. Shake on it?'

They shook.

Reaching her bedroom, relieved that she now had a clear sense of her role, Jemima made straight for the picture of Honor at the ship's rail. 'When and where was this taken?'

'A year ago, on the promenade deck of the RMS *Llanstephan Castle*, on the voyage over.'

It was such a detailed answer, Jemima asked Elaine if she'd also been on the voyage.

Elaine confirmed it. 'As was Hildebrand. It was where we all met.'

'All of you?'

'We were all passengers in first class. I and my husband embarked at Durban, on the Eastern Cape. As did Hildebrand, though we didn't know each other until later, when we got talking. Mrs van Doorn and Honor joined the ship at Cape Town, for the western leg of the voyage.'

'You were travelling east to west?' Jemima wanted to be sure. It was amazing how tiny details, stored up, could prove important.

Elaine nodded. 'On that occasion, the ship took the clockwise route around Africa. My life changed on that voyage, utterly and for ever.'

A story for later.

A closer study of the photograph suggested that Miss van Doorn's top and trousers were made of linen. 'From the size of the darts and the side-buttons, I'm guessing they are wide-leg yachting slacks with a sailor top tucked into the waistband.'

'You would be right.' Elaine looked impressed.

'Coco Chanel shocked the world with such an outfit two years ago. Still, it's a daring choice for a very young woman, even when relaxing in the sunshine aboard ship. I bet she bought it secretly, and her stepmother was shocked.'

'Again, correct. Cornelia ordered her to go and change at once.'

'Who took the picture?'

'I did. Using my late husband's camera.'

Jemima picked up a slight stumble over the words 'late husband'. She let it pass. 'As for the hat with the flower, I'd say it was bleached raffia.' Jemima had already noted the hat's absence from the wardrobe. 'Nor did I see any white linen. Everything in this photograph appears to be missing.'

Elaine agreed. 'What does that suggest?'

'That at least she didn't leave the house naked. Did Miss van Doorn like to swim?'

'Here?'

'Anywhere. I'm particularly thinking of the river.'

Elaine Cleeve gave a visible shudder. 'Swim in that current? I wouldn't, not for a thousand pounds.'

'I'm not asking if you would, Elaine. What about Honor? Did she like nature, getting close to the earth? Is she the sort who would plunge into cold water and let the current take her?'

'I know what you're suggesting,' Elaine said unsteadily. 'If she'd gone swimming and drowned, her body would have been found.' She glanced at her watch. 'Can you spare me, Jemima? Only I must put out Mrs van Doorn's clothes for dinner tonight.'

'Do we dress formally?' Jemima mentally ran through the contents of her trunks.

'"Informal but elegant" sums up our style,' Elaine told her. 'Mrs van Doorn dresses for dinner as hostess, and I make an effort. Hildebrand will turn up looking as if he has been called in from cutting logs. He has an open invitation and eats nearly all his meals with us. Dinner's at eight, but we always gather in the drawing room for cocktails at seven.'

Elaine left and, having finished the last of the Welsh cakes, Jemima took a leather journal from her bag. Turning to the first empty page she wrote:

I am at Castle Gloaming and have been handed a mystery to solve. I hope it will prove a simple case of a headstrong girl running away from home, but Honor van Doorn left everything necessary for a journey behind and nobody has mentioned a 'goodbye' letter. She yearned for London, but no sane young woman would travel so far in summer slacks and without shoes.

Honor had mixed with a youthful set on the boat coming over. An optimistic idea was that she'd formed an attachment to a young man and had gone off with him. An elopement, in other words.

A less positive option was abduction. Honor van Doorn, heiress, was a prize for someone, though nobody had mentioned a ransom note either. There was another possibility, of course. That she hadn't left at all.

From her window, Jemima gave the gatehouse an uninterrupted study. Crimson curtains were drawn across the upper windows and she wondered if Lord Muirhaven was 'at home' or carrying out some manual task.

Speak of the devil. She saw him emerge from the main building below and cross the courtyard towards his gatehouse. He entered the central passage and was swallowed by shadows. There must be a door, the entrance to his bachelor quarters.

'Your father was a second son,' Jemima muttered. 'Growing oranges in the Eastern Cape is unlikely to have furnished him or you with a fortune. So why aren't you pursuing Honor van Doorn more purposefully?'

For aristocrats, a wealthy wife was a tried-and-tested route out of poverty. Perhaps Hildebrand's reluctance was simply that he was wise enough to know that Honor, with or without money, would make him unhappy.

Jemima put her shoes back on and found her way to the stairs. Once she had learned her way around Castle Gloaming, she might sense which direction Honor van Doorn had taken, and why.

Chapter Nine

A patch of apparent wilderness behind a sturdy wall, which Jemima had glimpsed from her bedroom window, proved to be a sheltered kitchen garden. She walked first around a vegetable patch where lettuce, radish and spinach looked ready for picking, and leeks and onions were well established. Hazel pyramids supported runner beans whose infant tendrils were eight or nine inches high. Everything was in ruler-straight rows, suggesting the hand of a gardener.

Jemima picked a sprig of curly parsley and chewed it, thinking that the castle must once have been self-sufficient, but that wouldn't be the case now. She knew there was a pony. Supplies would be fetched from Trevor or Llangollen further away.

Leaving the vegetables, she took a path through a cutting garden filled with peonies, campanula, lupins and bleeding hearts. There was purple honesty, now slightly over. This path led to an area of white and yellow flowers, the wilderness she'd seen from her bedroom. Close up, it didn't seem quite so wild. Narrow paths had been mown in a spiral, and she could move through without getting sprinkled with petals and pollen. There were more plants than she could put names to, but wasn't this hogweed? There were swathes of it, lime-green, dome-shaped florets busy with ladybirds and brimstone butterflies. It was all very different from the curated parks of London.

'I wonder why the gardener let the weeds run riot in this patch.'

A person Jemima hadn't noticed, because she was bent over, stood up at this comment. It was a woman, wearing a housecoat over her dress, and a headscarf knotted under her chin. She was dark-eyed, with a pronounced nose. She came towards Jemima, holding a plant she had just pulled up by the root.

'We have two gardeners,' she said, her accent placing her firmly in these parts. 'My husband Beddoe and the lad, Ifor. This garden is my territory. You haven't seen a weed, whatever you might think, because nothing here grows by accident.'

Regretting her indiscretion, Jemima expressed her admiration for everything, adding, 'I have a tiny town garden, no space for more than a pot or two of herbs. You are Mrs Beddoe, the house-keeper?'

The woman obliged with a nod. 'You must be Mrs Flowerday. I hope you found your room to your liking.'

'It's perfect and thank you for taking my things to it. What is that you've dug up?'

'Angelica.' Mrs Beddoe held up the plant for Jemima to see. Liquorice-black soil clung to pale brown roots. 'I dry all parts of the plant for Mrs van Doorn. It's good for digestion and sleep, and against the migraine headache.'

Ah, for the special tea that had been requested. 'You are an herbalist, Mrs Beddoe?'

'Not by training, but I grew up amongst these plants and learned their craft.' The housekeeper pointed to various in turn. 'There's Soloman's seal for the lungs. There's mugwort, for food poisoning and monthly cramps. St John's wort for melancholia. I make a tea of that for Miss van Doorn. Well, I did until...' Mrs Beddoe shook off the subject as she might a ladybird from the back of her hand. 'There's nettle for a blood tonic and against hay fever. There's hogweed to cleanse the blood in spring. And there,' she pointed to a clump of plants the size of small saplings, 'is their Goliath of a cousin.'

'Giant hogweed's poisonous, isn't it?' Jemima had been taught at school that its sap could blister the skin painfully.

Mrs Beddoe agreed in an offhand way and pointed in a different direction. 'There is belladonna, for sleep and the ague.'

Jemima regarded a plant with hood-shaped flowers the colour of bruised skin. 'Isn't belladonna what I'd call deadly nightshade?'

Mrs Beddoe gave the plant a secret smile then pointed to a cluster of umbrella-like heads and said, 'That is hemlock.'

'Goodness.' Jemima went over and peered at it, noting purple veins and blotches on the stems. Those marks aside, hemlock appeared very similar to the angelica Mrs Beddoe had dug up for Mrs van Doorn's tea. 'Don't you worry, growing things that are poisonous?'

'Many things are so,' Mrs Beddoe informed her gravely, 'including the rhubarb in your jam, if you use the wrong part of the plant. A poultice of henbane and hemlock takes the pain from ageing joints and I make it for my husband. The druids drank a brew of mugwort and betony, to aid their visions, and took mistletoe for eternal youth. Though only a fool will swallow a mistletoe berry.'

This was unlike any gardening conversation Jemima had enjoyed over a fence in her time. 'I'll remember,' she said.

'Nothing is dangerous so long as you know what you are touching.' Mrs Beddoe gazed once again at the giant hogweed. 'Have you ever provided floral displays for a castle, ma'am?'

To be fair, never.

'Or a cathedral?'

Ditto, no.

'I buy flowers in London's Covent Garden,' Jemima said. 'I'm pleased if I create something colourful on a windowsill.'

So far, Mrs Beddoe had given not a vestige of a smile and now was no different. 'You will have noticed a marble plinth in the great hall, no? I cut hogweed yesterday and arranged it with willow and artichoke heads in the Chinese vase that sits on it. My husband grows plants for that purpose, plants that fill the eye.'

Jemima hadn't noticed the plinth, because Lord Muirhaven had taken her through the hall at such a clip. However, she saw the sense in Mrs Beddoe's words. 'Everything here is on a massive scale, isn't it? A few pansies in a jar wouldn't cut the mustard.'

'Will you be staying long?'

Mrs Beddoe's manner was polite, but Jemima was under no illusion. This woman was taking her measure. Unsure how much the housekeeper knew of Honor van Doorn's disappearance, she answered that she hadn't yet decided.

'If you can find Miss van Doorn, your presence will be worthwhile.'

Ah, so she knew. 'Did you or your staff see her the morning she left?' Jemima had already been told that they had not, but scullery maids, gardeners, stable lads, were up and about at first light and might have noticed something and not thought it worth mentioning.

Mrs Beddoe shook her head. 'We only knew anything was wrong when Mrs Cleeve came asking if Miss van Doorn was with us. The young lady often got up early to walk by the river and would knock at the kitchen door for a cup of coffee.'

'On the day she went, bare footprints were found crossing the lawn, in the river's direction. Do you think they were hers?'

'We saw nothing.' Mrs Beddoe was showing signs of wanting to end the conversation, which, in Jemima's experience, was the best moment to press a point.

'Where would someone hide around here?'

'Well, now. In the attics, but they have been searched. As has the tower. Into the forest?'

'She's been gone the best part of two weeks. She can't be hiding in the trees like a child.'

'Nor do we think it, Mrs Flowerday.'

'Then what do you think?' Jemima was convinced the house-keeper was on the verge of divulging something, so she waited and was rewarded.

'I had a canary once that I kept in a cage.' It was said in a soft, distant voice. 'I'd leave the door open for the little creature to fly out. It would explore further each time, but it always came back. Always.'

'So you think Honor van Doorn—'

Mrs Beddoe cut her off. 'What am I doing, gossiping? I must take this plant to the drying room and then see to dinner.'

'You're the cook too?' Jemima followed her out of the garden and into an outbuilding that appeared to be a cross between a storeroom and a still room, with ropes of onions and herbs hanging from rafters.

'There are three of us in the house to do the indoor work,' Mrs Beddoe said as she laid the angelica in a shallow sink. 'Two girls and myself.'

'One of them brought tea to my room, and Welsh cakes, which were lovely.'

'That was Gwen.' With a nod suggesting that was all she meant to say, Mrs Beddoe poured water from a pitcher over the plant in the sink.

Jemima went back to the garden, ruminating on all she'd seen and heard. Here was a lesson in the dangers of presumption. What she'd imagined as a wilderness was nothing of the sort. Every plant, whether tall, blowsy, leggy or shy, in the hands of a wise woman offered a cure for some ill or other. Even the dangerous growth had its purpose.

She left the garden through the wicket door she'd come in by and was crossing the main courtyard when she heard hinges grinding. Evening sunlight poured in through the main gate.

Getting there before it swung shut, she saw a man striding over the dry moat towards the river. The blue neckerchief, the loose-limbed gait, were Lord Muirhaven's. Hildebrand. That name, with its pagan overtones, suited him.

'I will stick to calling him Lord Muirhaven, for all that,' Jemima decided. 'Being a mere eighteen months into his title, he might be touchy about it.'

Jemima had surmised that his apartment door was within the gateway passage, and she was right. It opened to her tentative push and she stared inside, into a room of lime-plastered walls. A desk filled a window embrasure. That, along with a rug, a bishop's chair and a set of shelves, was the totality of the furniture. The shelves were empty except for a framed photograph. A landscape, though not a Welsh one. The sense of immense distance, the curve of the hills and a flat-topped tree told her, 'Africa'.

In the corner, narrow stairs invited her onward. Dare she? They must lead into one of the turrets. Since there was only one door, the other turret must be accessible only from this side. It demanded investigation.

She wondered what she'd say if somebody walked in on her. 'I'm looking for Miss van Doorn.' Or, 'I'm searching for a body, if that's no trouble.'

Was she searching for Honor's remains?

Her investigator's mind had begun its journey, and her feet had no choice but to follow. She went up the stairs.

Chapter Ten

At the top was a squat tower room, where remnants of daylight squeezed through arrow-slit windows. A niche behind a curtain proved to be a rudimentary bathroom with a sink, water jug, shaving mirror and a towel horse. The room next-along was a bedroom, shaped like a half-round of cheese and big enough for a single bed, chair and a clothes rail. Curtains hid the view, the crimson ones she'd noticed from her bedroom window. A short corridor took her from one turret to the next and she was conscious of the blocked-up murder hole beneath her feet. She reached another circular tower room with windows front and back, velvet chairs, a fireplace and more bookshelves, this time with something on them. Lord Muirhaven enjoyed adventure stories. *Moby Dick*, *The Coral Island* and Scott's *Ivanhoe*, among others. There was a display of wooden masks with chiselled faces, some of which looked threatening. African also, she assumed.

These eyeless watchers apart, this seemed to be a comfortable den, complete with a card table and a game laid out. It looked like poker, though with only a single chair pulled up it seemed that one person had been playing both sides. On a console were candlesticks, decanters of tawny liquor and cut-crystal tumblers. Lord Muirhaven liked a drink.

A second flight of steps led down to a dining room with a round table of veneered cherry, seating for eight and a grandfather clock. The walls were painted duck-egg blue. A glazed door cut into the curved wall seemed to lead out into a small courtyard. Interesting, she thought, as there appeared to be no kitchen in the apartment, unless she'd missed a door. Hadn't Elaine mentioned that Lord Muirhaven dined with them, at the castle? If dining ever took place here, then food must be brought over from the main house.

It was a little while since anyone had cleaned this room. In fact, someone had written a message in dust on the tabletop. Jemima felt a ripple of excitement. A cry for help from Honor?

I am a prisoner.

It turned out to be nothing of the sort, merely a series of symbols with no obvious meaning. Taking out her notebook, Jemima sketched what she saw: three wavy lines and, above them, a five-pointed star and another offset to the right a little higher up. Above the first star, a half-moon. It put Jemima in mind of a pub sign. Specifically, the Moon and Stars in the old town of Rye on the Sussex coast. Simon had taken her there on a daytrip while they were courting. If it was anything other than an absent-minded doodle, Lord Muirhaven had done it to remind a housemaid that she needed to be more active with her duster.

The main gate clanking shut made Jemima freeze. She went to the glazed door and, to her profound relief, it was unlocked. She stepped out into the evening air, which was filled with midges and the odour of damp soil and wild plants.

'A secret garden,' she said, finding it charming, apart from the midges, which were biting. She feared she was entirely walled in, but there had to be a gate out. Her hip collided with a table, the metal sort found outside Parisian cafés, and she grabbed its edge to stop it falling. A brass ashtray fell off and a number of cigar butts, which she picked up, listening acutely for footsteps that might indicate she'd been detected. Following the turret's flank,

Jemima saw a wicket gate set into the garden wall, half obscured by nettles and other weeds. She pushed them aside and tried the latch. It was stiff, as was the gate, but she wriggled through into the main courtyard. Forcing herself not to look back, she walked towards the main house.

Before she'd reached the front entrance, she felt a stinging sensation in her fingers. Had she cut herself on the edge of the café table or was it the nettles? She went directly to her room to find out. While she'd been out, someone had lit paraffin lamps. Castle Gloaming must be without electricity, then. A lamp also burned in her bathroom, where she inspected the fingers of her right hand. Red patches were forming around her knuckles.

'Yes, nettles,' she muttered. She ran cold water over the redness and washed her hands thoroughly.

With a little time to kill before pre-dinner drinks, she lay down on her bed. If anyone asked how she'd spent the last hour, she would tell them she'd, 'Scrambled around the place, the better to appreciate the building and its grounds.'

While crossing the main courtyard, she had taken in the tower, its great height, and the wooden parapet nestled beneath its conical roof. According to the housekeeper, it had been included in the search for Miss van Doorn. Still, Jemima felt it essential that she climb up and look out from that crow's nest, somehow conquering her great dislike of heights.

'But not tonight.'

When it was time to prepare for dinner, Jemima went to her dressing table where someone had placed an envelope with her name on it. Inside was a cheque for two hundred pounds, made out in ink, and signed by Cornelia van Doorn. As promised, her fee had doubled.

But rather than pleasure, Jemima felt a crawling unease. What if Honor van Doorn could not be found or, worse, was found as human remains? She muttered, 'Where are you, child?'

The river, came the cool voice of logic. Honor went to the river, there's your answer.

Placing the cheque in her dressing-table drawer, Jemima went to select a dress suitable for dinner with an earl, a diamond widow and a plain-speaking secretary.

Chapter Eleven

Elaine Cleeve was waiting in the domed hall as she came down. Jemima had chosen a black silk-velvet shift dress which reached to mid-shin, wearing it with a beaded cardigan whose long sleeves ended in a point that concealed the nettle rash on her fingers. Style without ostentation was the intention.

'I hope I'm not late,' she said.

'You are punctuality itself. Mrs van Doorn is on her way down... ah.' Elaine glanced to the side. 'Well done, Mrs Beddoe, girls.'

A discreet doorway had opened beside the staircase to admit the housekeeper carrying a tray of glassware. She was followed by two young maids wearing white aprons and caps, bearing snacks on silver trays. All three made their way to the drawing room and there might have been a collision as Lord Muirhaven chose that moment to stride in. He saw them in time and loped to the drawing-room door, opening it with a cry of, 'Onward, ladies.'

When it was Jemima's turn to pass, she caught a fragrant whiff of bay and lemon. He had tamed his black curls for the dinner hour and the application of hair oil had brought out strands of grey. It did not diminish his appeal. What would be his appeal, she amended, if one were not married and beyond ideas of that kind.

He wished her good evening, as if he had glimpsed her thoughts. He was dressed for cocktails in a claret-red smoking jacket with a black satin collar and cuffs, a lightly starched shirt, its open collar filled with a silk paisley cravat. The corduroy riding breeches had been replaced with dress trousers and Jemima assumed his shoes were black and polished, though she didn't look down. The outfit implied a desire to conform... but not too much. There was a reckless dash about Lord Muirhaven, she decided. Unless, of course, he simply didn't know what English gentlemen wore for dinner.

'My apologies for not being around to give you a tour of my gatehouse,' he said, his smile intensifying as he perceived her blush. 'I went swimming in the river and wasn't fit for polite company.'

'In the river?' She spoke to hide her mortification, though it did astonish her. She'd seen him leaving the castle and had assumed he was off on some errand. 'You surely didn't grapple with that current? It looks so very dangerous.'

'With respect, that's the point,' he said carelessly. 'Otherwise, I'd find a pond to sit in.'

She wouldn't go into a swollen river at gunpoint, but a certain stamp of male enjoyed stepping over the edge. They relished danger and sometimes induced others to join in their risk-taking. A vision of a pale-haired girl floating face down, white clothes caught in the half-submerged branches of a tree, brought a shiver.

Lord Muirhaven bent his head to look into her eyes. 'Did you enjoy your exploring?'

No doubting it, he knew.

'I need to apologise. I trespassed, but how did you rumble me?'

He half closed one sharp, grey eye. 'You are not the only solver of puzzles at Castle Gloaming, Mrs Flowerday. You knocked over the bistro table outside and set it back on its feet.'

'You heard,' she said.

He shook his head. 'I heard nothing. I used this.' He tapped his nose. 'At some point, you had taken a bath with the rose-geranium salts Mrs van Doorn provides for guests. The scent lingered on the stairs and I followed it all the way down to my courtyard. Don't be surprised. I grew up among people who hunt and use all their senses. Though that courtyard gets little light, a sliver of flagstone free of moss showed how the outdoor table had been moved.'

'You win.' Jemima was determined not to be unsettled. 'I did enjoy myself, most particularly your collection of masks. Where did they come from?'

'Do you suppose I won them in battle?' That smile again. 'I bought them at the market at Beira, in Mozambique.'

This man you wouldn't want to play poker with, Jemima thought. You'd never know how many aces he had up his sleeve. Four, or even five.

Elaine approached, and perhaps perceiving that Jemima was being toyed with, took the conversation into her steady hands. 'I heard that Mrs Beddoe gave you a tour of her herb garden earlier.'

Lord Muirhaven hadn't given up his teasing.

'Which did you prefer?' he asked Jemima. 'God's garden or the Devil's patch?'

'I'm sorry?'

'Didn't you realise?' Lord Muirhaven raised his voice so Mrs Beddoe and the maids would hear. 'The paths spiral past plants dedicated to the saints. St John, Benedict, Margaret and Our Lady. Keep going past the fumitory and rue, you'll find henbane and monk's hood and worst of all—'

'That's enough, Hildebrand.' Elaine nodded sharply towards the door. Mrs van Doorn had arrived.

She had changed into another chiffon dress, this one banded with gold satin. A lace shawl softened the radiance of the diamonds on her wrists but left a scintillating collaret on full show. Matching earrings caught the light. She cast a smile around the room. 'Mrs

Flowerday, so glad to see you again. Have you been offered a drink? What is your preferred aperitif?'

Jemima usually went for a medium-dry sherry, the drink least likely to have her staggering into a dining room, but seeing a cocktail cabinet crowded with crystal decanters, an ice bucket and olives laid ready, she said, 'Gin and French?'

Mrs van Doorn asked Lord Muirhaven to do the honours, adding, 'My usual, please. You too Elaine?'

'As always. Gin and It, Hildebrand. Arctic cold, steady on the gin.' Elaine implied a small measure with her finger and thumb.

This conversation had Jemima wondering where their ice came from, as they had no electricity to run a refrigerator. From town, then straight into the cellar? She watched Lord Muirhaven tilt the gin decanter over ice cubes four times before passing round the drinks.

He gave a pink-tinted glass to Mrs van Doorn. 'Gin and bitters, ma'am. Mrs Flowerday, gin, ice and dry vermouth. For you, Elaine, gin, ice and sweet vermouth. Gin and bitters for me.' He proposed the toast. 'To new friends.'

'New friends,' they chorused, though Jemima thought, surely, the toast ought to be, 'Absent ones.'

The maid, Gwen, whom she'd encountered earlier, offered olives on sticks while the other maid presented rounds of toasted rye bread spread with a paste Jemima couldn't identify.

Elaine noticed her confusion. 'It is laver. Seaweed, boiled and pounded with anchovy and tabasco. Try it, I dare you.'

The taste was hot, salty and strong. After the initial surprise, it proved perfect with gin and olives. 'I am converted,' Jemima said, accepting another along with more olives, which left her looking for somewhere to put the sticks. One of the social challenges of the age, the bane of cocktail hour. Unless a maid or a waiter with a tray happened to be close by, or an ashtray sat within reach, you had to hang on to them. She'd once seen a drunken young man at a party push his redundant sticks into a lady guest's chignon.

Her solution was to go to the fireplace where a blaze had been lit and left to sink to the glowing stage. Despite the warmth of the day, this last evening of May had turned chilly. The cavernous fireplace had been built with attention to historical detail, including recesses for salt. Something sat in one of these nooks and as she stooped to throw her cocktail sticks onto the embers, a small face with bright eyes stared back at her. Reaching in, Jemima pulled out a miniature doll dressed in corduroy trousers, a check shirt and waistcoat. It... *he*... had been fashioned from wool-cloth and stuffed with something dry, like wheat or seeds. She smelled soot and rosemary, and a note of thyme, perhaps? He wore a blue neckerchief and little boots made from window cleaning leather. The eyes were silver press studs, the snap fasteners one used to close the necks of silk blouses. Jemima had read about these dolls – poppets they were called – secreted in walls or fireplaces. They were a form of witchcraft.

Jemima was no believer in magic, but what made her shiver was the real hair on the poppet's head. She couldn't resist a glance at Lord Muirhaven. Returning the figure to its nook, her mind went to the moon and star symbols she'd seen in his dining room. All at once, they felt less 'pub sign' and more 'tarot card'.

It felt like the moment in a concerto when the key slips from major to minor. Jemima watched Lord Muirhaven drop another rock of ice into Mrs van Doorn's drink. Cornelia was sitting on the sofa, he leaning over its back, his arm against her shoulder. Only a fool would miss the way his knuckles rested momentarily on the lady's ring-heavy hand.

He doesn't want to marry cold-fish Honor, but he's not going to let a fortune slip away.

Finding the fireside suddenly too hot, Jemima went in search of a cooler spot from which to observe the room. An attractive, middle-aged lord and a rich, older woman had every right to like each other. It wouldn't matter a jot were it not for a girl missing for eleven days.

'Did you find Mrs van Doorn's cheque, Jemima?' It was Elaine Cleeve, coming to stand beside her. Elaine wore hyacinth silk, the beaded straps showing she had good shoulders and the caramel tan that was so desirable these days, and so hard to achieve in the British climate.

'I did,' answered Jemima.

'And... that settles things?'

'Yes, on one condition.' Seeing Elaine's mouth tighten, Jemima added, 'I'm not angling for more money. It is this: If Miss van Doorn is still missing by Sunday morning, we call the police.'

Chapter Twelve

To reach the dining room they trooped upstairs, and the effort was worthwhile to catch the last of a showy sunset. Everyone went to the window to look out over the castle's lawns. Jemima tracked the line of a ruined curtain wall bathed in dark-blue light; the gloaming that the castle's Scottish renovator must have had in mind.

From here, the shrubbery was out of sight and Jemima made a mental note to check from which part of the castle Honor's last walk would have been visible.

Lord Muirhaven drew out chairs for the ladies, placing Jemima in the seat of honour on Mrs van Doorn's left. The room was as richly furnished as those downstairs; Byzantine in its use of gilding. A satinwood dining table dominated, and Jemima was glad their places were laid all at one end and not spread out like points on a lonely compass.

After soup, spring lamb was served and Lord Muirhaven carved while Mrs Beddoe brought dishes of roast potatoes and vegetables from a sideboard. Jemima had endured many a dinner at her parents-in-law's Suffolk mansion, where the starched cuffs of footmen and the creaking stays of the elderly butler came between her and the enjoyment of her food. She appreciated the more relaxed atmosphere here. If only she hadn't seen that little stuffed doll. It had changed her feelings about this place.

Mrs Beddoe carried out her tasks unobtrusively. Lord Muirhaven poured the wine. The conversation flowed. Jemima was asked about London, who was who, what fashions prevailed. She passed on some gossip, though nothing that touched on her London clients, and described the wedding of Lady Elizabeth Bowes-Lyon to Prince Albert, Duke of York, which had taken place the previous month. Several of her clients had been invited and describing their outfits took them to the cheese course at which point, Mrs van Doorn indicated that she, Jemima and Elaine should retire to the drawing room for coffee and leave Lord Muirhaven to his port.

This would abandon him to his own company, unless one discounted a pair of stuffed otters in a cabinet at the far end of the dining room. Still, it offered a chance to pose questions to Mrs van Doorn and Elaine in private. Now that Lord Muirhaven knew she was capable of snooping, he would be on his guard. She'd carelessly thrown away her chance of observing him in secret.

In the drawing room, the three women sat close to the fire as a decided chill had come with the dark. It must be the nature of a castle, Jemima thought, to retain the cold in its stones even when the days were bright. Herbal tea was brought in. Jemima had declined coffee and the other two never drank it after midday. Mrs Beddoe poured a tisane of valerian and angelica for Mrs van Doorn, and peppermint tea for Jemima and Elaine. Over the clink of fragile china, Jemima asked the first of her questions.

'Did Miss van Doorn receive any letters in the days before she disappeared?'

'From whom?' Mrs van Doorn enquired.

'Anyone. Letters in general.'

Mrs van Doorn shook her head, but Elaine disagreed. 'I saw her walking back from the gatehouse one morning, looking down at something. A letter, quite possibly.'

'When would this be?'

'Oh... maybe ten days before she went. Vanished, I mean.'

Jemima asked Elaine where she'd been standing when she saw this event.

'In the room you're using. I was checking bedding and curtains for moth.'

'Oh?' Fabric moth cocoons hatched in springtime, but surely that was the housekeeper's job. Jemima said as much.

'Mrs Beddoe only has two pairs of hands and while the girls are excellent, this is a very big place. I do what I can to lighten the load.'

Jemima made a mental note that Elaine Cleeve was one of those sorts that employers like to call 'a treasure'. Was she very well paid? Or doing extra jobs because she was bored and insufficiently occupied?

'You saw Honor coming back from the gate, reading a letter, yes?'

Elaine nodded, then backtracked. 'It was raining hard, and Honor had draped a raincoat over her head, but I'm fairly certain that's what she was doing.'

'Would she have known the postman would call at that particular time?'

'Post-girl, actually. And, no, we never know quite what time she'll call, but you may have noticed, there's a cage fixed on the entrance gate. When there was a postman, I'm told he would bring mail to the kitchen door. These days it's the postmistress's grand-daughter who does the round and the gate is too heavy for her. Beddoe cut out a letter box and fixed a wire basket to catch what-ever came through.'

Jemima wanted to be clear. 'Honor would know this?'

Elaine nodded. 'Though most times, Hildebrand brings our letters to us.'

'But Honor fetched her own on that occasion.' Jemima was

nagging the point for a reason. 'It suggests she was expecting something important.'

'I suppose she was,' Elaine agreed. 'I hadn't thought of it. This is why we need you, Jemima.'

Jemima let the compliment pass. Her focus was Honor van Doorn. A girl fetching a letter in the rain is a girl with something to keep private. Her eye landed on the fireplace, where the poppet nestled, apparently undiscovered by others.

'Firstly, Castle Gloaming deserves some explanation,' Jemima said. 'Why does Lord Muirhaven inhabit the gatehouse, when he could surely take a wing here without intruding on you, Mrs van Doorn?'

'It suits Hildebrand,' said Mrs van Doorn. 'The gatehouse was converted originally for the first earl's steward, being convenient for an unmarried man. Hildebrand has no taste for castle living.'

Elaine decoded the statement for Jemima's benefit. 'He grew up in a single-storey house made of wood and thatch. The kind where you step from your bedroom onto a veranda, onto a lawn.'

Jemima understood. 'Whereas you do like it here, Mrs van Doorn.'

'I always wanted to be queen of a castle,' her hostess admitted. 'And I pay a generous rent. Hildebrand has no other income.'

An impoverished peer, as Jemima had suspected.

'Does the African farm not provide an income?

'Its name was Clear Acres,' said Elaine, sipping her peppermint tea. 'It's gone. Sold. It never was profitable. His father died in debt. People assume aristocratic families are wealthy, and the first earl *was*, but as we've already discussed, he spent a fortune on this place. On his demise, death duties drained most of what was left. From what Hildebrand has shared with me and Cornelia, his own father left England on the heels of the family quarrel and bought the first property he came across.'

'Exhausted orange groves.' Cornelia van Doorn sighed. 'These Englishmen come in, without any knowledge of the terrain.'

'Instead of restoring them,' Elaine continued, 'Leopold Woolton lived it up in Durban or went hunting, leaving the land to be managed by hired hands. The brothers never reconciled. The elder brother inherited the earldom in his turn, but chose not to marry, and as Leopold pre-deceased him, Hildebrand inherited.'

'Did you say his mother died young?'

Elaine nodded. 'He was just a baby. He doesn't talk much about her.'

'That is sad. And now he's stuck with a title he never wanted, and no wealth to support it,' Jemima concluded. Which brought them back to the matter of Honor, and the fortune her future husband would share. 'Any chance the letter that came for Honor might be in her room?'

'It could be,' said Elaine.

'She will have burned it.' Mrs van Doorn looked defeated. She was nursing her sedative tea, taking small sips. 'The girl became secretive, Mrs Flowerday, I'm sorry to say.'

Jemima agreed that Honor's letter was probably ashes by now. 'But with your permission, I'd like to search for it.' She took a deep breath. 'I'd also like to see up inside the tower.'

Mrs van Doorn lowered her cup to her saucer and her rings glinted in the lamplight. Everywhere were brass lamps with glass shades, lit by unseen hands. 'This means you are staying? Elaine said so, but I'd like to hear it from you, Mrs Flowerday.'

'I'm staying,' Jemima said, 'but I hope Elaine mentioned my conditions. If I get the slightest sniff of foul play, or danger to your stepdaughter, I will walk to Trevor and telegraph the police.'

Mrs van Doorn understood perfectly and tugged on a bell rope beside the fireplace. 'All I ask is that you do your absolute best in the hours between.'

'You have my promise.'

Having summoned a maid to clear away, Mrs van Doorn gathered her shawl around her shoulders and rose. 'Hildebrand suggested a game of cards earlier, but I haven't the energy.'

Jemima was ready for bed too. Elaine said she'd wait up and make sure Hildebrand was served his coffee. 'I might give him a hand or two of whist. We're both night owls.'

Tired as she was, once upstairs, Jemima walked past her bedroom and along the gallery to Honor's room. With a lantern in her hand, she located the fireplace. The grate was clean, not a singed paper in sight. Hardly surprising, as the maids would have cleaned the room since Honor's disappearance.

Ah well. It was why it was called 'investigation'. If the obvious was laid on a plate, there'd be nothing for her to do.

Chapter Thirteen

Friday, 1 June

Jemima slept soundly that night, woken by birdsong at dawn. A beautiful first-of-the-month looked to be in prospect. Perfect for a visit to the post office at Trevor, where she hoped the postmistress had a good memory and the inclination to talk.

Crossing the river, Jemima spared a moment to look down. Lord Muirhaven must be a powerful swimmer to entrust his life to these waters. Perhaps his outdoor life in Africa had prepared him physically. Her note to Vicky was in her coat pocket, a convenient excuse for leaving the house before breakfast. From the river, she crossed the meadow, her shoes sending the dew flying. When she looked back, she could see her tracks in the grass and it recalled Elaine's impressions of Honor's final footprints. Elaine had seen them in the dew, crossing the lawn, and she hadn't mentioned a second set coming back. This strengthened the belief that Honor had made a one-way journey in the direction of the river.

Jemima's shoes were wet and her ankles damp by the time she reached the canal. They dried as she walked the beaten path. The *Miss Nettle*, whose line she'd tripped over the day before, was gone. A different vessel was moored a short way on, a cargo of roofing slates on board. A tethered horse paused in its cropping of the grass and whickered at Jemima as she passed.

At Trevor railway station, Jemima asked directions to the post office and was directed to the main street with the warning that it was yet rather early. A sign on the post-office door stated *Ar Gau*, which could mean 'We're Open' or 'We're Shut', Jemima wasn't sure. She knocked and the door was opened by the postmistress who wore a long, dark skirt and a high-collared blouse of the kind Jemima's mother had favoured in 1900.

The woman addressed Jemima in Welsh, and when Jemima smiled blankly, tapped her watch. 'Not open until eight o'clock, madam.'

Unwilling to wait around, Jemima offered apologies. 'I was hoping I might send a letter home, but also save your postie a walk to Castell Glan yr Afon.'

'Glan yr Afon?' echoed the woman. 'A guest there, is it?'

'I am, and I'd be happy to take any letters you might have and save your girl a trip.'

She was invited in and she immediately handed over the letter for Vicky.

The postmistress glanced at the front. 'Mayfair. A London lady, are you?'

'I am, and may I say how gloriously green your countryside is. I'm quite envious.'

'It's green because it rains.' The postmistress retired behind the counter, opening a stamp book and carefully tearing out a penny ha'penny one.

Jemima paid, asking, 'Anything for the castle?'

The postmistress called 'Lowri!' bringing a girl of about fifteen from the rear of the shop. The girl wore a uniform, a buttoned jacket and a brimmed felt hat. A leather satchel was slung across her chest. After a quick chat in Welsh, the girl reached into her satchel and handed a white envelope to the postmistress, who read the address on the front before giving it to Jemima.

'For Mrs van Doorn,' the postmistress explained, unnecessarily. 'From her bank, I dare say, by the Wrexham postmark. Nice quality paper, see, and a typed address. You can always tell.'

Even more so were you to steam it open, Jemima thought. Not that she suspected the postmistress of committing that sackable offence. 'Anything for Miss Honor?'

'Lowri, anything for Miss van Doorn?'

The post-girl shook her head, adding a comment in Welsh.

'The last letter for her came about three weeks ago,' the postmistress translated. 'Miss Honor had a letter from London, but nothing since.'

'Oh... Good quality paper and typewritten, as from a bank?'

'Ivory bond,' came the answer, 'handwritten in beautiful script. The postcode was WC1, if I remember rightly.'

Jemima smiled to herself. Long live inquisitive post-office staff. 'WC1 sounds like Bloomsbury,' she said.

The postmistress had never heard of it.

'It's charming if you like Georgian architecture, and it's a literary enclave.'

'Well then,' observed the postmistress.

At that moment, a new customer peered around the door, as if to check the post office really was open early. A conversation started that Jemima could not follow. She wished everyone good morning and left with Mrs van Doorn's letter in her pocket, congratulating herself on a successful fishing expedition. Honor van Doorn had received a formal communication from central London days before she disappeared. From fearing the girl was dead, she now felt more hopeful. A letter, a secret journey.

Oh, but that unsuitable clothing, the handbag left behind and the absence of shoes. A worrisome bell would not stop jingling. She set off for home and reached the fork in the canal in time to see the *Miss Nettle* mooring at the spot where she'd last seen her. It struck Jemima that there was no horse nibbling the grass, nor a tow rope. A throbbing sound and the churning of the water as the boat edged to the side explained why. The *Miss Nettle* was engine driven. A funnel between the cabin and the midsection belched steam and Jemima supposed she was witnessing mechanical innovation. Dare she stop and ask? A sturdy figure in a waxed coat and fisherman's hat stood at the tiller, directing the vessel so that its stern gently kissed the bank. As Jemima watched, the helmsman picked up a length of rope and leapt with it onto land, picking up a metal spike and a hammer from the grass.

It wasn't a helms*man*, it was a helmswoman. Jemima had mistaken oilskins, trousers and lace-up boots for male attire. Three meaty hammer blows drove the spike into the soft ground. The woman wound the rope around it, testing the tension before loping to the front of the boat to grab a rope she must have thrown to the bank earlier. She hauled in the boat's bow.

'I admire you,' Jemima said as she watched a clove hitch being tied in the mooring line. 'Doing it single-handed must be difficult, if it's windy or the water's choppy.'

The woman turned and both she and Jemima gave a simultaneous double-take. On Jemima's part, it was because the woman was Black. To be more accurate, of mixed parentage. The woman's shock seemed to arise from the fact that Jemima was wearing her chic brown cloche and velour, wrap-over coat, an outfit that passed unnoticed on Bond Street, but might be a touch *en vogue* for a towpath of the Ellesmere Canal.

The woman, whose black hair was turned up under her hat and who seemed at first glance neither youthful nor old, stared at Jemima through kohl-rimmed eyes and said, 'You again.'

'You saw me fall yesterday? I apologised. At least, I tried to.' Jemima strove to sound unruffled, but the woman was glaring. 'I'm Mrs Flowerday. Jemima Flowerday.'

'Olive Nettle.' The woman added resentfully, 'You stared in through my cabin window. I don't like that.'

Jemima gaped. She had done exactly as she was being accused... but what she had just heard overset every expectation. The woman had spoken not with a Welsh accent, but in one akin to that of Mrs van Doorn and Lord Muirhaven. Olive Nettle was South African. Jemima burned to ask if she knew Lord Muirhaven, but a glint in the dark eyes warned her off.

She looked around for a conversational gambit, and seeing the metal bucket full of feathery leaves on the cabin roof said, 'I take it you're fond of parsley.'

'It's not parsley. Don't touch it!'

'I wasn't going to.' Jemima preferred the curly-leafed variety anyway. Vicky held the contrary opinion, favouring flat-leaf, and the sisters grew separate pots in their backyard. Each to their own. 'Do you enjoy living on the water?'

Olive Nettle squared her jaw. 'Would you like to haul wet ropes and clean weed off a propellor twice an hour?' she fired back. 'You in your high-price shoes and hat?'

Jemima's hat hadn't cost much, as a friendly milliner had made it for her at cost. Her shoes *were* expensive, being handmade, but they were five years old and would go on, with care, until she was fifty. 'If I lived on a boat, I wouldn't wear this ensemble,' she conceded. 'Like you, I'd wear oilskins and trousers.' Oilskins and trousers. It sounded like a music-hall song. 'Quite a lot of women wear slacks these days.'

Olive Nettle made a sound of disgust and clambered back on board, with one last glare at Jemima. 'It's rude to walk close to a boat, staring in. Don't do it again.'

'I won't.'

That last comment had clinched it. Definitely South African. Jemima watched the woman edge along the gunwale towards the stern. The *Miss Nettle* had been built to carry a cargo, having only a small cabin to the rear. Most of the rest of the space was taken up with a canvas superstructure. The woman paused to check the tension of the ropes holding it in place.

Jemima gave up. 'I'll be on my way.' Stepping like a circus pony over the taut mooring line at the front of the boat, she noticed a profusion of pots and containers. It was a herb garden in miniature, including tomato plants and sprouting potatoes. A wicker chair was wedged amongst the pots, a newspaper folded in half on its seat. The lower half of a colourful illustration and the words 'Wedding Number' brought Jemima to a stop. How on earth...

Jemima heard the cabin window scrape open and a pale arm edged into view. A log, aimed by Olive Nettle, landed on the bank a few inches from Jemima. The window snapped shut. Jemima walked on.

Chapter Fourteen

She arrived back at Castle Gloaming to find the young housemaid Gwen waiting for her. The girl indicated that Jemima should follow and led her to a room off the great hall where Mrs van Doorn and Elaine were having breakfast. A sideboard was laid with covered dishes and Jemima discovered her favourites: bacon and mushrooms. There was bread, warm from the oven and yellow butter to spread. Explaining her errand: 'My sister will fret if she doesn't hear from me', Jemima handed over the letter entrusted to her. The postmistress had been sure it was from a bank in Wrexham, and Jemima was curious to see if this was so.

However, Mrs van Doorn made no move to open it.

'I'd like to brave the tower after breakfast, before I lose my nerve,' Jemima said to Elaine. 'Will you be my guide?'

'Of course, but I warn you, it's a testing climb. You need good lungs and knees.'

'It's where Honor goes to do her painting,' Mrs van Doorn said. She had placed the letter face down on the tablecloth. 'Where she went, I should say.' Her voice dipped, as though a cloud had passed across the sun.

Jemima was pouring coffee for herself. 'Your stepdaughter's an artist?' Nobody had thought to mention it.

'Not really. It's how she passed the time. She has no friends here.' Mrs van Doorn smoothed a wrinkle in the cloth. 'No young people to mix with. None suitable, I should say.'

'Was she lonely?' Jemima sat down and stirred sugar into her cup.

Mrs van Doorn didn't quite answer the question. 'I have blamed myself for taking up Hildebrand's offer to reside here. I thought living in a castle would be delightful. Romantic. It has isolated my stepdaughter.'

'Castles in Spain are the stuff of dreams. Castles in Wales are romantic only in novels,' Elaine observed. 'I did warn you, Cornelia.'

'You did, I know you did.' It was said contritely, but it closed the subject.

Elaine asked Jemima, 'See anything interesting during your walk?'

'Well...' Jemima had made up her mind not to mention the unfriendly boatwoman. A South African of mixed race, living on a canal two miles away, exceeded the bounds either of probability or coincidence, and the fact that nobody had mentioned it felt significant. 'I saw and heard fish a-leaping and spotted my cormorant again, but sadly no flash of a kingfisher.' She added in the same poetic vein, 'I will never tire of seeing the aqueduct rising out of the mist. It must be how our distant ancestors viewed the pyramids of Egypt. Oh, and of course, I met the postmistress.' The discovery of a letter from London WC1, arriving for Honor around three weeks ago, was this morning's greatest prize. 'A pleasant lady who, I suspect, knows who is writing to whom, from where and how often.'

Mrs van Doorn gave a little start. 'You're not suggesting the postmistress opens our letters?'

'No indeed, that's against the law. Though I'm sure, in her quieter moments, she reads postcards. There have to be some perks to the job.'

Speaking of which, Jemima set about enjoying her breakfast.

*

Afterwards, Elaine suggested they 'take on the tower'.

Mrs van Doorn wished them well, and said, 'Nobody will think the worse of you if you lose courage halfway up, Mrs Flowerday.'

Jemima was determined not to. She was not sightseeing; she was searching for traces of Honor, and clues to the girl's intentions.

Elaine led the way across the great hall and conducted Jemima down an echoey corridor where traces of ancient stonework were visible and the air grew increasingly stale. Opening an iron-studded door to reveal spiral steps, she said, 'Onward?'

'Onward.'

Their footsteps rang and the curving walls amplified their breath. Slit windows at intervals gave just enough light to go by, but it was a relentless climb and when they reached the top and entered a circular room, Jemima was panting.

She had constrained her fear of heights until this moment, only there wasn't much to alarm her. The room was cleanly plastered with a card table in the centre on which stood a glazed vase containing dried-out stems. The table was the fold-away kind, easy to carry up and downstairs. Other than that, there was an easel with a schoolroom chair next to it.

Mrs van Doorn had said that Honor came up here to paint but this room gave no sense of being the studio of someone with a vocation.

'When was Honor last in here?'

'Likely the day before she disappeared. She came most days, once the weather warmed up.'

Jemima asked Elaine to be more precise.

'From about the middle of March, I suppose. Before then it would be too cold to stand around up here.'

'And she came with her pencils and paints, and brought the table and easel up here to work at?'

'Yes, though I expect Beddoe carried the heavier things for her.

Or Ifor, the garden boy. Honor would slip away all the time. One got used to it. Cornelia's indifferent health and habit of taking naps gave Honor a lot of freedom. Whether she came up here every single day, I couldn't tell you. I made a practice of not asking.' Elaine said it firmly. 'I didn't ever want to be accused of spying on her. Are you ready to step outside?'

A Gothic arch on one side of the room contained a door, which opened inwards. Elaine held it wide, showing Jemima the wooden parapet she had already viewed from the ground. Anxious tremors rushed to her stomach and knees, the first signs of primal panic.

It didn't help when Elaine said, 'I can't bear heights, so I'll stay here if you don't mind.'

'Is the platform safe?'

'It's built of oak and the first earl would bring some of the most important people in the land up here to enjoy the view.'

In that case... Jemima sternly reminded herself that she wasn't being paid to cower inside and, gulping a breath, stepped out onto the planks. Instantly, the breeze whipped around her face and lifted her hair. She hadn't put her coat or hat back on, and it was quite chilly. A rail at waist height gave some comfort, and she gripped it as she made a faltering circuit of the tower.

The roof was home to cawing birds. Bright eyes and beaks poked out from under the tiles as she made a second, more confident, circuit. The view on the side opposite the doorway was of a line of smoky blue hills that might be Snowdonia. On the door side, the treeline showed the meander of the River Dee all the way to the aqueduct. A boat was crossing in the direction of Trevor. From here, she could look down on Lord Muirhaven's gatehouse.

'Are you all right?' came Elaine's anxious voice.

Jemima stepped back inside the room. 'Did Honor paint landscapes? I can't imagine any view more inspiring.'

'Well, imagine again.' Elaine pointed to the vase on the card table. 'She preferred still life. Pastels and watercolours and, I'm sorry to say, she hadn't much talent.'

Jemima stared at the dried stems in the vase. They were mostly daffodils, tracing-paper petals with brown veining, a few twigs of pussy willow stuck among them. Pussy willow was among the first harbingers of spring, coming into bud in March. About when Honor began using the tower, though Jemima was starting to suspect she hadn't done any actual painting in a while.

'Was she as lonely as Mrs van Doorn implied?' Jemima asked.

Elaine's hesitation hinted at professional tact. 'It's fair to say that living here was only ever Cornelia's wish. She saw herself opening fetes and being lady-patroness of a castle.'

'Except...?' Jemima prompted.

'There is no real society here. There are respectable people, of course, and a flourishing light-opera scene in Wrexham. But this is Welsh Wales. A different character from anything she expected.'

'And Lord Muirhaven had no idea either,' Jemima suggested. 'Growing up amid the orange trees, seeing nothing much of the world, it wouldn't occur to him that anyone desiring high society should head for London. Even so, I am intrigued that he has made no effort to take up his position. I wouldn't have him down as a shy man.'

Elaine's shrug was uncomfortable. 'I can't answer for Hildebrand.'

'No, of course not. But what of you, are you also going slowly mad amid the greenery?' Seeing Elaine twist her wedding ring as if consulting a memory, Jemima added, 'You are here because life dealt you a difficult turn. May I ask what happened?'

'My husband died,' came the unembellished reply. 'He drowned. Are you also bereaved, Jemima?' Elaine glanced at Jemima's wedding finger. 'I suspect you are too. It makes three of us, the "not-very-merry widows" of Castle Gloaming.'

'I'm not a widow,' Jemima said.

'But you make your own living. You are independent. Is that a choice?'

'A necessity. I don't mind explaining as I believe you'll understand.' In the stripped-down way she'd acquired through repetition, Jemima explained how her husband Simon had been severely injured during the war, on a battlefield in France. 'A shell exploded close by, killing several of his comrades. He managed to drag one of them to a foxhole, where he was later found. They thought he wouldn't survive his injuries, but he did. He was sent home and I thought I had my husband back... sadly, what they couldn't mend was his mind. He is at Netley, a hospital near Southampton.'

'Southampton?' The name brought a jolt from Elaine.

'Of course, where your ship docked,' Jemima said. 'Remind me which one you were on?'

'RMS *Llanstephan Castle*. I spent some days in port, talking to the police,' Elaine said with visible distaste. 'My husband, Cecil, died on the voyage.'

'You said he drowned?'

'He went overboard. Fell into the sea.'

'Oh, my goodness. How?'

Elaine shook her head. 'I don't suppose I will ever know, because I only realised he was missing when I woke in our cabin next morning. I assumed he'd gone out for a breath of air. I didn't worry at first and went up for breakfast. By mid-morning, I was starting to fret. The ship was searched to no avail. We were a day away from Cape Town by that point, but the captain turned us around to search.'

'How very distressing for you.' Jemima couldn't help asking, 'What time did he fall in, d'you think?'

'I suppose it was the dead of night, else he'd have been seen on deck. We'd had dinner in our cabin the previous evening. Cecil had been unwell from the off. He suffered from seasickness and wouldn't join the other passengers on deck as we rounded the tip of Africa. It's a ritual on board, to pop corks at Cape Agulhas as you leave one ocean for another. Cecil never much enjoyed what he called "organised fun". I went up on my own and it was a beautiful dusk followed by a wondrous night of stars, the moon diamond-bright. After a while, I went down to persuade Cecil to come up to the rail, but he said he was going to play billiards and maybe a hand of cards with some chap later. I decided to call it a night, and turned in. I didn't see him again. The ship went all the way back to Cape Agulhas.'

'No trace found?'

'Those seas are vast. If you sail south from there, you eventually reach Antarctica.' Elaine shivered, as if the idea of her husband drifting out into the deadly cold disturbed her. 'They had to search; it's maritime tradition, but nobody expected to find a body. Apart from me, of course.' She dashed a hand at her cheek. 'Hope springs eternal. When we reached Cape Town late, the passengers embarking there were thoroughly miffed.'

'Not all, surely,' Jemima said. 'I believe you told me that the van Doorns joined the ship at Cape Town and, clearly, a friendship sprung up between you.'

'Oh, that's Cornelia all over.' Elaine smiled. 'We found ourselves gazing out over the same section of rail on the promenade deck one morning and got talking. We discovered a lot in common. She had also lost her husband at sea and was journeying towards a new life in England. I was journeying towards heaven-knew-what. Obscure widowhood, struggling on the little savings I had. I don't know how you've been left provided, Jemima, but Cecil died with debts.'

'Is that why you were going to England, to escape the creditors?'

The faint blush Jemima was growing familiar with entered Elaine's cheeks. 'You don't miss much, do you? Like me, Cecil was

English, but shortly after we married he announced we were going to emigrate. No discussion, he'd made his mind up.' Elaine shrugged. 'I hadn't much to keep me in England as my parents were dead, my one sister married and she didn't take to Cecil.'

'What was his trade?'

The blush deepened. 'I don't think you'll like what I'm going to say.'

Jemima promised to stay neutral.

'Big game. He booked tickets for wealthy Englishmen wanting to come out to shoot. Not that he joined in,' Elaine added hurriedly. 'He was their travel agent.'

Jemima didn't like it, not one bit. She had once been handed a sporting rifle by her father-in-law on their Suffolk estate and ordered to 'bag a pheasant'. She had aimed for a cloud, injuring her shoulder, and had been sent back to the house in disgrace. But none of this was Elaine's fault.

'With your husband dead, you still had to carry on to England, to face life alone,' Jemima stated.

'Yes, except there was no home waiting for me. The best I could hope for was to find a job in a shop, and a room in a hostel for distressed gentlewomen. I hope I haven't given you the wrong impression of Cecil but he was a complicated man. We'd been in the Cape about six years when war broke out. He joined up in 1916 and was sent out to the Dardanelles. He was there for the slaughter at Gallipoli. Like your Simon, he never really recovered. He could be wonderfully amusing then, suddenly, he'd turn and be frightening. Though he never hurt me,' Elaine added quickly. 'He would fall into melancholy and his headaches...' She shut her eyes, afflicted by the memory. 'He took morphine, they were so bad.'

'Had he taken morphine when he went overboard?'

'Almost certainly.' Elaine pushed the wedding ring she'd wound over her mid-finger joint, back into place. 'He'd been drinking too, during his game of billiards. I'm told he made a decent fist of it, even so, and won a few rounds of poker in the smoking room after.'

'You were told this by the chap he made the arrangement with? Could this man not offer any more insights or information?'

'No, because he left Cecil alone to finish off a glass of whisky sour. They'd shaken hands and said goodnight. I believe Cecil finished his drink, then went out for a smoke or to look at the stars.'

Stars kept cropping up. Jemima thought of the five-pointed ones drawn in the dust of a table, and a half-moon above. Like the sign of the Moon and Stars in Rye Old Town. Mine's a pint, please landlord. Or in the case of Cecil Cleeve, whisky sour and morphine.

'He went to the ship's rail and leaned out too far?' Jemima suggested.

'If the boat rolled, he might have overbalanced,' agreed Elaine. 'The currents are strong there. Did I say that already?'

'You can be forgiven for repeating yourself when it comes to so deep a trauma. Did Mrs van Doorn offer you a job on the voyage?'

'She did and I will always be in her debt. I count her a dear friend.'

'You know what they say, "A friend in need".' One thing niggled at Jemima. 'You said a moment ago that you spoke with the police in Southampton. Surely the death would have been reported at Cape Town?'

'No. The *Llanstephan Castle* is a British Royal Mail ship, and the captain's first act was to inform the directors of the Union Castle Line. They called Scotland Yard who passed the investigation to the Southampton police. Two of them boarded as we came into port.' Elaine shivered. 'DI Pollard was one. I forget the other's name.'

It must have been a brutal experience, Jemima thought, a grilling on top of a shocking bereavement.

Jemima was growing cold and it was time to leave the tower. 'Is there any of Honor's artwork I can see?'

'In her room.' Elaine seemed pleased to move to a different topic. 'I had one of her sketches framed as a surprise for her birthday in January.'

They left the tower room.

In Honor's room, Elaine pointed out the painting, a watercolour study of holly and ivy in a glass jug. Jemima lifted it off its hook and studied it. What she saw bore out Elaine's verdict on Honor van Doorn's talent. Absent.

She put the picture back on its hook. 'Where's the rest of her work?'

The question seemed to take Elaine by surprise. Something else she had not thought about. 'I don't know.'

'If she's been going into the tower to paint and draw since March, there ought to be a body of work. At least a few sketch books.'

'I see. You're right.'

They looked under the bed, in and behind the wardrobe, and in a blanket chest without result.

Elaine suggested asking Mrs van Doorn at lunch. 'Which is in an hour, by the way.'

'Do I need to dress?' Jemima was wearing one of her comfortable skirt and jersey outfits, the kind she liked because they allowed her to walk, kneel, bend and wield a tape measure.

'You're fine. Hildebrand will turn up in the usual garb.'

'He eats every meal here, did you say?'

'Since Cornelia got rid of the maid that used to wait on him, yes.'

Interesting. 'Why did she do that?'

'Oh, you know. The girl was young, rather pert. It wasn't working.'

At 12.30 p.m., the three women sat down to salad and cold ham in the dining room. Lord Muirhaven didn't join them, though a place was laid for him. After waiting some time for Elaine to bring up the matter of Honor's missing paintings, Jemima mentioned it.

Cornelia van Doorn looked mystified. 'You're certain there's nothing up in the tower? That's where she went to paint. Honor couldn't stand anybody standing over her, watching her work.'

'Understandable,' agreed Jemima. In her early days as a dress designer, she'd hated sketching while a client looked on. However, her suspicions were tending elsewhere and as soon as lunch was over she announced she would take another look at the painting in Honor's bedroom.

'What is your interest in it?' Mrs van Doorn was going to take a stroll around the gardens and had invited Jemima to join her.

'I want an idea of who your stepdaughter was. Is.' They had all fallen into the unfortunate habit of referring to Honor in the past tense. 'What might have motivated her to leave? Has Elaine mentioned that she left without money, a coat or even shoes?'

Turning to her secretary, who looked very much as if a cat had been let out of a bag, Mrs van Doorn repeated, 'No shoes?' in an anguished voice. 'You didn't say, Elaine!'

'It is Mrs Flowerday's supposition that she was unshod,' Elaine replied tersely. 'We have no actual proof and, anyway, I didn't want to worry you.'

'I need to know everything. Everything.' Mrs van Doorn pressed a hand to her temple, presumably to quell a headache. 'I don't believe I will walk after all. Would you have Gwen or Mairwen come up and brew a cup of my special tea?'

Elaine refused point-blank. 'The maids are busy. I'll walk out with you, because exercise and sunlight are the best medicine. I'll make your tea for you afterwards in your suite. Will you mind if we abandon you?' she asked Jemima.

Jemima minded not at all and went up to Honor's room. The little painting with its signature of 'H. van D.' did not hold her attention very long. Her real intention was to establish if, from this room, one could see the shrubbery. And indeed, one could.

Going into every room on this side of the castle convinced her that the only other place with a view of the shrubbery was the long gallery. And, of course, from the top of the tower. Jemima returned there, but the prospect of a toiling up all those steps and getting a stitch again deterred her, as did the growing suspicion that Honor van Doorn had not spent day after bleak day painting in the tower room. Rather than return to the great hall, she continued on along the passage, further than she'd come with Elaine, and discovered a sturdy door. An iron key protruded from the lock, but the door opened at a pull. Jemima walked out into a compact courtyard.

'I think,' she said to herself, 'I have discovered how Honor van Doorn left Castle Gloaming.'

Chapter Fifteen

A gate in the courtyard wall invited Jemima onward. She went through it on to a terrace, beyond which was the lawn where Honor had impressed her bare footprints.

The shrubbery, she discovered, was a plantation of lilacs long past their best, and overgrown bay trees with dry leaf litter beneath. The ground was thick with bluebells gone-to-seed. Anyone entering this enclave would quickly be hidden from sight. The air was still and markedly cooler than the castle lawn. She pressed on towards the river, following its sound, passing an egg-shaped brick building with a low door. Peering in, she was hit by frigid air which, when she bent and entered, she discovered emanated from a plinth of thick slate. On it was a tin bath holding ice shards, their edges reflecting the minimal light. A hammer and a pick lay beside it.

Well, at least she now knew how the gin got cold.

She left, happy to be back in fresh air, and on her way to the river. The path sloped down, gently at first, growing steeper until it became a series of broad steps. She counted them until she reached forty, at which point she couldn't hear herself over the river's voice. At the water's edge, she turned to the right, no idea where she was heading, but letting the river lead the way.

After thirty minutes or so, the aqueduct appeared above the treetops. A scramble up a jagged path brought her to a lane and, from there, hot and out of breath, she arrived at the point where the canal began its course across the valley, with nothing below but pillars and a dizzying drop into the foaming waters. A path ran along one side of the aqueduct and Jemima mustered the courage to walk a short way along it. With nothing but a steel rail between her and nothingness, one glance over the edge made her innards lurch.

The canal itself was wide enough only for one vessel at a time. Two boats travelling in opposite directions could never pass and it troubled her until she saw distant figures ahead of her, running, and she deduced that this was some kind of information-relay. Lads sprinting from one side of the aqueduct to the other to hail the boats approaching in the opposite direction.

'Hold your position, my dad's coming across!'

A narrowboat that had been approaching for some minutes was now alongside her. Jemima recognised the *Miss Nettle* from the black funnel and green-painted cabin and the plants in the bow. The boatwoman, Olive Nettle, was guiding the tiller, her gaze fixed ahead and either she didn't recognise Jemima, or didn't see her. So slowly was she going, Jemima could have stepped aboard with no difficulty.

There was the newspaper she'd spotted earlier, still folded on the chair, a stone on top to stop it blowing away. This time, the masthead was visible and though Jemima couldn't make out the date, she didn't need to. Half the world would know the faces gazing from the front page.

Was it Olive Nettle's reading choice, or that of the figure whose pale arm had briefly emerged through the cabin window? Jemima began to laugh as myriad suspicions blended into one clear idea. She was still laughing as she retraced her steps. From here, you could see Castle Gloaming's tower and it followed that, from the tower, you could watch the boats pass by on the aqueduct.

Twelve days ago, early in the morning, Honor van Doorn had vanished leaving nothing but footprints in the dew. Anxious enquiries at the railway station had drawn no information of a young woman answering Honor's description having caught a train.

Of course not. Why bother with a train when a more private form of transport glided by several times a day, every day?

Jemima lost no time in returning to the castle. She found Elaine in the breakfast room, bent over a set of accounts. Apologising for the interruption, she requested that Mrs van Doorn be fetched.

'Why, what's happened?' Elaine peered at Jemima and asked if she realised she had bits of greenery on her shoulders and sleeves.

Jemima looked and saw that tendrils of the plant known variously as cleavers, goosegrass and sticky bob had attached to her, probably as she made her way down from the aqueduct. She picked them off, but her explanation was stolen by violent screams from the great hall.

She ran out and was in time to see Mrs van Doorn almost falling down the stairs in her urgency to reach the ground floor. The screams came from her mouth, and her voice split as she cried out on seeing Jemima, 'She's back. My stepdaughter is back!'

Chapter Sixteen

Between them, the housekeeper and Elaine supported Mrs van Doorn to the drawing room, leaving Jemima free to run to the front entrance where loud thuds indicated that somebody wanted to come in.

Opening the door, she saw Lord Muirhaven with a mud-daubed girl in his arms. Jemima got her first sight of Honor van Doorn in the flesh. As he strode in, Jemima saw he was also holding a white hat, its brim scrunched in one hand. She recognised it by its oversized silk flower, its colour in real life a vibrant scarlet. She hurried to fling open the drawing-room door and watched Lord Muirhaven lay down his burden.

Honor was slight of build, but taller than Jemima had realised from her picture. Her blonde hair was smeared with the same mud that pasted her face and hands. As Jemima had predicted, she was wearing a white linen sailor top and trousers, filthy and torn.

Mrs van Doorn had escaped the concerned clutches of her secretary and housekeeper and cast herself on her knees beside the sofa where Honor lay. 'Oh, my child, my child. Say something, Honor, please. *Please*, darling.'

Honor van Doorn's lashes fluttered, revealing guileless blue eyes. 'Mamma Cornelia, my feet hurt.'

Jemima looked and pulled in a short breath. Muddy as they were, it was obvious that Honor's bare feet were blood streaked.

'We need to clean those,' she said to Mrs Beddoe, who went at once and returned with a first-aid box, Gwen following with hot water and towels.

Honor's feet were cleaned and gravel picked from her flesh. Even when her wounds were bathed with dilute surgical spirit, she made not a sound. Jemima was impressed.

Mrs van Doorn cradled her, moaning, 'My poor, brave girl. You are home, you are safe.'

'Safe, but in quite a state,' Jemima observed. 'Who did this, Miss van Doorn?'

Blue eyes, wide and wounded, locked onto hers. 'A man,' Honor whispered.

'But who? Tell us.'

'A rough man. I don't know who.'

'Describe him.' Jemima threw a glance at Lord Muirhaven who had retired to sit on an ottoman on the other side of the room and was watching in silence.

'Dark-haired. Wild. A beard. He smelled awful,' Honor gasped.

'Age?' asked Jemima.

'I don't know. He – he blindfolded me.'

'For all of the twelve days you've been missing?'

'Yes.'

'How, then, did you discern his hair colour?'

Honor looked momentarily confounded. 'I... I just did. I don't know, it was so confusing.'

'I understand. Where did he keep you all this time?'

'In a cave, I think, or a cavern.'

'Either or both?'

'I don't know! Why are you questioning me?'

Honor's story, as Jemima was later to write in her journal, quickly unravelled and could be succinctly described as bunkum. Repeated 'I don't knows' interspersed with details such as having had a sack thrust over her head and being dragged from the castle garden and tied up in a cavern... or a cave... not only sounded unconvincing, but proved so when Jemima sought permission to roll up Honor's trouser leg. The skin from ankle to knee was lily-white. Completely clean.

Jemima's son, Tommy, devoured hair-raising adventures in which half-human beasts abducted unwary humans, or occasionally faithful dogs, leaving heroic boys like himself little choice but to rescue them. Jemima detected a strong similarity in Honor's story, though whether Honor shared Tommy's reading matter she neither knew nor cared. Mrs van Doorn's joy at seeing Honor alive was enough for now.

Lord Muirhaven's reaction was of more interest. He had moved from the ottoman to the sofa opposite the one where Mrs van Doorn sat beside her stepdaughter. His shirtsleeves and the front of his waistcoat were streaked with mud, but he seemed oblivious of it as he leaned forward to take one of Cornelia's hands between both of his.

While Honor drank the hot, sweet tea the older of the two maids brought in for her, Mrs van Doorn's hand lay sandwiched in a clasp that seemed to Jemima to be both protective and tender. The occasional glance Lord Muirhaven spared for Honor was strikingly indifferent. If Mrs van Doorn still had hopes of a marriage in that quarter, Jemima reflected, she was backing the wrong horse. Did she not feel the man's interest focussed on herself? Could any woman be so completely without vanity?

'Let me understand, Honor,' Lord Muirhaven said in a teasing voice, 'all this time, you've been kept tied hand and foot? You must have been perishing cold.'

'Dreadfully,' Honor agreed, taking a sip of tea, wincing because it was too hot. 'And so very, very frightened.'

'I should say so,' agreed His Lordship. 'This man, this hairy abductor... did he harm you in any way?'

Honor shook her head. 'Only frightened me.'

'That's a relief. Shall we send for the police?'

'No, please...' New tears followed their predecessors down the dirt tracks on Honor's cheeks. 'I can't talk about it. All I want is a bath and to sleep.'

'That is exactly what you will have,' cried Mrs van Doorn, pulling her hand free. 'Drink your tea and eat your Welsh cakes, darling girl. We won't ask you anything more.'

'Thank you, Mamma Cornelia.' Honor managed a grateful smile. 'I missed you.'

'And I you, darling.'

And so endeth the drama, thought Jemima and wondered if there was a word to describe a situation where all parties agreed, by unspoken consent, not to probe the chief witness's testimony, but to sweep it under the rug and drink tea? She would ponder it later. Meanwhile, she wondered if she might resurrect the job she'd come here to do – designing two sets of summer clothes. If so, would the double fee hold good? Honor's miraculous return had stolen Jemima's thunder, glad though she was to see the girl in one piece. The cheque was still in her dressing-table drawer and Jemima decided she would give it back only if asked.

Elaine and Mrs Beddoe conducted Honor upstairs to be bathed and put to bed. Mrs van Doorn wanted to go with them, but Elaine was adamant.

'You've had a shock. I'll have Mrs Beddoe light your kettle and make your special tea, then you can rest in your room.'

It left Jemima, Lord Muirhaven and Mrs van Doorn to digest the turn of events. An imp in Jemima's soul prompted her to urge that someone should, really should, fetch the police.

'I mean, if there's a wild man in the woods abducting maidens?'
Mrs van Doorn twisted her hands together. 'On no account.'

Lord Muirhaven shot Jemima a frigid look.

'But this man, this monster,' cried Jemima, 'holding Honor prisoner in a cave... or cavern. I volunteer to go. I will ask the stationmaster to put a call in to the nearest Criminal Investigation Department.'

This time, Lord Muirhaven's look said, 'You've had your fun.' He reclaimed Mrs van Doorn's hand and said, 'Let's all admit it, Cornelia. That girl's story was hogwash.'

'Hog... w-w-what?' stammered Mrs van Doorn.

'Wash,' he repeated. 'Rubbish, balderdash, delusion.'

The diamond-studded hand was again pulled away abruptly. 'Honor doesn't lie.'

'I didn't say she lied. I am saying she created a fiction because she can't deal with reality. Whatever the cause, we don't want the police here,' said Lord Muirhaven. 'We let it pass and say no more.'

Jemima found this interesting. Wasn't he just the tiniest bit curious to know where his tenant's seventeen-year-old daughter had been for nigh on two weeks? 'What is it you fear Honor can't deal with?' she asked him.

'I don't know,' he said irritably. 'You're the genius in the room, you tell us.'

'It's not my place to guess,' Jemima said, 'but when a young woman keeps a secret from her elders, it usually boils down to romance or waywardness.'

'Honor is not wayward!' Mrs van Doorn's voice strained upwards.

'Then it's romance.'

'You're saying she has a young man? How?' Mrs van Doorn shook her head, genuinely perplexed. 'How would she meet anyone? There's only old Mr Beddoe and his nephew who helps in the garden and tends the pony.'

Jemima had not yet seen 'young Ifor', fetcher of luggage among his other duties, but a thought sidled in. 'How young exactly is he?'

'Seventeen or eighteen,' said Lord Muirhaven.

The perfect age for Honor to fall in love with. 'Is Ifor handsome?'

'I suppose,' said Mrs van Doorn. 'If you like dark eyes and a brooding kind of gloom.'

Jemima laughed out loud. 'Well, I'm sorry. "If you like dark eyes..." Think about Jane Eyre, Catherine Earnshaw, Lizzie Bennett.'

'I don't know any of them,' declared Mrs van Doorn. 'Honor wouldn't care for a boy from a labourer's cottage. Her head is full of bigger dreams.'

'In that I agree with you,' said Jemima soberly. She toyed with the idea of mentioning what she had seen that morning on the bow of the *Miss Nettle* but decided to fudge. She said, 'In my opinion, Honor engineered her disappearance.'

'Why would she? Honor wouldn't know where to begin,' cried Mrs van Doorn.

Jemima was adjusting her ideas of her hostess. Rather than being a victim of unworldly innocence, Cornelia van Doorn was blinkered. Locked inside her own world view, finding it impossible to accept that others saw life differently. 'It's not for me to guess at Honor's motives,' Jemima said, 'but you'll recall Elaine mentioning the letter that came.'

'Elaine *thought* Honor might have had one,' insisted Mrs van Doorn, 'but probably she was mistaken.'

Dear, dear, this was uphill work. 'I'd better tell you,' Jemima said, 'that the postmistress confirmed a letter arrived for your step-daughter with a London postmark. It adds up. A desire for London, a letter from the same, followed by a twelve-day disappearance. If I had to place a bet, Mrs van Doorn, I'd say your stepdaughter enjoyed a trip to the Smoke.'

'Enjoyed?' Spots of colour jumped into the pale cheeks. 'She was kept prisoner. How can you say she enjoyed that? I believe my stepdaughter. I always will. Ah, bless you, Mairwen, my special tea.'

The elder of the two maids had arrived with a tray.

Mairwen. Jemima had liked the name on first hearing and looked more closely at its owner. Mairwen was a few years older than Gwen and seemed designed for this place with her dark hair and eyes, and similar disinclination to speak. The hands holding the tea tray were pale and long-fingered, the nails neat, suggesting she took great care of them.

'Anything else, madam?' Mairwen asked in a low voice.

'Not for me. You, Mrs Flowerday?'

Jemima needed nothing, other than a minute alone to think. With the day almost spent, and dinner in under two hours, the party split up, but as Jemima made for the stairs, a voice called her back.

'You said London.' Lord Muirhaven was striding towards her. 'What's your evidence?'

'That's my privilege,' Jemima answered. Having done her sleuthing, she'd been reflecting that it would be a relief to sketch summer dresses and ponder on bias-cut versus straight grain, on beading versus Russian embroidery. But Hildebrand's tone pushed her to a question of her own. 'Mrs van Doorn ran down to greet Honor before you were through the door. So, who saw her first?'

'Me. I was taking my shower on the riverbank.' Seeing Jemima's expression, he barked a laugh. 'There's a spring that spurts out of the rocks, a little way on from the bridge. Standing beneath it is my preferred method of washing.'

'I thought you swam in the river.'

'I was teasing, Mrs Flowerday. Only a fool would wade into that flow. Washing in my apartment means lugging water pitchers up and down steps. I prefer the natural option.'

'It must be cold in winter.'

'Glacial.' He grinned. 'But I'm a hardy colonial. Who else can boast they wash in company with otters and kingfishers?'

Jemima thought that she'd rather bathe in the company of soap and a flannel, but Lord Muirhaven's arrangements certainly sounded invigorating. 'Did Honor stumble along the riverside path as you took your shower?'

He nodded. 'Luckily I'd finished and was dressed when she rounded a bend, all in her white.'

'Her clothes were very soiled. Surely, there wasn't much white to be seen.'

'White beneath the dirt. You're very specific, Mrs Flowerday.'

She accepted it as a compliment. 'In my line of work, accuracy is all.' That went for sewing and sleuthing. 'She was dishevelled when you first saw her?'

'She certainly didn't roll in the dirt as I stood watching. She came into view messed up, fainting with exhaustion.'

Quite so, Jemima thought cynically. Tired out, having run like the clappers to get back to the castle before I could report her presence on the *Miss Nettle*. Clever girl must have been watching from inside the cabin and realised I'd rumbled her. 'What did she say at that moment, Lord Muirhaven?'

'Nothing. She was sobbing and almost distracted, as if she feared she was being pursued.'

'You don't believe her abduction story, for all that.'

Lord Muirhaven raised his palms. 'Twelve days in a cave, with a hairy man-beast? No. But there's a grain of truth in every story. I don't see it as my job to drag secrets from Honor's soul. Nor is it yours, pardon me for saying.'

'I thoroughly agree. That responsibility resides with Mrs van Doorn, with Elaine's support, perhaps.' Changing the subject, she asked where Mrs van Doorn's bedroom suite was located.

Lord Muirhaven pointed to the mezzanine that encircled the

domed foyer. 'Her rooms are the Countess's Suite, named for my grandmother, who spent much of her life here.'

From this, Jemima established that Mrs van Doorn's suite lay on the opposite side of the staircase to hers. From her window, Cornelia would look down onto the kitchen gardens. She would see the gatehouse and main courtyard from an oblique angle. It was perfectly possible that she'd spotted Lord Muirhaven crossing with Honor in his arms and flown from her room, almost falling in her haste. Hildebrand must have carried Honor from the river's edge. Well, he was tall and strong, and Honor wasn't a strapping girl.

'I take it you left the castle's entrance gate wedged open when you went to bathe,' Jemima said.

Lord Muirhaven looked puzzled. 'I can't say I remember. Why do you ask?'

'I was wondering how, otherwise, you'd have opened it with a fainting damsel in your arms? Unless you put her on the ground while you did so.'

Her flippancy clearly annoyed him and his tone changed. 'I was in the grip of extraordinary emotion, seeing the girl alive and well. The minutes afterwards have gone from my mind.'

'Understandable.' Jemima smiled. 'It must have done your heart good to see her.'

She could have added, 'Who would not rejoice to see the youthful heir to a fortune come home, mostly unscathed?' but discretion prevailed. One last question, though.

'Do many other South Africans live around here? I met one, I believe. She owns a boat called the *Miss Nettle*.'

For three heartbeats, Hildebrand, Lord Muirhaven, stared down like a man who has seen a grave open to reveal his own bones. He collected himself, saying robustly, 'I don't know what you're talking about. Who calls a boat "Nettle"?' He leaned in and whispered on the back of a teasing smile, 'Castle Gloaming is affecting you... as it does us all. You're starting to see things that aren't there, Mrs Flowerday.'

Chapter Seventeen

Oh, no I'm not, Jemima reflected to herself in a moment of solitary pantomime. As she walked outside – she'd decided a stroll through the herb garden would suit her better than continuing upstairs – the circling cries of rooks – or were they crows? – took her gaze to the top of the tower.

'Home to roost,' she muttered, wondering why that phrase betokened trouble.

In the kitchen garden, late sunshine flowed like aged champagne. Shadows were long, the air chilling like wine on a marble shelf. Would they bother with pre-dinner drinks this evening? Most likely, she and Elaine would dine à deux, unless Lord Muirhaven joined them. 'If I'm a judge of character, he won't risk me being alone with Elaine, asking questions about a South African diaspora.'

She ambled around the vegetable beds, going up the long edge of one plot and returning down the other side. With six beds to inspect in this plough-wise fashion, several minutes went by. She was able to appreciate how rich the soil was, how well dug.

She strolled in the same style around the cutting garden, leaning into a clump of vibrant honesty to rescue a ladybird on its back. The skirt she'd put on that morning for her walk to the post office was sage green with a nubbly texture and when she stepped back from the bed, there were purple petals on it. She brushed them off.

A boy was watching her. He was on the far side of the garden and appeared to be cutting up shrub prunings, slicing through stems with shears, throwing the bits onto a heap. It must be the brooding Ifor. Jemima got the impression of a well-grown young man with a mop of dark curls. He wore a hessian apron, the sort with pockets for penknives and balls of twine. She had assumed the poppet in the fireplace represented Lord Muirhaven, but here was another contender.

Though did it matter? Country lore and lovelorn hearts were not her territory. She entered the spiral herb garden just as Mrs Beddoe came round a corner of the castle with a basket over her arm. After greeting Jemima, she snipped some fennel fronds, laying them in her basket. After that, came marjoram and a plant Jemima took to be cow parsley only to be corrected.

'Sweet cicely, or garden myrrh if you like.' Mrs Beddoe held out a ferny leaf. 'Try some.'

Jemima chewed cautiously. 'It tastes of aniseed. It's not that different from fennel.'

'But from a different family. Sweet cicely is one of the Apiaceae family. Or umbellifers, which is easier to say. Like carrots and parsley.'

'And hemlock?'

'Yes, that too, though they call hemlock "fool's parsley", don't they?'

Did they? Jemima had much to learn.

'Sweet cicely aids digestion, which is why I put it into salads,' Mrs Beddoe told her. 'I distil the root in brandy too, to sharpen the appetite and settle the stomach, as the monks used to.'

'There were monks here?'

'No, but at Valle Crucis. A Cistercian abbey,' Mrs Beddoe

explained, perceiving that Jemima had never heard of it. 'It was built by Prince Madog who also built Castell Glan yr Afon. See, Mrs Flowerday, everything changes but nothing does.'

A sharp cry made them both look round. Mairwen was approaching, in obvious distress. She began speaking before she reached them, in Welsh, and Jemima had to wait until the housekeeper had heard her out.

'She's been turned off,' Mrs Beddoe said.

'Turned off?' Jemima repeated. 'You mean—'

'Sacked. Dismissed.'

'On what charge?'

With a visible effort at keeping her anger under control, Mrs Beddoe explained that Mairwen had been to see Miss van Doorn in her room. 'She ought not have.'

'I only went in to ask where my dress was,' Mairwen burst out.

'Your dress?' Jemima repeated.

'The one I keep for best. I realised this morning it was missing. She took it, I know she did.'

'Well, you should have asked me to brooch the matter,' Mrs Beddoe said gruffly. 'It doesn't do, marching into a young lady's bedroom.'

'I can't see it's a sacking matter,' Jemima said. 'I'll go speak with Mrs van Doorn.'

Mrs Beddoe forbade it. 'You will make things worse. Anyway, it was young miss who had hysterics and Mrs Cleeve who insisted Mairwen be turned off.'

Elaine? That was strange, though everyone was in a fluster at this moment. 'Tell you what, I'll have a word with Lord Muirhaven,' Jemima said. 'You're *his* staff, are you not?'

Again, she was forbidden. 'He won't step in. Mrs van Doorn pays our wages. It gives her all the power. Her and Mrs Cleeve, and I'm not sure which is worse. I've a notion Mrs Cleeve sent Eleri away.'

'Who?'

'The maid who looked after Lord Muirhaven. Please ignore me. I'm speaking out of turn,' said Mrs Beddoe.

Mairwen had begun to cry and Jemima felt a wave of pity. Rich girls like Honor van Doorn had no idea the consequence of turning off a maidservant. Often, they had nowhere to go or, even if they did, their families could not afford to keep them. The disgrace of a dismissal prevented them easily finding new work.

'You must let me do something,' Jemima urged.

'Let us deal with this our own way.' Mrs Beddoe pressed down the herbs in her basket and bid Mairwen to pluck sorrel. The girl went to a different part of the herb bed and came back with a bunch of mid-green leaves.

Taking it from her, Mrs Beddoe said, 'The sharpness of sorrel heals the kidneys and brings peace to the soul. It counters a spiteful temper and is a balm for grief.'

'Into the salad it goes?' suggested Jemima. 'I have to say, talking to Mrs van Doorn would be quicker.'

'We have our own ways, Mrs Flowerday.'

Mrs Beddoe led Mairwen away, to the kitchens where herbal magic would no doubt be spun to induce Mrs van Doorn to relent. While they'd been talking, Ifor had wheeled his barrow to the furthest end of the garden where he appeared to be scything at a thicket of weeds. On impulse, Jemima went over and introduced herself. Ifor lifted his cap, though he immediately went back to his work. The brief interaction proved something. Ifor's eyes were sloe black.

'*He* did not inspire the charm in the chimney breast,' Jemima said to herself as she returned to the castle. 'The poppet looks out through eyes of steely grey and whoever made it has, as I do, a passion for detail.'

She felt tired suddenly, and her earlier wish for a quiet moment in her room re-asserted itself. A lie-down on her bed before a hot bath and a leisurely get-ready at her mirror would fill the time before dinner. At the head of the stairs, however, she once again changed her mind.

Chapter Eighteen

Instead of going to her suite, Jemima went to Mrs van Doorn's room. The Countess's Suite, Lord Muirhaven had called it. She approached quietly and, hearing voices on the other side of the door, pressed her ear to the paintwork.

Elaine Cleeve was speaking, saying something which at first appeared to concern Mairwen.

'... time to send her out into the world where she'd be answerable only to herself.'

Mrs van Doorn's response told Jemima that it was Honor who was being discussed.

'I promised my late husband I would guard his daughter and I cannot "send her out" as you put it. I failed once, letting her mix with unsuitable company. She met people on the *Llanstephan Castle* who filled her head with ideas of emancipation that would have turned her father's blood pale.'

Jemima's opinion was that emancipation was another way of saying 'freedom', something all creatures craved.

Elaine seemed to be of a similar mind, though she expressed herself more tactfully. 'You and I were born in a very different age,' Jemima heard her say. 'I was fifteen before I heard the first telephone ring, and Honor's age before I set eyes on a motorcar. War wiped the canvas clean and the young are painting themselves a new picture.' Elaine paused, and Jemima predicted what was coming next. 'Which prompts me to mention Honor's art. She has a driving need to express her creativity.'

'I don't understand this art business,' Mrs van Doorn answered sullenly.

'Mrs Flowerday considers Honor has real talent.'

I do? Jemima silently echoed. Hardly, and neither do you.

'Let her spread her wings, Cornelia, let her blossom,' Elaine continued. 'Then, in due time, when she announces her wish to marry, you will know it's to someone she's chosen for herself.'

'I don't want her to choose for herself!' Mrs van Doorn's violent anguish passed through the door, making Jemima start.

'Face it, Cornelia,' Elaine retorted, 'Honor doesn't want Hildebrand. You wouldn't press the child into a union that is clearly distasteful to her?'

'But why is it distasteful?' came the reply. 'Hildebrand is charming, polite and she'd be a countess.'

'An unhappy one. You want more than that for her!'

'I want Honor to have a position,' Mrs van Doorn persisted. 'Then she is safe.'

Safe from what? Jemima wondered. Weary of being on the wrong side of the door, she retreated then walked forward, clearing her throat before tapping. Was it her imagination, or did a nervous silence descend before Elaine opened the door?

'Jemima, do come in. I'm about to brew a pot of fennel-seed tea. A wonderful digestif if taken in advance of a meal. Will you join us?'

'Why not.' Jemima smiled at Mrs van Doorn who, unlike Elaine, was unable to pretend that all was well. 'How is Honor, sleeping still?' She wondered if anyone would mention Mairwen. 'I can't imagine she'll be appearing at dinner, though she must eat to build back her strength.'

'Elaine left her sleeping,' Mrs van Doorn said. 'Have you been outside, Mrs Flowerday?'

Jemima had already brushed a few lingering petals off her sleeve. 'I strolled through the garden and chatted with Mrs Beddoe. Isn't it admirable that she does so much with so few staff?' Jemima was determined to soften Mrs van Doorn's feelings towards Mairwen. 'Those girls deserve medals. And Mrs Beddoe is quite the herbalist.'

'She's quite the *witch*,' Elaine contradicted amiably.

'I won't have such talk,' Mrs van Doorn said sharply.

'Of the benign variety, is all I'm saying.' Elaine was at the sideboard lighting the kerosene beneath a spirit kettle. 'What Mother Beddoe doesn't know about herbs, infusions and natural lore... Did you know, her husband will only plant seeds when the moon is waxing? One learns so much from them.'

The mention of the moon again recalled the diagram drawn on Lord Muirhaven's dining table. The power of magic, Jemima believed, lay in the mind of the perpetrator, but that didn't make it ineffectual. There were odd energies here at Castle Gloaming and Jemima sensed them gathering. Act one was over. Bring on the second act.

Sitting down on the well-sprung sofa to await her tea, Jemima looked around. This was a comfortable room, with double doors separating it from – presumably – the bedroom and bathroom. The large fireplace would make it snug in winter. The grate was filled with dried flowers, including handsome globe artichoke heads. Elaine came and sat with them while the kettle simmered. It made a gentle, sibilant sound.

'I'm sure Mrs van Doorn won't mind if I tell you that, a moment ago, we were discussing Honor's burning wish to live in London,' Elaine said to Jemima. 'You know the capital better than any of us, so give your opinion. Is it safe for a girl of seventeen?'

Jemima considered her answer. 'My daughter Molly is ten going on eleven, but one day I will have to make the decisions Mrs van Doorn faces now. My answer is that no girl that young ought to be in London without friends or family.' She turned to Mrs van Doorn. 'But that shouldn't mean a blanket no. It is your intention to take a house, and accompany her, after all.'

Mrs van Doorn shook her head and the diamonds in her earlobes scintillated. 'I've changed my mind. I won't go to London. It was a bad idea.'

'But... were you to take a house and chaperone Honor to parties and other events, she'd be no more at risk there than any other young person,' Jemima said.

'But they don't want to be chaperoned,' Mrs van Doorn burst out. 'You weren't on the boat, Mrs Flowerday. You didn't see the after-dark parties, the girls in flimsy dresses, showing their arms, knees, everything. The champagne corks popping and jazz music blaring. Girls and boys smoking cigarettes together. Honor was a quiet mouse of a girl when we boarded the *Llanstephan Castle* at Cape Town. By the time we docked at Southampton, she had turned into one of those dreadful "new women". Talking of going to college and cutting her hair and using slang like a kitchen boy.'

'None of this is shocking to me,' smiled Jemima. 'As Elaine implied, the war changed everything. Wanting to go to college does not make a modern young woman unusual. Honor may be frightened of asking you, and this nonsense about being kidnapped may be a ruse to show you how passionate she is.'

'That's all done with.' Mrs van Doorn gestured the subject away. 'We're not going to mention it again.'

'Very well. But you can't ignore that Honor has dreams beyond this place.'

'To be an artist?'

'Yes, and in London,' Jemima said, stating her firm belief.

Mrs van Doorn brushed this away too. 'She hasn't got what it takes.'

Truth impelled Jemima to agree that what she'd seen of Honor's work showed little present genius. 'But everyone starts somewhere. We must all be allowed to take risks, to learn and even fail.'

'Fail?' echoed Mrs van Doorn. 'Why would anyone wish to fail? You are very strange, Mrs Flowerday. I don't understand you at all.'

The kettle's voice rose to a tinny, rattling sound. Jemima, meanwhile, thinking she heard a noise outside the door, got up to check. There was nobody there and she supposed she'd heard steam sputtering through a narrow spout. Elaine went to make the tea, selecting one of two caddies, spooning contents into a pot. Jemima had said all she could in Honor's defence. Mrs van Doorn was impervious to appeal.

Elaine brought the first cup to Mrs van Doorn, saying, 'Jemima, did I mention? Dinner is delayed tonight and Mrs Beddoe will serve it at nine, so it's cocktails at eight.' She poured tea for Jemima and herself, and they sipped in silence until Mrs van Doorn lowered her cup.

'Have you stepped into the library here, Mrs Flowerday?' she asked.

'Not yet.'

'You should. Read the first Countess of Muirhaven's memoir. It will give you a better feel for Castle Gloaming, and the pleasures and duties of an earldom.'

Elaine chipped in, sounding suddenly irritated, 'I'm sure Jemima has more interesting things to do with her time.'

'I would like to read the memoir,' Jemima countered. 'All people are worthy of study, and I never tire of looking at pictures of fine clothes. What was her name, the countess?'

'Hilda,' said Mrs van Doorn. 'I believe that's where "Hildebrand" comes from. She was not herself of noble blood, which is why I feel a kinship. She married her husband when he was a young industrialist and his ennoblement changed their life.'

'Exactly,' said Elaine. 'Hilda went from a contented wife to being a peeress of the realm, out of her depth. Not to put too fine a point on it, she was left on the starting line while her husband raced up the social ladder. He learned to despise her.'

'You exaggerate, Elaine,' Mrs van Doorn protested.

'I read between the lines. My point is, on the wrong head, a countess's coronet can be a crown of thorns.'

'Pah.'

Elaine came back with vexation, 'I appreciate you and Hildebrand made a pact on the voyage here, Cornelia, but there comes a time to accept reality.'

'Pact?' Mrs van Doorn repeated, sounding as though she didn't like the direction the conversation was taking.

'Honor and your money in return for his title.'

'Well!' gasped Mrs van Doorn.

'It's true. I will never lie, even though I depend on you, Cornelia. Bad marriages have no upside, whoever they're between.' Elaine sought Jemima's eye. 'You agree, don't you?'

'I agree that bad marriages are to be avoided. I don't necessarily agree that those between people of different backgrounds are inevitably harmful.'

'But in this case, Honor knows what she wants, as does Hildebrand. Or rather, what they don't want.' Elaine gave Cornelia van Doorn's hand an apologetic pat. 'You know the lie of the land, hmm, where his preference tends?'

Was that a blush alighting on Mrs van Doorn's cheeks? And was Elaine trying to influence her employer's feelings?

I see no good in this, Jemima thought, and said impulsively, 'Bring your stepdaughter to London, Mrs van Doorn. I'll not only fit you out in style, I'll find you a house and someone to guide you through the season. My mother-in-law, Lady Winterfold, might provide introductions. If, by the close of summer, Honor still has her heart set on an artistic life, you will know it is not a whim. You might by then have found your own friends in London.'

She expected an acknowledgement, if not a thank-you.

'No. No. No,' cried Mrs van Doorn and with each 'No' banged a fist on her knee. 'I will not be told I cannot have what I have set my mind upon. Everything I do is for Honor's own good and if she runs from the wonderful chance I am giving her, it's all over. She will face a future with nothing. There will be no money.'

Jemima exchanged a glance with Elaine. 'You mean you'll cut her out of your will?' Jemima pressed.

'I don't know. I'm tired. May I be so rude to ask you ladies to leave me?'

Jemima was the first to go. On the threshold outside was a scattering of something she at first thought was purple confetti, before realising they were petals of the honesty flower, possibly off her skirt. Or perhaps someone had come with flowers for Mrs van Doorn and overheard the three of them discussing Honor's artistic talent, or lack of. Perhaps that someone had heard Mrs van Doorn threaten to disinherit Honor if her stepdaughter left Castle Gloaming.

If nothing else, it promised to make dinner an interesting occasion.

Chapter Nineteen

Walking into her bedroom, Jemima immediately noticed that her wardrobe was open. She never did that. It encouraged moths, and sunlight could create subtle differentials in colour. The bed cover was minutely wrinkled, suggesting that somebody had sat down briefly.

Jemima made an audit of her clothes. Within a minute, she knew exactly what was missing. She took herself to Honor's bedroom, entering without knocking.

'Miss van Doorn?' she articulated coldly.

The room was empty, as was the en-suite bathroom. Jemima would have marched out, except that her eye caught on a detail. In the waste bin, a wicker basket with a silk lining, a bunch of flowers had been discarded, head down. It felt odd, disposing of flowers that way. They were a mix of yellow broom, possibly from the bush beneath the breakfast-room window. Ah, and stems of honesty. There were also florets of Queen Anne's lace and sprigs of purple lavender. At the bottom of the bin was a screwed-up nugget of waxed paper. She left that where it was.

'I know now who came to Mrs van Doorn's door, then flitted away. What is she up to?'

As Jemima went downstairs, annoyance became disquiet, then sharpened into downright suspicion. After a cursory glance into the drawing and breakfast rooms, she called in at the kitchens, but nobody had set eyes on Miss Honor. It was conceivable the girl planned another flit.

Jaw set, she headed to the tower.

She paused to rest at every half landing so that when she reached the top, she still had her breath. The door to the parapet was open, allowing her a perfect view of a young woman in a tobacco-brown coat leaning against the parapet, looking east towards the aqueduct. To the west, the sun was gathering in its rays, casting bronze on the rail.

'Miss van Doorn, you make a pretty picture.'

Honor spun round, mouth dropping.

'Why are you wearing my clothes?' The coat, with its lush velvet collar, outsize pockets and single, deer-horn button closing it low on the hip, never failed to turn heads in London when Jemima wore it. Yet it was too short for Honor, and the colour was wrong. Earth colours flattered Jemima, but made Honor look like an unripe bean in a sundried pod. She'd even taken Jemima's cloche hat and a pair of kidskin gloves. The cloche, pulled down low to emphasise the fragile lines of her jaw, looked all right, but that made Jemima all the angrier. As for the gloves... 'How dare you raid my wardrobe?'

'I only borrowed—'

Jemima raised a palm. 'There are three things one never takes without asking. Two of them being clothes and a person's bedtime reading. I won't name the third as you're not yet of age.'

Honor stared at the ground and her throat bobbed. 'I had no choice.'

'Everyone has a choice. Including you, when you took Mairwen's one and only good dress for your last escapade. Frankly, I'm tired of listening to hogwash, Miss van Doorn.'

'Hogwash?'

Clearly, a word both Honor and her stepmother were unfamiliar with.

'The wild-eyed abductor. And now being told you have no choice but to steal my things. Put simply, you are an opportunist liar, but not brave enough to own it.'

Shame invaded the girl's cheeks and the dam walls broke, sobs and tears flooding out. 'I'm sorry, Mrs... Mrs...?'

'Flowerday.' Jemima remained unmoved, except to add, 'Nothing entitles you to take my outfit. Or to engineer the sacking of a housemaid.'

'I know.' The girl covered her face with her hands, the admission squeezing between her fingers. 'But Mairwen needn't have been so rude, forgetting her place, asking questions. I have to get away, and I can't risk anyone knowing. I thought if I slipped out looking like you, nobody would stop me.'

There was some logic in that, not that it softened Jemima's heart. Honor's clothes were pale and flimsy, more suitable for garden parties than hiking up steep paths or scrambling along canal banks. 'Your stepmother believes you're still sleeping. She was so very distressed when you simply vanished.'

Honor wiped a tear with the heel of her hand. 'Mrs Beddoe made me lemon-balm tea to make me sleep, but it gave me bad dreams. And then Mairwen came in, badgering me.' She broke off to cry some more.

Jemima stood her ground. The histrionics of a spoiled child-woman strained her tolerance. Still, this was a moment to test out her powers of deduction and so she joined Honor at the parapet rail, keeping her back to the sheer drop below.

'What a vantage point this is. No English raiding party could ever have crept up on Glan yr Afon undetected.'

'Glan-yr-what?' asked Honor. 'Oh. Castle Gloaming. Sorry. I don't speak Welsh. Gwen tried to teach me some words, but it's fiendishly difficult.'

'Tell me what you were doing in London last month.'

'London?' Honor made a motion with her mouth, like a fish discovering the limitations of fresh air. 'I've never been—'

'Miss van Doorn,' Jemima sliced through the bluster. 'You're not an idiot, despite your valiant efforts to appear so. Like Dick Whittington's cat, you have been to London. And even if you did not look at the King, you caught a glimpse of His Majesty's near relations.'

Honor shook her head, at a loss. 'I didn't, I was taken prisoner—'

'If you so much as mention being kidnapped by a hairy wodewose or a bearded troglodyte, I will have no choice but to summon—'

'Not my stepmother!' the girl shrieked, pulling herself up on tiptoe as if she intended to pitch herself over the top of the rail.

'The police.' Jemima pulled Honor away from the edge.

'No, please.'

'Then you have one minute to tell me the truth.' Feeling the silky texture of her own coat on somebody else's arm, Jemima's anger returned. 'I daresay you're planning to go back to the canal to wait for a lift on the *Miss Nettle*. Where to after that?

Chapter Twenty

Honor's answering question was predictable. 'How did you know?'

'A process of deduction,' Jemima said. 'I was told you wanted to go to London. As no trace was found of you getting on a train, for a time I feared you'd come to grief.'

'I grieve all the time,' the girl said with feeling.

'You misunderstand. "To come to grief" implies a fatality. When someone goes missing leaving their possessions behind, foul play or even suicide is a disturbing possibility. When I learned you'd had a letter from London shortly before you disappeared, I felt more hopeful. Perhaps you had gone there... but I couldn't work out how. You don't drive, you didn't appear to have an accomplice.'

A furtive glance towards the aqueduct did not escape Jemima who breathed, 'Isn't it splendid, how it glows in the setting sun. Your mode of transport was in front of my eyes, but I had to walk along the canal path twice before the penny dropped.'

'The penny...?'

'Another English idiom. We scatter our speech with them, but often use them inaccurately. It all fell into place when I spotted *The Illustrated London News* on the *Miss Nettle*. The special edition celebrating the marriage of their royal highnesses, the Duke and Duchess of York. I surmised that the *Miss Nettle* must either have navigated to London within the past month or had taken a passenger who spent time there. It's a long, slow journey south by canal, so here's where I am forced to conjecture... that this passenger used the boat to get her to a railway station where she wouldn't be recognised. She took a London train, concluded her business, then rejoined the boat at the same place, completing her journey without anybody at home knowing about it.'

Honor's face didn't disappoint, too green to hide her astonishment. 'You worked that out from one newspaper?'

'Somebody on that boat had to have been in London before the souvenir edition of *The Illustrated London Aforementioned* disappeared from the stands. Push one domino over, the whole lot tumbles.'

'You won't tell my stepmother?' Honor begged. 'Poor Olive will be in such trouble, and I'll never be allowed out again.'

'Olive, the stalwart who sails the *Miss Nettle*. A friend of yours?'

'Yes.' It came out as a kind of gasp.

'A fellow South African. Olive Nettle is an unusual name. Is it real?'

'Sort of,' said Honor. 'People can't pronounce her real one, so they call her Nettle. And because she's prickly.'

'Where did you meet, in Cape Town?'

'On the canal bank.'

The answer came too quickly.

Jemima waited a second or two then said crisply, 'I have a handyman at home who does odd jobs. He's a cockney and when I say something he can't quite believe, he answers, "Garn!" Rather than say it myself now, I will ask you again. Where did you meet Miss Nettle?'

'On the *Llanstephan Castle*.'

On the ship. Now Jemima had a link to work with. Was Olive Nettle one of the 'new women', one of the 'bad influences', Mrs van Doorn feared so much? 'Let me surmise. You were walking alongside the canal one day, and the *Miss Nettle* happened to go past. You called out to Olive, "Good heavens, we meet again. May I get on board?"'

Honor grasped at the explanation. 'Yes. She plies between Trevor and Chirk. Chirk is a few miles from here.'

'Where there's a railway station and trains to Shrewsbury and from there, to London, Euston.'

Honor didn't answer directly, but her expression flickered. 'Olive goes to Chirk two or three times a week, but never goes further. She hasn't got much money and fuel is expensive, she says.'

'What's her job?'

'She's an artist.' Honor spoke almost with reverence. 'A real one. She has a studio in a big, old house with other painters. They call themselves "The Chirk School". A man there sells her paintings for her. That's how she lives.'

'You met a fellow South African artist on the RMS *Llanstephan Castle*, and later, on the Ellesmere Canal,' Jemima recapped. 'You cemented a friendship born of a shared love of art and water.'

'That's right.' Honor nodded fervently.

Mm. It was the opposite of a convincing explanation, not least because Olive Nettle's presence in Wales was an enigma. Rather than question Honor further, Jemima mentally placed herself on the aqueduct and opened her mind to what came in. If she dared look down, she'd see the Dee swirling below. If she glanced over the treetops to the castle, she'd see this parapet where they now stood. A figure standing here, simply standing?

'You like coming up here to paint, I'm told,' she said.

'Yes. Yes I do.'

'I came up earlier with Mrs Cleeve. I didn't see any of your work, nor any materials.'

'I don't leave anything lying around.'

'Really? You lug all your stuff down those stairs after every session, then back up the next day. Where do you store them?'

'In my room.'

'Honor, I meant it when I asked for the truth. Lie to me, I will report your supposed abduction to the police. They'll go looking for the perpetrator and, of course, they'll interview you and your stepmother.'

Honor van Doorn looked at Jemima as though she hated her. The antipathy lasted a second or two then, once again, her lip trembled. 'You don't know what it's like to be watched and told what to do all the time. I come up here because Stepmother can't follow. The stairs are too much for her.'

'You come up here not to paint, but to watch the horizon.'

Honor made no contradiction.

'Or do you come up here to signal? I'm told you like to get up early. Flashing a lantern at first light could signal to a boat making its way across the aqueduct. "Flash, flash. Moor up and wait. Flash, flash. I'm coming to join you." Simple enough for you to leave by the courtyard door that opens from this tower, dash to the shrubbery and then to the riverside. You're young and fit, you'd reach the aqueduct in fifteen minutes. You'd board the *Miss Nettle* and then travel to the town you mentioned.'

'To Chirk?' Honor shook her head. 'It's three hours by water so I'd be missed.'

'Mrs Cleeve told me you like to walk on your own.'

'Not all day, not for seven or eight hours. You are very clever, Mrs Flowerday, and everything you've said is true. I flash a lantern to let Olive know I want to join her. If she sees the light, she waits. I'll ride a distance with her, drawing and painting as we go. Olive teaches me. I get off the boat after an hour or two and walk back.'

'Leaving your work and art materials on board.'

'Yes. I'm learning to paint in the new style, you see. Olive is so

110

modern, but Stepmother hates anything up to date. If she had her way, I'd be locked up here in a long dress and a veil until Hildebrand marries me. I won't. I don't like him.'

Jemima thought about the painting in Honor's room, holly sprigs in a vase, tight little dabs, amateurish. 'For home consumption, you paint safe subjects,' she said thoughtfully. 'Kittens in baskets, if you could find some, nothing that reveals the real you. You yearn to escape your stepmother's leash, but don't want to alienate her too far. She holds the purse strings, after all.'

Honor bit her lip. 'You think I'm money-grubbing and ungrateful.'

'What I think isn't important. I was asked to find you and you saved me the trouble by coming back. Now, you're planning the next getaway, in clothes that I and my sister spent many painstaking hours creating. You're even wearing my best gloves!'

Leaving the girl to blush, or not, Jemima glanced at Honor's feet. She saw ankle socks and flat deck shoes. She'd seen those shoes in Honor's cupboard on her first day here. Teamed with a hat, coat and gloves, they were little short of a crime, but – of course – Honor had lacerated herself tearing home barefoot and needed footwear to accommodate her bandages. The fact that she was planning another escape despite her injuries spoke of a steel core. An ability to do whatever it took to achieve her ends.

'Let's talk about your reason for going to London. You received a letter with a WC1 postcode,' Jemima said. 'I'm guessing... from London University.' Blood raced into Honor's cheeks. Jemima coolly went on. 'I'm a passionate admirer of the first university in Britain to award degrees to women. You were invited to present yourself for interview, having applied there to study. Correct?'

'No.'

Had she misinterpreted the blush?

'Not the university,' said Honor. 'The Slade School of Art.'

'Of course.'

'They allow women in as equals and I'll die if I can't go.'

Jemima quite understood that at age seventeen, the denial of a dream was akin to death. 'The Slade is part of the University of London campus,' she said thoughtfully. 'It has always been ahead of the times.'

It all spilled out. Honor had left early in the morning of 20 May, arriving in London two days later. She'd stayed in a hostel near Euston Station, with resources enough for two nights and some food. Jemima asked her where the money came from.

'It was mine.'

'I'm told you have only pin money. London is expensive.'

The girl sighed. 'Olive paid. The trip cost two pounds, eight shillings and sixpence since I suppose you'll ask.'

Dishonest people rehearse their answers, and too much detail is always suspicious, yet Jemima sensed she was hearing secrets being laid bare.

'So – did the Slade take you?' she asked.

Tears pooled in Honor's eyes and she dug her gloved hands deep into the pockets of Jemima's coat. She whispered, 'Yes. They offered me a place there and then, when I showed my portfolio.'

'What, on the spot?'

Honor nodded.

'I am speechless. That's extraordinary.'

The tears spilled over. 'But I'm not of age. I can't go without Stepmother's permission. And she—'

Won't give it, Jemima thought. 'You haven't asked her, though? Not yet.'

'No, and please, *please* don't tell her.'

'You were coming to speak with her earlier, bringing flowers as a peace offering. But you heard what we were saying and scuttled off.'

'You said I had no talent.'

'Not exactly. I said you were at the beginning of a career. If the Slade thinks you have what it takes, my opinion doesn't matter.' Honor must have overheard her stepmother threatening to cut her off from her fortune. Kudos to Honor for sticking to her goals despite it. 'Soon enough, the Slade will want an answer,' Jemima said. 'You can't put it off forever.'

'I won't.'

'You're running away, only you'll have to come back again and get Mrs van Doorn's blessing. Is Olive crossing the aqueduct tonight?'

Honor nodded. 'I got off the boat this afternoon only because you'd seen me.'

Jemima hadn't at any point seen Honor on board the *Miss Nettle*, but it might have appeared that the game was up. 'Where is Olive now?'

'On the move, I hope. She'll moor up on the Chirk side of the aqueduct when it's dark. There's a buyer interested in a painting she's done and she wants to meet him tomorrow.'

'When the *Miss Nettle* passed me on the aqueduct this afternoon, it was going towards Trevor. Isn't that the wrong direction for Chirk?'

'Olive was on her way to Llangollen, to buy logs. She'll go on to the next winding hole—'

'The next... sorry?'

'Winding hole. Where the canal widens so she can turn. She'll come back this way any moment. Before sunset.'

'And you will signal your intention to join her. You'll run along the river path to the canal, but I'll tell you one thing – not in my coat, gloves and hat.'

The western sky was suffused with a gingery light and birds were flying back to the tower roof to roost. In an hour, it would be too dark for Honor to go anywhere.

'How do you recognise her boat from this distance?' Jemima asked.

'Olive keeps a metal bucket on the cabin roof. It catches the light.'

Ah, the bucket with the parsley. Or 'not parsley' as she had been tersely informed.

'You must have keen eyes.' Jemima saw no sign of any luggage with Honor, though she was unlikely to have brought it up the stairs. 'Will I find a suitcase in the little courtyard at the base of this tower? Or in the shrubbery or the icehouse, perhaps? Don't gasp, Honor. My deductions are not sorcery. I read human nature. Olive will be looking out for your lantern flash any time now. By tomorrow afternoon, if you get away with it, you'll be on your way to take up your place at art school. But you'll still be underage. What's your plan?'

Honor's reaction suggested she had one, but wasn't ready to divulge it.

'Forge Mrs van Doorn's signature? Employ an actress to impersonate her, to give her blessing in person?' Jemima guessed.

'I might,' Honor said in a way that told Jemima she had considered both options.

'There's still the money, child,' Jemima said patiently. 'Or lack of.' She checked her watch – it was still, just, light enough to see the face. Ten past seven. 'Where is your lantern?'

Honor made a movement of the head, indicating the other side of the tower. 'Will you help me go, Mrs Flowerday?'

Jemima imagined her daughter Molly in a few years, confiding to a young teacher that she meant to run away to Paris, or New York, to follow a dream. What if that teacher, for motives of idealism, let her go? I would be distraught, Jemima acknowledged, and angry. But I can't let this girl be cornered into a marriage she dreads.

Jemima spent the next minutes trying to dissuade Honor from her plan, until the sight of Hildebrand walking towards the main house reminded her that she was expected for cocktails at eight, and that Honor would be missed at some point during the evening. 'Wait till the morning,' she advised. 'I will speak again to your stepmother, as will Mrs Cleeve, who is on your side. What seems impossible one day, resolves the next.'

'It won't resolve.'

'How about you write a note apologising for causing your step-mother distress? Hear me out. Mrs van Doorn wants the best for you—'

'For her!'

'She holds the purse strings and you cannot risk those strings tightening. Being penniless here at Castle Gloaming is survivable. Being penniless and alone in London is not.'

That seemed to sink in. 'You don't think I could manage.'

'I'm darn sure of it. No woman can exist in London on less than a hundred pounds a year, unless she lives in as a maid.'

That fell exactly as Jemima intended. Honor's mouth jerked in antipathy.

'You think a letter to Stepmama would help?'

Jemima nodded. 'She loves you and wants you to return that love. Be humble. Retrieve those flowers. A pretty ribbon around them, with a little note showing contrition, will take away anger. Over the coming days, we'll work on a plan and, I promise, if it's humanly possible, I'll get you to London. My bet is that in a year from now your stepmother will be proudly attending your first end-of-term exhibition.'

Rather than bring a smile, that image sent Honor deeper into indecision, leaving Jemima feeling she had no option but to remove Honor's means of signalling to her accomplice. She walked round to the other side of the tower and saw a lamp hanging from a nail.

As she reached for it, the air burst into a deafening clamour. Birds flew out from under the eaves, cawing in panic. Jemima screamed and ducked, horrified by wings so close to her head. She was instantly ashamed and stood up, realising then that somebody else was screaming.

'Don't, *don't!*'

It came from the other side of the tower, ending in a howl of terror. Jemima ran, stumbling to where a moment ago she'd left Honor standing.

There was no one there. Jemima's cloche hat was on the parapet planks. Sick with dread, she looked over the rail.

Oh, dear God, no.

Far below, spreadeagled on the ground, was a dark shape, arms spread wide. Jemima crouched with her hands to her head. For at least a minute she stayed in this attitude, until, pulling herself together, she took to the stairs.

They seemed to go on for ever and she staggered like a drunk. She aimed for the great hall, reaching it at exactly the moment Mrs van Doorn came out of the drawing room.

'What's the matter?' Mrs van Doorn asked, panic in her voice at the sight of Jemima's face. 'You look as though you've seen a ghost.'

'Stay here,' Jemima said curtly. 'Please, I beg you.' She hurried out through the main door, running down the steps and making her way to the flank of the castle where the tower rose. She steeled herself to confront the horror of a broken body.

There was nothing there.

Chapter Twenty-One

'Mrs Flowerday?' Lord Muirhaven came out of the shadows. Something was slung over his arm. He held it up. 'Is this yours, did you drop it?'

It was her coat.

'It was on the ground,' he said. 'I was picking a flower for my buttonhole when I heard a scream.'

Mrs van Doorn joined them. 'Will someone please tell me what is going on? Where is Elaine? Where is Honor?'

Jemima had no idea where Elaine might be. 'Honor and I were at the top of the tower, when – oh. Bless me.' Her legs gave way and she sat on the ground. 'I thought she'd fallen, but it was only my coat.'

'Fallen?'

'It was only my coat.' Jemima began to laugh, a hysterical sound that poured out despite her attempts to stop it.

Lord Muirhaven crouched beside her and she felt the brush of his sleeve, his satin cuff against her cheek.

'You're in shock. There now, take a breath. All is well.'

'I will only agree with you when I see Honor alive,' Jemima gasped.

'Elaine will know something,' he answered. 'She usually does.'

Almost to the second, Elaine Cleeve joined them. She too asked what was going on.

Lord Muirhaven took charge. 'A rumpus, signifying nothing.

Mrs Flowerday has suffered the most appalling shock. Let's get her inside and give her a shot of brandy.'

They ushered her into the drawing room and, to her astonishment, Honor was there, at one end of a sofa, still wearing Jemima's skirt and top. Jemima's brown kid gloves lay beside her.

Mrs van Doorn took her stepdaughter's hands. 'Darling child, must I worry every minute of every day?'

Honor stared ahead, her gaze fixed.

'Speak,' pleaded Mrs van Doorn.

Lord Muirhaven placed a balloon of brandy in Jemima's shaking fingers and she took a gulp as she waited for Honor to speak.

The girl found her voice. 'Someone tried... to hurl me off the top of the tower.'

There was a horrified gasp from Mrs van Doorn.

'Who?' demanded Elaine. 'Who would do that?'

Honor shook her head. 'They came up behind me. One moment I was looking out at the sunset, the next...' She steadied herself. 'Someone grabbed my coat to make me overbalance. I gripped the rail for my life.' She raised her hands, showing bloody tips where a nail appeared to have been ripped away. Everyone drew in a breath. 'They'd have pushed me to my death if the coat hadn't come off and the birds hadn't flown into the air.'

'Are you saying your attacker was scared off?' Elaine sought Lord Muirhaven's eye.

Honor nodded blankly.

'I saw you up there.' Lord Muirhaven addressed Jemima. 'You were looking down from the parapet and someone was with you. Was that Honor?'

'You have that wrong.' Jemima's nerves were reviving thanks to the brandy. 'What you saw was Honor wearing my coat and hat, and me dressed as you see me now. I was looking for something on the other side of the tower when the attacker struck.'

'Did you see anyone or hear anything?' Lord Muirhaven asked.

'Not a sound,' Jemima acknowledged. 'Whoever it was must have waited until they knew Honor was alone and vulnerable. I take it you saw nothing from the ground?'

'As I told you' – Lord Muirhaven indicated a spray of yellow broom in his buttonhole – 'I was purloining these flowers from under the breakfast-room window and wasn't directly beneath the tower.'

'You heard a scream, though,' Jemima reminded him.

'I did. I ran towards the tower and stepped on *your* coat. I looked up at that point, but saw nothing but the rooks circling.'

Elaine interrupted to ask Hildebrand if he would, please, mix the cocktails. 'We could all do with a drink, I imagine.'

'Do we summon the police?' Jemima asked.

Hildebrand thought not. 'It's dark now and someone would have to trek to Trevor and drag the one police constable there from his fireside. Or take the pony trap into Chirk, which is two hours' travel.'

'Would you be willing?' Jemima pressed. It was hard to construe this blatant attack on Honor as anything other than attempted murder.

Lord Muirhaven was unpersuaded. 'I don't drive a horse and trap at the best of times. We'd have to send Beddoe. Even then, there's no saying a policeman would accompany him back here. Police in these parts are used to dealing with sheep theft and drunkards, not complicated matters.'

Elaine gave her opinion that sending for the police would be to blow things out of proportion. The incident, horrible as it was, was a prank that went too far.

'A prank?' Jemima was incredulous. 'This wasn't a bag of flour placed on top of a door, Elaine. Honor could have—' At the last moment, she softened what she'd intended to say. 'It could have ended badly.'

'You're best placed to say,' Elaine came back a touch acidly, 'as you were the only witness. Bring in the police and you'll be first up for interrogation.'

'I will gladly give my account,' Jemima replied. 'Unfortunately, I saw nothing useful.'

'You didn't see Mairwen skulking about with an angry look on her face?'

'Let me be clear,' Jemima replied when Elaine's meaning became clear, 'you're accusing the maid?'

'Well, she has been sacked, hasn't she? Her kind always bear grudges.'

'Please.' Mrs van Doorn lifted a hand. 'No more. No police, no scandal. Honor is unharmed and I want the tower door locked. Hildebrand, you have a key?'

'Mrs Beddoe has. I'll give the order.' All this while, Lord Muirhaven was mixing Mrs van Doorn's pink gin. He gave it to her with a formal bow.

Honor was taken to the kitchen to have her injured hand dressed.

At a few minutes past nine, they proceeded to the dining room, Hildebrand taking Honor's arm, Elaine supporting Mrs van Doorn. Jemima, who'd had no opportunity to change, was given dispensation to 'come as she was'. She lingered behind. Her coat had been brought inside and was folded on the ottoman. She didn't have the heart to check for damage. That could wait. Her hat was still at the top of the tower, though. Hopefully, it would take no harm overnight.

Her last action before leaving the drawing room was to put her gloves in her skirt pocket. A Christmas present from Molly and Tommy, they were more precious to her than frankincense and myrrh. She joined the others in the dining room, whereupon Mrs van Doorn asked if she would mind giving up her seat to Honor.

'I should like her as far from the door as can be, just for tonight, Mrs Flowerday.'

Jemima had no objection and was about to take the seat Honor vacated when Lord Muirhaven advanced a better idea. 'Let Miss van Doorn sit on your left, and I will take Elaine's seat beside her. You don't mind, Mrs Cleeve?'

Elaine rose, saying, 'Not at all. I enjoy musical chairs, even without music.'

Lord Muirhaven explained his thinking. 'This way, Honor is sandwiched between you and me, Cornelia. Whether she wishes it or not, we must keep her safe.' Lord Muirhaven seemed pleased with his arrangements, while Honor looked mutinous.

Mrs Beddoe and Gwen waited at table. Mairwen's dismissal was not mentioned. Nor did Elaine repeat her accusations as to who had tried to push Honor off the tower. After the first course was served, the servants withdrew through a door at the far end of the room.

Tucking into lemon and spinach soup, Jemima marvelled at how composed Honor appeared. That wasn't to say she looked anything other than miserable, but whereas Jemima kept re-experiencing that moment of visceral horror in shivers across her skin, Honor seemed to have distanced herself from it. A talent, Jemima decided. Lord Muirhaven, now sitting diagonally opposite her, seemed unaffected too. Somebody should paint his portrait, she thought. He was a remarkably good-looking man, though her designer's eye objected to the yellow-gold broom flowers in his buttonhole which clashed with the claret velvet of his jacket.

If she'd had her hand on the Bible, Jemima would agree with Elaine that Honor's attacker was Mairwen. The maid had access and motive. 'Giving Miss Honor a nasty fright' was as good a revenge as any. Jemima doubted Mairwen had intended murder; it took a particularly twisted character to attempt to push someone to their death.

Mrs van Doorn cut into Jemima's musing, asking her if she had enjoyed tonight's sunset. 'Such an intense shade, it turned the drawing-room windows almost to blood.'

'Thanks to the stained glass,' Lord Muirhaven chipped in. 'The architect who dreamed up this place provides us with nightly drama.'

'A brilliant-red sunset usually means rain,' Elaine observed.

'I thought it was the other way round.' Jemima's thoughts jumped to her hat, which would not survive a soaking. '"Red sky at night, shepherd's delight".'

'We get more than our fair share of rain here,' Elaine replied. 'The usual rules don't apply.'

'It is why Wales is so green,' Lord Muirhaven countered in a voice that suggested he'd heard that phrase a thousand times.

Honor yawned. Deliberate or not, she made little attempt to conceal her loathing at being among them.

Jemima tried to catch Mrs Beddoe's eye, thinking she might ask if Ifor, or Beddoe himself, would oblige her by fetching her hat. But the housekeeper remained aloof. The weather continued to stoke the conversation and, through the fish course, Mrs van Doorn spoke in an unstoppable guttural about May's unseasonal showers and the rainbow that had spanned the river valley a week ago. 'So clear, I could have reached out and touched it.'

Lord Muirhaven told her she was a hopeless romantic. 'Beddoe says that once heavy rain sets in, it doesn't know how to stop and, before we know it, we're cut off.'

Over the meat course, which was a pie made from leeks, potatoes and yesterday's lamb, Mrs van Doorn asked Jemima if she had ever visited Polesden Lacey in Surrey. 'Where the Duke and Duchess of York spent their honeymoon.'

'Just because she lives in the south, it doesn't follow she knows everyone.' Lord Muirhaven softened the reproof with a laugh. He got up as Mrs Beddoe brought a shallow serving dish in from the side room, meeting her halfway. 'Allow me. Ah, a fine salad and all from our garden. You are looking after our health, Mrs Beddoe.'

'I hope so, sir,' Mrs Beddoe said repressively.

Putting down the dish in front of Honor, Hildebrand presented her with a pair of bone-handled salad servers. 'Let's see you toss a salad, Miss van Doorn. It's an art that must be learned if society is to remain civilised. There you go.' He almost forced the servers into Honor's hands, one of which was bandaged with white lint.

Elaine tapped Jemima on the wrist. 'My mother held it true that God gave us lettuce as a vehicle for a good dressing. Always oil in first, then salt, then vinegar last.'

Jemima reminisced about her mother's home-made salad cream, made from pounded, hard-boiled egg yolk, cream, mustard, lemon and vinegar. 'So much better than bottled.'

She glanced across the table to see Honor passing the salad servers back to her neighbour, saying coldly, 'I can't. It hurts.'

Lord Muirhaven made a show of demonstrating how it should be done. The satin cuffs of his dinner jacket rode up and the gold bezel of his watch caught the candlelight. He gave Jemima a tilted smile before proffering the salad dish to Mrs van Doorn, saying, 'First choice is yours.'

'Not this evening. Salad slows the gut, one can have too much.'

'I won't force you, Cornelia. You, Mrs Flowerday?' He swivelled the bowl, so the handles of the servers pointed to Jemima.

She placed a helping of leaves on her side plate. Crisp lettuce, radish tops, sorrel, sweet cicely and was that angelica? She took some. The dressing Hildebrand had mixed in was dark, suggesting there was honey in it.

'I've never been to Polesden Lacey,' she belatedly answered her hostess. 'Only seen it from the outside.' She and the children had picnicked on Box Hill last summer, from where Polesden Lacey's roofs and chimneys were visible.

Piercing a sprig of angelica with her fork, her focus sharpened. Were those beads of salad dressing on the stem? Using her napkin, she wiped it clean. Purple, bruise-like spots remained and she wasted no time. 'Nobody touch the salad. I mean it – Lord Muirhaven, stop!' Hildebrand was about to put a loaded fork into his mouth.

Jemima held up the green stem so all could see. 'Hemlock. Enough of it here to kill us all.'

Chapter Twenty-Two

Dinner descended into turmoil. Mrs Beddoe was summoned back to the room. She marched in with the air of someone forced to partake in a fuss about nothing. But when Jemima invited her to look closely at what lay on the side of her plate, her colour changed.

'I don't understand.'

'It is hemlock?' Jemima pressed her. 'No doubting it?'

'It is. But I don't see how, I honestly don't.'

'You've badly messed up,' Lord Muirhaven accused. 'You could have poisoned us all.'

Mrs Beddoe defended herself robustly. 'I know every plant in the garden and I do not make such mistakes.'

'Perhaps it wasn't a mistake,' he said grimly.

'You are accusing me of intent, Lord Muirhaven?'

'Someone put the stuff in the salad. Someone who likes unfunny tricks. Two such antics in one evening is no joke.'

'But you don't believe that someone really is trying to harm us?' Mrs van Doorn sought his answer, breathing fast.

Lord Muirhaven sighed. 'I don't want to believe that, so let us carry on with dinner.' He instructed Mrs Beddoe to clear the table. 'Bring in the dessert. I presume there's no herbage in the pudding?'

Jemima picked up her plate and followed Mrs Beddoe into the annexe off the dining room, saying, 'Before you fetch dessert, let's search this salad in case there is anything else we need to be aware of.'

'You don't think I did it deliberately, Mrs Flowerday?' Mrs Beddoe's confidence seemed shaken.

'No,' Jemima said quietly, 'but it won't take long for fingers to point elsewhere.'

'At Mairwen?'

'Sh.' Taking the salad dish from Mrs Beddoe, Jemima went to a sideboard that was stacked with used plates. Pushing them aside, she laid out a linen cloth and tipped the salad onto it, spreading the leaves out with a carving fork.

With Mrs Beddoe holding a lamp close, Jemima went through every stalk and stem. When she was done, she was satisfied that there was no more hemlock in the salad. 'Just that one, rogue piece. Will you make sure it's safely disposed of?'

Mrs Beddoe said she would burn it directly.

Jemima re-took her seat at the dining table and, after a moment, Mrs Beddoe came out of the side room. In the charged silence that fell at her appearance, she cleared her throat and said, 'On consideration, I believe it must have been my mistake. The hemlock, I mean.' She looked straight at Mrs van Doorn, then at Lord Muirhaven, adding before she left the room, 'Mine and nobody else's.'

You're a good woman, Jemima thought. You look after your girls. When she was sure Mrs Beddoe was out of earshot, she asked Mrs van Doorn, 'Will you dismiss her for this?'

Cornelia van Doorn glanced at Lord Muirhaven.

'I shouldn't think so,' he said. 'Now she's admitted it, it seems like an honest accident and no harm done.'

Dessert was tinned pineapple and cream, though nobody had much appetite for it. At eleven, Mrs van Doorn indicated the ladies should withdraw. Lord Muirhaven got up too.

'I don't want to drink port,' he said, 'but a hand of cards might settle my brain. Any takers?'

Honor begged to be allowed to go to bed. Mrs van Doorn thought a game might help her to relax and so all of them except Honor trooped down to the drawing room, where the whist table was set up. Mrs Beddoe brought in coffee and peppermint tea.

'Do you require anything else, madam?' she asked stiffly.

Jemima wondered what conversations had taken place in the kitchen.

Mrs van Doorn said no, that was all for the night. 'But please make sure there is fresh water in the kettle in my room, Mrs Beddoe, as I will need my night-time angelica and valerian.'

'Assuming you trust her not to have added a dash of hemlock,' Elaine said under her breath, but audibly enough for Mrs Beddoe to hear.

'Of course I do,' Mrs van Doorn answered quickly with a nervous laugh. 'Why on earth would anyone want to poison me?'

Mrs Beddoe assured her that she would personally check the kettle and ensure both tea caddies were replenished. 'Thank you for your trust, madam.'

Elaine apologised as she poured coffee for Lord Muirhaven, and peppermint tea for the rest of them. 'That slipped out, I'm afraid. I hope she'll forgive me.'

Jemima accepted a cup, and worried about her hat. The wind was getting up, buffeting the window, but leaving the room to fetch it would break up the whist four. Waiting for the others to seat themselves, her eye was drawn to the fireplace. The poppet's steel-bright eyes searched her out, reminding her that someone in this building practised spellcasting. Which, in turn, implied a belief in the extraordinary, and perhaps a desire for power.

Thank you for your trust, madam.

Someone had attempted to push Honor off the tower tonight

and someone – not necessarily the same person – had slipped a poisonous plant into the salad. Mrs Beddoe had shielded Mairwen from blame, but the maid had a motive as well as access to the kitchen garden. She knew her way around the plants. Mrs Beddoe had sent her to pick sorrel in Jemima's hearing and Mairwen had gone straight to it.

A poppet, a push, a poison. All the work of the same hand?

'Would you partner Elaine?' Lord Muirhaven asked Jemima from the card table. 'Mrs van Doorn and I make a devilishly good pairing, whereas you and Mrs Cleeve have the look of angels.'

'A battle between dark and light?' Jemima asked as she took her seat. She forced herself to appear enthusiastic though she was feeling jaded.

The other two joined them, and Lord Muirhaven shuffled. Jemima was fascinated to see him spread the cards out on the baize, first in a line then a circle, then into a figure-of-eight before drawing them together again, so fast her eye could hardly keep up. He must practise in the empty hours. Ah, remember that card game laid out in his apartment. His movements were making her dizzy, so instead of looking at his fingers, she focussed on his wrist. He'd taken off his watch and she saw its shape in pale skin, where the sun didn't reach.

He caught her looking, cocked an eyebrow, and began to deal.

Jemima picked up her cards. Oh, dear, a glut of diamonds. Woefully low-value ones too. All at once, the red shapes began to swim and she blinked fiercely. She played the first hand badly and apologised to Elaine, who clearly took the game seriously. Lord Muirhaven and Mrs van Doorn swept up all the points of that game and the next.

'I suspect you're not on peak form,' Elaine commented.

'No. I...' Jemima could hardly string words together. 'I'm dog tired.'

'"A drowsy numbness pains my sense",' quoted Lord Muirhaven.

'"As if of hemlock I had drunk",' Jemima finished. 'Except I neither drank nor ate it.'

'You look pale, though,' Lord Muirhaven said. 'How about you, Elaine? Flagging yet?'

'No, sharp as a dagger,' Elaine replied. 'You, Hildebrand?'

'Diamond-bright. So sparkling, I could be a ring upon dear Cornelia's finger.'

'Then I'll show no mercy' – Elaine smiled – 'because you're unbearably smug when you win.'

But after they'd ceded the third game, Elaine shook her head. Picking up the pad of score sheets she'd brought in with her, she said, 'No more. It's past one in the morning and Mrs Flowerday is all in.'

Jemima was grateful for the reprieve, and she and Elaine went upstairs together, she dragging because her limbs felt weak. 'I'm so sorry to have played like a drip.'

'Think nothing of it.' At the top of the stairs, Elaine stated her intention of lighting the spirit kettle for Mrs van Doorn's night-time tea. 'Mrs Beddoe won't have lit the flame, and Cornelia likes to have everything ready, just so.'

'You'll check nothing's been added that shouldn't have been?' Jemima urged.

'Of course. I'll drink some myself first,' Elaine said, adding with a faint smile, 'let's not see danger in every corner. I believe Mairwen followed you up to the tower to give you a scare. I can't think why, but I don't suppose she meant harm.'

'To give *me* a scare?' Jemima's mind started to churn, like wheels on mud. 'Surely, you mean Honor. Oh, but I see! Honor was wearing my things. Even Lord Muirhaven assumed she was me when he saw us from below.'

'I thought as much,' Elaine said. 'The outfit Honor had on tonight was never one of hers. I assumed you'd lent it.'

'No. It was plundered, along with my hat and gloves.'

'And coat?' Elaine gave a dry shake of the head when Jemima confirmed it. 'Now I understand.'

'A cloche hat shadows the face and hides the hair,' Jemima added. 'Anyone coming upon us from the tower room might have thought Honor was me.'

'Especially if her back was turned.' After all, Honor had described looking out at the sunset moments before she was attacked. 'It might have been you whom the prankster wanted to frighten, Jemima.'

Frighten – or fling her to her death on the flagstones below? Surely it wasn't possible that Mairwen, a girl she'd hardly spoken to, felt so bitterly towards her?

Elaine said abruptly, 'You should leave.'

Her Welsh idyll was over? For some reason, Jemima felt a tug of disappointment. 'I was going to speak with Mrs van Doorn tomorrow about the matter of clothes. It's not too late to begin designing summer things. After all, it's why I came.'

'After everything that's happened' – Elaine sounded almost angry – 'a London season isn't the remotest possibility. You've seen how Cornelia changes her mind with whiplash speed, and she won't budge, not until she's ready. My advice, take your cheque and go home, Jemima.'

Jemima's sense of fair play rebelled. 'I promised Honor I'd help her. She has a place...' she checked they weren't being overheard, 'at the Slade School. I wrung the confession from her earlier, when we were up on the tower. Her disappearance was a secret trip to London, for an interview, and the Slade granted her a place on the spot. That doesn't happen often, I promise you. To deny her the chance of taking it up would be cruel. I'd go as far as to say immoral.'

Elaine sighed. 'I wish I could change Cornelia's mind, but so far I've failed and, honestly? Your job here is done. Good night, Jemima.'

With no more to say, Jemima made for her bedroom. A distant click indicated that Elaine had gone into Mrs van Doorn's suite to get the kettle going.

On the parquet floor outside her bedroom door, Jemima noticed a smattering of mauve petals. They hadn't been there earlier, and it suggested Honor had acted on her advice; writing a letter to her stepmother, taking flowers. Let's hope there was a bouquet waiting for Mrs van Doorn in her suite with a written apology.

As she turned the knob of her bedroom door, Jemima thought she heard someone call 'Hat!'. It seemed to come from the hall, whose dome amplified every sound. Was her mind playing tricks, reminding her that her cloche was awaiting rescue? She'd rather leave it till the morning. She went to bed and slept until woken by a heavy dash of rain against her bedroom window. Her hat would be ruined. Though it must be the early hours, and she felt quite unwell, Jemima prepared to make one more trek up the tower.

Chapter Twenty-Three

Jemima hoped Lord Muirhaven hadn't already given the instruction to lock the tower door. Carrying her lantern in one hand, holding hard to the banister rail with the other, she went down and saw light under the drawing-room door. She and Elaine had left Mrs van Doorn and His Lordship there together. Had they decided to play on at two-handed whist?

She didn't investigate, wanting only to get her errand done. Thankfully, the tower door had not been secured, though it seemed to have become five times heavier since she last opened it. The stairs were no easier; she felt as though she was climbing in chain-mail. Never underestimate the power of a fright, Jemima told herself. Body and mind were close-coupled and an assault on one was an assault on the other.

Out on the parapet, the wind flung rain at her face and whistled around the curve of the tower. At least her hat was where she expected it to be, and not too wet. She put it on quickly because raising her hands caused her to flash her lantern. She didn't want to rouse those birds.

She stepped back into the tower room and went down, almost missing her footing twice. By the time she reached the great hall, Jemima was certain she had a fever. Her temples burned, though she also felt shivery. It didn't stop her noticing that the light still shone beneath the drawing-room door, which was slightly ajar. Nor did it stifle her curiosity when she heard voices from the room.

Going close enough to peer in, she saw Mrs van Doorn seated on the sofa and Lord Muirhaven on his knees before her. Both were speaking over each other, she anxiously, he reassuringly.

His voice was the louder. 'We'll break the news to Honor in the morning. Or wait until she's recovered. Until then—' He broke off, because Mrs van Doorn had seen Jemima and got to her feet. Lord Muirhaven got up in a scramble, and when he saw Jemima he looked first angry, then guilty, as if caught out.

'I – I'm so sorry.' Jemima felt a blush travel to the roots of her hair. 'I needed to rescue—' She indicated her hat.

Mrs van Doorn blurted out, 'He's asked me to marry him.' Extending her left hand, she showed Jemima a gold band with a square, green stone. 'He's asked me to be the next Countess of Muirhaven. And I' – Cornelia van Doorn inhaled a breath that reminded Jemima of the kind you take on a high diving board – 'I have said yes.'

Jemima was later to record the remainder of that night in her journal with a single word: *Bizarre.*

In her bathroom, taking off her watch so she could cool her wrists under the tap, she made a haphazard note of the time: 2:45 a.m. Having earlier persuaded herself that she was overtired or 'coming down with a bug', she now knew something was seriously wrong. With that admission came the horrible dread that, despite her statement to the contrary, she had partaken of hemlock. Her heart was racing and everything was blurred. The headache that had been a dull throb a short while ago was now a painful drumming, and she *burned.*

She sank onto the bathroom floor. For hours, it seemed, she lay on the tiles, falling in and out of consciousness. The strangest images unfurled behind her eyes. Events from her life raced past, towing more recent memories with them. Her husband Simon came and stroked her face, and the woman on the canal boat spoke in her ear. She felt herself being turned, Olive Nettle's dark eyes boring into hers, knowing and unblinking. She heard the same voice... or thought she did.

'Open wide, sister, drink.'

I'm hallucinating. At some point, she turned over and vomited before passing out. Later, she came round and got up onto her knees, then to her feet. Stooping over the sink, she drank as much water as she could take from her cupped hands.

Lord Muirhaven's smirking comment – *Castle Gloaming is affecting you* – came back, loaded with portent. Quite how she'd ingested hemlock when she didn't eat any...

She looked down at her wet hands and saw the marks on the backs of the fingers which she'd put down to nettle rash. They were very red and starting to blister. 'I touched hemlock in Lord Muirhaven's gatehouse courtyard, trying to get out before he caught me.'

What a fool. What if she'd died and left her children motherless? Elaine Cleeve was right, Jemima decided. It really was time for her to leave Castle Gloaming.

Chapter Twenty-Four

Saturday, 2 June

Daylight through Jemima's undrawn curtains woke her. She sat up with a deep headache and a desperate thirst. Dear heavens, the bathroom!

She cleaned up as best she could and after drinking more water and changing into fresh clothes, descended the stairs, once again gripping the banister. When the drawing-room door came into her line of vision, she paused. Had she really interrupted Cornelia van Doorn and Lord Muirhaven pledging themselves to each other last night, or had it been a figment of a fevered brain? And what of the dark face swimming above hers, telling her to open her mouth and drink? Delusion, she decided. The mind was a remarkable instrument, capable of summoning imaginary help at moments of crisis.

Jemima entered the breakfast room, craving tea and hoping to find Gwen or Mrs Beddoe, as she doubted she had the strength to lift a heavy pot. The room was empty, however, the breakfast table unlaid and the sideboard bare. Surely breakfast had not been finished and cleared? Going to the window, she saw that the rain was coming down harder than ever. She couldn't walk to the railway station in such weather. Nor would she countenance a journey by pony and trap. She had great compassion for horses and, anyway, the wheels would get mired on the primitive roads. Unless ordered out, she must stay until the sun returned.

A cough made her look round. Mrs Beddoe came in with a salver of condiments, salt, pepper and mustard. Jemima wished her good day.

'And to you, Mrs Flowerday. I'm afraid we're all behind this morning, but it comes down to being one maid short.'

'Mairwen's gone?'

After a hesitation, Mrs Beddoe replied that she had not. 'But as she isn't being paid, she isn't working. To be frank with you, we're all wondering when our salaries for May will arrive. Mrs van Doorn has never been late before.'

'Mrs van Doorn's stepdaughter has never gone missing before,' Jemima pointed out. 'She's had much on her mind.'

'But she has Mrs Cleeve to think of these things for her.'

Jemima couldn't argue with that. She didn't like to say so, but in her experience, very rich people were often the worst payers. It made her feel guilty about the two-hundred-pound cheque upstairs in her dressing table.

'I can wait a while,' Mrs Beddoe was saying, 'but Gwen, Mairwen and Ifor, they send money home, see, and it matters.'

'Would you like me to mention it, if I can find the moment?'

'I would be obliged.' After a pause, Mrs Beddoe craved pardon for speaking bluntly, but added that Jemima did not strike her as one of those haughty Englishwomen who only cared about their own comfort.

'I should hope not,' Jemima answered fervently. 'My parents ran a grocer's shop. My sister and I got a good education, but we came home each day with chores to do. We also had an hour's work every morning, stacking shelves, before leaving for school.'

'A useful youth is the path to a useful life, I always say, Mrs Flowerday. It shows in your attitude, unlike some.'

Jemima felt it wisest not to ask. 'May I ask how Mairwen is?'

'Sad. Angry.'

'Angry?'

'With me, for saying I accidentally put hemlock in the salad. She says I should have held my ground and demanded a proper enquiry.'

'Do you think Mairwen might have put it there, as a joke?'

'A joke? Of course not! Nobody would do that.'

'Yet it was there. It was either deliberate, or an error. Have, um, have any of you in the kitchen fallen sick?'

A shake of the head and an air of surprise was a clear no. 'I did what I said I'd do, burned all that salad in the range.' Mrs Beddoe looked more closely at Jemima. 'Are you saying you've been unwell?'

'A little. Well, to be truthful, I was very sick. I think I must have touched hemlock outside in the gardens.' Jemima wasn't going to mention her excursion into Lord Muirhaven's territory.

Mrs Beddoe asked her to describe her symptoms, listening intently. 'Hm. I'm not sure. I've never heard of anyone having visions from hemlock, and you only touched the leaves you say? You didn't eat any?'

'Certainly not.'

'One touch wouldn't make you so ill.'

'Then why do people wear gloves to handle it?' Jemima showed Mrs Beddoe her blisters.

The housekeeper inspected them, and repeated, 'Hemlock is deadly if eaten, but a touch won't kill.'

'And I'm not dead. I was lucky.' Jemima asked where Mairwen would go when she left Castle Gloaming.

'Her parents have a place not far from Trevor, in the hills. A barn and a couple of fields, no more. They'll find work for her till she finds another position.'

'Or she marries. Is Mairwen in love with Lord Muirhaven, by any chance?'

Mrs Beddoe gaped. 'What makes you ask that? Mairwen isn't in love with him nor he with her. I see everything, Mrs Flowerday, so I would know. What put that into your head?'

'I see things too and I believe someone is suffering unrequited love for His Lordship and has made a charm. Such tokens usually represent the object of desire. I wondered for a moment if it might be Ifor, but he has the wrong colour eyes. The poppet has eyes of steel-grey, like Lord Muirhaven.'

'Poppet?' Mrs Beddoe asked sharply.

'I didn't tell you before, but please, don't hold it against Mairwen.'

'What is it to do with Mairwen?'

'I suspect she created it,' Jemima said. 'I studied her yesterday. She has the fine, smooth fingers of a good seamstress, whereas Gwen has square hands, and bitten nails. It's not proof, but it's a feeling.'

'Where is this poppet-creature?'

'In the drawing-room fireplace. Perhaps Mairwen enjoyed a brief affection for Lord Muirhaven, which passed, and she forgot to remove the effigy. I'm sure it's harmless, but if she was in love with him people might say it gives her a motive for disliking Honor van Doorn.'

Mouth pursing, Mrs Beddoe began to lay the table, clattering knives, forks and spoons while muttering to herself in Welsh. When Gwen came in with tea and coffee, the housekeeper spoke to her likewise. Gwen put down her tray and went straight out.

'Would you be kind enough to pour tea for me?' Jemima asked Mrs Beddoe, explaining that she still felt weak as a kitten.

The housekeeper obliged in silence, then left the room.

Jemima drank her tea and managed some dry toast. She was surprised Mrs Cleeve wasn't yet down as it was almost nine. Then again, they had retired well after midnight.

'Did I really interrupt Lord Muirhaven proposing to Cornelia van Doorn?' she whispered to herself. I did. Tea had cleared Jemima's head, and she was able to separate hallucination from reality. 'I spoiled their moment. Poor things, but really, what were they thinking of? What *are* they thinking of?'

Jemima got up to see if a spoonful of scrambled egg might shift the last of the fog from her brain, when a shrill noise like a peacock's cry made her stop what she was doing. It had come from close by. Hearing it again, she went out to investigate. It came from upstairs, from the mezzanine, amplified by the dome. And again, horror trapped in a bell jar. Jemima ran upstairs and, looking towards Mrs van Doorn's suite, saw Elaine Cleeve on her knees outside the door. She was screaming through hands clasped to her mouth. When Jemima reached her, she grasped at Jemima's hem.

'Don't. Go. In.'

Jemima released Elaine's grip and entered the sitting room of the Countess's Suite, where she'd sat the previous afternoon. This time, the double doors were wide open, revealing the room behind and the gilded rails of a bed. On the threshold between the rooms, a satin coverlet lay as if dragged. Jemima went closer, then stopped. Instinct told her to look to her right.

Behind the sitting-room sofa, locked in a foetal pose, lay Cornelia van Doorn. She wore a nightgown of oyster-pink satin, stretched over her knees which were drawn in towards her navel in an agonised attitude. Her head lay at an angle, her eyes wide open. At some point, she had vomited violently and her mouth was set in a hideous rictus grin.

Jemima crouched beside her and picked up one hand. It was cold.

She heard someone come in and got to her feet to see Honor, in silk pyjamas, coming towards her. The girl's hair was loose around her shoulders and there was a feverish gleam to her temples.

'What has happened?' Honor asked harshly. 'Stepmama—'

Jemima moved quickly and steered Honor back out into the passageway. Elaine had stopped screaming and was using the wall for support.

Seeing Honor and Jemima, she said in a fractured voice, 'She's dead, isn't she?'

'I'm afraid so,' Jemima confirmed. 'This time, somebody must summon the police.'

She had the presence of mind to make note of the time. It was twelve minutes past nine.

Chapter Twenty-Five

Southampton Docks

The ship's officer made himself known to the plain-clothes policemen waiting on the quay. After greetings were exchanged, he handed a neat package to the senior of the two. It was sealed with tape and knotted string.

'All yours, Detective Inspector Pollard. I have to tell you, I am very glad to be handing this over. I've had to keep it in my cabin, locked away, and – frankly – I haven't enjoyed sleeping with it.'

'Where was it found, d'you know?' DI Pollard inquired.

'On the boat deck. It dropped where the oakum had come loose, disappearing between the deck planks and the ship's side. Look, I'd better get back on board, but good luck.'

'Luck?' Pollard repeated. 'What for?'

'Finding out how the poor fellow came to leave it behind.'

Chapter Twenty-Six

Within an hour of Mrs van Doorn's body being discovered, Mr Beddoe had harnessed the pony to the trap. He and his nephew Ifor set off together. Ifor was to be set down on the top road, by the aqueduct, from where he would hitch a lift on a boat to Trevor. At Trevor, he would seek out the doctor and ride back to the castle in the doctor's horse and trap. Beddoe, meanwhile, would continue on to Chirk where there was a police house containing a sergeant and two constables. The idea was to bring a constable or two back with him.

None of it would happen quickly, as Jemima was acutely aware. With Elaine catatonic with shock, Honor distraught in her room, and Lord Muirhaven pale and silent, it fell to her and Mrs Beddoe to manage the situation. They spoke in the passage outside Mrs van Doorn's suite.

'It is crucial nothing is touched or tidied up in there,' Jemima warned. 'Do you have a key?'

Mrs Beddoe selected one from the chatelaine at her waist and secured the door under Jemima's eye.

Jemima repeated, 'Nobody must enter until the doctor or the police arrive, whichever is first.' The lesson had been learned from her previous encounter with murder, at Merry Beggars Hall, when crucial evidence had been, literally, washed away by the scullery maid.

'It feels wrong to leave Mrs van Doorn on the floor, in such condition as you describe. Can we not at least lay her on the bed?' Mrs Beddoe entreated.

'I'm afraid not. The doctor must see her in situ. She shouldn't be moved until both he and the police have viewed her.'

'Bryn Probert is our village PC,' Mrs Beddoe said. 'He's a tidy sort. Beddoe wanted to fetch him, not those from Chirk who we don't know.'

'The thing is, Mrs Beddoe, PC Probert would have to call in senior colleagues anyway, and this saves time. It is vital that tests on Mrs van Doorn's system are done quickly.'

'But I went to school with Bryn's mother and Beddoe sings with him in the men's chorus.'

Jemima sighed. The ties that kept a small community tightly together could present problems. Mairwen, who *must* be questioned without fear or favour, was also one of their own. No doubt her parents attended the same chapel and sang in the same choirs.

'When the police arrive, Mrs Beddoe, and the doctor for that matter, might we speak English because there are things I want say to them. Things which concern you.'

'Me?'

'And Mairwen and it won't help if two conversations are going on at once.'

'Are you blaming me for Mrs van Doorn's death – or Mairwen?' Mrs Beddoe looked suddenly ready for combat. 'I was nowhere near these rooms last night. None of us staff were. We sleep down below, beside the kitchen.'

'But you *were* in the suite, Mrs Beddoe. I heard Mrs van Doorn ask you to check the water in the kettle before you retired. Did you?'

'Of course, as I have every night since she came to live here!'

'The presence of a deadly plant doused in French dressing, served at dinner by you—'

143

'Not served by me. Lord Muirhaven took the dish from me. And you know very well why I claimed responsibility. *Duw,* why did I do that? They'll say I killed her!'

'Yes,' Jemima acknowledged. 'It will be the first evidence the police will follow up and I would like to understand how it happened, so I can speak for you. Help me, and I won't just save the police some time, I may prevent innocents from being charged. Having said that, Mairwen has the strongest motive for harming Mrs van Doorn.'

'Being sacked is no motive.'

It was though. A burning sense of injustice could fan a person's rage. 'Mrs Beddoe, unless you really did blunder when harvesting the salad herbs—'

'I don't blunder. Why else would Mrs van Doorn trust me to make her herbal teas? I am skilled.'

The *tea*, Jemima thought. She'd drunk a fair amount of fennel and peppermint tea since arriving, as had Elaine Cleeve. It was the other tea, the 'special' preparation of angelica and valerian that should go off to a laboratory and be put under a microscope. Elaine, whatever she was experiencing mentally, was showing no sign of being poisoned and Jemima was still inclined to believe that her symptoms had resulted from skin-contact with hemlock. She must somehow have transferred sap to her mouth.

'You put last night's salad in the kitchen range, I think you said?'

'I burned it all.' Mrs Beddoe had scraped out the serving dish directly onto the fire. 'We have a kitchen cat and Ifor has a terrier and I didn't want them getting to it.'

'What about the chopping boards where you prepared the salad, and the knife you used?'

'Scrubbed. You can't be too careful.'

Which meant the evidence of preparation was gone. 'Mrs

Beddoe, may I suggest you itemise everything you picked in the garden for last night's dinner. Leave nothing out.'

'If I have time,' Mrs Beddoe said gruffly. 'With all the comings and goings, doctor, police, the undertakers, I need to make Welsh cakes. Several batches.'

'Is Mairwen still in the castle?'

Mrs Beddoe nodded. 'She can't walk to her parents in this rain.'

'No, and it would look bad if she left.' Jemima frowned. 'Why are you looking at me that way, Mrs Beddoe?'

'Because I can't make you out. Are you here for good or harm?'

'The only proper course in a situation like this is to weed out the truth. I will attempt that.'

'But you believe there's a murderer among us,' Mrs Beddoe persisted.

'I simply don't know. Yet. Let's hold the fort and our tongues until the authorities arrive.'

The housekeeper didn't argue. 'Should I prepare luncheon? Nobody ate breakfast, and His Lordship often comes over for his midday meal.'

It was still only quarter past ten, but if cooking helped Mrs Beddoe cope with catastrophe, then lunch was to be encouraged.

'I suggest we eat in the breakfast parlour, Mrs Beddoe. The police may want to examine the dining room.'

'Very good, though I expect Mrs Cleeve will have her own ideas.'

'In due course, but at the moment her nerves are overset.'

Mrs Beddoe cleared her throat. 'Will she hold the purse strings, do you think, with Mrs van Doorn deceased? Only, we still need to be paid.'

Jemima offered reassurance. 'Mrs Cleeve will know which firm of solicitors manages Mrs van Doorn's affairs and she'll no doubt take up the reins. She won't string things out, if I'm any judge of character.'

The women went their separate ways. The conversation left Jemima with plenty to mull over. The victim had been a stepmother and employer, friend and tenant. And a fiancée, briefly. All those dwelling beneath Castle Gloaming's roof had lost a great deal with her death.

But which of them might have had the most to gain?

Chapter Twenty-Seven

Making her way downstairs, Jemima calculated how long it would take for the doctor to arrive. Taking the heavy rain into account, she concluded he'd turn up as they sat down to lunch. She'd suggest an extra place at table.

Jemima paused under the dome, resting a hand on the marble plinth in the centre of the hall. A china vase, the one that took four gallons of water to fill, held fresh stems of corkscrew willow. The hogweed that had made such a spectacular display the day she arrived had been replaced with branches of white-flowered mock orange. Despite its sweet scent, Jemima perceived that the water in the vase was a little whiffy; it hadn't been changed. Mrs Beddoe didn't strike her as the kind of woman to let things slip, but late payment of wages blunted even the most diligent servant. Dirty water, breakfast served late... it told a story.

In the drawing room, she found Lord Muirhaven nursing a very early whisky and Elaine sitting with her hands tightly folded. They shared a sofa, a gap between them. Elaine's eyes were swollen and she looked haggard. Her short curls were tangled, as if she'd had no time to brush them that morning. Perhaps she'd gone straight from her room to Mrs van Doorn's only to find—

Jemima mentally blocked the image of Cornelia van Doorn in her death agony. Distancing herself from trauma was something she had learned to do as Simon's wife. She was good at it, as long as she fastened her mind on other things.

She asked Elaine if she would like tea. 'I could go ask or make it myself, Elaine?'

Elaine shook her head. 'I feel sick.'

Jemima was instantly on her mettle. 'In what way?'

'Just sick.' Elaine buried her face in her hands and rocked.

Jemima sat on the broad sofa arm and put a hand on her shoulder. 'Once her body is removed somewhere more appropriate, you'll feel more settled. How do you feel, in yourself, Lord Muirhaven?'

'What the hell does that mean, "in yourself"?' Aggression shot through Lord Muirhaven's voice.

The whisky in his glass wasn't his first, Jemima suspected. She wondered who, apart from herself and poor, late, Cornelia, knew of the marriage proposal? Had he told Elaine?

'I'm asking if you might have suffered any symptoms of poisoning during the night.'

'No. I felt a bit off after I went to bed. Nothing that kept me awake.' He brushed away Jemima's attempts to prise more detail from him. 'What the hell happened?' he repeated. 'And what are we going to do?'

'Wait for the authorities,' said Jemima.

'And get skewered for murder.' He said it as though it were a fait accompli. 'We're all vulnerable, you included, Mrs Flowerday.'

'Why me?' she asked.

'Ignore me.' Hildebrand quaffed from his glass. 'Of course you're innocent. Why would a dressmaker kill the woman who's paid her handsomely to run up a few frocks? Oh, hang on, you haven't made any. You were brought in because your letter in a sleuthing magazine piqued Cornelia's interest. She summoned you to solve a mystery. It's what she did.'

'Explain, Lord Muirhaven.'

'Cornelia acted on caprice, but was terrified of scandal because she believed it would prevent her being accepted by English society. You were a perfect solution, discretion incarnate.'

'I am indeed. Yet when I offered to help establish her in London, she turned me down flat.' Jemima went to the fireplace and pulled the bell rope. 'I could do with more tea, and you both could too, I'm sure.'

'I'm sticking with a proper drink,' Lord Muirhaven said savagely. 'I'm not one of your tea-obsessed Englishmen.'

'He'll have some,' Elaine said quietly.

While waiting for someone to come from the kitchen, Jemima took her coat from the ottoman. Time to face the damage. She held it up in front of her. One pocket hung limply, probably torn off during Honor's struggle with her adversary. She'd have to get out her needle case, but not now. It also needed a sponge-down as there was blood on one cuff. She flinched, thinking of that excruciating injury to Honor's hand. A fingernail ripped off. The girl must have fought for her life.

Jemima turned the coat around to check that the back was undamaged. It looked fine, needing no more than a gentle brush. She turned it again to re-examine the front, and something jumped out at her. The deer-horn button, placed level with the hip and large as a guinea piece, fastened by being passed through a brocade loop. It took patience as it was designed to be snug, otherwise the coat would flap open. Honor had been wearing the coat with the button fastened, but now it was undone. Could Lord Muirhaven have done it when he picked it up off the ground?

The man himself interrupted her thoughts. 'Who tops your list of suspects? Who would want to kill Cornelia?'

Suspecting his antagonism sprang from distress, she answered patiently, 'Speculation helps nobody. It might have been an accident.'

'You don't believe that, Mrs Flowerday. What's the motive, in your view?'

'I refuse to conjecture.'

'Generally then, what are the principal motives for murder?'

'Greed, rage, hatred, vengeance and desire. In no particular order.'

Lord Muirhaven raised his glass in an ironic toast. 'Which of us has any or all of those in their heart?'

'That's for CID to discover.'

'CID?' Elaine jerked, looking anxious. 'You mean—"

'Criminal Investigation Department,' Jemima confirmed. 'If the doctor believes it to be an unnatural death, the local police will notify them. They'll be headquartered in the nearest city.'

'God help us,' muttered Lord Muirhaven. 'Will you speak with them, Mrs Flowerday?'

'You need to take the lead, Lord Muirhaven. You are the master of this house.'

'I'm no use,' he cried. 'I don't trust men in uniforms, and they don't like me.'

'I should be taking charge but' – Elaine turned tear-stained eyes on Jemima – 'I don't know what to do...' She tailed off on a keening note.

They're falling to pieces, Jemima realised. If she was to judge, she'd say that Mrs van Doorn's death had devastated them. Each had enjoyed a relationship with Cornelia and both had much to lose: Elaine would forfeit her income and her home; Lord Muirhaven's losses were financial too. As to his heart, Jemima could not bear witness.

'If you genuinely wish me to engage with the doctor and the police, then I'd first like to establish where everyone was at various points yesterday,' she said.

'Why?' Lord Muirhaven returned to his earlier animosity.

'Because they will ask, and if you flounder and contradict yourself, they will pin you like a botanical specimen to a board.' She went to the door. Nobody had answered the bell, so this was a good moment to go into the kitchen. 'I'll suggest that everybody present yesterday, with the exception of Mr Beddoe and Ifor, gathers here. Elaine, would you fetch Honor down?'

'She won't come,' Elaine said, blotting her eyes with a hanky.

'Tell her that I'm going to ensure that the tower door is locked, as per Lord Muirhaven's instructions, as well as her usual exit to the outside. Tell her, if she ever wants to escape, her only option is co-operation.'

Elaine went and Jemima reminded Lord Muirhaven that he must ask Mrs Beddoe to lock the tower.

'I will. And, Mrs Flowerday?'

'Yes?'

'No tea. I can't stand the stuff.'

Jemima's progress to the kitchen got no further than the great hall, where the sound of hooves in the courtyard took her to the door. A horse-drawn cabriolet was drawing up, its hood sheltering the gentleman holding the reins. He wore a rainproof mantle and a bowler hat. Ifor, looking very sodden, sprang down from the rear platform. A dun cob with a kind eye, water streaming off its flanks, was brought to a stop and the reins passed over.

The doctor had arrived.

Chapter Twenty-Eight

The doctor plucked a medical bag from under his seat and got down from the box. His first comment was directed in Welsh to Ifor, who was releasing the horse from the traces.

Jemima introduced herself as Ifor led the animal away. 'Mrs Flowerday. I'm a guest at the castle, but here to help as much as I may.'

'Dr Rees-Parry. Shall we get out of the rain?'

Mrs Beddoe had to have the hearing of an owl, or had posted a lookout, because she emerged from the servants' wing as Jemima ushered the doctor inside and closed the front door.

'Would you take Dr Rees-Parry's coat? And serve tea in, say, forty minutes?' Jemima asked the housekeeper, adding, 'I will need the key to the Countess's Suite.'

When she took the doctor into the drawing room, Elaine had not yet returned, and must still have been trying to prise Honor from her room. Jemima made introductions, and the doctor asked if Lord Muirhaven would be good enough to show him where the body was.

The reply was a shake of the head, and a gravelly, 'I can't.'

Dr Rees-Parry looked taken aback, but allowed Jemima to lead the way instead.

On the mezzanine level, she advised him to prepare himself. 'The death Mrs van Doorn suffered was not – my goodness!' Honor was waiting at Mrs van Doorn's door, still wearing her silk pyjamas and a long cardigan to keep out the chill. Her hair was unkempt, and tear stains on her cheeks revealed she had not taken off her makeup since last night.

'What are you doing?' Jemima demanded. 'You can't get in, the door's locked.'

'I need to see my stepmother.' Honor gave the doctor a stare that matched her voice. Frightened. Childlike. She was hugging herself, as if to press the shivers back inside. 'Who is this?'

'Dr Rees-Parry. Get dressed, Honor. Mrs Cleeve is looking for you. Mrs Beddoe is making tea and Welsh cakes.'

'How can you think of food when they're all saying my step-mother was poisoned?'

'At some point, everyone will think of food,' was Jemima's clipped answer. 'And nobody's saying it. Go to the drawing room and wait.'

'Are you giving orders to me?'

'Not at all, I am saving the doctor the trouble.' Allowances had to be made for shock and sudden bereavement and as Honor pushed past, Jemima said, 'It will help to think about the last conversation you had with your stepmother, and your last sighting of her. The police will ask.'

Did the girl hesitate? Perhaps, but she made her way to the stairs without speaking.

Jemima unlocked the door of Mrs van Doorn's sitting room, again warning the doctor of a distressing scene, adding that everything had been left as found. She did not accompany him in, but waited on the threshold. She heard a sharp intake of breath followed by something muttered in Welsh which she translated as, 'My good God.'

Dr Rees-Parry spent around twenty-five minutes with the body. Jemima stood guard, listening to the opening and shutting of the medical bag, wishing she understood Welsh. When he joined her he was in his shirt sleeves, and spatters on the fabric implied a thorough examination had taken place.

'Well,' he said, in a tone that warned of grim things to come, 'I have seen cases of poisoning in my career, but rarely one as pitiful or violent as this. The poor, dear lady. I wonder if she was attempting to leave her room to summon help.'

Jemima had already come to that conclusion, as a bell rope by the sitting room fireplace would almost certainly ring in the servants' quarters. And, of course, Elaine slept nearby.

'It must have been a most painful death,' Jemima said. She wouldn't forget the rictus grin, the bent fingers and knees drawn up to the chest. 'As her bedcover was in the doorway, I presume she was in bed when the symptoms struck and dragged herself out. Do you think that likely?'

The doctor agreed it made sense. 'She may have been trying to leave her apartment and collapsed before she could get around the sofa. She died where she lies. I understand from the young lad that the police are on their way.'

'Ifor's uncle has gone to Chirk to raise the alarm and, hopefully, the police won't drag their feet.'

The doctor consulted his fob watch. 'Mid-afternoon is my estimation. Can you tell me what this lady consumed yesterday that might have led to her poisoning?'

'You have no doubt, then, it was poisoning?'

'An autopsy will take place. Until then, I go on the evidence of eyes and nose. So?'

'I can't entirely say what Mrs van Doorn consumed yesterday, but I too had a violent reaction to something.' Jemima described the night she had endured, and when asked if she had any idea what might have brought on the attack, she answered in two words.

'Hemlock, Doctor.'

Having re-locked the door, they went downstairs. Jemima suggested Dr Rees-Parry go into the drawing room while she rallied the servants. 'You can ask each in turn and get a full picture of what Mrs van Doorn might have eaten and how it was prepared. Unless you wish to speak to everyone separately?'

'All in one room is fine, so long as they don't talk all at once.'

Jemima assured him she would moderate proceedings, if he would trust her.

'You seem very able, Mrs Flowerday.' He detained her, asking, 'In your opinion, are we looking at accident or intention?'

'That's for the police, but Mrs van Doorn's death has not come out of the blue. As you will learn, it is the latest in a series of strange and unsettling incidents.'

The doctor agreed that, if that were the case, they would not speculate, but wait for the law.

In the kitchen, she found Mrs Beddoe cutting sultana-rich dough into rounds. Gwen was hunkered before the range, opening the dampers to increase the heat. Mairwen was looking out through a window set high in the wall. She had abandoned her maid's uniform and cap for a drop-waist, mauve dress, but was recognisable by the dark hair caught in a net against the nape of her neck.

Jemima announced that the doctor wanted them all in the drawing room. 'Bring in tea and Welsh cakes, but don't delay.' Her worry was that Honor would do something to obstruct proceedings, perhaps even attempt another flit.

Mairwen said without looking round, 'I'm not going in.'

'You must,' Jemima said. 'In fact, help me light the drawing-room fire. It's turned chilly.'

'Gwen can do it,' Mrs Beddoe said, rather quickly.

Jemima conceded. 'All three of you must present yourselves, however, and Ifor too.'

Mairwen turned. 'Why me? I didn't do anything to anybody. But they're not going to believe it, are they?' She gave a metallic laugh. 'I'm the perfect suspect, the one with the grudge. I was out in the kitchen garden, too. I know how it goes.'

She's been crying, Jemima realised, and has rubbed her cheeks with a coarse cloth. Since I doubt she cared much for her late employer, she weeps from fear. 'All the more reason to face the music, Mairwen. If there are to be accusations of poisoning or attempting to push Miss Honor off the tower—'

'You think I did that? I wasn't up there.' Mairwen sought corroboration from Mrs Beddoe, who carried on cutting rounds from her dough. 'That place gives me goosebumps and Gwen's the same.'

'I do hear you, Mairwen,' Jemima said, 'but it's not me you need to convince. Fetch Ifor and come to the drawing room, soon as you can.'

'"Soon as you can"' Mairwen echoed. 'You're good at giving orders—'

'That's enough.' Mrs Beddoe paused, cutter in hand. 'Mrs Flowerday is right. You will be questioned and if you spit fire or refuse to help, the police will think you have something to hide. Gwen, *bach*' – she got the attention of the younger maid – 'make the tea then fetch logs and coal for the fire upstairs. Mairwen, do as you're told, get Ifor.'

Mairwen ignored the command. 'Everyone's against me.'

Mrs Beddoe opened the knife drawer in the side of her table and removed something which she slammed down next to her skillet. It was the poppet. She turned angrily on Mairwen. 'You've made your choices, girl. Where there is sin, there's—'

A price? Jemima was eager to know, but Mrs Beddoe remembered at the last moment to switch into Welsh.

Chapter Twenty-Nine

Walking into the drawing room, Jemima was struck by a sense of breath tightly held. Elaine and Lord Muirhaven were in their customary place on one sofa. The doctor sat on the sofa opposite. Honor was perched on the ottoman, apparently still in deep shock.

The doctor had asked if, in her opinion, Mrs van Doorn's death was accident or intention. Jemima's first thought was that Lord Muirhaven was the least likely person to have killed her. A man who has been accepted in marriage by a wealthy diamond widow has every incentive to keep her alive, at least until after the wedding. Elaine had even less cause as, in her words, she had been Mrs van Doorn's dependent, albeit an outspoken one.

What of Honor, who had gone up a rung from 'heiress' to 'beneficiary'?

'Refreshments are on their way.' Jemima went about the room pulling out chairs. Everyone should be able to sit unless they preferred to stand. She glanced into the fireplace and wondered if Mrs Beddoe had removed the poppet before Mrs van Doorn's death was discovered, or immediately after. 'Shall we hear Dr Rees-Parry's opinion on what he saw upstairs?'

Honor's chin jerked upward. 'It's obvious. Someone poisoned something she ate or drank. We were all there at dinner, weren't we?'

'We were,' Jemima agreed. 'All of us here, bar Dr Rees-Parry, were sitting at table and witnessed the least subtle poisoning attempt in history.' She turned to the doctor, who was following attentively. 'There was a piece of hemlock in a salad served last night, which got there accidentally. Nobody touched it, and Mrs van Doorn refused salad anyway. We must look for a different cause.' Jemima could not resist a glance at Honor who was shaking her head. 'You think differently, child?'

Honor gave an angry shrug. 'Calling it an accident is highly convenient.'

'I agree,' said Jemima, 'except that as a means of killing, one sprig of a deadly plant in a large salad that is going to be shared among five people is too random.' Unless, she thought, the intention was simply to make somebody – anybody – ill. Though why? As a warning, or a gesture? Still – why? She said to Honor, 'Killers usually have a target.'

'Did anybody else feel unwell after dinner?' The doctor put the question generally.

Honor shook her head, as did Elaine. Lord Muirhaven, last to answer, admitted to feeling a mite queasy during the night.

'I touched the dish and handled the salad servers,' he said. 'Would that be enough?'

Dr Rees-Parry wouldn't commit. 'Could be. Or not. It depends.'

Mairwen came in with coal and logs and, for a while, the only sound was the grate being scraped and the hearth swept. Jemima wondered if Mairwen appreciated the extent to which Mrs Beddoe had protected her. Had that poppet remained in place and the police found it, their questioning would have taken a very particular course. Who loves whom, who is jealous of whom? They'd have found out in the end who made it and placed it.

Gwen arrived with tea, followed by Mrs Beddoe with a platter of buttered toast, gentleman's relish in one pot, jam in another. 'I'll return when I've taken my Welsh cakes from the oven,' she told them. 'The girls have permission to stay.'

'Should Mairwen be here at all?' Elaine demanded.

Mairwen was still kneeling in front of the fire, lighting a twist of paper.

'Of course she should,' Lord Muirhaven snapped. 'Unless you're volunteering to take on her work? Mairwen should never have been sacked in the first place.'

'We know why she was,' Honor piped up, her mouth jerking.

'For challenging you, who took her property,' Jemima put in.

'Not so, because she questioned my right to have a life outside these walls. She should talk!' Honor cradled her bandaged fingers, and Jemima got the first intimation that she rather liked to be the centre of attention. 'Mairwen has a...' She saved up the moment. '*Lover*.'

Mairwen got hastily to her feet. 'Don't you dare.'

'No?'

'Or I might tell this company a few things about you, Miss Honor.'

For a moment the young women battled it out, their eyes their weapons.

Then Honor gave a shrug and said in a high, tense voice, 'Don't let me interrupt your work, Mairwen.'

For a moment Jemima believed Mairwen would throw her coal scuttle at Honor. In the end, she clearly thought better of it and muttered something in Welsh that carried the timbre of contempt. Fearing the household would split into warring factions, 'downstairs' against 'upstairs', Jemima asked Gwen if she would kindly pour the tea.

'Your Welsh cakes, Mrs Beddoe?' she prompted.

'Oh, yes. Excuse me.' The housekeeper left.

'Meanwhile, Dr Rees-Parry will tell us, in as much as he's able, how Mrs van Doorn met her death.' Jemima indicated the floor was his.

'Respiratory failure as a consequence of poisoning, causal substance as yet unknown,' the doctor answered briskly.

'What do you estimate as time of death?' Lord Muirhaven asked in a voice rough with emotion.

This time, the doctor took a moment. 'I am not a pathologist, merely a general practitioner, but there are visual tests in cases of an unattended death. These being—'

The under-gardener, Ifor, shuffled nervously into the room. Dr Rees-Parry paused until the young man had made his way to a place near the window, separate from the rest of them, before picking up his thread.

'First, I noted the body's temperature. I then performed a muscle-stimulation test. Third and fourth were assessments of rigor mortis and livor mortis.'

'Rigor... that's the stiffening of the limbs, isn't it?' Jemima prompted. *The Weekend Sleuth* often printed articles on criminology and forensic technique.

Dr Rees-Parry nodded. 'How far rigor has advanced gives a rough gauge of the length of time dead. Taking that and other indicators into account, I estimated the lady's death occurred approximately seven hours before.'

It was now ten minutes to midday, so if the doctor was correct, Mrs van Doorn had surrendered life as dawn broke, at around 4 a.m. She had appeared in sound health when Jemima gate-crashed her romantic moment with Lord Muirhaven in the early hours. A little overwrought as she confided her exciting news, but otherwise coherent. It was awful to think that Cornelia van Doorn had been doomed, even as she accepted the chance to become a countess.

'How much hemlock to kill?' she asked the doctor.

'All parts of the plant are toxic,' Dr Rees-Parry responded. 'Particularly the root, or any part when dried as the toxin is then concentrated.'

She showed him her blisters, explaining how she'd come by them. The doctor asked if she had experienced burning in her mouth.

'No,' said Jemima. 'Just to my skin. I thought it was nettle rash at first.'

Asked how soon after this she'd experienced symptoms, she pondered and said, 'We dined very late and didn't rise from the table until gone eleven and I felt odd as we sat down to play cards. I couldn't focus and performed badly.' She spared Elaine a wan smile. 'I couldn't for the life of me remember who had put what down.'

'Indifferent card skills are not, to my knowledge, a common symptom of plant poisoning,' the doctor observed drily.

'No, but the cards in my hand seemed to swim. I put it down to tiredness. I felt all right for perhaps an hour after that. It was only after I went up the tower to fetch my hat that I began to feel distinctly unwell.'

'You went up the tower?' Lord Muirhaven repeated. 'At that hour – why?'

'As I said: to fetch my hat.'

'But it was night, and raining.'

'By those very words, Lord Muirhaven, you display a masculine contempt for fine millinery. I couldn't leave my cloche to the elements. Coming down the stairs was quite an endeavour and by the time I reached my bedroom, I could hardly stand.' For a moment, she was back in her bathroom, believing she would die and imagining things that weren't there. *Open wide, sister, drink.*

She'd heard someone shout 'hat!' in the great hall before her symptoms worsened. She should have taken it as a warning, drunk water, gone to bed.

The doctor, who had taken out a notebook, asked if Mrs van Doorn had mentioned feeling similarly unwell during or after dinner.

They all shook their heads.

'Apart from Lord Muirhaven and Mrs Flowerday, did anyone else experience sickness or fever?'

Nobody spoke. Jemima waited for Lord Muirhaven to expand on his experience and when he didn't, she prompted him. 'You said you felt "off" and "queasy" but what did that entail?'

In reply, he lifted his empty tumbler. 'Pouring a last nightcap at God knows what time, I could hardly put bottle to glass. Everything was blurred.'

'How many nightcaps had you drunk?' asked the doctor.

'Too many, is my point. We drink plentifully at Castle Gloaming and I suspect that Mrs Flowerday, schooled in the genteel niceties, is not used to it. If you want to diagnose her illness last night, look over there.' He pointed to the cocktail cabinet, with its glimmering population of decanters.

'You're suggesting my symptoms were overindulgence?' Jemima was outraged.

Lord Muirhaven made no apology. 'I mix my gin strong, madam, and take far too little account of the more delicate constitution of the fair sex.' He turned back to Dr Rees-Parry. 'I deserve a lecture, but could you leave it till later? I promise I will mend my ways.'

Jemima seethed. Even before these slurs upon her sobriety, she'd been losing respect for Lord Muirhaven. He had failed to defend Mairwen against Honor's verbal attack. As Castle Gloaming's owner he was the guardian of those who worked there. He should have stepped in. Ah, but His Lordship liked to keep his head below the parapet, so to speak, while others managed the daily concerns of Castle Gloaming. He had admitted to being slightly unwell during the night. Now he blamed the drink. Let that pass. On another vital matter, he would not find her so accommodating.

Fixing him with her most open expression, Jemima said, 'Last night, when I found you and Mrs van Doorn together, her hands were shaking visibly. Had you been plying *her* with strong liquor?'

'She liked her pink gin, you know perfectly well,' he said, straight back. To the doctor he said, 'This fuss over the hemlock is irrelevant, Dr Rees-Parry. Mrs Beddoe has already admitted it was her error. Nobody touched it, it can be ruled out.'

The doctor asked Gwen, who had finished handing around the tea, what her opinion was.

Jemima was surprised when Gwen answered in English, nervously but otherwise clearly. 'As His Lordship says, Mrs Beddoe did it by mistake and she will never again gather herbs except in the full light of morning.'

The doctor spoke in Welsh. Watching Gwen, Jemima saw a flicker of understanding pass between the two. Gwen answered in Welsh also, nodding as if she agreed with what had been said.

'You will have to translate,' Jemima said coldly.

'Gwen is offering a different perspective on Mrs van Doorn's death, of it being an outsider's work.'

'What outsider?'

'A ne'er-do-well who strayed into the grounds. Castell Glan yr Afon is remote, but not inaccessible. It can be approached from the river, the canal and the lane.'

Jemima burst out, 'Doctor, none of us want it to be murder, but you mustn't influence Gwen. Such questioning is for the police.'

'You asked my opinion. Lord Muirhaven believes the presence of hemlock is a distraction, an irrelevance. You yourself pointed out that a single piece of the weed in a salad intended for – what? – five people dining together, would be too random to imply an intent to kill.' Dr Rees-Parry puffed out his cheeks. 'Murderers like better odds than that, I'd say. Only an imbecile would take the chance.'

'You're suggesting that an intruder killed Mrs van Doorn, by other means?' Jemima wished she knew what he'd said to Gwen, and she to him.

Perhaps realising he had trespassed into police territory, Dr Rees-Parry returned to his own turf. He had come across several cases of hemlock poisoning in his career, he said. 'I'm sad to say all fatal, all Boy Scouts on adventure holidays from the city. They don't know what they're eating, see. Every one of them was frothing and vomiting within half an hour of ingesting leaves or seeds. Half an hour,' he stressed.

Jemima considered it. Her symptoms had become acute three to four hours after getting up from the table yesterday. As for Mrs van Doorn, she'd seemed fine when Jemima last saw her at around 2:30 a.m., though by four she was dead. Cornelia's symptoms had arisen sometime in the wee hours of this morning.

The doctor had carried his point.

'I have only ever come across one deliberate case of the poisoning,' he said, then made them wait as if imagining a circus drumroll. 'That of Socrates, condemned to drink a bowl of hemlock in wine, in Athens, two thousand three hundred years ago.'

Bowing to the doctor's better knowledge of Greek history, Jemima said no more. *Condemned* was a brutal word. She envisaged Mrs van Doorn, her knees drawn up like those of a skeleton in an early Christian burial, bluish fingers bent into claws. Fingers... wait...

'Where's her ring?' she demanded.

'Ring?' echoed the doctor. 'I counted several. Her fingers were loaded with jewels.'

'Yes,' Jemima agreed impatiently, 'she wore many diamonds. I'm talking of a ring with a square, green stone. An emerald, probably.' She turned to Lord Muirhaven, giving him a chance to reclaim his dignity in her eyes, and come clean. 'Mrs van Doorn had it on the fourth finger of her left hand when I came upon you together here last night, Lord Muirhaven.' She allowed him a few more seconds' grace but in the face of his silence, finished by saying, 'It wasn't on her body this morning.'

His hand forced, Lord Muirhaven stood rather unsteadily and addressed the room. 'Last night, I gave my dear friend Cornelia a ring. Why should I not?'

Jemima waited for him to add that it was to seal an engagement, but when it seemed he'd said all he meant to, she pushed harder. 'Your own ring, or ordered specially?'

'A Muirhaven heirloom, Mrs Flowerday,' was the reply.

'Passed down through generations?'

'From Countess Hilda, my grandmother.'

'Where is it now?'

Honor, evidently working out the implications of this conversation, burst in scathingly. 'You made advances to my stepmother? Oh, my word, Hildebrand, even you wouldn't sink that low.'

Lord Muirhaven sat down again, head in hands.

Jemima waded in. 'It is true. In the early hours, Mrs van Doorn accepted a proposal of marriage from Lord Muirhaven.'

Honor slowly shook her head. Mairwen, who had spent a few minutes sweeping ashes from the grate, tipped them back into the fireplace then left the room. Taking her emotions at this news away with her?

Gwen hastily followed. Ifor, the only member of the staff left in this upstairs domain, looked distinctly uneasy.

Jemima could have stayed, listening to Honor pouring scorn on the man who had briefly bid to become her new stepfather, but instinct told her that 'downstairs' would yield richer pickings. Lifting the lid on the teapot, saying, 'Hm, needs a refill,' she invited Ifor to carry the tea tray down to the kitchen.

She helped him load it, then followed him out of the room.

Chapter Thirty

They found Mrs Beddoe, Gwen and Mairwen by the kitchen table. Smells of baking filled the air.

The housekeeper was holding the poppet and the other two were gazing at it. Jemima sensed a decision being made.

'May I see it again?' Jemima held out her hand.

'Only for a moment.' Mrs Beddoe handed it over.

Jemima held it to the light, viewing it with a mind more open to its meaning. For a certainty, it was Lord Muirhaven. Along with the cowlick of black hair – *real* hair – the silvery eyes and painstakingly replicated clothes, she perceived another detail. A watch. It was on the poppet's left arm, where the wrist would be on a man, embroidered in gold chainstitch.

'How long was it hiding in the fireplace?'

'About seven or eight months, isn't that so?' Mrs Beddoe threw the question at Mairwen, who responded with a glum shrug. 'When strangers come into a community like ours,' Mrs Beddoe continued, 'they make ripples. A new face is more alluring than the one you've seen at chapel every Sunday for years.'

Jemima squeezed the poppet, making a dimple in its belly. 'Honor implied something more than attraction when she accused Mairwen of having a lover. I don't like to pry, but the police ask the most awkward questions. Is it true, Mairwen?'

The tension in the room grew tangible.

'Yes,' Mairwen said at length. 'I'm not a child, why shouldn't I?'

'You slip away at every possible opportunity, don't you, Mairwen?' Mrs Beddoe said. 'I tell you you're a fool, that it will finish your reputation around here. But you don't listen.'

'I'm surprised you allow it, Mrs Beddoe,' Jemima said. Most housekeepers she'd come across would have nipped an affair with Lord Muirhaven in the bud or got rid of the girl. But then, Mrs Beddoe had already demonstrated her partiality for Mairwen.

Mrs Beddoe answered, 'She's in love, and foolish enough to believe that life will give her what she wants so badly.'

'Then she's in the same boat as Honor.'

Something in that made Mrs Beddoe ask for the poppet back.

Jemima raised it to her nose and, as before, caught the odour of soot and herbs. 'What's this stuffed with?'

Mairwen answered. 'Hawthorn berries mostly, thyme and rosemary. It's country magic, Mrs Flowerday. Nothing dangerous.'

Mrs Beddoe took over. 'In the deep past, our forebears handfasted beneath the thorn tree and would pin a spray of its flowers over their heart. Thyme and rosemary are for purification. There is nothing wicked in the object you are holding.'

'No,' agreed Jemima. 'Though it's self-evidently ineffective, as Lord Muirhaven proposed to Mrs van Doorn last night.'

'That, now.' Mrs Beddoe shook her head. 'Mrs van Doorn had no need of a husband and was old enough to be his mother.'

'Not his *mother*,' Jemima objected. 'Even so, I agree it feels odd.' To propose marriage to a woman after a day of unsettling events … One might almost think Lord Muirhaven's timing was deliberate. And another thing, assuming he had put the emerald ring on Mrs van Doorn's finger, how did he happen to have it so conveniently on his person?

'The poppet, Mrs Flowerday.' Mrs Beddoe extended her right hand.

Jemima relinquished it, saying, 'It points to a belief in magic and might seem to embody jealousy of any woman Lord Muirhaven preferred. I'm afraid' – and she meant that literally – 'this little doll provides a motive for murder.' She turned her eyes back to Mairwen.

'You're saying they will call it witchcraft and that will be a hangman's rope, with Mairwen's name upon it?' Mrs Beddoe took the poppet to the cooking range, lifting out another batch of Welsh cakes which she slid onto a cooling rack. She opened the firebox and with the air of one releasing a liability, dropped the poppet into the shimmering glow, ignoring Mairwen's cry of distress.

'It's done.' Mrs Beddoe closed the firebox and took her Welsh cakes to the table.

Jemima could ask the question that had brought her there. 'What did Gwen say to the doctor in the drawing room, please? I'm on your side, and I need to know.'

A discussion in Welsh took place, before Mrs Beddoe answered, 'She informed him there was a stranger within these walls last night.'

'From outside the castle... who?' demanded Jemima.

Mrs Beddoe looked at Gwen who shook her head. 'We cannot say.'

'But Gwen saw someone?'

'No.'

'Then how does she know?' Jemima felt no exasperation, as she herself often acted on instinct.

The answer came as no surprise.

'We just do, Mrs Flowerday. We have our ways.'

Chapter Thirty-One

Mr Beddoe returned mid-afternoon, accompanied by a policeman riding a Welsh cob. Jemima, hurrying out to greet them, thought it a solemn sight. Beddoe huddled under a hopsack cloak, water dripping off his hat. The trap pony was muddy to its shoulder. The policeman's weatherproof cape covered his horse's rump, and he resembled a tent at the end of a sodden camping trip.

Ifor came and took the cob's bridle so the police officer might dismount. Jemima greeted the newcomer, named herself and asked him if he spoke English.

'Of course.' He introduced himself as Sergeant Maddox. 'Your position here, madam?'

She explained her situation. 'Everyone is at sevens and eights, so I've taken the tiller for now. Shall we go in?' She led the way inside, where the clip of feet heralded Mrs Beddoe's arrival.

Mrs Beddoe greeted Sergeant Maddox in Welsh, and he answered at some length, once again leaving Jemima with the impression that information was flowing over her head. Butting in, she offered the sergeant tea and a chance to get out of his wet things.

'I have already offered,' Mrs Beddoe told her stiffly. 'I shall bring a tray up to him. His orders are to guard the body until the detectives arrive.'

'CID is on its way, then?' Jemima asked the sergeant. 'From Chirk?'

'No, from Mold.'

Mold, Jemima learned, though she had to ask twice, was Denbighshire's county town. A telegraph from Chirk had requested their attendance.

'They won't be here quickly, will they?' she said gloomily.

'Not for hours,' Sergeant Maddox agreed, adding that they'd be coming by train and would commandeer transport from the station at Trevor.

Dr Rees-Parry joined them, and Jemima had an idea he was relieved to escape the drawing room. Lord Muirhaven had retired to his gatehouse, leaving Elaine and Honor to keep each other company, if could be called that. The doctor suggested that he conduct Sergeant Maddox upstairs for a viewing of the body.

Determined to witness the event, Jemima asked Mrs Beddoe for the key to Mrs van Doorn's rooms. After the housekeeper reluctantly surrendered it, Jemima moved quickly, saying, 'Follow me upstairs, gentlemen.' She was fleeter of foot and had unlocked Mrs van Doorn's door before they'd reached the mezzanine. She waited, holding the door to Cornelia's sitting room open for them. They entered the murder scene.

She lingered until she heard Sergeant Maddox make an inhalation and repeat *Duw* several times. Confident nobody's eyes were on her, she nipped to the sideboard where the tea-making paraphernalia was kept. There were two teacups and saucers on a tray, when yesterday there had been three.

The burner of the spirit kettle felt cold when Jemima laid her knuckles against it. Using a clean handkerchief to avoid fingerprints, she lifted the teapot lid and sniffed, picking up a bland, sappy aroma which gave little away. Glancing round to make sure she wasn't being observed, she took a pinch of the mash from the bottom of the pot. This, she put into an empty jar she'd taken from the breakfast room. The mash retained a vestige of heat.

171

Again guarding against leaving prints, she opened the two caddies in turn. The first contained the distinctive aniseed-scented fennel seed. The second was half full of a greenish mix Jemima presumed to be Mrs van Doorn's sedative tea: angelica and valerian. She inhaled.

Hm. Mildly aromatic with perhaps a slight hint of celery or parsley? 'Grassy and earthy' might best describe it. Jemima was satisfied they were the same leaves that she'd extracted from the teapot. She removed a pinch between thumb and forefinger.

'Mrs Flowerday?'

'Sergeant?' She turned and waited to be ordered to reveal the hand she was hiding behind her back.

'Leave the door key in the lock, please. It stays with me for the time being.'

'Of course, Sergeant Maddox. I'll have a comfortable chair brought up for you too.' She left them to their work.

Rather than go down, Jemima made her way to her bedroom. In her bathroom, she laid the jam jar against her cheek. The base of the jar felt slightly warmer than room temperature, consistent with the leaves having touched boiling water in the early hours. Elaine had spoken of lighting the burner before she went to bed, and it was fair to assume that Cornelia van Doorn had stuck to her routine, making herself a cup of angelica and valerian tea before she retired. Made it and drank it. And then died.

Jemima cleaned and dried a china soap dish and emptied the greenish pulp into it. She stared hard at it and sniffed it again, wishing she could get her hands on a microscope. She compared the mash to the dried leaves she'd brought with her but couldn't say conclusively that they were the same.

Going downstairs, she went around trying doors. By this method, she found the library, where, she reasoned, there would be one book at least dedicated to the structure of plants.

Chapter Thirty-Two

The library looked out over the lawn through one of the square bay windows that gave the castle its air of civilised grandeur. The glass was tinted green, which turned the view to a mossy mosaic. Green serpentine marble lined the walls and even the table had a jade-coloured leather top. On this day of heavy rain, the effect was of being under water. Still, Jemima chose not to light a lamp as she inspected the shelves.

Whoever had collated this library had liked industrial history and – perhaps unsurprisingly – canal building. Volumes bound in brown and claret leather with gilded titles proclaimed that the world was a serious place. She also came across a set of volumes on the Muirhaven family. There was Countess Hilda's memoir, and Jemima felt a pang as she remembered Mrs van Doorn recommending she read it.

She eventually found a section on natural history and reached up for *Wildflowers of Field and Hedgerow*. It was part of a set of three, covering different aspects of the British landscape. She took her selection to the table, opening it at 'A'.

Angelica. *Angelica archangelica.* An umbellifer, family Apiaceae, an herb said to cure the plague, found often in old monastery gardens. Apiaceae is familiar to us as the carrot family, and includes parsley, celery and parsnip.

Though it was beautifully illustrated, it was hard to compare the pen-and-ink sketch to the plant with umbrella-shaped flowers in Mrs Beddoe's kitchen garden, or the spent leaves in Mrs van Doorn's teapot. Jemima intended to turn next to 'V' for Valerian, but the book fell open a few pages along where a yellow ribbon bookmark was attached to the head of the spine. At the letter 'H'.

Hemlock. *Conium maculatum.* A plant deadly to humans and animals. Sometimes known as 'fool's parsley'. It is at its most poisonous in the spring, see footnote *

*There is no known cure.

Chapter Thirty-Three

The day wore on without any sign of the detectives from Mold. Sergeant Maddox stood guard, the doctor paced. Lord Muirhaven kept to his apartment while Mrs Beddoe produced tea and Welsh cakes on the hour. At around five, still with no let-up in the rain, Elaine and Honor retired to their rooms and Jemima managed to find Mrs Beddoe alone in her kitchen.

'May I ask your opinion of something?'

The housekeeper invited her to join her at the table. Jemima then presented the residue she'd fished out of the teapot. 'Can you identify this?'

'Dried leaves and stem of angelica and a lesser amount of valerian for insomnia,' was Mrs Beddoe's instant response as she held the jam jar up to the light.

'And nothing else?'

'Nothing, Mrs Flowerday, except boiling water of course.'

'We'll have to wait for a laboratory report to be absolutely certain,' Jemima said. 'There's only one other sure way of testing for poison... not one I'm willing to try.'

'Indeed no,' agreed Mrs Beddoe, who then stood up and proved that she had very good hearing by saying, 'Ifor must be going out. That's the pony trap, crossing the courtyard.'

Jemima went to check and discovered that Mrs Beddoe was

right. Ifor was leading the pony towards the great gate. Ignoring the rain, she hurried out after him to ask where he was going.

'To the railway station, to see if those CID have arrived.'

'Yes, surely, they ought to be here by now. Sergeant Maddox must be wondering how many more hours he'll be left here on his own.'

Ifor was clearly anxious to be gone. 'It's not so far to Mold and the fastest route is to go via Wrexham and change there for Trevor. Go inside, madam, don't get wet.'

Jemima appreciated his concern and told him to take care on the roads. Inside again, she stamped the wet off her shoes and looked at her watch... 5.20 p.m. There were a good three hours of daylight left.

Still, the more hours that passed, the weaker memories grew. She retired to her room. After drying her hair and changing into dry things, Jemima took out her journal and brought her notes up to date.

Yesterday, with time on my hands, I ventured into the kitchen garden. It was between 3.15 and 3.30 p.m. and the date was Friday, 1 June. I met Mrs Beddoe collecting salad leaves and herbs for dinner. She showed me sweet cicely, describing it as an aid to digestion. She later admitted to adding a snippet of hemlock by accident

'Wait though.' Jemima spread out her hands. Her blisters were fading, losing their sting. 'Mrs Beddoe wasn't wearing gloves and had she picked hemlock, she'd have sores like these to show for it.' She pictured the housekeeper in the kitchen just a while ago, studying the contents of a jam jar. There had been no trace of blistering or redness. It strengthened Jemima's certainty that Mrs Beddoe had taken responsibility for the hemlock incident to defend Mairwen.

Mairwen, who had come into the garden, tearful at her dismissal, could have put on gloves for a later foray. Or nipped off a sprig with scissors, when nobody was about. Ifor had been in the garden that afternoon too. 'Wearing an apron, wielding cutters.' Jemima couldn't have said if he had been wearing gloves or not. 'Though if you have secateurs, would you need them?'

Why would Ifor want to harm those he depended on? The Beddoes were his aunt and uncle, the garden and the pony his world.

What about Gwen? A row of bland question marks ran through Jemima's brain. What did she know about Gwen, her secrets, her impulses? Nothing at all. Ditto, Mr Beddoe. But she didn't believe they were suspects. Of the servants, only Mairwen had any motive for harm.

What about the 'upstairs' folk? Where had they been in the latter part of the afternoon? Mrs van Doorn had been in her apartment until cocktail hour, directed there by Elaine, who had advised her to rest and allow Mrs Beddoe to make her 'special tea'.

Elaine must have joined her employer at some point, as Jemima had found them together in the Countess's Suite. As for Lord Muirhaven, after their pithy exchange of views in the great hall, Jemima hadn't seen him until much later, when she looked down from the tower and saw him walking from his gatehouse. Perhaps he'd spent the intervening hours practising his card skills. Hemlock grew in his courtyard garden, as she had discovered to her cost, but was he even aware of it?

That left Honor. Following her 'miraculous' return, the girl had been spirited upstairs by Elaine and Mrs Beddoe to be tubbed and put to bed. At some point, she had got up, entered Jemima's room and 'borrowed' clothing. Could she also have snuck into the kitchen garden? There had been flowers in the waste bin in her room; lavender and purple honesty. And hemlock? Jemima hadn't noticed any, just some waxed paper, screwed up at the bottom. She might have overlooked a sprig or two.

'If she added hemlock to the salad, and to her stepmother's tea caddy, then I am imagining a girl of seventeen to be a poisoner on the scale of Catherine de' Medici.'

It should be impossible, for one who had seen nothing of life to act like a premeditated killer. On the other hand... Honor might be silly enough to play a prank that went horribly wrong.

'That ridiculous abduction story. *And* she stole my coat, hat and—' Jemima's mouth dropped. '*And* my gloves.' That changed everything. Jemima paced her bedroom, her heart beating a slow tattoo. 'When I found her at the top of the tower, she had on my kidskin gloves.'

Heart still pounding, Jemima went back to her journal and picked up her pencil.

Suppose Honor went out that fateful afternoon and picked a bouquet for her stepmother. She would hardly do so wearing my clothes, and as I didn't see her outside, it was likely done while I was in the Countess's suite with Mrs van Doorn and Elaine. Let's say she came up to the suite with her bouquet and paused at the door. Note, the purple petals on the threshold. Instead of coming in, she returned to her room, tossing the flowers head-first into her bin. Shortly after, she went into my room and raided my wardrobe. Why? Why reject the impulse to make amends and begin the process of running away a second time? What did she hear that altered her plans?

Jemima recalled the three-way conversation between herself, Mrs van Doorn and Elaine. 'I know Honor overheard Elaine and me trying to persuade Mrs van Doorn to let her spread her wings.

And me being lukewarm about her talent. She may have heard me offering to help them find a London house and, if so, she'd have heard her stepmother's granite opposition. And, finally, the threat to disinherit her.'

Taking up her pencil, Jemima added more lines.

Where the sums involved are great, and represent a
person's only chance of freedom, murder might seem a
logical act.

Add to that, if Honor had an inkling that Lord Muirhaven planned to propose to Mrs van Doorn and supplant her, there would have been a sense of time running out. 'Even if she did not foresee it, she might have felt that the only way for her to live the life she chose was to put a period to her stepmother's existence.'

Jemima went to her wardrobe and took out the sage-green skirt she'd worn the day before, with her gloves in its pockets. She was about to remove them, when a dent appeared in her theory.

She returned the skirt to the rail.

Honor would not get her inheritance until she came of age, and that was four years away. Until then, she was under the thumb of guardians and lawyers. While it didn't cancel out the motive, it weakened it. Not to forget the attempt on Honor's life, suggesting she was more victim than perpetrator.

Jemima's thoughts swung back to Mairwen, angry and dis-affected, and with more ease of access to the gardens than Honor. In love with Lord Muirhaven, too.

'He was planning that night to propose marriage to another woman. Did Mairwen see the ring, and assume he meant to present it to Honor? Then later, when she realised she had almost killed the wrong rival, did she murder Mrs van Doorn?'

With a sigh, Jemima closed her wardrobe door. She wished the detectives would come. With nothing now to do, she lay on her bed and caught up on some lost sleep. She was woken in the dusk by the great gate opening and a pony's hooves on the cobbles.

CID, at last? Fumbling to find the shoes she'd kicked off earlier, Jemima was slow making her way down. The front door was wide open, and she saw Ifor next to the cart, holding the reins, he and the pony bathed in lantern light. Dr Rees-Parry stood in the doorway, a lamp held aloft, speaking with him.

Jemima was left nursing incomprehension, until the doctor perceived her. Agitated, he addressed her in Welsh too.

She shook her head. 'English, please...'

'I forget sometimes,' he said. 'The lad brings unwelcome news. Seems the CID gentlemen chose to take the rural train route through the Vale, rather than come by Wrexham. A tunnel has flooded outside Ruthin and all the passengers have had to disembark.'

'The Vale' and Ruthin meant nothing, but the implication was clear.

'They're not arriving tonight?'

'They will have to return to Mold and try the better route. And as tomorrow is Sunday, there may not be a train at all.' The doctor made a circuit of the hall, stamping his frustration into the marble tiles.

Jemima closed the front door and waited until the doctor paused.

'I'm needed at home in my surgery,' he said, raking lines through his greased-down hair. 'My wife will have cancelled patients and if I wait much longer our local roads may become impassable.'

'Then you should go,' she said. 'We have Sergeant Maddox.'

'Who is needed at his police station. It's a mess, I don't mind saying.' He looked up into the sky-blue dome and gave a *tsk*. 'Vanity, vanity.' Abruptly, he asked, 'Are there cellars here?'

'I'm sure there's a wine vault,' Jemima answered. 'I can't imagine

Castle Gloaming – sorry, Castell Glan yr Afon – being without one. I can't vouch for how well it's stocked.'

'I'm not after wine. I'm thinking of the body. I don't wish to be indelicate, madam, but we cannot leave Mrs van Doorn where she is much longer. It wouldn't matter so much if it were winter...'

'No. Of course. Is there a district mortuary?'

'Chirk,' came the brisk answer. 'At the cottage hospital. We could transport the body by boat, but not until morning and we'd have to get it to the canalside. Normally, see, the body could go in the chapel crypt at Trevor.'

'A local farmer might lend a cart, and we could take the deceased by road to Trevor. There is a road leading there, I suppose?'

'Yes. But we can't do it at this hour and if the rain doesn't stop, getting a cart up here, with the lane running rivers, will prove a Sisyphean task.'

'Undoubtedly.' Jemima made a mental note to look up the word when she was next in the library.

'The body needs to be moved tonight, that's a fact,' said the doctor.

'Then the cellar it must be. Let me consult with Mrs Cleeve.' Jemima was on her way upstairs, worrying that a damp wine cellar might not be sufficiently chilled to preserve the body, when the words 'Arctic cold' slid into her head. She paused, a hand on the banister. Where had that come from?

Steady on the gin. The *plink-plink* of ice in a glass.

She ran downstairs again, saying breathlessly, 'I know where we must take Mrs van Doorn, Doctor.'

Chapter Thirty-Four

Mr Beddoe took the scullery door off its hinges. Then, with Ifor taking one end, brought it upstairs. Elaine was visibly upset by this turn of events and stopped them before they reached Mrs van Doorn's suite. To Jemima and Sergeant Maddox, she expressed her revulsion.

'Does she really have to be taken to the icehouse?'

'I honestly believe it's the best solution.' Jemima could vouch for its frigid temperature.

'The doctor has advised it,' the sergeant added. 'And Lord Muirhaven agrees.'

Hildebrand had been summoned from his gatehouse and was sitting on a blanket chest in Elaine's bedroom, which was across the corridor. He was visible through the open door, watching the proceedings while appearing strangely detached.

'I won't have her laid on rough wood.' Elaine dashed into her room and brusquely ordered Lord Muirhaven to stand up. She opened the blanket chest, letting the lid fall again with a crash and emerged with a silken bed throw. Jemima helped her place it over the door which Ifor and Beddoe were holding flat, like a bier.

'What's going on, what's happening?' Honor appeared from the direction of her room. She was wearing one of her pale dresses and a cardigan hung loosely on her. With the lanterns lit, she looked haunted, her cheeks hollow.

Jemima explained.

'But that's too undignified,' Honor cried and turned on Elaine. 'You should stop it.'

'She can't,' Jemima intervened. 'We must ensure the body is fit for an autopsy.'

'Autopsy?' Honor echoed.

'The formal investigation into the cause of death. I'm so very sorry, Honor, but at this stage your stepmother's body is not yours, nor Elaine's. It falls under police jurisdiction.'

Sergeant Maddox requested that the ladies retreat while they removed the deceased. 'There is no need for you to bear witness.'

Elaine went without argument, and Jemima saw her ushering Honor towards the stairs. 'Ladies' included her, of course, but there was something she badly wanted to know which only a view of the body could satisfy. She bent her head and cast her eyes down.

It didn't dupe the sergeant. 'You too, madam. We have pall bearers enough.'

That was true. He and the doctor, Beddoe and Ifor, made a sturdy crew. Lord Muirhaven had sat down again on the blanket chest, cradling his brow in a morose thinker's pose.

Jemima went to him and said, 'Someone will have to guide the way. Why don't you take a lantern, and walk in front?'

He shook his head. 'It's too much.'

'Then I must do it.'

This time, he looked at her. 'Does nothing daunt you, Mrs Flowerday?'

'I've learned resilience.' Seeing him waver, she all but thrust a lantern into his hand, 'Stiffen the sinews, do your part.'

On cue, Sergeant Maddox's voice rang out. 'Take the bier into the room, men.'

From the doorway, Jemima watched Beddoe and Ifor manoeuvre the silk-draped door into the Countess's Suite. Dr Rees-Parry would supervise the lifting of the body. Jemima felt compassion for Ifor, for whom this must be the stuff of nightmares.

'Steady as we go,' warned Sergeant Maddox. 'That's it. Lay it on its side.'

It. The body. Rigor mortis would not have diminished. The victim should be covered, Jemima decided, otherwise it would be too awful for those not accustomed to seeing death at its worst. Evicting Lord Muirhaven from Elaine's blanket chest, pushing him into the corridor, she whipped out a plain coverlet. The body had been placed on the bier and now a struggle was going on to get it around the door frame and out. Jemima offered the coverlet to the doctor.

He thanked her. 'A ladylike touch, very good. Very kind. I will lay it over her.'

Jemima averted her gaze as the distorted form was draped. That done, she allowed herself one glance, and in the light of Hildebrand's lantern, counted the rings on Mrs van Doorn's clawed hands. There were five, but the engagement ring with the green stone was not among them.

'Sergeant Maddox?' she said quietly, going to the policeman's side. 'Should we remove Mrs van Doorn's jewels?'

'Jewels?'

'Her rings. And there's a diamond bracelet and a gold watch. Were rumour to get out that there are diamonds in the icehouse, we might get unwelcome visitors.'

'Madam, you have a point. Gentlemen!' A delay ensued. The valuables were laid in a porcelain dish which Jemima took from Elaine's dressing table. She asked Sergeant Maddox to record an inventory.

At last, the cortege set off. They would exit through the tower doorway and make their way to the shrubbery. Let them do their job, she thought. They did not need her.

She had no lantern, but there were candles on the sideboard where Mrs van Doorn's kettle and tea things were laid out as before – and matches. Lighting one, Jemima stood alone in the place of death and allowed a prayer for peace to wash through her mind.

She might now make a thorough and careful inspection of the scene of the crime.

'Am I sure it was a crime?' After consideration, she answered herself. 'I am sure it wasn't an accident or misadventure or suicide. Therefore, what else can it be?'

Chapter Thirty-Five

Jemima stepped over Cornelia van Doorn's silk coverlet that still lay, rumpled, on the floor, and entered the bedroom. The bed itself showed signs of its late occupant. Blankets and sheets had slipped to the side nearest the double doors, implying that Mrs van Doorn had struggled to get herself out.

The bed was centrally placed with cabinets either side, each one draped with a lace cloth and supplied with an oil lamp with a frosted-glass chimney. A cup and saucer sat on the left-hand cabinet. Its pattern of roses and butterflies matched those on the sitting-room sideboard. Mrs van Doorn's final cup of tea?

There was a finger-tip's depth of greenish liquid at the bottom. Clear, but for a speckling of tiny grounds of whatever plants had created it. Jemima inhaled, and her nose received the same sappy, nondescript notes she'd got from the teapot.

Mrs van Doorn had come to bed in the early hours and made herself a tisane. Angelica and valerian, a safe sedative. She would have found her spirit kettle simmering, thanks to Elaine's dutiful attentions. Assume she undressed for bed... where would she brush her teeth?

A door led into a bathroom with a slipper bath big enough for a sailor to put to sea in. There was a double sink, a wide mirror and a shelf with iron brackets. Jemima shone her candle along its length and discovered face and hand creams, an expensive scent, tooth powder and aspirin. A bottle of nail lacquer in Mrs van Doorn's almond-blossom shade lay on its side. Nothing in the bathroom suggested that the victim indulged in dangerous medications. Nor did it suggest that Cornelia van Doorn had stumbled in here to be sick. Jemima returned to the bedside. No... she had become ill here, in her bed, with symptoms that must have been sudden and severe.

At some point, she had removed her ring.

Jemima made a slow turn. The bedhead faced the window. A writing desk was placed beneath the window with a chair in front, though this was not tucked in close, suggesting Mrs van Doorn had sat at her desk after the maid had last tidied. In Jemima's experience, chambermaids always tucked chairs in, to signal they were doing their job.

On the left-hand side of the desk was a vase of wilted flowers. Jemima examined it. Stems of honesty had rained bright petals onto the desk. Cow parsley was reduced to green spikes, petals sugaring the surface. Welsh poppies hung their heads in defeat, while pot marigolds shone bright as guineas, the last survivors. Was this Honor's peace offering? Had she left flowers in a vase for Cornelia to find – or followed Jemima's suggestion and brought a neatly tied bouquet? Jemima's eye alighted on a roll of blue satin ribbon on the bedside table, beside the cup.

She ran her fingertips across the pillowcases and discovered that one was slightly gritty. Taking the pillow into the bathroom, she shook it over the bath. In the candlelight she saw a dusting of miniscule white petals. From this, she deduced that Honor had laid a bouquet, tied with blue ribbon, on her stepmother's pillow. The fact that Mrs van Doorn had taken the trouble to put the flowers in water implied that the gesture had been well received.

Honor had left a note too.

Jemima found it on the writing desk, pushed towards the back. Taking care not to touch it, she read what was written there in a schoolgirlish script.

Dearest Stepmama,

Please let us be friends. I do not want to upset you, but you know I cannot always be what you want me to be. I came to talk with you today, as we used to, but you were busy. Send Elaine with a message in the morning and I will wait on you like a good, good stepdaughter.

Yours with love,
Honor

Below it, in wavering letters, three words had been scored in pencil. Words Jemima had come to associate with Cornelia van Doorn:

No. No. No.

And after that, in letters that ran wildly off the page:

H is trying to kill me

Chapter Thirty-Six

Sunday, 3 June

A chapel bell tolling across a sodden valley was not a cheerful start to the new day, but that she could hear it as she lay in bed told Jemima that at least the rain had stopped.

Dr Rees-Parry had announced last night that he would depart after breakfast. Sergeant Maddox believed he had left his police station in the charge of young constables long enough and intended to go at the same time. It would leave the occupants of Castle Gloaming in a strange limbo, awaiting the delayed arrival of CID.

When Jemima went downstairs at a few minutes after eight, she found a buffet breakfast. On Sundays the staff attended chapel in the next valley while family and guests shifted for themselves. A spirit kettle had been left simmering, and she made herself a small pot of coffee.

Others arrived one at a time and by half past eight Jemima, Elaine, Lord Muirhaven, Sergeant Maddox and the doctor were all present. Honor was presumed still to be asleep. Jemima kept the coffee coming as the others helped themselves to food. They ate in silence, until Sergeant Maddox repeated his intention of returning to Chirk.

'The lad has tacked up my horse and I won't keep it standing.' He formally handed Lord Muirhaven the key to the Countess's

189

suite, which Jemima had surrendered the previous evening. 'I expect you will take charge, my Lord.'

Hildebrand looked askance at the key. 'Charge, how?'

'Ensure the icehouse is guarded and that nobody leaves the estate, other than to attend divine service. That means everyone: guest, resident, servant.'

'Yes, yes,' Lord Muirhaven agreed, in a tone that suggested he had no real intention of doing so.

Had Jemima craved importance, this would have been her moment to offer to oversee everything. She stayed quiet, preferring to swim deep, like a pike, and come up for air only when necessary. Mrs van Doorn's postscript – *H is trying to kill me* – had turned a bright, oscillating spotlight on two members of this household. Hildebrand and Honor.

Which of them Cornelia had feared, Jemima couldn't yet say. She had left the letter where she found it. CID must reach their own conclusions. Meanwhile, she would build on her suspicions through observation and careful questions.

With this in mind, she asked Sergeant Maddox if 'not leaving' the estate would prevent her taking a stroll. 'Now it's stopped raining.'

'You may walk where you will, Mrs Flowerday,' replied the sergeant. 'So long as you remain in the vicinity.'

Leave here, when a likely case of murder had taken a critical turn? Heaven forbid. Lord Muirhaven hadn't put the key to Mrs van Doorn's suite in his pocket. It still lay on the table, and Jemima's palm itched. Abruptly, she got up, went to the sideboard and picked up the coffee pot. 'Lord Muirhaven, your cup is empty, may I?'

He indicated he would like a refill.

When Jemima had first started out as a couturier, in 1919, the fashion in sleeves had been long and fitted to the wrist. As the twenties dawned, a less practical shape had emerged from Paris.

Orientalism, *grâce* à Paul Poiret, had established the bell sleeve. How many teacups had been knocked off tables by the trumpet-end of a cardigan... such as Jemima happened to be wearing? Cups, or keys, indeed.

Jemima poured fresh coffee for Lord Muirhaven. 'Anyone else?' She raised the pot then almost dropped it. 'Whoops, that was nearly a nasty mess. More coffee, Dr Rees-Parry? Coming over.'

After breakfast, when everyone was in the great hall seeing off the doctor and Sergeant Maddox, Jemima nipped back into the breakfast room and retrieved the key from the floor. She doubted anyone had noticed her sleight of hand. Sleight of sleeve. But that was the point of trickery. Those being duped were always looking elsewhere.

She had her key and none but her would step inside Mrs van Doorn's suite until CID finally made it by whatever trainline they had switched to. She intended to search the desk for further clues. But not now, with everyone milling about like shepherd-less sheep. A spell in the fresh air would clear her head.

Chapter Thirty-Seven

With the ground too wet for exploring, Jemima made do with a circuit of the castle. It brought her back to the kitchen garden where, with sunshine squeezing from its cloud cage and falling on dewy lushness, she felt she was entering an Impressionist painting. Later, the midges would be busy, but not yet, and the soft bounce of the air reminded her of her first day here. It was hard to equate a scene like this with death.

Completing her circuit in the courtyard, she looked up at the tower. It was the colour of elephant hide and Spanish leather. Who had attempted to push Honor off its summit?

If not Mairwen, what about Lord Muirhaven, wishing to rid himself of his future wife's turbulent stepdaughter? Jemima imagined him as she'd seen him from the tower, striding across the courtyard on his way to cocktails. He'd stopped to pick a sprig of yellow-flowering broom for his buttonhole... just here. She paused by a flowerbed to the right of the main door. To have been able to attack Honor just minutes later, he would have had to career up the tower steps like a man possessed and get back down again just as speedily.

It felt unlikely, but not impossible.

For some reason, Jemima felt drawn to the river and pointed her feet to the gatehouse. She noted the metal cage on the inside of the riveted door, empty of letters as it was Sunday. Lifting the latch with both hands, she slipped through. When the door shut with a reverberating clang, she tried to get back in by turning the hoop handle. Even with two hands, she couldn't do it. Oh, well. She knew a different way back.

Crossing the dry moat – now not so dry with a pool of iron-rich water at the bottom – she reached the river bridge. The Dee was in spate, the stone piers wearing foamy white collars, the water brown as beer and deafeningly loud.

Jemima turned along the river path. Honor had returned from her 'abduction' adventure by this route, making for the main gate. Yet Honor must have known she could not open it unaided.

A splashing sound above her head made Jemima leap to the side, sparing herself a soaking. A natural spring gushed from the rocks that formed the castle mound with enough force to gouge a hollow in the path. This must be Hildebrand's outdoor bathroom. Tucked in against the wall was a wooden bucket with a sponge and a bar of green soap. Highly invigorating, Jemima reflected, and private enough.

'And I think it's why Honor arrived back plastered in mud.' She spoke her thoughts, drowned out by the river's thunder. 'She stumbled along, saw Lord Muirhaven who, if he's to be believed, had finished his shower and was dressed, and she called out to him. Lord Muirhaven had described seeing Honor as she "rounded a bend, all in her white".

'Not so white after she slipped in this muddy hollow. Lord Muirhaven rescued her, as she intended he would.'

Disinclined to experience Honor's mudbath for herself, Jemima turned back. At the gate, she reflected on something she'd read in *The Weekend Sleuth*.

'A wise detective will survey the scene-of-crime, but also the surrounding area. He will ask, "Why this place and not some other?"'

It was a good question and, applied to Honor van Doorn, Jemima had to ask, 'Why not return to the castle by the path she was familiar with, through the shrubbery? Then sidle in through the tower door and regain her own room, unseen?'

Because she *wanted* to be seen, answered the bludgeoning voice of the river. Honor jumped off the *Miss Nettle* and made her way back to the castle. She slipped and fell – deliberately, to support her claim of abduction? – and allowed Lord Muirhaven to find her.

'He scooped her up and carried her to the castle entrance.' Jemima put her hand against the stalwart gateway. 'He would have been forced to put her down at this point, because no man, however strong, could open this door with his teeth.'

Jemima had already challenged him on that score. What had he said? 'He couldn't remember, having been in the grip of extraordinary emotion, seeing the girl alive and well.' Jemima had assumed his emotion had been relief.

Were we being primed to look at this the wrong way? Jemima wondered. Honor's disappearance had left Lord Muirhaven with a clear run at marriage with the more accommodating Cornelia. 'A fortune in his grasp... and then the inconvenient stepdaughter returns.'

Jemima looked up, her gaze passing over the gatehouse turrets to where the tower cut into the clouds. Two jet-black birds landed on the parapet as if choreographed. She'd forgotten, were they ravens, rooks or crows? Now she'd lost her thread. Ah, yes. Lord Muirhaven had brought Honor in from outside and done little to challenge her absurd abduction story. He'd colluded with Cornelia's desire not to involve the police. And, lo, within hours of Honor's reappearance, Cornelia van Doorn was stating her intention to cut her stepdaughter out of her fortune. Not much later, someone had tried to send Honor hurtling to her death.

A few hours after *that*, Cornelia had Lord Muirhaven's ring on her finger.

'He described Cornelia as impulsive,' Jemima said to herself. 'Was he rather too eager to plant that impression? What if he worked on her after Elaine and I got up from the card table, persuaded her to marry him and to cut out Honor completely?'

And what if Honor had heard and acted on an impulse of her own, poisoning her stepmother?

Could there have been two potential killers in the castle on that fateful night?

H is trying to kill me.

Mrs van Doorn had written those words at the bottom of Honor's letter of apology.

Jemima doubted that Lord Muirhaven was the 'H' in question, as Cornelia's death left him far worse off. 'There's still the matter of the hemlock in the salad, who put it there and why.' And what of the stranger that Gwen and Mrs Beddoe believed had been present? Castle Gloaming was remote but, as Jemima had proved to herself, it was linked by paths to lanes and to the canal.

If Lord Muirhaven had ambushed Honor at the top of the tower, why had he failed in his mission? Creeping up on an unsuspecting girl, he should have been able to tip her off balance in one movement.

'Did my coat catch on something, giving Honor a moment in which to scream and fight back?'

It was a beguiling idea, that a garment she had made might have preserved a human life. It didn't change the conundrum she'd created. Two murderers being active at Castle Gloaming at the same time. Quite a coincidence.

Another bird joined its fellows on the parapet, reminding Jemima that coincidence was always the weakest answer. Find the logic. Two birds land on a prominent ledge, and a third joins them, not by chance, but because it is a good perch. Honor had gone to the top of the tower to signal to her friend Olive. Lord Muirhaven had seen her there, but mistaken her for Jemima. 'If he had raced up to commit murder, it would have been to murder *me*. I don't see his motive, even if he doesn't like me.' Besides, he hadn't been notably out of breath when, a short while later, he had found Jemima in a state of shock, collapsed in the courtyard. Theories come, theories go.

Back to square one.

'Bore da!'

Jemima spun around. She hadn't heard anyone approach, too lost in her thoughts, her ears acclimatised to the river's roar. It was Lowri, the post-girl. Jemima was surprised to see a satchel slung across her chest.

'Are they making you work on Sunday?'

Lowri explained that she'd brought mail because her grand-mother felt it should be delivered as soon as possible, 'Because of what happened to the lady.'

'I'll take care of it.' Jemima took a wad of envelopes and a postcard, a sepia print of churning waters, taken from a bridge. 'View of the river at Chirk' was inscribed in white lettering. Jemima turned it over and read the message.

The Captain shouts, 'Turn the ship around!'
One hundred pounds, Hildebrand, and we keep sailing.

There was a sketch beneath the words. Wavy lines surmounted by two stars, above the stars, a half-moon. The symbols Jemima had seen drawn in dust on Lord Muirhaven's dining table. It felt like a direct message, or a threat.

A sharp clanking sound on the blind side of the gate warned that the latch was being lifted. Jemima had enough time to turn the postcard over before Lord Muirhaven's appearance sent Lowri hurrying away. He watched her departure, as if trying to work out if it really was Sunday, before seeing the postcard in Jemima's hand.

'What else has come?' he asked, taking it from her.

Jemima sorted through. There were several brown envelopes for Elaine. Tradesmen's bills, Jemima guessed. The final one, a long, white envelope with a Wrexham postmark, was addressed to Mrs van Doorn.

Hildebrand tried to take them all, but Jemima stepped around him, saying, 'I'll deliver them to Elaine. I'm going back inside now.'

She searched for Elaine without success, and with questions lining up in her head, let herself into the Countess's suite. As careful as before not to leave fingerprints, she put the letters into a drawer of the writing desk.

One hundred pounds and we keep sailing. It reeked of blackmail.

'What are you doing in here?'

A light, accusing voice made Jemima jump. Honor van Doorn stared at her from between the open double doors. A second's appraisal told Jemima that Honor hadn't bathed or brushed her hair in hours. A satin dressing gown knotted over her pyjamas was crumpled, suggesting she'd slept in it. She was cradling the fingers of one hand inside the other, and the sight of a scruffy bandage around the two middle fingers, stained rust red, rang an alarm.

'You need that nail bed looked at in case it's going septic,' Jemima said. 'I wish the doctor was still here.'

'Don't fuss.'

'I'm not fussing,' Jemima answered. 'But I have children, and I've seen how a graze or cut turns nasty if not properly cleaned. Come on. Downstairs.' She ushered the girl out, locking the door of the Countess's suite behind her.

In the kitchen, she found the staff seated around the table, drinking tea. From the cheerless silence, Jemima assumed the chapel service hadn't dispelled their sorrows. Seeing her steer Honor in ahead of her, all but Mairwen stood. Jemima urged them to sit down, asking Mrs Beddoe if she could look again at Miss Honor's injury.

'It's clearly bled recently and if you have something like surgical spirit...?'

'Use mouldy bread and garlic,' Mairwen suggested.

Giving Mairwen a look, Mrs Beddoe rose and left the room, returning with a wooden box from which she took wads of cotton wool and a brown bottle. 'Castor oil and infusion of mugwort. Shall we take that bandage off, Miss?'

Honor presented her wounded fingers and Jemima couldn't hold back a shudder as Mrs Beddoe unpeeled the blood-caked binding. She saw Honor flinch, heard the suck of breath, but there were no tears. Honor endured the process without a whimper.

I'd have looked away, Jemima thought. She is stoic.

The wound site was unpleasant, however, the exposed nail bed raw-looking. There were other wounds on the finger, short, deep tears in the flesh.

'That happened as you clung to the parapet?' Jemima asked. The oak rail must be rough and splintered, to have lacerated the skin that way.

Honor nodded, and turned her gaze on Mairwen, who stared straight back. 'I keep reliving the moment when I thought I was going over.'

'That's what shock does,' said Jemima.

After Mrs Beddoe had applied a clean bandage, Honor asked if she might go back to bed. 'I'm so tired.'

'Can't I make you a snack? Scrambled egg, perhaps?' The house-keeper peered into Honor's eyes. 'You need sustenance. I can see it in your irises.'

'I can't eat, Mrs Beddoe. I have no appetite.'

'I will bring you something later, then,' the housekeeper said, but let her go.

Jemima accepted the offer of tea and mentioned having seen Lowri. 'I would have insisted she come in after walking all this way, but Lord Muirhaven frightened her off.'

'Why was she here, on the Sabbath?' Mairwen demanded, unease in her voice.

'Her grandmother sent her with mail. Including a postcard.' Jemima wasn't sure what prompted her to say that, but it had an effect. Mairwen went to the sink to begin washing up, though nobody had asked her.

'Lowri saw His Lordship once, wearing nothing but a towel around his waist,' Mrs Beddoe said with a swallowed, '*tsk*'. 'She's been brought up strict, see, and it's not right, a gentleman making his ablutions outdoors.' She extended her frown to Jemima, who had gone out in only a skirt and jumper. 'No coat, Mrs Flowerday? A warm morning after rain can catch the lungs.'

Jemima explained that her coat was 'laid up, temporarily unfit' and she hadn't a spare. Mrs Beddoe rattled out an instruction to Gwen in Welsh and the outcome – a raincoat.

'It won't be your usual style,' Mrs Beddoe said, shaking it out, 'as it was the late countess's. She passed it to me many years back, but I could never get the buttons to meet at the front.'

The coat was indeed of a bygone era with a corduroy-lined collar and deep pockets, the kind Jemima liked. It was belted, the waist trim, and it would graze her ankles. There was a hood, so she could look forward to gliding, monk-like, around the grounds. She thanked the housekeeper.

'How long will this go on?' Mairwen threw out as Jemima made to leave.

'The police investigation?'

'No, the looks I'm getting from the likes of Honor van Doorn. It's obvious, isn't it, what killed that woman.'

'Mairwen!' Mrs Beddoe shot out. 'Don't speak ill of Mrs van Doorn. She was a lady.'

'In what way is it "obvious"?' Jemima's curiosity was whetted.

'She drank tea in her room that night,' Mairwen answered. 'What else could have killed her? For a bit, you thought it was the hemlock in the salad, but that was only a...' Her hands jerked as she searched for the words. 'What do you call it when you lure a duck into the shallows, to trap it?'

'Dinner?' Ifor suggested, earning himself a fierce look from Mairwen.

'A decoy?' Jemima offered.

'That's it. Decoy.' Mairwen clapped her hands together. 'The hemlock was to make the police think that one of us down here was a murderer. It was the tea she drank in her room later that killed her.'

Mairwen fetched a wooden caddy down from a shelf, spooned a measure of leaves into the cup she had drunk from and reached for the kettle. Mrs Beddoe asked her what she was doing.

'You always refill Mrs van Doorn's caddy from here,' Mairwen said. 'It's the same leaves. I'm going to find out if they are safe, or deadly.'

'Don't be a fool,' Mrs Beddoe admonished. 'Anyway, it will prove nothing.'

Jemima seconded that. 'If any poisonous substance was mixed into the leaves, it would have been done in Mrs van Doorn's bedroom, not here where it might kill everyone and anyone. Mairwen, you're young. You're a daughter, a friend. You have no right to gamble with your life.'

Mairwen lifted the cup to her lips. 'Who cares if I die? If I can't be happy the way I choose, what's the point of living?'

It was Ifor who walked around the table, took the cup from Mairwen and emptied its contents into the sink.

Mairwen lowered her head, as if in the grip of despair.

'Because Lord Muirhaven wanted to marry another woman?' Jemima asked gently.

Mairwen flashed a quick, proud look, but didn't deny it. 'I was never going to fall in love with a farmhand or the blacksmith's son, me being who I am.'

'Love can flower across the social divide, but not often. It's a risky business.'

Mairwen didn't reply, but left the room, returning with a pair of brown leather boots. They looked neat and well made. 'These were the Countess's too.' She glanced at Mrs Beddoe, seeking permission. 'Mrs Flowerday might as well have them, no?'

'If she wants.'

Jemima thanked them both, and said she'd try them on in her room. Unlike coats, boots either fitted or they didn't and she didn't want to look like one of Cinderella's ugly sisters, hauling on too-small footwear.

Mairwen followed her out.

'Thank you for keeping my secret, Mrs Flowerday.'

'Secret?'

Mairwen whispered, 'The poppet. Mrs Beddoe nearly skinned me alive, but it was for love, not hate. Only, if the police hear of it, they'll say I had a motive to kill the van Doorns.'

Both van Doorns. Was that a slip, or a lucid observation? 'You did have a motive, Mairwen. Love and revenge. Of course they'll ask about it.'

Mairwen's chin came up. 'Still, I'm not a criminal. I didn't hide hemlock in the salad or hurt Mrs van Doorn or try to push Honor off the tower. But they'll say I did because it makes their job easy.'

Jemima couldn't argue. The inclination of the police to cling like baby sloths to the wrong decision was a constant complaint of *The Weekend Sleuth*. 'If I knew who took hemlock into the kitchen, I might point them elsewhere.'

'Who's saying it did? Get into the kitchen, I mean.'

'It was in the salad, Mairwen. I picked it out.'

'Why does it have to have been in the kitchen, though?'

'You're suggesting it was added later... in the dining room?' Realising she had once again slithered down the slope to lazy assumption, Jemima asked how the dishes came up from the kitchen.

'I'll show you.' Mairwen went to the stairs and Jemima followed.

Chapter Thirty-Eight

In the dining room, Mairwen drew something in the dust that had settled on the satinwood table since that last meal.

Jemima asked if she was writing her name.

'No.' She sounded touchy and used her elbow to erase her handiwork, but not quickly enough.

'Did you draw something on Lord Muirhaven's dining table, in the gatehouse?' Jemima asked. 'The sea, the moon, the stars.'

A blush was affirmative enough. Fearing Mairwen would dash off to hide her embarrassment, Jemima turned from her. She walked around the table, touching each chair as she went. 'We sat here, at this end. Mrs van Doorn was in her usual place. We had a very good soup, after which things went downhill.' She gave Mairwen a placatory smile. 'What are you going to show me?'

Mairwen strode to the far end of the room, into the annexe where Jemima and Mrs Beddoe had dissected a salad in candlelight. In full daylight, she could appreciate that the room was quite large, with sideboards equipped with serving utensils and warming plates.

'This is how the food comes up.' Mairwen indicated two wooden cubby holes set into the wall, furnished with shelves and pulleys. Dumb waiters.

'Is the kitchen directly below?' Jemima asked.

Mairwen nodded. 'When the castle was rebuilt, the earl back

then would sit twenty-four down to dinner, or more. He didn't want footmen parading up and down the stairs, so these were put in.'

Jemima imagined Mrs Beddoe in the kitchen, placing dishes on the shelves and Gwen or Mairwen up here, cranking the handle. 'The salad arrived this way?'

Mairwen bothered her lower lip. 'Most likely, yes.'

Jemima waited. Hesitations spoke volumes, but Mairwen was waiting so she asked, 'Was it Gwen on Friday night, up here, working the pulley?'

'No,' Mairwen said at last.

'You? I didn't see you.'

'I kept to the side. Let sleeping dogs lie, Mrs Beddoe says. I'm not supposed to come out of the kitchen, but if I said what I saw—'

With utmost effort, Jemima limited her response to eyebrows raised.

'It was after the meal, Mrs Beddoe let me help Gwen tidy up in here.'

'Tidy how, exactly?'

'Polish the table, sweep the carpet and the chair seats.'

Considering the dust on the dining table, Jemima assumed they hadn't gone at it with much vigour. She said as much.

'Gwen said why should we, with us not being paid. She sends her money home, and I do too. Our families need it.'

'What was it Mrs Beddoe was anxious you shouldn't mention?'

Mairwen walked back into the dining room, and stood behind the chair that would have been directly to Mrs van Doorn's left. 'I got on my knees to sweep up the crumbs under the table. Other times, we'd lift the table between us, me and Gwen, and give the rug a good brushing.'

'But you felt disinclined.' Jemima detected the end point of this conversation, like a late train coming round a corner. 'And while under the table you saw...'

Mairwen opened a drawer in a monstrous mahogany sideboard and took out a rolled linen napkin. She opened it, revealing a limp piece of greenery.

Jemima's eye flew to the purple blotches on the stem. 'Show me exactly where you found it.'

Mairwen pointed to the chair behind which Jemima was standing. 'There, underneath.'

Jemima pulled the chair out. The rug beneath was Persian, jewel colours in geometric patterns. 'Point to where it was lying, but don't touch the carpet.'

Mairwen pointed. 'There, in that red bit. I thought someone had dropped some salad off their plate, but the moment I swept it up, I saw what it was.'

'Hemlock.'

It could have dropped off someone's lap, or fallen from a pocket, but Jemima strongly doubted it had come from the salad bowl. Though long past its sprightly, green best, this sprig of hemlock had never seen oil and vinegar dressing.

'Should I have told Sergeant Maddox?' Mairwen was anxious. 'Gwen said not to and Mrs Beddoe said I should—'

'Let sleeping dogs lie,' Jemima finished for her. She didn't suppose the sergeant would have been interested, his task being no more than guarding the body. CID would have to know. Jemima put the chair back. 'This is where Miss van Doorn sat.' She tried to remember what Honor had worn at dinner – long sleeves or a draped shawl? – when Elaine Cleeve entered the room.

'There you are Mrs Flowerday, I've been – Mairwen?' Elaine's voice flattened as she saw the maid. 'What are you doing up here?'

'I asked her to show me the dumb waiter,' Jemima said.

'She shouldn't be here.' Elaine glared at Mairwen. 'Your presence is tolerated in the kitchen, where—' Elaine's eye fell on the hemlock stalk, framed by the white linen napkin. It lay on the table, and triggered a tirade aimed at Mairwen. 'How dare you, after what you did – how dare you bring that vile stuff into the house?'

'I didn't bring it,' Mairwen declared.

'Don't lie. I know what you are, what you did. You should be locked up. If I had a choice, you'd be—'

Jemima told her to stop. 'Mairwen didn't bring this plant here. She found it, that's all. Under the table.'

'Why didn't she say?'

'For the reason you have demonstrated, from fear of blame and blind prejudice.'

'I am neither blind nor prejudiced,' declared Elaine, 'but I saw how Cornelia suffered. I walked in on her—' She screwed up her face. 'I found her body.'

'You did, but you have no evidence against Mairwen.'

'She dabbles in the dark arts. She's sly. She can't read or write, but she reels off spells. A homily for everything.'

Jemima reached for the napkin, intending to put the hemlock specimen somewhere safe, but Elaine got there first. Making a hasty parcel, she took it to the empty grate, poured on liquid fuel and struck a match. The cloth caught with a whoosh. When no more than smoking cinders were left, Elaine seemed calmer. She ordered Mairwen back to the kitchen.

'You have no right saying I can't read.' Mairwen had watched the burning without emotion, but anger flared now. 'I try, but my sight goes funny. I won't stay here, in a house where you need eyes on both sides of your head, and behind you.'

'If you go home, inform the police. But you should leave, I agree,' Elaine said stiffly.

At the door, Mairwen cast one last rock. 'I want my wages first. You're meant to be in charge now, so pay us, unless you're taking it all for yourself.'

206

'How dare you!'

Mairwen left, slamming the door behind her.

Elaine sighed. 'I handled that badly, but the sight of that plant...'

'You're overwrought, Elaine. We all are. But you were cruel to the girl.'

'True. Give me letters to write and unpaid bills rather than servants to manage.'

'Why are their wages outstanding? I thought Mrs van Doorn was magnificently rich.'

'She is.' Elaine glanced at the boots Jemima was holding, and the coat over her arm. 'Absolutely she is. I watched her pay her dining room bill on board ship in cash, wads of it. But now her bank is making a meal of sending new funds. Everything comes from Cape Town and communications are slow. Speaking of which, I believe there's mail for me.'

Jemima said she would put the letters in the breakfast room. Mentioning that she'd locked them in Mrs van Doorn's desk would alert Elaine to the fact that she had the key. 'Was that why you wanted me?'

'Not entirely. It's Honor.' Elaine sighed. A tolling bell could not have sounded more fateful than the final word. 'Gone.'

Jemima was astonished. 'But I was with her not forty minutes ago! I had Mrs Beddoe re-dress that wound to her finger. Are you sure she's not in the garden?'

'I've searched every room of the castle and walked around the garden in both directions. I cannot find hair nor hide of her.'

'Have you thought of the tower?'

'It's locked. Hildebrand finally saw to it. Anyway, I spoke to Beddoe who was on guard at the icehouse, and she passed him, heading towards the river.'

'Oh, the little fool. We must get her back.'

'Of course, but I can't ask Hildebrand because he's...' Elaine cleared her throat. 'Unwell.'

He wasn't an hour ago, Jemima reflected. Perhaps puzzling over a postcard, with its cryptic demand, had given him the gripe.

Elaine was saying, 'I can't ask Beddoe, obviously, as someone must stay by the icehouse. As for Ifor, apparently he's sworn never to go near it again. Honestly, these people, soused in superstition.'

'Someone needs to find the poor girl.'

'I'd go after her myself but—' Elaine broke off then tried again. 'I'd go but... the river.' Her face twitched. 'I'm terrified of water.'

'Since losing your husband overboard, on the ship?'

Elaine nodded. 'I've had nightmare after nightmare about drowning. I couldn't walk alongside it, I just couldn't.' A gleam of sweat showed on her brow.

'A volunteer is the man who doesn't get away quick enough' had been one of Jemima's father's quips. Clearly, there was but one person fit for this job. Jemima repaired to her room, feeling this was as good a time as any to try out her new acquisitions. The coat, when belted, made her feel like an old-fashioned tailor's dummy wrapped for posting. The boots were the perfect size and nicely worn in. She left the castle shortly after midday with little doubt of Honor's destination. The canal. Her intention, freedom.

One hundred pounds and we keep sailing. The message to Lord Muirhaven had reeked of blackmail, but also carried a promise. *Pay up and we'll be out of your hair.*

Walking through the shrubbery, she recalled Lord Muirhaven's reaction when she'd asked if any other South Africans lived in the neighbourhood. Something savage had flashed in his eyes, though he'd quickly mastered himself.

'Castle Gloaming is affecting you... as it does us all,' he'd said with a smile. 'You're starting to see things that aren't there, Mrs Flowerday.'

True, but she had witnessed horrors that were all too real. Nodding good day to Beddoe as she passed the icehouse, she prayed that death had finished with Castle Gloaming.

Chapter Thirty-Nine

A walk that had taken about forty minutes on the previous occasion, this time took over an hour thanks to the slippery conditions. Jemima clambered up to the aqueduct at just after 1 p.m. She unbuttoned her coat and flapped it to cool down as she gathered her breath.

Jemima had followed a messy set of footprints this far. Female ones, from the shoe size. There was no sign of Honor, but having got a head start, the girl could by now be ensconced on the *Miss Nettle*. Last night, she'd expected Olive to moor this side of the aqueduct. And indeed, the footsteps turned right on the canal path, heading in the Chirk direction.

Jemima could have followed to see where they led, but a strange, new compulsion came over her: to face her fear of heights. Honor would be run to ground soon enough, here or in Chirk. But never again would Jemima get the chance to walk across the tallest aqueduct in the world.

Dragging up her courage by the roots, she walked onto the path that led into thin air.

When she reached the point where the river was directly below, she regretted her impulse. Whether we believe in God or Mr Darwin, she told herself, we are not designed to be this high up. Using her hands like blinkers either side of her face, she forced herself on. To her left, the rail protected her from oblivion. To her right, the canal's edge merged with the sky. And worse was heading towards her.

A boat, from the Trevor direction.

It was horse drawn. Jemima imagined one of those awkward jigs people dance when they meet in a doorway. 'After you, sir, no after you, madam.' Who would take precedence, she or the horse, and who might fall into the water? Or be pitched over—

Her nerve failing, she turned and hurried back the way she'd come. When she finally raised her eyes, it was to see Lord Muirhaven striding up from the lane from which she had emerged not five minutes before. He was recognisable by his tartan shirt and sleeveless waistcoat, leather hat and this time, a red neckerchief. She assumed he was coming her way, but he took the path towards Chirk. The set of his shoulders told her he was looking for something. Or someone.

Jemima pulled up her collar and followed him.

A few hundred yards on, she saw him stop beside a stationary boat. Jemima recognised the green-painted cabin, the black funnel.

Without hesitation or apparently seeking permission, he stepped on board.

Chapter Forty

He got on at the stern end and Jemima saw him rap against the cabin door, then open it. Tucking his head down, he vanished into the living quarters. The cabin would be too low for him. He'd have to hunch. Averting her face, Jemima continued past the *Miss Nettle*'s starboard window, which had a curtain drawn across. At the bow, she stopped. If Olive and Honor were on board, three would be a crowd in that tiny cabin. She could only imagine what it would feel like to have an angry Lord Muirhaven barge into your private world, dominating the space.

Where the boat was moored, timber piling created a rudimentary wharf. The usual ropes were attached to metal spikes, hammered into the soft ground. Jemima wondered what time Olive had pulled in and if Honor had managed to signal to her. If so, it wouldn't be in her usual fashion as the tower was now locked. The metal bucket was no longer on the cabin roof, but in the well deck, amongst the tomatoes, potatoes and herbs. The chair was there too, but *The Illustrated London News* had gone. Instead, a painting was propped up on the seat; a square of canvas with a rag draped over it.

Whose painting, Olive's or Honor's? Gripped by irresistible curiosity, Jemima clambered onto the gunwale and stepped down.

It was a flower painting, though not the kind you'd see in a polite gallery. This was an explosion of red, carmine, cobalt blue and yellow. Nor were the flowers any you'd see growing wild in the British Isles. When Jemima placed a fingertip against a petal, pink pigment came off on her skin. It must be just finished, as it was signed. A capital O over capital N. Olive Nettle.

The work was bold even by modern standards, and Jemima was reminded that Olive had tutored Honor away from her watercolour dabbles, into a place at the Slade. 'I'd like to have been a fly on the wall,' Jemima said to herself, 'during lesson one.'

Hearing a dull bump from the cabin end, she entered the boat's midsection. She went from light to darkness, moving stealthily beneath the weatherproof canvas that enclosed this part. There was a resinous smell in here. As her eyes grew used to the dimness, she saw that the hold was filled with sawn wood, stacked equally on both sides. Shelves stored ropes and mooring pins, candles in waxed paper, paraffin and bottles of turpentine, such as artists used.

A muffled scraping sound drew Jemima on. At the furthest end, she untied the canvas flaps and poked her head out. When her skull met something hard, she realised she had reached the boat's engine room. A huge, cylindrical boiler explained why so much wood was on board. She'd seen this vessel in motion, releasing a thick vapour haze from its funnel: *Miss Nettle* was steam powered. There was an access hatch in the rear wall, its outline visible behind the boiler, but there was no way through. If Lord Muirhaven detected her presence, and came at her from the bow, she'd be snared. She could hear him speaking behind the cabin wall. The boat was, in effect, a big sound box.

'Think you and your friend can wring more out of me?' she heard him say. 'Scare me with your drawings in the dust?'

She'd been right, then. He was being blackmailed. Since he knew of this boat, he must know Olive too. He had the women trapped, but what could Jemima do?

She heard a low grunt of laughter. 'You're not saying much, so, listen to me. We all had something to gain from our association but now, you've gone too far. I've covered up for you long enough, letting you come and go.'

He clearly knew more about Honor's past disappearances than he'd ever let on to her stepmother.

'You cannot have this life you crave. The world won't allow it, girl.'

You mean, you won't, Jemima supplied. He wasn't going to let Honor get away from Castle Gloaming. He must be thinking of the fortune she had coming to her. Why wasn't anyone speaking? Why had Olive not objected, or tried to defend Honor? Nothing about Olive Nettle had suggested a woman easily cowed.

Was it because Honor was there, alone?

Jemima was sure of it when she heard Lord Muirhaven say, 'You don't deserve what's going to happen to you, but you pushed me to it, you and your absent friend.'

What's going to happen...

Jemima heard something strike the cabin wall, followed instantly by the shattering of glass. Frightened into stillness, she stayed where she was... until black smoke began to wreathe around the sides of the boiler, seeping through the edges of the hatch.

Fire. Jemima heard the clash of boots on metal and knew that Hildebrand, Lord Muirhaven, had leapt clear. He'd left Honor inside and the smoke was thickening. Jemima did not panic. Years ago, as an apprentice shop assistant, she'd been trapped in a top-floor room when the department store she worked in had been set ablaze. Later, she would prove that her friend, Peggy, had not been to blame but at the moment of crisis, her ability to slow down her thinking and apply logic had saved her. Putting the same skills into practice, Jemima reversed along the midsection like a terrier emerging from a badger set. When she was once again standing in the well deck, she saw flames shooting from the cabin roof.

Olive's bucket, crammed with the parsley-like plant, was by her foot and full of water. Jemima carried it out onto the bank and ran to hurl its contents onto the flames licking at the cabin window. A sizzle followed by a guff of steam allowed her one glimpse through curtains that were alight to something that would haunt her for months to come.

A girl on a bed.

The impression vanished, replaced with boiling flame. *You're starting to see things that aren't there, Mrs Flowerday.*

Jemima's bucket was yanked from her hands. Men appeared from nowhere. The boat that had been crossing the aqueduct had pulled in and its crew set about trying to douse the flames, scooping canal water into buckets thrown by a woman on board. A boy was struggling to untie the tow-horse's rope. Everyone was shouting, and all in Welsh. They tried their best, but flames fuelled by dry logs, paraffin and turpentine were unstoppable.

Jemima could do nothing but watch the *Miss Nettle* being reduced to a smoking carcass. Only then, as she stood helpless, did she know what she had seen. A human form, lying on a pallet of charred bedsprings in the cabin, burned beyond recognition.

Chapter Forty-One

Jemima left her name and directions to Castle Gloaming with the woman on the boat that had stopped to help. 'Tell the authorities it's the *Miss Nettle*.' She said nothing about the charred body in the wreckage. It would be found in due course and identified as Honor van Doorn.

She gave the scene a last look, knowing her testimony alone would not prove murder. Words overheard were weak evidence and burning, however ugly its aftermath, was the great cleanser. Even Lord Muirhaven's footprints on the tow path were churned up with all the others.

But as she reached the place where the lane joined the canal path, she noticed something in the overgrown verge. It was a bent piece of brass. Blood glinted on its surface and on the vegetation immediately around it, suggesting it had been hurled away in haste.

With no clean handkerchief in her pocket, she unclipped a stocking and slid her hand inside before picking the object up. She guessed it to be some kind of wrench; L-shaped, with a square head that would fit around a substantial bolt or rivet. The square end was the bloodiest part with strands of hair mixed in messily. Dark hair, not blonde.

Olive's, then, not Honor's.

Feeling the implement's weight in her hand, Jemima could tell herself that Lord Muirhaven had struck a merciful, killing blow. His victim had felt nothing of the fire that consumed her.

'And what I am holding, my Lord,' Jemima rasped in a voice roughened by smoke and rage, 'is evidence that will hang you.'

The walk home forced Jemima to tread, literally, in the killer's footsteps. For a while, the need to proceed cautiously consumed every thought, but as she climbed the last yards to the castle grounds, the reality of everything she'd witnessed hit her.

Beddoe was no longer at his post, but as she passed the icehouse, it impinged on her that should Lord Muirhaven see her with the murder weapon... well, she knew what he was capable of. Pausing, she took off her coat, concealed the wrench within its folds and draped it over her arm. Conscious that she smelled of smoke, wore only one stocking and might have smuts on her face, she entered through the front door, praying nobody would see her.

She reached her room without challenge, placed the wrench under her bed and pulled the coverlet down to hide it. That done, she undressed and put her smoky clothes into a wicker laundry bin in the bathroom. She'd find a bag ... an old pillowcase would do... and take them home with her. Running a bath, she threw in fragrant salts and soaked away the physical evidence of the last two hours. She washed her hair and scrubbed her nails. Afterwards, she put on a plain dress, fresh stockings and added a string of garnets. A touch of bravado. She must present a self-assured persona.

Putting her watch back on, having removed it for her bath, she saw the afternoon was quite advanced. Had Mrs van Doorn still been with them, tea would be next.

At her dressing-table mirror, she combed a trace of glycerine and orange-flower water through her hair and left her room, wondering if she should lock the door.

'No,' she told herself. 'It would be more likely to rouse suspicion.'

Walking down the stairs, she was struck as always by the immensity of the hush of a great house. The birds caught in perpetual stillness under the dome seemed symbolic of the lifeless state of Castle Gloaming. Built to display the pomp and wealth of one man, it had outlasted its age and its purpose. As if to test her tolerance of excessive ornamentation, she caught her beads on a parrot head. A wooden one, carved into the newel post at the bottom of the stairs. Garnets skittered across the floor and Jemima scurried to retrieve them, which gave her the opportunity to see that, close up, the floor needed mopping. Much of what looked to be the intricate veining of marble was in fact dirt.

There simply weren't enough staff for a place this size. Jemima wondered if Mrs van Doorn had balked at paying too many people's wages. Hadn't Mrs Beddoe spoken of another girl being turned off?

She retrieved thirty garnets. Two missing.

They'd rolled up against the marble plinth where Jemima also found a crumpled ball of card. Opening it out, she saw it was one of the whist score sheets Elaine had brought to the drawing room for their game that awful evening, when diamonds had swum in front of Jemima's eyes and she'd thrown away almost every point. This was a fresh sheet, torn from the block.

If she remembered rightly, Elaine had taken the pad upstairs with her when she and Jemima had retired. Why would anyone screw up an unused sheet, and drop it as litter? Unless... she glanced up at the rails of the mezzanine... unless, it had not been dropped but *aimed*.

Jemima ran back upstairs. From the top, she threw the crumpled ball which landed a few stairs down. She tried again, using the palm of her hand as a bat. The sphere went a little further. She tried again with one of her garnet beads wrapped inside and bowled it, saying, 'Catch!' as it left her hand. It flew almost to the plinth. Jemima went slowly downstairs, pocketed the ball and continued to the library, her intended destination. She had wondered how Lord Muirhaven came to have an engagement ring ready on his person, the night he asked Mrs van Doorn to be his wife. She should have known there was no such thing as coincidence. Lord Muirhaven was a resourceful man, but even he would occasionally require an accomplice.

In the library, she took *Wildflowers of Field and Hedgerow* from its shelf and allowed it to fall open at the page marked by a yellow ribbon.

Hemlock.

No, wait a minute... the botanical drawing looked completely wrong. The description was wrong too. Jemima fetched a magnifying glass she'd noticed before on top of a Davenport desk, sat down at the library table and studied the page.

Hemlock water-dropwort. *Oenanthe crocata*. An umbellifer, family Apiaceae, a plant found in wet, damp and marginal places. Highly toxic to humans and animals.

Had someone tampered with a book she'd studied only a few hours ago, or had she absent-mindedly moved the ribbon before returning it to the shelf? Jemima read more about Oenanthe crocata.

Sometimes known as dead man's fingers from the appearance of its root. Traditionally used as a poultice for skin eruptions, but should be handled only by an expert practitioner. By legend, in certain Mediterranean communities, hemlock water-dropwort was used to kill criminals. Death is preceded by convulsions, rapid heart rate, sometimes psychosis, lung collapse and brain haemorrhage and resulting, postmortem, in a fixed, rictus grin.

Jemima pictured Cornelia van Doorn's clawed hands and bared teeth. In a low voice, as if giving a closing statement in court, she murmured, 'What conclusion can we draw, gentlemen of the jury. I beg your pardon, *ladies* and gentlemen of the jury?'

That hemlock was not the cause of Mrs van Doorn's death. In Mairwen's words, it was a decoy. 'Hemlock water-dropwort killed her,' Jemima breathed. The symptoms fitted. With its feathery leaves, *Oenanthe crocata* would be easy to mistake for the more benign members of the family Apiaceae. The bucket Olive carried around on the roof of her cabin suddenly took on a more sinister character. The woman had been adamant – *It's not parsley. Don't touch it!*

'Hemlock water-dropwort? Oh, my Lord. If Gwen was right, and a stranger was in the castle the night Mrs van Doorn was poisoned, could Olive have been responsible?'

Or did it point to Lord Muirhaven who had proved he had access to Olive's boat. As did Honor.

How extraordinary, Jemima thought, that she'd moved the ribbon to this page. Without it, she'd never have discovered the existence of this lethal plant. It felt divinely guided. Only when she took the book back to its place did she discover a less spiritual reason. She had taken *Wildflowers of Wetland, Stream and Marsh* from the shelf instead of the one dedicated to fields and hedgerows.

She took down the book she'd intended to read, and yes, the yellow ribbon was where she'd left it, keeping the page for hemlock. Somebody had been here before her and had marked places in both books. Who had been researching the deadliest plants in the landscape?

Elaine would hiss, 'Mairwen!' but it couldn't be so. Mairwen couldn't read.

Jemima doubted that Beddoe or Ifor could access the library without rousing attention, though others might do so without question.

Jemima returned *Wildflowers of Wetland, Stream and Marsh* to its place and sandwiched *Wildflowers of Field and Hedgerow* between a pair of dictionaries on a different shelf. It felt a risky thing to do, as it might alert somebody dangerous that she was on to them.

As indeed she was. She had followed their footprints, speculated on their motives, seen their handiwork. Only their face eluded her. For now.

The events of the afternoon were catching up with her, and Jemima's thoughts strayed towards tea and Welsh cake. However, as she returned the magnifying glass to the Davenport, her eye alighted on the book Mrs van Doorn had recommended: *The Memoir of a Countess*.

She took it down and resting it on the desk, opened it at the frontispiece which displayed a large, hand-tinted plate. Hilda, Countess of Muirhaven, looked solemn in her robes and coronet, her hair piled in one of the lavish pouffes that used to take ladies' maids hours to create with padding and false tresses. Another hand-tinted picture showed Hilda as an older woman in a more naturalistic setting. In fact, it looked like the terrace outside. Hilda was gazing across the lawn, her left hand resting on the rim of a garden urn.

Jemima reached for the magnifying glass. Under enlargement, the countess appeared to be wearing an engagement ring, a row of pearls or opals with diamonds between, and a plain gold wedding ring. Neither resembled the one placed on Cornelia van Doorn's finger. She leafed through the whole book, hunting for a square-cut emerald.

When her search yielded nothing, she took another book down: *The History of the Earldom of Muirhaven* and after patient page-turning, found a photograph that caused her to say, 'Ha. You are caught out in another lie, Hildebrand.'

Tea. Jemima felt she'd pass out if she didn't have refreshment. She must nerve herself to encounter Elaine, who would ask if she'd found Honor. What on earth would she tell the woman?

She wanted to say: 'I have no idea where Miss van Doorn may be, but I did witness Lord Muirhaven committing murder.' She must hold her composure and say nothing. Olive had died aboard her boat, while Honor was out there somewhere, alive and hopefully well.

Chapter Forty-Two

Jemima found Elaine at the kitchen table, in conversation with Mrs Beddoe. The housekeeper was complaining she was running short of 'all the staples'. She'd need the pony trap tomorrow for a trip to Llangollen. 'And ready cash, please, Mrs Cleeve, as we're to the limit of our credit at Blethyn's.'

Blethyn's being a grocer's shop, Jemima assumed. Her parents had owned Paget's of South Wimbledon and, growing up, she'd overheard many a fraught conversation over customers who were late paying off their tab.

Elaine had mentioned that funds were being held up in Cape Town. If so, Mrs van Doorn's death was hardly going to ease the money supply, and unless Mrs Cleeve had access to a post-office account or similar, the pantry shelves would soon be bare.

Jemima cleared her throat, making both women look up.

'Have you found her?' Elaine asked, getting up.

'No, and you need to sit down. Boil water, please Mrs Beddoe. We'll need tea.' Without preamble, she broke the news of the burning of the *Miss Nettle*. She did not mention the somebody had perished.

'Well, I'm sorry, but what has that to do with Honor?' Elaine demanded.

'Honor used that boat to get herself to London last month, and I'm certain it was a journey she intended to repeat.'

Elaine looked winded. 'She told you that?'

'She admitted it, but I'd worked it out anyway. Are you aware that Honor was friends with the woman who owned the boat? The same woman was teaching her to paint.'

'Was?' Elaine caught on to the past tense.

I might as well tell her. News would fly in this direction soon enough. 'I'm afraid the boat's owner was on board when the fire started, and did not get out.'

A wave of agony seemed to course through Elaine's body.

Mrs Beddoe, having put the kettle onto the hot plate, came forwards saying, 'You mean the Nettle woman? The foreigner?'

Jemima nodded.

'Dear heavens. Ifor said there was smoke from that direction, but we thought it must be a bonfire.'

Jemima described following Honor's footprints to the aqueduct. 'I went towards Trevor hoping to spot her.' She didn't mention that she had deliberately walked in the wrong direction, to test her own mettle, or that she had witnessed the destruction of the boat close at hand.

'So she's dead.' Mrs Beddoe spoke the words as for an epitaph. 'Does Mairwen know?'

'Mairwen?' Jemima echoed. 'No, why?'

'They were friends. Whenever Mairwen needed to go to her parents' place, she'd ask for a boat ride to Trevor. It only saved her a mile or two on foot, but she liked being on the water.'

This was news to Jemima. 'You had better break it to her, Mrs Beddoe.'

The housekeeper carried on making the tea. 'I will, when she's back. Last I saw of her, she was buttoning up her coat, offering to fetch butter and cream from the farm. I think she just wanted a walk.'

Elaine lifted her head. Until this moment, she had been studying the grain of the table. 'Do you think she'll come back?'

'Mairwen? Yes, of course,' said the housekeeper.

'I mean Honor.'

That was harder to predict. With Mrs van Doorn gone, Honor no longer had to battle for her right to study art. On the other hand, she still needed a guardian's permission and who was now her guardian? A wise soul would have stayed here, preparing her arguments for whoever took control of her affairs. But Honor was young and in her own way as stubborn as her stepmother had been. Chances were, she'd find that lack of money was the greatest obstacle of all.

'She'll be back, I predict, in four or five days,' said Jemima.

Elaine gasped. 'So long?'

'That being the time it'll take her to get to London, discover how expensive it is, and realise she has no choice. Elaine, may I ask you a question?'

Elaine looked reluctant, but said, 'Yes.'

'The ring Hildebrand gave Cornelia must have meant something to him, to place it among all those sparklers on her fingers.'

'With respect, that's not a question,' Elaine said.

Jemima reframed it. 'Where did he get the ring he presented to Mrs van Doorn?'

'He told you, it was Countess Hilda's. A family heirloom. She was his grandmother.'

Jemima shook her head. 'No. It was never hers.'

Elaine's sigh accused Jemima of game-playing. 'What are you trying to say?'

'I found the countess's memoir.'

Tea was poured. Jemima thanked Mrs Beddoe and stirred several sugars into her cup. Sensing the housekeeper was interested in their conversation, Jemima said, 'I'm sure you can spare a moment to sit with us, Mrs Beddoe, but would there be any Welsh cakes? Sorry to ask.'

A tin was fetched. A chair scraped and there were three at the table.

Jemima picked up her thread. 'There are many portraits of the countess in those family history books, and that emerald ring is not on her hand at any point. It is, however, on the hand of the Honourable Leopold Woolton. Hildebrand's father. He wore it on his little finger.'

For effect, she waved her own pinkie, then addressed Elaine again. 'D'you know, when Mrs van Doorn showed her engagement ring to me, my immediate impression was that it was rather plain. Of course it would be, being a man's signet ring. Fancy Hildebrand not remembering that.'

'May I assume you have asked your question?' Elaine said coldly.

'Not entirely.' From her dress pocket, Jemima brought out a crumpled ball of card which, without warning, she tossed at Elaine.

Mrs Cleeve made a defensive feint and the ball landed back on the table. 'Really, Mrs Flowerday!'

Ah, we are no longer using first names. Understandable, Jemima thought. What she said was, 'Your friend Hildebrand did a better job of catching the ring when you threw it down to him in the great hall.'

'You have gone completely mad, Mrs Flowerday.' Elaine rose to her feet.

Jemima also stood. 'Not only did you know that Lord Muirhaven meant to offer marriage to Cornelia van Doorn, you encouraged him.'

'How on earth could I do that?' Elaine's cheeks formed hollows, and her mouth turned up at the sides. The dimples of fear.

'By bringing them together,' Jemima said. 'For instance, you, not Mrs van Doorn, got rid of the maid who prepared Hildebrand's meals.'

'That was Eleri,' Mrs Beddoe cut in. 'A nice girl. Hard-working.'

Jemima continued, 'Providing him with meals three times a day, not to mention having cocktails and playing cards, gave opportunity for intimacy to arise.'

'Between him and *Honor*,' Elaine said, as if Jemima had muffed the simplest sum in the maths book. 'Cornelia dearly wanted them to unite and, yes, I played matchmaker. But it was always Honor who was the intended bride.'

Jemima shook her head. She didn't believe it, not anymore. 'You mentioned a pact being struck on the boat from Cape Town,' she said. 'Cornelia's wealth in exchange for a title.'

'Yes, and I repeat, for him and Honor.'

'No. Doesn't wash. I can see Honor taking one look at a man of forty and thinking he had nothing to offer her. Cornelia herself told us, Honor was off with the young set, dancing the bunny hug and dreaming of short skirts and even shorter hair. She somehow formed a friendship with Olive Nettle on that voyage too. Olive was an artist, inspiring and a rule-breaker. Honor didn't want to marry a stuffy aristocrat almost of an age to be her father. *Cornelia* had the dream, she was the malleable one, who might be persuaded to lavish her fortune on a penniless aristocrat. After all, Honor's father had been poor and Cornelia raised him up with her money.'

'You know nothing, Mrs Flowerday.'

'Oh, but I do know human nature, Elaine. What's the better bet, a woman in her sixties, suffering indifferent health, or a slip of a girl with her head filled with ideas of a career and independence? *And* with an inconvenient fifty-odd years of life ahead of her.'

'That is a disgusting charge and I refute it utterly.'

'He'd want a son, though, wouldn't he?' Mrs Beddoe put in. 'They all do, to keep the title alive. Mrs van Doorn couldn't do that for him.'

'It's generally what we suppose,' Jemima conceded. 'But he might have thought, "I can always have a second marriage." After all, if Cornelia lived to be eighty, he'd still be in with a shout of fathering children.' She turned again to Elaine. 'I think you and Hildebrand had that planned, and you enabled Honor to leave for London as a way of removing her from the picture.'

Ridiculous, said Elaine's face. But the more Jemima thought of it, the more it made sense.

'I cannot imagine Honor writing to the Slade, getting an interview, planning a journey all alone.'

'You've already said she had help. That Nettle woman,' said Elaine.

'That was transport. Olive wouldn't know how to apply to an art school either. It needed someone who understands how these things work, who can find an address, which "Dear Sir or Madam" to write to. A secretary, in other words. You hoped she'd be offered a place and stay away.' Jemima paused a moment. 'But you must have realised that without her stepmother's consent, the scheme would fail. Oh, but of course.' She gave a smile that said, *You idiot, Jemima*. 'It went over my head at the time. I asked Honor how she intended to get over that problem. Would she forge Mrs van Doorn's signature or hire an actress to pose as her stepmother. Her answer, "I might." Now I realise that was exactly your plan. I'm sure you can forge Mrs van Doorn's signature like a dream, Elaine.'

'That is slander, Mrs Flowerday, and I have listened to your impertinent questions too long.' Elaine stalked out.

After a silence, Mrs Beddoe said, 'What are you doing, Mrs Flowerday?'

'Unravelling a fiendish knot.' Jemima took a Welsh cake. 'These are very good.'

'You think Lord Muirhaven and Mrs Cleeve were duping Mrs van Doorn?'

'Pretty much. I believe they engineered Honor's time away in London, and hoped she'd stay away for good.'

'You don't think they killed poor Mrs van Doorn?'

'Far from. She was the golden goose.'

'Then who did?'

'I know what it wasn't, Mrs Beddoe. It wasn't hemlock.'

'I told you that already. So has Mairwen.'

Jemima took another Welsh cake. Energy was seeping back into her limbs. 'But you suppressed vital information. If you or Mairwen had mentioned finding hemlock on the dining-room carpet I could have spent the last two days working out how it got there.'

'Or you would have looked even harder at Mairwen. What will you do now?'

Rather than answer, Jemima said in a dreamy voice, '"A drowsy numbness pains my sense as though of hemlock I had drunk". Keats.'

'If you say so.'

'Could we dine in state tonight? I think we should use the dining room.'

Mrs Beddoe shook her head. 'Who'd want to sit in there after what happened?'

'Nothing happened, did it? Will you give notice that it is dinner at eight, cocktails in the drawing room at seven.'

'I don't know. You heard me say, the cupboard is bare.'

'"Better is a dinner of herbs where love is, than a stalled ox and hatred therewith".'

'Book of Proverbs,' said Mrs Beddoe. 'I didn't have you down as a Bible reader, Mrs Flowerday.'

'I read everything, even the labels on bottles of shop-bought salad dressing.'

Jemima watched Mrs Beddoe cast a shocked glance at the kitchen cupboard.

'How did you know?' the housekeeper demanded.

'My parents were grocers. Pope & Haddiscoe's epicurean vinai-grette, the one with English mustard and Scottish honey, was always the best.'

Leaving the kitchen, Jemima's smile crumbled. She had angered Elaine Cleeve beyond any hope of reconciliation. She had exposed Lord Muirhaven's lies. She had identified the plant that had, poten-tially, killed Cornelia van Doorn as hemlock water-dropwort. Or, if she wished to be theatrical, 'murderer's parsley'.

Now all she had to do was prove how it got into the victim's system. Oh, and sit down for dinner with Lord Muirhaven and his collaborator. With Honor gone, and Cornelia dead, it would be only the three of them. Throwing that crumpled ball of card across the table at Elaine, she had revealed her hand.

Jemima was beginning to feel distinctly outnumbered.

Chapter Forty-Three

The photograph that had revealed the provenance of the emerald signet ring was in a chapter of *The History of the Earldom of Muirhaven* headed 'African Sojourn'.

Jemima had returned to the library rather than retreat to her room, where a murder weapon lay hidden. There was always solace in books, even books about people one did not know or naturally trust. The photograph showed a man standing beside a boy mounted on a pony, the man's hand resting on the boy's shoulder. Their bush hats and matching cotton drill jackets, light eyes and black hair suggested father and son. The caption agreed:

> The Hon. Leopold Woolton and Hildebrand his son,
> Oosthoek, Eastern Cape

A second photograph showed father and son standing in front of a thatched bungalow where trees threw shade across a parched-looking lawn. And here it became interesting to Jemima. A few paces behind them stood a Black woman in a cotton print dress clasping the hand of a little girl. They weren't named, but in a subsequent photograph they were.

> Emily Ntuli, housekeeper at Clear Acres
> and her daughter, Olive

As with all the other pictures, this one had been coloured in by a professional tinter. The pattern on the woman's robe was red-and-pink check and the little girl wore a short dress of the same fabric. She was lighter skinned than her mother, her dark hair twisted into plaits, tied near her scalp with ribbons.

Consulting the Muirhaven family tree on the flyleaf, Jemima had learned that Leopold's elder brother had succeeded to earldom in 1892. Leopold had pre-deceased him ensuring the title passed – a year and a half ago – to Leopold's son, the present Hildebrand. All perfectly unremarkable, bar the inexplicable presence of an 'Olive Ntuli' in a photograph and an Olive Nettle on the Ellesmere canal. They were almost certainly the same person but Jemima wanted to be sure. She feared the police would ignore the inconvenient business of identifying the body on the boat and it horrified her to think of Lord Muirhaven getting away with murder.

'I need that breakthrough, the link, the careless mistake that springs the case wide open,' she whispered, closing the book.

The Weekend Sleuth liked to remind its readers that, while details were the detective's friend, they were the criminal's undoing. With this ringing in her mind, Jemima made her way upstairs again, this time to Cornelia van Doorn's bedroom.

Chapter Forty-Four

Jemima walked through the sitting room into the bedroom, going straight to the desk, ignoring the letters addressed to Elaine which she really must hand over. The one for Mrs van Doorn, with its Wrexham postmark, should be reserved for the eyes of the police. Jemima suspected it came from her bank, as the postmistress had also suggested. Hadn't it been on a trip back from Wrexham that Cornelia had found a copy of *The Weekend Sleuth*, discarded on a train seat?

How much influence had Elaine wielded in summoning Jemima to find Honor? An untested amateur would have suited her purposes as much as they'd suited Mrs van Doorn's, if the object was to keep the police away.

Jemima wondered at herself for trusting Elaine Cleeve on sight. 'It was the navy-blue suit,' she muttered. 'I'll be harder nosed in future.' The thought of Elaine having a free hand on this desk made her impulsive. She opened the letter.

It was from the Wrexham branch of the Provincial & Overseas Bank, dated Friday, 1 June.

Dear Mrs van Doorn,
    I write to inform you that your account remains overdrawn and request immediate settlement of the

outstanding debt. In our meeting last month, you informed
me that South African funds were to be transferred to
cover the shortfall. My subsequent investigations suggest
there are no such funds.

None? Jemima had once received a stern letter from her bank
manager when she had overspent on a client's wedding trousseau.
It had upset her for a week. Mrs van Doorn's bank manager had
more to say, and it did not make comfortable reading.

My colleagues in Cape Town have informed me that your
account there is also seriously overdrawn. Until you clear
your debts entirely, your account will remain suspended
and interest levied at the standard percentage. All cheques
drawn on your account will be returned, unpaid.

'What, including mine?' It was a low punch. Jemima had resisted
Mrs van Doorn's generosity at first, but how quickly one got used
to having money, or at least, the idea of it.

She stuffed the letter in a drawer and slammed it shut. If
Elaine still anticipated funds from Cape Town, she'd be disappointed, but not nearly as much as the tradespeople of Llangollen.
Did Elaine have any idea of the financial mess she was facing?
Possibly not. Mrs van Doorn had given every appearance of solid
wealth. The diamonds, the Régal dresses, her plans for a London
season...

'Unless of course, she never intended such a thing and it was
all a ruse to bring me here. To disrupt my life for her own ends.'

Waiting for angry feelings to subside, Jemima plonked herself
down on the sitting-room sofa in front of the empty fireplace.
Right here, Cornelia van Doorn had blocked her stepdaughter's
hopes of a place at the Slade. No, no, no!

'Because she couldn't afford it,' Jemima said, in the tone that comes as a thought matures. 'She couldn't have Honor skipping off to London, requiring an allowance, clothes and art materials. She needed the girl to marry Hildebrand *toot-sweet*, become a countess, safe from creditors and poverty.'

Cornelia had wanted to protect Honor from the catastrophe that was closing in... but to safeguard herself also? As Jemima knew well, an English peerage is no guarantee of credit, but it offers a certain protection. Her own bank manager, though adept at stern letters, was all smiles when she went into the branch and was announced as the Honourable Mrs Flowerday. It shouldn't help, but it did. Massively.

'That's why Cornelia accepted Lord Muirhaven's proposal. Honor had made her loathing of Hildebrand so plain, not even Cornelia could persuade herself that a union was viable. So she threw herself on the sacrificial altar. Or perhaps she could not resist the idea of becoming a countess.'

How Lord Muirhaven and Cornelia would have fared together, Jemima could only speculate. His reaction when he discovered his diamond widow was flat broke would have been something to behold.

'Was she always broke, I wonder?' Was she a swindler, or a rich widow who'd spent everything she had? A few clues pointed to the latter. Elaine's description of Cornelia paying her way on the RMS *Llanstephan Castle* with wads of cash sounded like a woman who had emptied her bank accounts before skipping the country to evade her creditors. Her habit of wearing all her diamonds at once, teamed with anxiety and the need for sedative tea, pointed to a woman who feared she might once again have to get away quickly. Lying low at Castle Gloaming fitted the theory.

'I don't think she was on the make. I think she was absolutely on her uppers and was terrified of being rumbled. I can imagine that putting Honor through school and bankrolling a second husband wrung her dry. Then there was the cost of travelling to England first class, and the rental on this place...'

On a whim, Jemima went to the sideboard and once again stared at the tea things, so domestic and innocent. Was anything in this place really what it purported to be? Using her sleeve as a guard, she lifted lids, peered in and sniffed. She came last to the spirit kettle, remembering how it rattled as it began to steam, the noise delaying the moment she heard Honor come to her stepmother's door. 'If I'd caught her, brought her in, mediated, how much might have been prevented?'

Returning to the bedroom, Jemima again read Honor's note to her stepmother, and one line jumped out: *I came to talk with you today, as we used to.*

Came to talk... Honor had come up bearing flowers, but had dashed away, scattering petals. Whatever she'd heard had propelled her to Jemima's wardrobe, and a second attempt at leaving. She had probably heard her stepmother declare, 'There can be no art school.' And perhaps the most dispiriting comment, 'There will be no money.'

Jemima repeated it slowly as a blanket of mist lifted from her mind. That was all Cornelia had said on the subject. She hadn't said, 'I will disinherit Honor.' Cornelia van Doorn had simply stated the truth: there would be no money for art school, or London, because it was all gone.

'I leapt to the wrong conclusion.'

If Honor had done the same, believed she was going to be disinherited, it offered a motive to kill.

Jemima stepped over the bed cover which had been left between the double doors when the body was moved. The detectives would need to see it, to understand the victim's final movements. The sight of it always brought a lump of pity to Jemima's throat. She imagined Cornelia coming up to bed for the last time. Newly engaged. Happy and elated? Or wondering, 'What have I done?'

Jemima could say for sure that she had made herself her calmative tea, taking her cup into her bedroom. She'd undressed and put on her nightgown, oyster-pink satin. Where were the clothes she'd worn at dinner and to play cards?

A lady's maid would have hung up the dress, to inspect in the morning for spots or marks. The underwear would have been discreetly bagged for hand-washing. But Cornelia had no lady's maid. She had Elaine. Who did her washing?

In the bathroom, Jemima received a partial answer. All the clothing Mrs van Doorn had worn that fatal night was in a lidded basket, beside the bath.

'She undressed and put on her nightgown. Perhaps she brushed her teeth and hair and took off her makeup. Quickly, I should think. She'd have wanted her bed.'

The placement of the teacup indicated Cornelia had sat up in bed to drink. In just her nightdress? 'She came from South Africa. She'd have found a rainy Welsh night too chilly for that.'

Jemima ran her fingers under the fallen bedcover, making a sound of satisfaction as she drew out a knitted bedjacket. She shook the pink folds. Out fell a signet ring with a square, green stone.

Jemima tried it on the fourth finger of her left hand. It went on easily, but she was of slight build. It would have been a tighter fit on Mrs van Doorn.

Too tight, perhaps.

Try it this way... Cornelia had come upstairs, made tea.

Why do I keep coming back to tea?

Elaine had lit the flame under the spirit kettle expecting her employer to follow her upstairs soon after. 'It must have been steaming away when Cornelia finally made it to bed. Not far off boiling dry. Maybe just enough hot water for a single cup.'

The victim had taken her tea through to sip in her bedroom, then discovered a note and a bunch of flowers... Jemima went and touched the pillow that still held a faint halo of pollen. How had Cornelia felt at that moment, wearing the ring that had been meant for her stepdaughter? She'd untied the ribbon of Honor's bouquet, filled a vase with water and placed the flowers on her desk. The ribbon had been neatly rolled. It suggested that, at this point, Mrs van Doorn had been able to function normally and was inclined to accept Honor's gesture in the spirit it was intended.

She had got ready for bed and sat propped up on her pillows drinking her tea. Still wearing the ring. She'd have seen its glint in the lamplight as she raised and lowered her teacup. It might have begun to constrict the blood flow to her finger, but if she'd taken it off in bed, she would surely have laid it safely on the bedside table.

The only conclusion Jemima could come to was that something had triggered a violent alteration in Cornelia's emotions. And back we come to the tea. One effect of hemlock water-dropwort poisoning, according to the book, was psychosis.

As the poison took hold, Mrs van Doorn would start to feel sick and giddy. Pain and disorientation would have worsened by the minute. 'She got herself out of bed, only her covers caught around her legs,' Jemima said, and walked to the double doors. 'Here, she dropped the coverlet and her bedjacket fell off her shoulders. She'd pulled the ring off her finger; she didn't want to marry Hildebrand. Everyone was her enemy now.'

Jemima looked again at the note from Honor. Had Cornelia written 'No. No. No.' and 'H is trying to kill me' in the grip of poison-induced psychosis? The added lines looked like child's writing, topsy-turvy letters, and were in pencil whereas the rest of the letter was in ink. Remembering how she'd staggered into her bathroom that same night, convinced she was dying, Jemima had no difficulty believing that Mrs van Doorn's handwriting would have deteriorated. What she couldn't believe was that Mrs van Doorn, in the grip of violent distress and desperate to summon aid, would sit at her desk to write a postscript to her stepdaughter.

Jemima lifted her hand and stared at the ring until the emerald winked back. 'Cornelia didn't write those words. Somebody else did.' 'H is trying to kill me' was a crude attempt to throw suspicion on the letter writer. In short, to frame Honor. Who would do that? Someone literate, so not Mairwen. Someone familiar with Mrs van Doorn's handwriting. Someone who had heard that lady's stubborn declarations many times and could repeat them with authenticity.

'My money's on Mrs Cleeve,' Jemima said out loud. 'Nobody has had more opportunity to study Cornelia than she.'

A slow hand clap behind her made Jemima whirl around. Lord Muirhaven and Elaine stood between the double doors.

'You are quite the sleuth Mrs Flowerday,' Hildebrand said, 'and at any other time, I would be keen to hear the rest, and understand your processes, but you are wanted downstairs.'

'For what purpose?'

'A sherry, and to answer some questions. Tell me – you were up at the canal earlier today?'

This man had bludgeoned a woman to death and left her body to burn. It wouldn't be true to say he looked untouched by it. On the contrary, there were new lines about his eyes, a tension to his mouth. But bowed down by the weight of evil? No.

'I was,' Jemima replied. 'I was searching for Honor. There was a terrible fire on a boat – a casualty.'

'So I understand.' He shook his head. 'Those boats are lethal, all wood and oilcloth, with fuel lying around. Rags soaked in turpentine.'

'Turpentine, why?' Jemima was savvy enough to sound genuinely curious.

'Oh, I believe the owner was an artist of some kind. You know what they're like.'

'I see. You're suggesting that the poor girl knocked over a paraffin lamp, started a blaze and couldn't get out.'

'It's not impossible.'

He even managed a sad smile. 'I've covered up for you long enough,' Jemima had heard him say. How that statement linked to Olive, she hadn't yet an idea, but it wasn't something you'd say to a stranger.

She couldn't resist a further prod. 'Were you there? Did you see it?'

'No, no I got the news when I returned from a walk.' Lord Muirhaven shot up his sleeve and glanced at his watch. Jemima's eyes followed the movement. There were red lesions on his skin near the clasp. The strap must be too snug for his wrist and she wondered why he hadn't had it extended, a couple more links added.

She asked, 'Who is it who wants to question me?'

'Oh, I beg your pardon. Our friend Sergeant Maddox,' said Hildebrand.

That was a surprise. 'From Chirk on his horse, at this hour?'

'No, by car as far as the road will allow. He couldn't have ridden because he's brought Honor with him. Sorry, didn't I say? I can't imagine her sitting pillion, though she's dressed for it.' He smiled, leaving the statement hanging.

Jemima said she'd assumed Honor would make her way direct to Chirk. 'But why is Sergeant Maddox involved?'

Elaine said with icy restraint, 'She went to the railway station at Trevor and caught an excursion train taking day trippers to Chirk Castle. Only, the stupid girl didn't buy a ticket and on arrival at Chirk, someone called the police station.'

'It's hardly an arrestable offence.'

'True,' agreed Elaine, all the sympathy wrung from her voice. 'Being found in possession of a stolen cheque is, however. She took the one Mrs van Doorn wrote for you.'

Lord Muirhaven chipped in. 'Two hundred pounds, Mrs Flowerday, and you're worth every penny, I'm sure. Maddox will ask if you gave it to Honor willingly.'

'Is that what she's claiming?'

'Come down and find out for yourself. One last thing.' Hildebrand still blocked the way out of the bedroom. 'Why are you wearing my father's signet ring?'

Chapter Forty-Five

The obvious riposte would have been, 'I thought you said it was the late Countess Hilda's' but Jemima opted for the truth.

'I found it on the floor, and wanted to test if it could have fallen off Mrs van Doorn's finger.' She held up her left hand. 'Even though it was designed for a man's smallest finger, it fits me nicely. I think it would have been very tight on your fiancée.'

'Not a flattering observation.' Lord Muirhaven had regained his effortless self-control.

'No two people take the same ring size,' Jemima pointed out. 'I'm sure she'd have suggested taking it to a jeweller to be enlarged.'

'We will never know, Mrs Flowerday.'

Jemima removed the ring, saying to Elaine, 'I'm going to ask that burning question you wouldn't let me put earlier. Mrs Cleeve, would you prefer to see this ring on your finger?'

She tossed it. This time, Elaine managed the catch.

I should have realised much earlier that those two were in league, Jemima scolded herself after they left her to make her way down alone. The signs were there. Elaine, getting rid of the girl, Eleri, who waited on him. And what about their chit-chat? Calling him 'Hildebrand' and saying things like, 'You're unbearably smug when you win.'

'I should have read more into their familiarity.'

Elaine was a partner in a magic show, subtly directing the audience's attention while the more flamboyant one pulls the rabbits out of the hat.

Sergeant Maddox and Honor were in the drawing room. The stained glass in the window glowed pomegranate pink in the lowering day. Maddox was planted near the unlit fire, Honor hunched on the sofa in the defeated posture Jemima had come to associate with her.

This time, she was wearing trousers, a man's shirt and waistcoat, a waxed jacket and a hat of the same fabric. Only the shoes were recognisably hers, the lace-up Oxfords Jemima had seen with various other pairs in Honor's bedroom. She had followed their prints along the river path. Unsurprisingly, the welts were caked in dried mud. A suitcase secured by a leather strap stood close to Honor's knees.

This was the girl's third attempt to escape, but had she checked herself in the mirror? With her blonde hair and willowy figure covered up, the bandage on her fingers looking again quite grubby, Honor van Doorn had given away the charms that would have got her through a ticket barrier. In cream lace, with well-timed tears and a plausible story, she'd have had station employees pulling every ruse to help her.

When Lord Muirhaven came in, Honor shrank deeper into herself. His first comment was that Mrs Cleeve was visiting the kitchen to ensure there was some kind of dinner tonight. 'You will stay and eat, Sergeant Maddox?'

'We'll see, sir,' the policemen replied, and put his first question to Jemima. 'I expect Lord Muirhaven has explained the situation?'

'He has,' said Jemima. 'Or, rather, enough to make me realise that a tiresome mistake has taken place for which I must apologise.'

'Oh?' The sergeant raised an eyebrow.

'Miss van Doorn borrowed an outfit of mine the other day, and the cheque you speak of would have been in the pocket. May I see it?'

Sergeant Maddox removed a folded rectangle from his top pocket and handed it to Jemima.

She made a show of inspecting it. That flourishing signature, 'C. van Doorn', was familiar from their exchange of letters, but Jemima was positive that the rest had been written by someone else.

Jemima asked Lord Muirhaven, 'Would Elaine have filled in the cheque for her employer?'

'Of course,' he replied. 'She prepared everything for Cornelia to sign, except her personal letters.'

'She has a distinctive hand,' Jemima noted. Elaine's letter 'O' didn't close at the top. It curled like a curtain hook. The loops were neat and whole in the signing of 'van Doorn', but not in the phrase *Pay the bearer two hundred pounds only*. That same broken 'O' appeared on the postscript to Honor's letter to her stepmother. *No. No. No.*

As *The Weekend Sleuth* was always drumming home, it's the detail, always the detail. Jemima turned away from Lord Muirhaven to give the sergeant a sweet smile. She said, 'It's my cheque and my sister Vicky is always reprimanding me for leaving important things in skirt pockets. I am abject, Sergeant Maddox, abject.'

Elaine Cleeve came in at that moment, to say that she'd asked for dinner to be on the table in an hour. 'Early, but the servants won't want to be up late.' She repeated Lord Muirhaven's invitation to the sergeant, adding, 'It's only cold ham and potatoes, I'm afraid. With everything going on, the menu has shrunk.'

Sergeant Maddox said that was a kind invitation, and he was glad the business with the cheque was settled, but there was still the matter of Miss van Doorn boarding a train without the means to purchase a ticket.

Everyone looked at Honor, who received the attention with a blankness Jemima found disturbing. This business was a distraction. CID, when they finally arrived, would need Honor present, alert and willing to answer questions. With this in mind, Jemima suggested Ifor could go to the station and pay for the ticket, taking a letter of apology to the stationmaster.

Hildebrand made a disparaging sound and rapped out, 'That's it, a smack on the wrist after all she's done? She goes on pretending to be the poor little girl that nobody loves, when the truth is, she had everything on a plate.'

Was that a flinch from Honor? Something in that must have struck home.

'Having Honor charged with evading a fare won't help anyone,' Jemima said.

'With respect, Mrs Flowerday, this is absolutely none of your business.'

'With respect, Lord Muirhaven, it is absolutely none of yours either.'

'There you are wrong. I make the rules now, where Honor is concerned.'

Honor came alive. 'You can't tell me what to do, Lord Muirhaven. You tried to dupe my stepmother into marriage, but you failed. Now I'm free.' Honor's hectic gaze sought Jemima's. 'My Uncle Geoffrey in Cape Town is my guardian now. He's Stepmama's brother and she said, if anything happened to her, he would look after me.'

A dry chuckle broke from Lord Muirhaven. 'Wrong, dear child. Your stepmother altered her will, handing the guardianship of you and your fortune to me.' He moved a hand, indicating Elaine. 'And to Mrs Cleeve. We jointly have the care of you, and it empowers me to say...' He paused, as Jemima noted he liked doing. 'Go upstairs and change out of those disgraceful rags. Put on a dress and come downstairs like the civilised young woman you are expected to be.'

Chapter Forty-Six

The news of her new circumstances broke the trance Honor had fallen into. She struggled to contain open-mouthed sobs, which Jemima suspected were a genuine symptom of shock. Hildebrand, Lord Muirhaven, was a brute who shouldn't have guardianship of a pet mouse, let alone a bereaved young girl. But as he had succinctly pointed out to Jemima, it was none of her business.

She approached Honor and put a hand on her shoulder, saying, 'Come along, I'll help. For a short time in my life, when I grew tired of being a shop girl, I put myself out as a lady's maid. I was good at it, you won't be surprised to hear, but the wages were pitiful and the hours inhuman, so I quit.' Getting no response, she lifted Honor's suitcase, at which the girl sprang to her feet.

'That's mine.'

'Indisputably, but let me take it.' Jemima left the drawing room, confident that the ewe lamb would follow the mother sheep.

The suitcase was remarkably light, considering Honor's intention of beginning a new life. But hadn't she proved that she liked travelling unencumbered? There would doubtless have been a pair of shoes, a hat, a coat, stored handily aboard the *Miss Nettle*. Jemima put the suitcase at Honor's bedroom door and waited for her lamb to catch up.

'I take it you were back upon the pilgrimage?' The reference meant nothing to Honor, so she added the magic word, 'London.'

'Yes.'

Jemima took the suitcase into the bedroom. It was 6 p.m, and the light through the bedroom window had a northerly precision which allowed Jemima to recognise that Honor's 'disgraceful rags' were clothes she had seen before.

'You're wearing Olive's things.'

'She gave them to me.'

'You didn't rifle her wardrobe, then?'

When Honor sat down on her bed, giving a negligent shake of the head, it struck Jemima that Honor might not know what had happened to the *Miss Nettle* and its owner. She told her as gently as she could.

Honor stared. 'Burned, completely burned?'

'Yes, but it's only a boat. Olive is gone, Honor.'

Honor shook her head. 'No.'

'I'm afraid I—' Jemima had been about to say, 'I saw the body' but knew that if Honor were to blurt that out to Lord Muirhaven, they'd both be at mortal risk. 'I spoke to a person who saw a body on board. You will have to be brave, my dear. I know Olive was your friend.'

Blue eyes offered a stark and emotionless rebuttal. 'She wasn't. We didn't like each other really. She thought I was a rich, spoiled brat. I thought her a jumped-up servant.'

'You accepted her tuition, her hospitality.'

'She was paid to teach me and let me ride on her boat. Even when we first met, on the *Llanstephan Castle*, she expected a tip for not telling Stepmama that she'd caught me smoking. Nothing was free with Olive.'

Nothing was free. Verb tenses say so much and Jemima could only marvel at how quickly Honor van Doorn had adapted to the idea of Olive Nettle existing in the past.

'Who paid her to teach you? You have no money.'

'Haven't you guessed?'

'Lord Muirhaven.'

To her surprise, Honor laughed. 'He hasn't a bean either. Mrs Cleeve paid. She'd give me what I needed out of the housekeeping money Stepmama provided.' When Jemima said nothing in reply, Honor stood up and with a patrician lift of the chin, announced that she could change her clothes without help, thank you.

Jemima walked out. She went to her own room, and there she found Elaine waiting. With a weary, inward groan, Jemima asked to what did she owe the pleasure?

'Is she all right?' Elaine was sitting at the little table where, on her arrival at Castle Gloaming, Jemima had written home to her sister.

'Honor is a survivor, I'm not sure anything touches her.' Jemima sat on the end of her bed, so she and Elaine were on the same level.

'Cornelia found it so,' Elaine agreed. 'She really tried. She loved Honor and so wanted to be loved in return.'

'Did she know that you and Lord Muirhaven were aiding her stepdaughter in her London ambitions?'

Elaine clearly wasn't expecting the question and tripped over her answer. 'We didn't... I mean, we were sympathetic. You heard me say as much.'

'You paid for Honor's painting lessons, squirrelling the money from what Mrs van Doorn gave you.'

A rush of colour to Elaine's cheeks was answer enough. 'We wanted to help. I know what you think about me and Hildebrand.' She extended her left hand, showing the emerald ring securely on the middle finger. 'We aren't having a "thing", but we do care about each other, and with Cornelia gone we have quietly and privately agreed to share our lives. After a decent period of mourning, we'll marry.'

'And Honor?'

'Is our ward until she's of age. We will acclimatise her to the reality in our own way, and I would appreciate your discretion.'

'Consider my discretion applied. Rather fast, if I may say, with Mrs van Doorn's body still lying in the grounds.'

Elaine gave a rucked smile. 'I was expecting that. You think Hildebrand to be inconstant.'

I think him much, much worse than that. Jemima did not say it out loud.

Elaine continued, 'Engaged to one woman on Friday, to another on Sunday.'

'I'm reminded of the rhyme of Solomon Grundy.'

'Born on Monday, buried on Sunday. Do you have an inexhaustible supply of clever sayings, Mrs Flowerday?' Elaine didn't seem to want an answer. 'The engagement will remain private until Cornelia is laid to rest, her death explained and vindicated. Before you judge me too harshly, Jemima—'

Jemima again. The sun has burst from behind the clouds.

'Before you judge me too harshly,' Elaine repeated, 'Hildebrand did not ask Cornelia to marry him.'

That was too much. 'He jolly well did. I was there, she showed me the ring – the one you now wear.'

'Hear me out. You interrupted them late in the proceedings. Cornelia asked Hildebrand to marry *her*. Begged him. He, being a gentleman behind that gruff exterior, felt he had no choice but to say yes.'

Hogwash, was Jemima's opinion, but she managed a show of contrition. 'Goodness, Elaine, dear. I got it totally wrong.'

Elaine smiled benignly. Jemima smiled back, feeling the effort in every tooth of her jaw. These people thought she was halfway to half-witted, but she would indulge their games for now.

'I'll bring Honor down with me. Are we having cocktails?' she asked.

'Um... there's no ice. At least, nobody wishes to replenish the ice bucket, you understand?'

'Perfectly.'

'Sherry will be served and Mrs Beddoe has promised more of those delicious laver toasts.'

'Let's dress up, then,' Jemima suggested.

Elaine grimaced.

'We should,' Jemima insisted. 'Out of respect for Mrs van Doorn who always looked pristine and stylish despite her tribulations.'

'Tribulations?' echoed Elaine.

Jemima, who prided herself on her reading of minute facial betrayals, thought, she doesn't know her employer was, to use a vulgar phrase, broker than the seventh commandment. Poor as a church mouse, rocks in her pocket and moths making hay in her purse.

'Despite living here, so remotely, I meant to say. I did admire her, keeping up appearances as though she were Countess already.' Jemima went to her wardrobe and pulled out a dress the colour of holly berries. 'I shall give this sweet thing an outing.'

'All right. You win. As a future Countess, I shall wear green.'

'We'll clash.'

'Won't we just.' Elaine flashed her left hand. 'Though I meant green to match my ring.'

Chapter Forty-Seven

Jemima rarely spent long dressing, but this time she lingered, waiting for steps in the corridor to tell her that Honor was on her way down. The girl vexed and intrigued Jemima in equal parts. Sweet and confiding one moment, callous and cold the next. However, Jemima could not forget how young she was. Honor's Cape Town education wouldn't have prepared her to navigate this swerve in her circumstances. To find herself the ward of Lord Muirhaven and Elaine Cleeve... what a blow. Jemima was thankful she had made sympathetic, but watertight, arrangements for her own children in the event of her death.

She took up her journal, casting an inquisitor's eye over her paragraphs. The later ones had been written after her brush with poisoning, but, even so, the shape of the letters showed her that even then, the handwriting was recognisably hers.

Elaine had made the addendum to Honor's letter. *When* was obvious. She had to have done it after she discovered Cornelia dead and before she raised the alarm. Horrible as the sight must have been, it hadn't stopped Elaine thinking and acting. *Why* was simple: *H is trying to kill me* would focus the investigating officers' suspicions on Honor.

The rich stepmother was dead. Get the heiress hanged for murder, or legally disbarred from inheriting and who would get the money?

Good question. The uncle and nieces in Cape Town might reasonably expect to be next in line. However, Jemima had greater respect for Lord Muirhaven than that. 'What's the betting that as well as naming him and Elaine as Honor's guardians, Cornelia was induced to change her will, making them the residual heirs in the event of Honor's demise.'

How would they react when they learned there was no fortune to fight over?

She shook her head. It had taken her too long to see the obvious, that Elaine and Lord Muirhaven had engineered Honor's initial escape to London. They had fed her artistic dreams and provided money. Then Honor had come back, fearing Jemima had seen her on board the *Miss Nettle*, and rattled their plans.

They needed another ploy. Chuck Honor off the tower?

It would be a crude solution. Lord Muirhaven's methods were more subtle, for instance, painting Honor as difficult but vulnerable. Creating anxieties.

Castle Gloaming is affecting you... as it does us all.

That business with the salad servers at dinner, all but forcing them into Honor's hands... and his comment as they moved places at the table: 'Whether she wishes it or not, we must keep her safe.'

Elaine's tack had been different. 'I will never lie to you,' she had assured Cornelia, 'even though I depend on you. Bad marriages have no upside. Honor knows what she wants. Hildebrand does too.'

Between them, they had sought to drive a wedge between Honor and her stepmother. Even those asides of Elaine's, designed to throw suspicion on the servants over the hemlock incident... 'She's quite the *witch*,' Elaine had said of Mrs Beddoe. 'What Mother Beddoe doesn't know about herbs, infusions and natural lore... Did you know, her husband will only plant seeds when the moon is waxing?'

And that under-the-breath aside when Mrs van Doorn had

asked the housekeeper to fill her kettle for her night-time tea: 'Assuming you trust her not to have added a dash of hemlock.'

Clever, pushing Mrs van Doorn to distrust her servants.

A door clicked further along the passage. Putting her journal out of sight, Jemima left her room in time to see Honor making her way towards the mezzanine in a swish of silken pleats and long legs, the blonde hair brushed to a shine, a swinging walk.

Another quick change. Which Honor van Doorn was on her way downstairs for sherry?

Jemima waited till the footsteps echoed up from the floor below, then took the opposite direction, to Honor's bedroom. She found Olive's clothes thrown on the floor. A soiled bandage was on the bed and there was a bloodstained pillowcase in the wastepaper basket, which interested Jemima very much.

But not as much as the contents of the suitcase she had earlier carried upstairs and which she now opened.

Chapter Forty-Eight

The first thing that tumbled out was Jemima's brown velour coat. Calm down, she told herself. There are more important things than the kleptomania of a spoiled minx.

The coat had been brushed, and the torn pocket repaired with a safety pin fastened from the inside, through the lining. A bodge job, which for some reason infuriated Jemima more than the bare-faced theft.

The button was fastened, as it had been when Honor wore it last, though this fact reminded Jemima that when Lord Muirhaven had brought the coat inside after its fall, it had been unbuttoned. Jemima had not thought this out until now, simply noting the inconsistency.

She imagined the moment her coat went off the top of the tower, flaring like a kite. She hadn't seen it happen, but she had seen it on the ground, splayed out. The grotesque belief that it was Honor's body had disordered her at the time, and it was only now that she asked the obvious question.

'Honor claimed an intruder came up behind her and tore the coat from her body. But if so, the button would have flown off and the braiding that secures it would have been ripped.' Jemima might have found the button lying next to the parapet rail. As it was, it remained securely attached, her workmanship unblemished.

What if the coat had been pulled clean over Honor's head during the assault, leaving the button intact? 'Then my coat would not have opened out when it hit the ground. Where does that get me?'

It got her to the conclusion that Honor van Doorn's account of the attack on her did not hold water. Jemima laid the coat on the bed and removed the safety pin from the pocket. On the underside of the fabric was a reddish orange streak. It looked like rust. 'Curious,' she said. 'I have never put a rusty nail in my pocket.'

Turning back to the suitcase, she ignored the few clothes packed inside, the map of London streets, the toilet bag and the letter from the Slade School. She was more interested in items that were wrapped in a tablecloth, probably the one from the occasional table in the window. Opening it out, she discovered a number of sketches as well as oil paintings on coated paper. Jemima laid them on the bed. The vibrancy of the pictures, which intermingled faces, figures, flowers and geometric designs, gave the same pleasure as she'd felt looking at Olive's undried painting on the boat. These were all signed HON, written vertically.

H
O
N

'Such talent. Such gimlet-eyed determination to pursue a dream.'

Jemima took the pillowcase from the wastepaper basket. The blood on it looked to be a day or two old. Truly, Gwen had given up on her chambermaid duties, or perhaps Honor had given instructions that her bedroom was not to be 'done'.

Something fell from the folds. Jemima picked up the object then squeamishly dropped it. 'Ugh, surely not.' She crumpled the pillowcase around it and returned it to the bin. A trip to Honor's bathroom, searching every surface, the cabinet, even the taps, soap and towels, confirmed her suspicions that Castle Gloaming was a place soused in deceit. A generator of cruel and deadly mirages.

Leaving the bathroom, she opened Honor's wardrobe and viewed the rail of clothes with their Régal labels. The linen trousers and top Honor had come home in lay in a heap on the wardrobe floor. She picked them up and felt along their seams. The dirt would never come out; they might as well be sent down for rags. But her purpose was served after she established that neither garment had a pocket.

There were three hats on the wardrobe's top shelf. One navy, suitable for church. An oilskin cap for wet-weather walks, and, newly returned, a white openwork sunhat with a scarlet silk flower.

Jemima held the hat up to the light. Unlike the linen outfit, it bore not a trace of mud. The flower had come loose, though. Stitches holding it to the band had been levered away.

A voice she had come to know sounded a warning.

Don't touch, sister.

Taking off her shoes so she could run silently, Jemima slipped across to the Countess's suite. She locked the door with a quiet click, crossed to the sideboard and pointed to the kettle.

Don't. Touch.

Yet she did, with the greatest care.

When you sup with the Devil, take a long spoon. Jemima used a hat pin from Mrs van Doorn's dressing table. She slid it into the kettle, felt the tiny perforations at the base and hooked something out.

The veil tore. In an instant, every shadow, every lie, every hidden cruelty stood exposed.

Never assume, never presume. Only then will you see what is hidden in plain sight.

Shaken, Jemima returned to Honor's quarters. She swaddled the hat in a bathroom towel. After repacking the suitcase, she made the first of a series of trips to the dining room, taking items away: Honor's hat, suitcase, her wastepaper basket. Jemima also reclaimed her coat as, for the time being, that was evidence too.

From her own room, she removed the murder weapon from under the bed, still preserved inside the stocking. She took that to the dining room too, and placed it, with all her haul, inside the massive mahogany sideboard.

There was a serving plate on the sideboard, a carving knife and a spirit kettle. Jemima lifted the knife. Her voice rich and resonant, she declared, 'What I will reveal tonight might induce a guilty person to desperate action.'

'Mrs Flowerday?' Mrs Beddoe was in the doorway. 'What are you doing?'

'I know who killed Mrs van Doorn and tonight you will hear. Mrs Beddoe, would you please put this blade away somewhere safe. Oh, is Mairwen back?'

'No.' The housekeeper took the knife, clearly uncertain if Jemima was in the grip of some kind of mental attack. 'She never returned with the butter and cream she went for. I expect she decided to go on home, take them there instead. You really believe you know what happened to poor Mrs van Doorn?'

'Not exactly *what*, but I know who and how. That's two out of three. You will also hear my theory as to who put hemlock in the salad.'

'Oh, dear.'

'Mrs Beddoe, as it's just you and Gwen to serve tonight, could I beg a favour? Would you leave as much time as possible between courses, and present as many as you can? We need more than cold ham and potatoes, please. For instance, bring in a salad after the soup.'

'Salad? What will Lord Muirhaven say?'

'Plenty, and that will be fascinating. Please trust me.'

Mrs Beddoe left having informed Jemima that sherry was being poured in the drawing room. Jemima returned to her room to pick up her evening bag. Papers from Mrs van Doorn's suite, including the tradesmen's bills she'd failed to pass over to Elaine, went inside. She was now ready to join the company.

In the drawing room, she accepted a sherry from Elaine who wore an elegant drape-neck dress of green spotted silk. Honor, her lips painted with what struck Jemima as an admirably firm hand, was sipping a schooner and looking at nothing in particular.

'How is your poor fingernail?' Jemima asked.

Honor snapped out of her reverie and displayed the fingers of her left hand. A strip of clean cotton was wrapped around the middle one. It wasn't a bandage from Mrs Beddoe's first-aid box and looked as though it had been cut from a handkerchief. 'It hurts like mad,' Honor said piteously.

'It must. You have a will to survive, Honor. A nail ripped right off as you clung on for your life to a parapet rail...' Jemima shuddered.

Elaine begged her, 'Oh, don't.'

Lord Muirhaven and Sergeant Maddox were discussing the non-arrival of CID, which led to observations on the flooding that had affected the county. The sergeant feared that more would occur when all that had fallen as rain flowed off the uplands. In the gloomy pause that followed, Maddox asked Lord Muirhaven if he had visited the horseshoe falls at Llantysilio.

'No? You should, sir, they are a piece of engineering. They funnel water from the Dee into the canal and when the river's high, the weirs and sluices gush.'

Jemima heard Elaine draw a nervous breath. She really was mortally afraid of water. Feeling this conversation was unlikely to advance her plans, Jemima interrupted, saying brightly, 'During my time here, Sergeant, I've learned so much about the natural world. Plants, herbs, the saintly ones' – here, a smile for Lord Muirhaven – 'and the devilish ones. In fact—' she caught Honor's attention. 'My dear, would you run to the library and find me a book?'

Honor scowled. 'Must I?'

'No, of course not. Only my ankles are tired and I rather feel one favour deserves another.'

Under the makeup, a blush touched Honor's cheeks. 'All right. What book?'

'It's called *Wildflowers of Field and Hedgerow*. There's something I want to show the sergeant.'

Honor left, more sherry was poured. Gwen came in with appetisers, rounds of black bread, toasted and spread with anchovy paste and the seaweed Jemima had learned to call laver. Sergeant Maddox took two, expressing appreciation. A true Welshman. For her, laver was an acquired taste, but she had to admit, its saltiness was perfect with a medium sherry.

Honor returned from the library saying, 'It's not there, but here's one that might do.' She handed Jemima *Wildflowers of Wetland, Stream and Marsh*.

'Thank you. Clearly, you knew exactly where to go.'

Honor shrugged. Said, 'Yes,' then, slowly, the colour behind her makeup drained.

The ribbon marking *Oenanthe crocata*, hemlock water-dropwort, was in place. The bad, bad cousin of the carrot family. Medium of murder.

'What did you wish to show me?' asked Sergeant Maddox, taking more of the appetisers.

'It can wait.'

Mrs Beddoe was at the door, signalling to Elaine that dinner was served.

Chapter Forty-Nine

Lord Muirhaven gallantly offered his arm to Jemima, who accepted it while holding the book on wetland flowers in her free hand. Sergeant Maddox offered an arm each to Elaine and Honor.

As they crossed the great hall, Jemima glanced at her escort's chest. He was wearing the maroon velvet dinner jacket, clearly a favourite, and she remarked on the absence of a buttonhole.

'Well, it hardly feels right.'

'Oh, no, it's always right. If only in memory of absent dear ones. Look.' She brought them to a stop beside the centre plinth. A new flower arrangement had been created for the Chinese vase. Perhaps Mrs Beddoe enjoyed doing it as it allowed her to go outside among her plants. 'Look, Bobbies' Buttons.' Jemima pointed to the stems of Kerria with their gold, globe-shape flowers, rising alongside blood-red dogwood and tawny willow wands. 'Pick a spray from the top where it's less twiggy.'

Seduced, persuaded or duped – where did one begin and another start? – her companion did as she suggested. He reached and the satin cuff of his jacket fell back, revealing his shirt cuff, which also rode up to expose his wristwatch. The watch itself shifted half an inch or so. Before, Jemima had assumed the strap was too tight. Perhaps it was, but where the sun had failed to touch his skin, Jemima saw not just the mottled lesions she'd noticed before, but a lone, glistening blister. Small, but utterly damning.

When they reached the dining room, nobody quite knew who should sit where. Jemima seized on the hesitation.

'I recall last time, Mrs van Doorn sat here at the head. I sat here.' Jemima patted the back of the chair that had been to her hostess's right. 'You were to be there, Lord Muirhaven.' She pointed to the chair opposite. 'But you kindly moved so that Miss van Doorn might sit on her stepmother's left. You ensured Honor remained beside you, so you could keep her safe.'

'You have a better memory than I.' Lord Muirhaven was fixing his buttonhole in place with a pearl-headed pin.

Jemima suggested that Elaine should sit at the head of the table. 'Perhaps with Honor at your left, where she sat before. I'll sit at your right and perhaps Sergeant Maddox could seat himself beside Miss van Doorn? That places you beside me, Lord Muirhaven.'

'Always a pleasure, Mrs Flowerday.'

The gentlemen pulled out the chairs, the ladies sat, everyone sat. A rumbling sound signalled the first course was being hoisted up in the dumb waiter. Moments later, Mrs Beddoe brought in a tureen. As the housekeeper went around the table, ladling out steaming white-onion soup, Jemima played her first gambit.

'Last time we dined together, Mrs van Doorn was present. The soup was spinach and lemon, but the meal was curtailed, Sergeant, by the appearance of *Conium maculatum* among the salad leaves.'

'Cony – you've lost me,' said the policeman.

'Oh, sorry. Too much study brings out the Latin. Hemlock. I spotted it, no pun intended, as its stem is covered in a kind of purplish Morse code,' Jemima explained. 'I stopped everyone from taking any and, fortunately, nobody was harmed. We were all in a spin as to how it got there. Mrs Beddoe' – she smiled apologetically at the housekeeper, who was standing back from the table with a frown tied to her brows – 'was the first to be blamed. And then Mairwen, the maid who was sacked. It took me an absurdly long time to work out how it got here, but now I would like to tell you.'

'Take care, Mrs Flowerday.' Lord Muirhaven angled himself to glower at her. 'Something warns me you are edging onto slanderous territory.'

'The truth is never slander. Would you like to know, Sergeant?'

'Indeed I would, madam.'

'It came up here on Lord Muirhaven's arm. Two sprigs, tucked under the gold links of his watch.'

A gasp from Honor drowned out Elaine's protest. Lord Muirhaven slammed his wine glass down on the table, telling Jemima, 'I warned you.'

'The enclave beside his gatehouse is bursting with hemlock. Like a fool, I brushed my hand against it on day one and paid the price.' She displayed her thumb and index finger, the blisters now long past the painful stage. '"Never touch without gloves". I was taught that at school. If Lord Muirhaven would roll up his sleeves, you will see what I mean. The sap of hemlock causes a rash and when the blisters are rubbed, by a watch strap, say, they get very sore.'

To her surprise, Lord Muirhaven rolled up his jacket and shirt sleeve and showed the lesions. 'It's because my watch is too tight. It needs a couple more links added, but you can't get that sort of thing done around here.'

'I should imagine not.' Jemima nodded. 'South Africa would be the place. Cape Town.'

'That's Western Cape. I lived near Durban, Eastern Cape.'

'You deny bringing hemlock into this room, concealed in your clothing?'

'I not only deny it, I consider it the ramblings of a disturbed mind.'

'Oh, well, you're right there,' Jemima conceded. 'My mind has taken injury while I've been here, but my logic remains intact. I agree, your wrist has been rubbed raw, but constriction does not create a blister like the one beneath your watch strap.'

Their soup was in danger of growing cold. Jemima started eating hers and after a moment, the others did too, though she felt wary eyes on her. After Mrs Beddoe removed the bowls, Jemima said, 'In a moment, I'll show you how Lord Muirhaven did it.'

Mrs Beddoe came back from the annexe with a large salad dish. Jemima got up and strode towards her. 'Allow me.'

She took the dish from the surprised woman and carried it to the table, placing it in front of Honor. 'All yours, my dear, would you toss the leaves?'

Honor looked horrified. 'My hand is hurt and I'll never eat salad again.'

'Spinach, a little sorrel, lettuce leaves like cherub wings, and sliced radish. Nothing to fear. Any dressing, Mrs Beddoe?'

The housekeeper marched away and came back with a bottle. Jemima shook it hard, then poured a generous amount over the leaves. Standing between Hildebrand and Honor, she made a big show of tossing the salad, making the leaves jump. 'Now, you see, I have already dropped a sprig of hemlock into the salad. I did it with one dextrous flick of the wrist as I relieved Mrs Beddoe of the dish. I did it in the middle of the room, where the candlelight doesn't reach, and not even Mrs Beddoe saw me do it. But then, I am slick with my fingers. You should see me shuffling cards, it makes people dizzy. That way, I ensure I always have the aces.'

'Are you calling me a card sharp, Mrs Flowerday?'

'I could believe it of you, Lord Muirhaven, but if you are, it doesn't bother me. I am going to call you far worse.'

'Take care, madam,' grumbled Sergeant Maddox. 'You malign a peer of the realm.'

'I'm an egalitarian, Sergeant. I malign without fear or favour. And so, the hemlock is nicely covered with a dark dressing, but I am not finished. I offer the bowl to Miss van Doorn, inviting her to toss the salad. I move the servers closer to her, and as I do so, I drop the second hemlock cutting into her lap, so that when she eventually gets up from the table, it will fall on the floor and be found under her chair. Thus incriminating her.'

Honor sent Lord Muirhaven a look of revulsion. 'You wanted it to look as though I'd brought it in with me?'

'Certainly not, my dear,' his Lordship said in a tone of silky dismissal. 'Mrs Flowerday was brought here by poor Cornelia to solve a mystery and is doing her best to ensure she goes home with her pay cheque.'

'Oh, the pay cheque,' Jemima said. 'I fear, as the drunken sailor said from the quayside, "that ship has sailed". Let me finish my story. You would do well to take notes, Sergeant.'

'I would rather enjoy my dinner,' Sergeant Maddox replied, now seeming more disgruntled than fascinated.

Jemima felt a pang of anxiety. The sergeant had to come onto her team, so to speak, else she was going out alone on a dangerous limb. Still, no choice but to battle on.

'Having set up Honor as the potential poisoner, I now need to ensure my dressed hemlock gets onto the right plate. May I offer you salad, Mrs van Doorn?' She held the bowl towards Elaine.

'Oh, how tasteless!' Elaine burst out. 'Lord Muirhaven was mightily fond of Cornelia. Protective too.'

'And yet,' Jemima replied, 'he offered the salad bowl to her first, saying, if I correctly recall, "May I serve you?" He was going to plonk hemlock on her plate all right.'

'And poison her at her own table?'

'Of course not. He'd be the one to spot it and raise the alarm. Unfortunately for his plan, on that evening Mrs van Doorn had no appetite for greenery.' Jemima fixed a dark eye on Lord Muirhaven. 'I will try to forgive you, my Lord, for presenting the bowl to me next. I took the leaf, and I suspect you would have let me eat it. I have Mrs Beddoe to thank for an impromptu botany lesson that afternoon, alerting me to the danger.'

'I am not a poisoner.' Lord Muirhaven remained calm. The tension was in the room, not in his face. 'If you are accusing me of killing my dear, dear Cornelia—' His voice broke. 'If you are, then I would beg you to pause. Consider whether I would bring down the woman I wished to make my wife.'

'I have, and I'm not.' Jemima let her words fly into the shadows, soft-winged hope bringing balm to raw, red nerves. There was a palpable relaxation around the table. 'I'm not accusing you. But Cornelia van Doorn was poisoned and not by accident. She was murdered by somebody in this room.'

Nobody leapt to their feet. Nobody broke glassware or even a plate. Elaine Cleeve folded her hands in her lap. Mrs Beddoe shut herself in the annexe. Honor regained her expression of blank incomprehension.

Belatedly, Sergeant Maddox took out his notebook.

Disturbingly, Lord Muirhaven began to laugh.

A few miles away, in the gathering dark, a train pulled into Trevor station and four men got off. All wore suits in shades of taupe and grey, and put on felt hats as they walked along the platform. Two were dark-haired and wiry. A third had the pink complexion and gingery hair of the Anglo Saxon. The fourth was stout, jowly and wore round, rimless glasses that would later prompt Jemima to describe him in her journal as looking like a farmer who ploughs by day and studies for a diploma in law at night. The stationmaster, who had been warned of their arrival by a telephone call, came out to greet them.

He welcomed them in Welsh first, then English, saying, 'I have found a car and driver. He will take you as far as is possible by road to Castell Glan yr Afon, though I should warn you, gentlemen, there will be a muddy walk to the castle gate.'

At the same moment, a figure approached the castle from the direction of the river. Unheard above the water's roar, boots cracked twigs and crunched on leaf litter. At the door of the icehouse, the footsteps paused.

At the locked tower entrance they stalled a second time, turned back and continued around the castle's perimeter to the kitchen door.

Chapter Fifty

'How do I know Mrs van Doorn was deliberately—'

The shriek stopped Jemima mid-sentence. She hurried into the annexe off the dining room. 'Mrs Beddoe, what is it?'

'Young Gwen, I don't know.' The housekeeper was peering into the vent of one of the dumb waiters.

Jemima leaned into the other and called, 'Are you all right down there?'

'She won't speak English if she's upset.'

'Then you do it.'

Mrs Beddoe repeated the question in Welsh. A tremulous voice answered.

'She says somebody has arrived,' Mrs Beddoe told Jemima.

'Who?'

Mrs Beddoe asked Gwen who. The answer was hard to hear, but Jemima caught a reference to 'Mairwen'. She'd come back, then. Good.

'Do you want me to continue serving dinner?' Mrs Beddoe asked.

'Oh, yes. I want to keep everyone in one place.' Jemima went back to the dining table.

'You were saying Mrs van Doorn was deliberately something,' Sergeant Maddox reprised.

'Poisoned. The violence of her death isn't proof of intent. The proof lies in the timing. I've demonstrated that the hemlock incident was a diversion, performed by Lord Muirhaven, and done with Mrs Cleeve's collusion.'

'With...' Sergeant Maddox had been writing, but now he lifted his pencil and looked at Elaine. 'You're accusing this lady too?'

'I'm afraid so,' Jemima replied. 'The reason nobody saw Lord Muirhaven drop hemlock onto Miss van Doorn's lap was because, at the critical moment, Elaine launched into a story about her mother believing lettuce to be God's excuse for a good salad dressing. It drew all eyes to her. I fell right into the hole and rabbited on about my mother's home-made salad cream. Call it sleight of hand. A music-hall magician can steal a man's tie from around his neck, if he persuades the gentleman that his shoelaces are on fire.'

'I was making conversation.' Elaine sounded outraged, offended.

The one thing she couldn't hide from Jemima was the almost inaudible drone of fear in her voice.

'What you were doing – you, Elaine, you, Lord Muirhaven – was setting up Honor as a poisoner.'

'To cast blame for murder onto Miss van Doorn?' queried the sergeant.

'Not murder, no. Their motive was to blacken Honor in the eyes of her stepmother, part of a strategy to deprive her of Mrs van Doorn's favour. They'd already helped her get to London. That failed, but they were banking on the probability that if she made a second dash for freedom, after an apparent attempt at poisoning, she'd be cut out of Mrs van Doorn's will. Lord Muirhaven and Mrs Cleeve had already persuaded Cornelia to make them Honor's guardians in the event of a tragedy, as we discovered earlier. It's not many steps from there to flattering an isolated woman into rewriting her will and marrying the man who wants her money.' Jemima took a breath, then continued.

'I haven't seen Mrs van Doorn's will, but I witnessed the moment Cornelia consented to marry Lord Muirhaven. Her death did him no favours.' She addressed those words directly to Lord Muirhaven, who stared back, unflinching. 'My charge against Mrs Cleeve is that she colluded in a dangerous prank that could have killed me, or somebody else, and allowed others to be blamed. I refer to the hemlock. Then worse, on finding her employer dead, instead of immediately raising the alarm, Elaine doctored a note written by Honor to her stepmother.'

Jemima opened her handbag. She placed the letter on the table and Elaine attempted to snatch it. Sergeant Maddox got there first.

'"No. No. No.",' he read. '"H is trying to kill me." Who is H? Who wrote this?'

'The main part was written by Honor. A handwriting expert will judge if those postscripts are the work of Mrs Cleeve. Or you could consult an averagely intelligent seven-year-old. Elaine' – Jemima shook her head – 'very badly done, in both senses. And rather foolish. Did you forget, in the heat of the moment, the 'H' could be Honor, or indeed Hildebrand?'

Lord Muirhaven gave Elaine a hard glance, suggesting all this was news to him. 'Did you do that?' he asked Elaine.

'No.' Elaine's colour was rising. 'No.' *Yes. Sorry. I didn't think.*

So Jemima interpreted the harrowed look Elaine threw towards Lord Muirhaven. He had no right to look so put out. His turn now.

'Mrs Cleeve's actions could be called vexatious,' Jemima said. 'Lord Muirhaven does not escape so lightly.'

He sat back, arms folded, putting on a good show of being amused.

'I have said already that I don't accuse either Elaine or Lord Muirhaven of murdering Cornelia van Doorn. But I know it was done, and I know how and who, if not exactly *what* caused it.'

Sergeant Maddox interrupted. 'If you are intending to accuse, and ensnaring others into answering, you are not only exceeding your rights as a civilian, Mrs Flowerday, but your actions could be construed as entrapment.'

Jemima acknowledged the hit. 'Shall I tell you in private?'

'Oh, don't spoil the fun,' Lord Muirhaven jumped in. 'I don't mind. Do you, Elaine?'

'I mind very much.'

'We can take it. What about you, Honor, do you want Mrs Flowerday and the sergeant to retire behind closed doors?'

But Honor was still looking at her letter, her irises flickering. She reminded Jemima of a little girl who has a painting to take home to her parents, only to find it scribbled on by another child.

'While Honor is gathering her thoughts, I say Mrs Flowerday should proceed.' Lord Muirhaven had adopted a joshing tone. 'I give her permission to slander me to her heart's content.'

'Very well.' Sergeant Maddox invited Jemima to continue.

She secretly believed he relished the idea of more revelations and had only been doing his dull duty earlier.

From the sideboard, Jemima took out her coat and laid it on the table, at the far end. 'It begins when I, Mrs Cleeve and Mrs van Doorn were in her sitting room, enjoying a cup of fennel tea. I was certain I heard someone outside the door, but by the time I got up and opened it, whoever was there had gone. However, I saw petals on the threshold and from that I deduced someone had come with flowers. Honor later confirmed to me that it was indeed her, and like all eavesdroppers, she heard no good of herself. Miss van Doorn?' Jemima pitched her voice so Honor could not ignore her. 'I'm afraid you heard us discussing your prospects and your talents.'

'You said I had none.'

'Not quite, but I can understand that from your point of view it wasn't a ringing endorsement.' Jemima explained to Sergeant Maddox how Honor had applied for art school, and been accepted, but was unable to take up her place unless her stepmother gave consent. 'She was in a bind, and I strongly sympathised. I don't like keeping birds in cages, and I don't agree with keeping daughters at home, counting the hours until they marry.'

'You encouraged Miss van Doorn to rebel?' Maddox sounded disapproving.

'Not rebel, just stand her ground. I also encouraged her to make amends with her stepmother, believing that outright opposition would only make things harder. I hoped to persuade Mrs van Doorn to take a house in London, which would enable Honor to attend the Slade. My plea fell on stony ground, for reasons I will explain in due course. Honor overheard this conversation and resolved to leave Castle Gloaming come what may.'

'Cornelia threatened to disinherit her,' Elaine spat out. 'That's why Honor murdered her. You did, didn't you? Killed her before she could enact her threat.'

Honor shook her head. Beneath her makeup she was pale as milk. 'I did not.'

'We'll come to that,' Jemima said. 'Today, in Mrs van Doorn's suite, I realised that I'd misinterpreted what I heard regarding the inheritance. Cornelia didn't threaten to cut Honor off from her fortune. What Mrs van Doorn said was, "There will be no money".'

'Exactly,' Elaine came back sharply. 'No money for Honor if she went to London. Cornelia absolutely was threatening to disinherit her.'

'No! She was stating the pure truth. There was no more money, not two beans in the pot. Cornelia van Doorn was telling us she was penniless.'

'Rubbish,' Elaine snapped. 'She was awaiting funds from Cape Town.'

Jemima dropped the tradesmen's brown envelopes on the table, letting them land with a thwack. She then passed around the letter from the manager of the Provincial & Overseas Bank. Had she been cynical, she might have believed the intakes of breath were deeper than those that accompanied the news of Cornelia van Doorn's death.

When the letter made its way back to her, she said, 'Don't ask me how, but she spent it all.'

'She was broke?' Finally Lord Muirhaven had heard something that rocked him to the core. 'What about the diamonds?'

'I don't know,' said Jemima. 'They might be real, or they might be paste. Whatever they are, they'll be sold to pay tradespeople in this neighbourhood.'

Lord Muirhaven looked as if he had been hit with an iron bar. So did Honor, who said in a small voice, 'I heard Uncle Geoffrey telling her before we left Cape Town, "Wherever you go, Cornelia, debts go too." I thought he was talking about her not paying my last term's school fees. That was embarrassing. She said she wouldn't because I didn't pass my exam. I didn't realise she couldn't...' Honor's voice trailed off.

Of them all, Elaine seemed the least poleaxed. Jemima surmised that, despite her denials, she had already scented the first smoke of the forest fire.

'Let me explain the rest,' Jemima said. 'After drinking fennel tea with Mrs van Doorn and Elaine, I went to my room. There I found my wardrobe had been ransacked. I suspected Honor and I tracked her to the top of the tower, planning her next escape bid.' Leaning down, she retrieved *Wildflowers of Wetland, Stream and Marsh* and opened it at the yellow ribbon, taking it to Sergeant Maddox.

'Hemlock water-dropwort,' the policeman read.

'There's another book on field and hedgerow flowers in the library, with a yellow ribbon marking the page for hemlock. Common hemlock. Don't confuse the two, they are very different plants, though from the same wide-ranging family. Mrs Beddoe can tell you more.'

The housekeeper had emerged from her annexe, and answered Jemima's question, 'Which is the more poisonous?' by pointing at the book in Sergeant Maddox's hand.

'The dropwort. Nobody with any sense picks it. They're both bad, but if you're careful with hemlock, it has its uses. *If* you know the dosage. But the dropwort, having it near will make your head spin. You'll be sick from the vapour if you cut a stem. They used to kill people with it in the old days, criminals and those they called witches. Horrible. Horrible.'

Jemima couldn't but agree. 'I had a dose – a tiny, tiny dose I believe. So did you, Lord Muirhaven.'

He shook his head. 'I don't think so.'

'You "felt off" you said, the same night I was dreadfully ill. The same night Mrs van Doorn was killed. Later, you passed it off as too much whisky.'

He frowned. 'We all got a dose?'

'Not Elaine, not Honor.' Jemima went to her coat, giving it a loving stroke. 'I really had to think it through. What did I touch that you touched, but which Elaine and Honor did not? Answer, my coat and my gloves.'

A short silence was broken by Lord Muirhaven. 'Honor wore your coat to go up the tower.'

'She also stole my gloves.' Jemima went to the sideboard and took out the green bouclé skirt she had worn on the final day of Mrs van Doorn's life. Using a napkin she'd earlier placed with this in mind, she removed the kidskin gloves from its pocket. 'Now we come to the "What". I propose that Honor found a supply of hemlock water-dropwort. I had already seen some, outside the castle, and took it to be—'

'Flat-leaf parsley,' said Mrs Beddoe. 'Many a life lost in that way.'

'I do question the Almighty's wisdom,' Jemima said, 'creating a family of plants that includes carrot, parsley, parsnip and both hemlocks. Honor acquired dropwort.'

'How could I? I don't know anything about plants!' Honor half rose, but sat back down as Sergeant Maddox cleared his throat. 'This woman is making up stories. Because she did it. She killed Stepmama.'

'You can accuse me when I've finished,' Jemima told her. 'You say you know nothing about plants?' She pointed to the book Sergeant Maddox had kept by his elbow. 'You consulted this and another in the series, marking the pages that interested you. Then you forgot, as unprepared criminals always do.'

'I never touched that book in my life!'

'No? This very evening, I asked you to fetch me *Wildflowers of Field and Hedgerow*, which I'd hidden in a section devoted to dictionaries. You came back with an appropriate substitute in under four minutes. Because you knew where to go. You had sat at the library table, researching poisonous plants.'

Honor looked across at Lord Muirhaven, then at the sergeant. 'It isn't true.'

'Tell us where you got the dropwort, Honor,' Jemima quietly demanded.

'It grows around the canal's edge,' Mrs Beddoe put in. 'And alongside the river.'

'And is collected by highly skilled, or highly foolish, people.' Jemima fetched the waste bin she'd brought from Honor's room, and again shielding her hand with the napkin, took out a screwed-up ball of waxed paper. She undid it and rolled something resembling a very tiny parsnip onto the table. 'Can you identify this, Mrs Beddoe?'

She could, only too well. 'It's the root of hemlock water-dropwort.'

You can see why they call it dead man's finger. Don't touch it. Don't even breathe near it.'

'I won't. How does it come to be in your waste bin, Honor?'

Honor's silence, the desperate dart of her tongue between tight lips, told Jemima the girl was backed up a blind alley. She didn't need to wring a confession out of her, as Sergeant Maddox was witness enough.

'Only Honor knows why she killed her stepmother,' Jemima said, ignoring the expulsion of breaths around her. 'But I do know when and how. As I said, I followed her up to the tower and found her waiting to signal to her friend Olive, who would pass by on her boat. Perhaps I haven't made it clear to you, Sergeant, but Olive was giving Honor painting lessons. Paid for by Elaine Cleeve and Lord Muirhaven.'

Neither Elaine nor Lord Muirhaven contradicted.

'I say "was" giving lessons, as she's no longer alive to bear witness. Honor would signal from the tower, and when Olive saw a light flashing, she would moor up after the aqueduct. Honor would join her and paint as they steamed along. On one occasion, Olive took Honor to the railway station at Chirk so she could get to London, and picked her up on her return. She then let Honor stay on her boat to work out her next move. I suspect Honor found my presence on the canalside uncomfortable. I peered through the cabin window, quite a breach of etiquette. She interpreted my curiosity as a threat and fled home. Now to the point. Olive kept a bucket of hemlock water-dropwort on her boat.'

'She used the roots to make rat poison,' Honor rasped. 'You get rats on the canal. There's no way to keep them off.'

'I mistook it for its culinary cousin and Olive put me right. She shouted, "It's not parsley. Don't touch it!" I can now appreciate her urgency. You brought some of the deadly root home with you.'

Honor shook her head fiercely. 'I wouldn't be so stupid.'

Back to the sideboard Jemima went. She took out a white object and held it up.

'A towel?' said Elaine.

'Oh, wait.' Jemima opened the towel and walked around the table, showing what was inside. 'Stay clear, everyone. Recognise this, Honor?'

'My hat.' It came out almost as a sigh.

Jemima knew that Honor knew the game was up.

'When Lord Muirhaven carried you in, after your dramatic return, he was clutching this hat. I was intrigued that while your clothes were smeared with mud, the hat remained pristine. I had also wondered later how you could have secreted a dropwort root when the clothes you were wearing that day had no pockets. It turns out, you were very careful with the hat because you'd hidden the dropwort root under the red silk peony, a few stitches removed to make space.' Jemima angled her parcel to show the vibrant flower on the side of the hat.

'It's a protea,' said Lord Muirhaven. 'Not a peony.'

'My apologies. It did the job, though. Miss van Doorn wisely wrapped the part of the root she did not use in something secure before she disposed of it...' Jemima indicated the waxed paper. 'High risk, even higher for the poor maid who would empty her bedroom bin, but I don't believe Honor has much time for the servant class.

'She had the means to kill, but knowing how dangerous this root can be, took the wise measure of stealing my gloves. I touched those gloves later, before we played cards, which is how I got a trace of the poison in my system.'

'And me?' asked Lord Muirhaven. 'I was only mildly ill.'

'You picked up my coat from the courtyard, where it had landed after Honor dropped it from the tower.'

'What do you mean, dropped it? She was attacked,' said Elaine. 'Are you saying that was a charade?'

Jemima agreed that, sadly, it was. 'At the top of the tower, I felt I must stop her running away again. The lantern she used for signalling was at the other side of the tower, and I went to fetch it, meaning to take it away with me. I admit, her scream was extraordinary, such lungs! I thought she was being murdered. It is clear to me now that in the few seconds she was out of my sight, she unbuttoned my coat and hurled it over the parapet, then dashed into the tower room and down the stairs. While everyone was in a panic, rushing out to the courtyard, she was planting poison in Mrs van Doorn's suite.'

Honor was shaking her head. 'No. This is insane.'

'You faked the attack in the tower, and your injuries.'

'Faked?' Honor held up her bandaged fingers. Fresh blood had seeped into the cotton strip, and Jemima suspected she'd been worrying it while she sat listening to the accusations.

Jemima sighed. 'If someone comes up behind you and tries to wrench a coat off your shoulders, it causes damage. A button flies off. Seams are ripped. None of this happened. When I saw Honor on the tower, wearing my coat, it was buttoned. My theory is, and it is only a theory, that having unfastened the coat, Honor smacked it against the tower masonry.'

'Why on earth would I do that?'

'To scare the crows, of course.'

'Rooks,' said Lord Muirhaven.

Jemima promised she'd try to remember. 'The birds added drama, and Honor likes drama. If anyone wishes to look, there is a rust streak inside my torn coat pocket where I believe it caught on a lantern hook. I can't prove it, of course.'

'You can't prove any of it,' said Honor in a dull voice.

'No, but I can tell you that when I went up to the tower later to fetch my hat, I saw no trace of blood anywhere. I had a lantern, I would have seen spots and splashes, since you had a fingernail ripped off, Honor. However, I saw the pillowcase in your room, absolutely drenched. Stomach-churning.'

'Nail beds bleed.'

'Don't they just. And I admire your ability to endure in a cause you're so passionate about. I won't ruin everyone's appetite by showing the pillowcase or the bloody fingernail I found wrapped within it... My dear, you did it yourself, in your bathroom using nail clippers. You thought you'd cleaned up, but you've had servants in your life too long. There's blood on the underside of the sink, above the pedestal where nobody remembers to look, and some on the shelf because you didn't clean the nail clippers well enough.'

Jemima let the silence hang, then said, 'It's all circumstantial. Except one thing. Mrs Beddoe?' The housekeeper came forward and reluctantly accepted a key from Jemima who said, 'Kindly bring Mrs van Doorn's tea caddies from her suite and the spirit kettle. Protect your hands, touch nothing directly.'

Chapter Fifty-One

While Mrs Beddoe carried out her request, Jemima asked Lord Muirhaven to light the dining-room spirit kettle. Unused for some time, it took a while to coax a flame, but after much priming of the pump, a steady blue halo appeared. When the housekeeper returned with Mrs van Doorn's kettle and other tea things, Jemima asked him to light that one as well.

'We'll need plenty of boiling water,' she said.

When spouts were steaming, she made tea from angelica and valerian, spooning the leaves from Mrs van Doorn's caddy and using the teapot from the dining-room sideboard. 'Mrs van Doorn's sedative, dried and mixed for her by Mrs Beddoe, who swears that nothing harmful was ever added.'

'Nor was it,' the housekeeper said stoutly.

Jemima poured boiling water onto the leaves and rocked the pot to let it steep.

'You're not going to drink it.' Sergeant Maddox was alarmed.

Jemima poured green, fragrant liquid into a china cup. 'Actually, I am. I'm hoping Honor will join me. She's a daredevil at heart.'

'All right.' Honor took the challenge. There was a defiance about her, either born of desperation or a sense of untouchability.

Jemima sipped her tea. Honor did the same. A tense five minutes passed.

'I feel fine,' said Jemima, having emptied her cup. 'I don't believe I'm going to die. Honor?'

'There's nothing wrong with the tea. I didn't poison my step-mother. I keep saying.'

'Mm. I could drink another.' Jemima repeated the process, adding more leaves to the same teapot, but this time filling it from Mrs van Doorn's kettle. Again, she poured two cups and offered one to Honor.

The girl stepped back.

'No?'

'No. No. No!' Honor swiped the cup and saucer from Jemima's hand and it smashed against the sideboard. She ran out of the room.

Jemima said, 'Let her go. She can't get far.' She took Mrs van Doorn's kettle to Sergeant Maddox, placing it on a table mat, flipping up the lid with the end of a spoon. 'Don't touch.'

When the steam had cleared, she invited the sergeant to look inside. Did he see the trivet in the base?

'I do.'

'It's what rattles when the water's boiling. I returned to Mrs van Doorn's suite today and did what I should have done straight away.' Using the same hat pin as before, Jemima lifted the trivet out. 'Now what do you see?'

'Er... something pale-looking stuck to the bottom. Is it a slug?' Sergeant Maddox grimaced.

'Not a slug. It's a sliver of root that was wedged under the trivet. I advise you leave it.'

'What kind of root, Mrs Flowerday?'

'Hemlock water-dropwort.'

'The water was poisoned?' Sergeant Maddox sounded shaken.

'No – the kettle. Anybody who drank tea brewed from its water once Honor had planted the root would die. The only person who did so was Cornelia van Doorn, making her sedative brew after she retired on the fateful night. Though Honor could not have been sure of that. She might have killed any number of people.'

'A murderer, then,' Lord Muirhaven said quietly. 'You really think Honor faked the attack on top of the tower?' He sounded disturbed and intrigued.

'Absolutely,' Jemima said. 'I kept wondering how anybody could race up and down the tower stairs so fast. The answer? They didn't. While I stood frozen, staring at what I thought was Honor's body on the flagstones below, she was already tearing down the stairs. On her way to her stepmother's sitting room which was empty, as Mrs van Doorn had repaired to the drawing room for evening drinks. Honor tampered with the kettle—'

Jemima stopped as though someone had flicked a paper pellet at her. There was always a fly in the ointment, however well thought-out your deductions. The kettle would have still been hot from the tea Elaine had made less than an hour earlier. No time to worry about that.

'She planted the dropwort in the bottom of the kettle, left her stepmother's apartment unseen, ran down the stairs and into the passage that leads to the tower. There she waited until she heard a rumpus in the courtyard, and staggered out claiming to have been attacked. For a girl of seventeen, she has a cold, clear head. The one thing she will not have realised is that fingerprints adhere even to the insides of kettles, and not even boiling water will erase them. That is your proof, Sergeant.'

An ear-piercing scream from the floor below brought everyone to their feet. In the great hall, they found Honor van Doorn crouched with her hands over her face, in apparent terror. At first, Jemima thought that Beddoe had come inside in his work clothes until the lighting of lamps by Mrs Beddoe illuminated the scene.

It wasn't Beddoe, it wasn't a man. It was Olive Nettle, her hair loose, eyes flat with rage and pain for which there were no words. Her unblinking gaze fell on those who had rushed down and were staring at her in stunned silence.

'Someone burned my boat,' Olive intoned. 'Someone killed me.'

Honor screamed again. 'Make her go away, make her go away!'

Jemima walked over and put a hand on Olive's arm, with a rush of inexpressible relief. 'You feel as alive as I am. The *Miss Nettle* burned, and I thought you were on board. What are you saying, "killed you"?'

Brown eyes, strangely familiar, bored into hers. 'The other half of me is dead and that devil did it.' Olive's gaze moved from face to face and stopped at Lord Muirhaven. 'He murdered the one I love and I won't stay silent. The time has come for the reckoning.'

For the first time since he had opened the gates to Jemima on her arrival at the castle, Lord Muirhaven had no practised smile, or suave put-down. He rocked gently back and forth on his feet, his mouth opening and closing. Then, without a word, he loped to the front entrance and let himself out into the night.

Jemima went after him, slowed down by a pair of French-heeled evening shoes. The courtyard was dark, but there was moonlight and she could make out his shape, heading for the gatehouse. He disappeared and she expected to hear the gate whine open, but instead a forceful hammering reached her ears. Fists on wood, and voices. A moment later, torchlight shone and Lord Muirhaven was running back across the courtyard, veering towards a gate in the wall that would take him to the lawn, and ultimately the river. A man in a baggy suit and a hat sprinted after him, shouting for him to stop.

He was caught at the gate and a second man in a suit and hat helped wrestled him to the ground and pin his arms behind his back.

Jemima ran to look and heard one of them say, through his

panting breath, 'Cecil Thomas Cleeve, I am Detective Inspector Pollard of Hampshire Constabulary, and I am arresting you for the wilful murder of Hildebrand Woolton, otherwise known as the Earl of Muirhaven.'

Chapter Fifty-Two

The arrest presented an immediate need – a strongroom in which to place the prisoner. Sergeant Maddox suggested the tower, but Jemima pointed out that, although it was secure when locked, there was an exit route.

'Off the top,' she said. 'You don't want to lose your man that way.'

'This is a castle,' DI Pollard barked. 'Surely you've got a blasted dungeon.'

The intemperate language might have been attributed to him being a heavy man who had ripped his trousers bringing down his target. Hildebrand – Jemima was unable to think of the prisoner as Cecil – had kicked out, catching him on the elbow. A blow to the funny bone affects the temper.

Because of this she answered soothingly, 'It's a modern castle, mostly anyway, all dungeons and oubliettes filled in. Take him to the library. There's only one door.' A desperate man could attempt to escape through the window, but as it was set high up and made of small, lead panes, he would only hurt his head. 'Moreover,' she said, 'the library has enough chairs and a fireplace. I take it you won't be removing your prisoner tonight?'

'Tonight?' Pollard echoed, as if Jemima were a certified imbecile. 'This is the most godforsaken outpost I've ever visited. So, no, we won't be dragging a man in handcuffs through the dark to a one-train station. Not till morning.'

'Then we had better ensure your comfort and that of your colleagues.' Jemima went indoors, touching Mrs Beddoe's arm as we went. 'What a to-do,' she said. 'Did you have any notion?'

'That Lord Muirhaven isn't Lord Muirhaven? I'm not sure I believe it.'

'It does add up,' Jemima said. 'He never dressed like a lord, and his manners are rustic. I suppose that was put down to him being foreign.'

'You are all foreign,' was the housekeeper's answer to that.

'On an occasion such as this, there is only one thing to do, Mrs Beddoe. Make tea,' said Jemima. 'And Welsh cakes.'

Mrs Beddoe called for Gwen and Jemima left them to it. Walking through the great hall, she saw Honor was still at the bottom of the staircase, her head bent, hands clasped around her knees. Jemima went to sit by her.

'The injury to your fingers... I thought you'd harmed yourself to add a flourish to your story of fighting off an attacker, but, of course, you had to put your fingers inside your stepmother's kettle to plant the dropwort. You scalded your fingers, which you disguised by injuring a nail so badly it bled and bled.'

Honor replied in a hoarse voice, 'My father taught me to deal with pain. He was a real man, a mariner.'

'Did you mean to do it?'

'Hurt my hand?'

'Kill your stepmother.'

'Oh. I had to.'

'Honor, please, think. You will be charged and if you say things like that, you'll be seen as a hardened criminal. I advise you to say as little as you can until a lawyer can be found.'

Honor unclasped her knees and looked directly at Jemima. Ifor was going around lighting the lamps. As the dimness lifted, Honor's face showed in all its carefully made-up blankness. There were no tears, but Jemima discerned a tightness. A clenching of the jaw. *She's not ashamed, she's angry.*

'They won't hang me,' Honor said. 'I'm too young. They don't hang girls like me.'

No, Jemima silently agreed. Had Mairwen found herself accused of an attempt to poison, she'd have had the book thrown at her. 'You will get a few years in brown overalls, followed by a second chance. Why did you do it? And don't say you had to.'

Honor gave the question due thought. 'Stepmama liked to pick up wounded birds. My father and I were that. He had no money, just a broken-down boat he took tourists about in. My dresses were patched. Stepmama fell in love with his poverty as much as with his looks.'

'You make it sound awful. Was it?'

'Not at first. Suddenly, we were living in a house with pillars at the door. And servants. And I went to a girl's day school and was walked there by a nursemaid.'

'It sounds magical.'

'The thing about being a broken bird, you get put in a cage,' Honor said bitterly. 'You get fed by hand, and if you sing nicely, the hand keeps feeding you. But if you stop singing and say you want to fly off and see the world, the cage door slams shut. My father couldn't bear it after a while, and he took his old boat out and never came back. He left me in the cage all alone. Money is lovely, but it steals a person's soul. You're better without it.'

'Just as well,' Jemima said acerbically, 'since I'm not going to be paid for my work here. And you were stupid, taking a cheque made out to me. Were you going to walk into a bank somewhere and pretend to be Mrs J. Flowerday?'

'Yes,' Honor said with a guileless stare that Jemima knew would dupe police and judiciary alike. 'It's easy being someone else.' Almost inaudibly, she added, 'When you don't know who you really are.'

'I'm offended.' Jemima was not going to have her capacity for pity abused. 'Pretending to be me wearing a jacket that looked as though it spent last winter lagging a boiler.'

'Olive never throws anything out.' The blankness shifted, and something more human took its place. 'Didn't you say she was dead?'

Jemima got up and gripped the newel post, trying to avoid the beady eye of the carved parrot head, the one that had ruined her garnet necklace. Unless she'd melted away into the night, Olive was in the courtyard and, at some point, would drink tea and eat Welsh cakes. So whose was the body on the *Miss Nettle*, burned beyond recognising?

Ifor was approaching to light the ball-lamps each side of the staircase.

Jemima asked him, 'What time today did you last see Mairwen?'

He looked at Honor, then at Jemima, and a dread seemed to strike him. He shook his head, as if by answering he would make something true.

'Ifor, please?'

'After you were with her in the dining room, she came down to the kitchen and I asked if she was going home. She said was going to the canal.'

'What time, Ifor?'

'It was a few minutes before twelve.'

A few minutes before twelve... Jemima had set off to follow Honor at a few minutes after the hour. Mairwen would have been a little way ahead of her.

Chapter Fifty-Three

In the library, Jemima had Ifor light all the green-shaded lamps while she laid a fire. She needed to ask Olive if she had seen Mairwen, who sometimes got a lift on the *Miss Nettle*, the quicker way of getting home.

Don't rush to conclusions, Jemima told herself. You don't know. Nobody yet knows. It may be all right.

Kindling, logs and coal were stacked by the hearth, and she got a tentative flame flickering. She asked Ifor to bring down extra chairs from the dining room. He looked glad to be kept busy.

After he'd left, Jemima found the book on hedgerow flowers where she'd left it, between two volumes of the Oxford English Dictionary. Honor was a killer, but not the impulsive kind. A cold-hearted planner.

'Still, if her lawyer does a decent job, the jury will be duped by the story of Miss Blue Eyes and the wicked stepmother.'

Blue eyes... Jemima fetched down *The History of the Earldom of Muirhaven* and turned pages until she reached the picture that had set her on the trail of an emerald ring.

The Hon. Leopold Woolton and Hildebrand
his son, at Clear Acres.

Jemima had spotted the ring at once, on the hand resting on the boy's shoulder, but another detail had failed to hit its mark, like a mis-thrown dart, bouncing off the board. Hearing someone come in behind her, she said, 'It should have smacked me in the face like a cold herring. But I was fixated on something else.'

The person joined her at the table. A faint smell of burned wood gave away that it was Olive.

'See here?' Jemima showed her the picture of Hildebrand Woolton with his father. 'It was taken—'

'At the farm at Oosthoek,' Olive finished. 'The Hon. Leopold Woolton. In his own way, good to me and my mother.'

Jemima looked at her. 'She was Leopold's housekeeper, it says here.'

Olive nodded. 'And more. I am Leopold's daughter, but after he died we were hounded off the farm. We went to live in Port Elizabeth, where we had no family and no money. Hildebrand, who inherited everything, didn't want to know us. For all I was his half-sister.'

'How did you survive?' Jemima asked.

'As you do. My mother took in washing and cleaned. She got me a bit of an education. I started to paint at school. When I was eighteen, I got a job on the ships. A chambermaid. That's how I know everything about Hildebrand, the real one, and the man out there who took his name.'

Pointing to the pictured boy on the pony, Jemima said, 'Whoever hand-tinted this photograph gave him blue eyes.'

'That's right. Hildebrand had very blue eyes as a boy. I didn't see him for years until he booked a passage on the ship I was working on.'

'The *Llanstephan Castle*?'

'That's it. He still had blue eyes, because eyes don't change, do they?'

'They don't,' Jemima agreed. It was here all along, the proof, for anyone who looked. No wonder Elaine had tried to discourage her from looking up the late countess's memoir. Because Cecil Thomas Cleeve, her husband, possessed light grey eyes. 'Do you know that man out there in handcuffs?'

'I know enough,' Olive said, her voice low. 'A swindler. A chancer. Worse.'

One more question, which Jemima could not hold back. 'Olive, who was on your boat? Who was killed when it burned?'

The door opened and Mrs Beddoe came in, visibly upset. 'Mrs Flowerday, you're good at working things out.'

'What is it?'

'It's Mairwen. I'm not sure now that she went home to her parents' place because Gwen says her boots are still in her room.'

'Does that matter?'

'She would never set off for the farm without them, not after rain such as we've had. The roads there are hardly roads at all. You're up to your ankles in mud most of the way.'

Jemima had a mental flash of the river path, following Honor's footprints. Only Honor's prints, she'd presumed. She turned to Olive and what she saw confirmed her fear. That she'd unknowingly followed two sets of prints, Honor's and Mairwen's.

'She was on the boat,' Jemima said to Olive. 'She was your love.'

'The other half of myself. He killed her. That man out there murdered Mairwen.'

Mrs Beddoe gave an agonised cry and slumped down on a chair. 'Why?' asked Jemima.

'It's dim in the cabin when the curtains are drawn,' Olive whispered. 'He thought she was me. He thought he was ridding himself of me.'

'Because you sent a postcard, demanding money?'

'No.' It was said with contempt. 'Because I was there at Cape Agulhas.'

A disturbance in the hall took Jemima from the library and she was in time to hear Sergeant Maddox informing Honor van Doorn that she was under arrest for murder.

Chapter Fifty-Four

Jemima established, with Sergeant Maddox's help, that the dark-haired, wiry men were CID from Mold, delayed by a flooded tunnel and forced to take a different line. They had met the English officers from Hampshire CID when their routes coincided at Chirk. Though they were pursuing different crimes, there had evidently been the sharing of information.

The detectives from Mold were investigating a sudden death at the castle. When they learned that Sergeant Maddox had just that moment arrested the deceased lady's stepdaughter for the crime, they were not best pleased.

'Without a proper investigation, formal charges are premature,' one said. 'We will carry out a full scrutiny of the crime scene – if crime it be – then interview all those present in the building, one at the time.'

'But Honor has already confessed,' said Jemima. She couldn't face an interminable night relating everything she'd discovered, only to be asked to repeat it five times and then hear herself dismissed as a meddling amateur.

Mrs Beddoe, red-eyed, poured tea and handed round the cups to those seated in the library.

'Confessed to whom?' asked the Welsh detective, adding sugar to his cup.

'To me,' Jemima told him, 'not twenty minutes ago. With the greatest respect, you have arrived somewhat late in the day.' She regained the key to Mrs van Doorn's rooms from Mrs Beddoe and presented it. 'Sergeant Maddox can take you to where the victim is temporarily lying, then conduct you to the scene of the crime. But before you go, I'm afraid there's a further murder for you to investigate.'

'We are not involved in the Cecil Cleeve matter, madam,' was the sharp response.

'That's not what I'm saying.' Jemima told them about the body on the *Miss Nettle*, with reluctance naming the suspected victim. 'Mairwen was one of staff here. She was on the boat, hoping for a ride down the canal to save her a long walk to her parents' farm.'

Olive stood apart, in the window embrasure. The true reason for Mairwen being on the *Miss Nettle* was nobody else's story. If Olive wanted to tell it, she would do so.

Sergeant Maddox procured a lantern and took one of the Welsh detectives to view the body in the icehouse. The other remained to keep watch on Honor, who showed little sign of grasping the gravity of her situation. Cecil Cleeve – Jemima was still struggling to think of him as that – sat in handcuffs between DI Pollard and his colleague, whose name was Detective Constable Rose. Elaine stood near the fire, the fingers of one hand gripping the wrist of the other. She had not spoken since Cecil's arrest, except to confirm her name when asked and that he was indeed her husband. The occasional glance she sent Jemima contained fear and malice in equal quantity.

DI Pollard spoke. 'Who is going to explain what's gone on here?'

Everyone looked to Jemima, who took a breath, only to be pre-empted by a low voice cutting in.

'There is no point you knowing what happened here, Mr Pollard, until you understand what occurred a year ago, on the southern seas of Africa.'

Olive's words and her appearance out of the shadows caused DI Pollard a moment's consternation, provoking Jemima to say, 'You must have seen a woman in trousers at least once in your life. If only the music-hall star, Vesta Tilley, on stage.' She introduced Olive. 'If you listen to her story, your time here will be considerably shorter.'

Olive surprised her by saying, 'They have already heard it. I reported the crime to DI Pollard of Southampton police a year ago, when he came aboard the RMS *Llanstephan Castle* after it docked. I gave him everything, and he and his colleagues ignored me. I even went to the police station to talk to him again and was escorted to the pavement by a woman officer.' Olive jutted her chin towards Pollard and addressed him directly. 'You were happy to think that a man had fallen overboard by accident and that was that.'

'That was *then*,' admitted Pollard, 'but new evidence has come to light and we now have reason to believe a crime may have taken place. We'd like to hear your story again.'

'One more time,' Olive sighed. 'It began a year ago.' She paused. 'A year minus a day, on the third of June 1922. A Saturday. We were on board ship and it was night in the place where two oceans meet.'

Chapter Fifty-Five

Olive held the room.

'We were on the round – Africa service, sailing from Southampton and on this occasion, going east to west. It is just what it says, a circuit of Africa on a mail ship of the Union Castle Line. We called first at the Mediterranean ports, sailed down the Suez Canal to Mombasa and Zanzibar, Beira, Durban, Port Elizabeth and Cape Town. After ten or so weeks at sea, we arrived back in Southampton. I was a chambermaid in first class.'

'On the *Llanstephan Castle*.' Pollard seemed anxious to establish that.

'Yes. On the night of June third, the dining room was buzzing with excitement as we were about to round Cape Agulhas, Africa's southernmost tip. This is where the Indian Ocean and the Atlantic Ocean meet, and travellers like to stand on deck. Champagne corks pop and there is always cheering.'

'Were the Cleeves on board at this point?' DI Pollard interrupted.

Jemima saw Elaine jerk at the sound of her surname in the plural.

'They came on at Durban,' Olive said. 'As did Hildegarde Woolton.'

'Lord Muirhaven,' Pollard clarified. 'The *true* Lord Muirhaven?'

Olive inclined her head. 'Also, as I told you when I reported the events last year, my estranged half-brother.'

'Were the van Doorns aboard at this point?' Jemima asked.

'If you mean the lady who took Mrs Cleeve under her wing, and this person,' Olive jerked a finger at Honor. 'They embarked at Cape Town, two days' sail from Cape Agulhas.'

DI Pollard invited her to go on.

'As I said, I was employed as a chambermaid.'

A servant. Honor had said as much and Jemima threw the girl a cold glance, though she might as well have thrown a feather for all the effect it had.

'I didn't have much to do with first-class passengers,' Olive continued. 'I cleaned their staterooms but they never *saw* me. The night we rounded Cape Agulhas the weather was calm, the seas a little heavy. The current races fast and feels wild if you're not used to it. The sky was black velvet and a million stars glittered. We staff eventually retired to our cabins and some friends brought champagne down, half-drunk bottles left on the promenade deck. We had a little party.

'After a while, my friends went to their cabins and I slipped out, picking up an unopened half-bottle of champagne I found in one of the guest lounges. A sacking offence, but I wanted a little celebration on my own, just me and the stars. I chose the boat deck because it's more likely to be empty at night, only the ship's watch on duty. I can still see that southern sky, Sirius the dog star, the brightest of all, and Canopus just above the horizon.'

'And a half-moon, I believe.'

Pollard turned a curious look on Jemima as Olive nodded.

'That's right, a bright, half-moon.'

I shall never forgive myself for mistaking her dust-drawing for a pub sign, Jemima told herself. 'Sorry, I interrupted.'

'I stood at the rail, between two lifeboats, the wind pulling my hair. I popped the cork of my champagne and felt free. My mother had died not so long ago and, though I was grieving, for the first time in my life I could think of my future. I was going to England, where nobody knew me, to make something of myself. My job took me to extraordinary places, but being on a ship is still like being in a big cage. I vowed to live life on my terms, and not end it like Mamma, in two rooms surrounded by unwashed shirts and unpaid bills.'

'You wanted to paint,' Jemima said.

Olive gave a one-sided smile. 'Girls from my world don't become artists. Painting classes are for white girls.' Her gaze shifted and Jemima believed that, for a few heartbeats, Honor van Doorn must have feared for her life. Olive gathered herself. 'Girls like me sell our time, we labour for a wage that goes no further than our food and clothes.'

'But you're an artist now,' Jemima pointed out. 'Something changed.'

'The world changed on the boat deck,' Olive agreed. 'I was drinking my stolen champagne, wishing on a star, when I heard footsteps coming from the second-class smoking lounge. It has a door onto the boat deck. I ducked behind a lifeboat. I couldn't afford to be seen. At first I thought it was two men – two drunk men – but then I heard a woman's voice. I realised there were three people, but one was not speaking.'

Pollard asked who she thought they were.

'Him.' Olive pointed to Cecil Cleeve. 'His wife.' She indicated Elaine. 'And my half-brother who was, I believe, semi-conscious.'

'By half-brother you mean Lord Muirhaven?'

'Correct. I heard he was on the passenger list, but didn't go looking for him. He took a small cabin – he was mean with money – and had every meal brought in to him. He didn't much like company, and he was seasick.'

'Did you know he would be joining the ship?' asked Pollard.

'Of course not, sir. I hadn't seen Brandy for years, not since he kicked me and my mother out. After his father died, he gave us a day's notice. We left nearly everything we owned behind at Oosthoek and walked to Port Elizabeth where we found a room, shared with another woman and her children. Hildebrand Woolton cut us off, though his father had promised to support my mother for her lifetime. I never forgave Brandy and, before you ask, he had no love for me.'

'But you recognised him when you saw him on the ship?'

Olive made a so-so face. 'Like I said, I heard that a Lord Muirhaven was on board. I had no idea it was my brother, because it was his uncle who'd had the title all the years I was growing up. Before that it was Brandy's grandfather. I heard this Lord Muirhaven was going to Great Britain because he'd recently become the earl. Still, I wasn't sure it was Brandy until I saw him.'

'You didn't search him out?' The way Pollard edged the question implied Olive was withholding the truth.

Jemima admired the calm rebuttal.

'I wouldn't have searched for Brandy if he was the last person on the earth. I'd been asked to take some bed linen into his section of the ship, and he was in a corridor, alone and smoking. He turned and he knew me. He said nothing, I said nothing. You want me to finish my story?'

A nod invited her to do so.

'On the boat deck, when strangers came out, I kept my head down. I heard scraping and bumping towards the stern of the ship. At first, I thought it was the davits creaking. They're the winches that secure the lifeboats. Sometimes the wind buffets the funnels and it can sound like doors slamming. But then I heard a woman's voice.'

'Saying?'

'Portside.'

'What did you make of that?'

'That I needed to stay very still because I was portside. If I was caught, I'd not only be sacked, I'd be made to pay for the champagne, at the table price. I couldn't afford it. At first I thought it was a courting couple, coming out for a kiss under the stars. I heard a man say, "Take off my jacket" and a moment after, the ship hit a trough. We plunged and I was going over. I heard the woman say, "Oh, God". Or was it, "God, oh, God" and the strangest thing... she said, "Watch".'

'As in "Watch what I'm about to do"?' Pollard asked.

'I thought so, yes. There was a sound like something sliding, like a big box or a roll of canvas. I heard gasps and grunts, and then something heavy smacking into the water below.'

'And what do you think it was?' asked Pollard.

'At the time, I didn't know, not really,' Olive said. 'When the alarm was raised, and Mrs Cleeve was screaming that her husband had left their cabin in the early hours and had anyone seen him, I did wonder. The story went, Mr Cleeve had gone upstairs to play cards with Lord Muirhaven, and drunk too much. Lord Muirhaven had gone to bed leaving Mr Cleeve to walk off the drink alone on the boat deck. It convinced everyone but me, because I knew by then I'd heard a man being thrown off the ship. And after the search was called off, and we pressed on to Cape Town, the man strolling about, calling himself Lord Muirhaven, was not my half-brother.'

'Hm.' Pollard screwed up his brow. 'You said you heard a man being thrown. As in, "a leg and a wing"?'

'"Rolled off" is more accurate. Unless you've got a gang to help, there's only one way to send someone overboard. You get the victim to the side. He might be dead, or drunk, or drugged, and you lean him against the rail and wait till the ship tilts. You raise his legs, tip him, and momentum takes him over.'

And there, Jemima thought, is the root of Elaine's horror of water.

'The woman who said, "watch", that was Mrs Cleeve?' she asked.

Olive couldn't be certain. 'I assume so. The woman had an English accent. That's all I can say for sure.'

'Why would she say "watch"?' Jemima pressed. 'It feels, I don't know, perverted.'

Olive had no idea. 'I'm reporting what I heard.'

'Sounds more than perverted to me,' muttered DC Rose. 'A murderess who does for her husband is worse than the man who does for him. In my book.'

'It wasn't her husband that Mrs Cleeve murdered,' Jemima said. *Do keep up.* 'She was conspiring *with* her husband in the killing of the real Lord Muirhaven.'

Ruthless and well prepared. Elaine had made a point of mentioning that her so-called late husband had been dependent on morphine.

'Let me get this straight,' Jemima said to Olive. 'Elaine and the man who has been calling himself Lord Muirhaven, are man and wife. She is not a widow.'

Olive stuck to her guns. 'All I know is that a man and woman murdered my half-brother late at night, out at sea. And that man there,' she meant Cecil Cleeve, 'took on my half-brother Hildebrand's identity afterwards. He moved into Brandy's cabin, wore his clothes, took his name, his passport, his papers, everything.'

Elaine covered her eyes and an emerald ring glinted in the candlelight. At the same time, Cecil Cleeve raised his hands to shake the handcuffs lower. He was a muscular man and they were tight on him.

'Wait,' cried Jemima. 'Now I understand.'

Chapter Fifty-Six

'Watch' wasn't an invitation. It was an instruction.

'Elaine was telling her husband to take the victim's watch from his wrist.' Jemima turned to Cecil Cleeve. 'You had to make the exchange as your watch had your initials on the back. Since the man you were putting overboard had to be identified as Cecil Cleeve, were he to be pulled from the water, he had to have your watch on his wrist and be wearing your clothes. You needed his signet ring too.'

DI Pollard's sergeant was extracting something from a box, but Jemima addressed the Detective Inspector. 'Cleeve is wearing a wristwatch that is too tight for him. There's nowhere local for him to take it, to have extra links fitted, so he takes it off when he's doing something energetic and puts up with it the rest of the time.'

The Detective Sergeant had now opened the box and was showing them a tarnished watch with a white face and gold bezel.

Jemima held out her hand, and the watch was placed in it. 'Where was this found?'

'On the boat deck of the RMS *Llanstephan Castle*. It had dropped between the deck and the gunwale. Found during the ship's last voyage by a crew member who was checking the lifeboats.'

'Fortuitous or cursed. Depends how you look at it.' Jemima turned the watch in her hand. The back was monogrammed; two intertwined Cs. 'Elaine Cleeve told her husband to undo Lord Muirhaven's watch and exchange it for his own. They needed to make the switch, but the ship was pitching too hard. He couldn't fasten his watch onto the victim's wrist and dropped it in the dark. He never found it.' A salty bloom obscured the face, but the hands were still visible. 'Lord Muirhaven's watch stopped at midnight twenty-three.' She looked at Olive. 'You said the murder happened on Saturday, June third. I say it was the early hours of Sunday. A year ago to the day.'

Cecil Cleeve shuffled out a laugh. 'I like an anniversary. You are astute, Mrs Flowerday, but a good lawyer will pick holes in your madness.'

Ego, Jemima thought. Card sharp, trickster, impersonator. He'll never believe he's been called to account until the noose is round his neck.

Not so Elaine. She crouched in front of her husband, clasping his knee. 'Tell them I wasn't there, Cecil.'

'Shush, my dear. No loose talk, ha? Best say no more.'

'What I don't get,' Pollard muttered, 'is how they pulled it off. It's one thing taking a man's identity once you've drowned him, but how do you convince everyone else?'

'Easy,' said Olive, without hesitation. 'Brandy was always a loner. His farm was remote, and while he had boys and men working for him, once he'd sold up I doubt they ever set eyes on him again – or the man claiming to be him. On the ship, my half-brother went straight to his cabin and never came out. I only saw him that once because he stepped out to smoke a cigarette.'

Pollard still didn't look convinced.

Jemima had left *The History of the Earldom of Muirhaven* open on the table and she drew the detective's attention to the picture of Hildebrand as a boy, and his father Leopold. 'The resemblance between Leopold and Cecil Cleeve is quite noticeable. Same build, same very dark hair. Perhaps they share a Scottish ancestry. If Hildebrand resembled his father—'

Olive confirmed that he did.

'Then, superficially, they could each pass for the other. Both men boarded the RMS *Llanstephan Castle* at Durban.' Jemima pictured the gangway: blue skies, straw hats, chatter, white decks gleaming in the sun. She said slowly, 'First class passengers embark at their leisure, sometimes hours before sailing.' She glanced at Olive, who nodded. 'The real Lord Muirhaven wouldn't necessarily have boarded with the Cleeves or be accommodated on the same side of the ship. But – what if they'd already met? Maybe in the port a day or two before. Same modest hotel. All on their way to England, chasing a fresh start.'

She waited for an objection. None came.

'The Cleeves were running short of money... or of easy victims. Perhaps Cecil had won too many poker games in Durban. Time to vanish. Lord Muirhaven was on his way to claim his birth-right.'

'Could it have started over a game of cards? Someone joked they looked alike, and that's when the idea tumbled upon Cecil Cleeve. With his wife, he spun it into a scheme. Audacious. Nobody in England or Wales had ever laid eyes on Hildebrand Woolton. As long as nobody on board knew them from Durban, or witnessed the killing, what was to stop Cecil claiming Muirhaven's name, his title, his future? They'd play it slow. Wait. Watch. Then, on embarkation day, I can just see it. Cecil in his dark glasses, clinging onto his wife's arm like a sick man. Straight to his cabin, to lie low until he could engineer a meeting with the introverted aristocrat who was his target.'

A flicker of panic crossed Elaine's face. Jemima knew she'd hit home.

She hadn't finished. 'The real Hildebrand emerged after two or three days to play cards with his "friend" and they ventured up to the smoking room on the boat deck. It was late, everyone had celebrated rounding the cape, they had the place to themselves. They played a few rounds of poker and it got convivial.'

To this point, Jemima had relied on speculation. Now she asked Elaine, 'What did you put in his drink, Mrs Cleeve?'

'Nothing,' said Elaine, with a return of cool assurance. 'I never knew the man.'

'Maybe, but you know human weakness all too well.' The Cleeves wouldn't have been rash enough to bludgeon their victim. Too messy. Too much blood. Strong drink would have rendered Lord Muirhaven semi-comatose. Too stupefied to fight back. Then it struck her.

My usual... Gin and It, Arctic cold, steady on the gin.

'You poured the drinks at the card table, didn't you, Cecil? Brought your own. Gin and bitters. Some gins reach seventy-per-cent proof, a single shot is like downing an entire bottle of champagne. Add an innocent splash of pink, drink it ice-cold, who would suspect anything? Three, four of those and your opponent's helpless. Did you win the game, Cecil?'

Cecil Cleeve seemed about to respond but clearly thought better of it. 'You should write a novel, Mrs Flowerday.'

'One day, I might publish a memoir. For a last-minute scheme, yours was clever and you were lucky. Elaine crept up from the cabin after midnight and found you playing cards with a man who could hardly sit straight on his chair. "Let's get you some air. The night breeze will do you good." That's how it was done. Afterwards, you, Cecil, went to bed in Lord Muirhaven's cabin. Come morning, Elaine raised the alarm. "My husband is missing!" I doubt anyone on board spotted the switch, except Olive. That's where your luck ran out, Cecil. On board, was the one person who knew the real Lord Muirhaven, and could spot the fake.'

Olive spoke. 'When I saw this man on the promenade deck after we left Cape Town for the west coast run, calling himself Lord Muirhaven and surrounded by admiring ladies, I knew in the blink of an eye what had been done.'

'But you said nothing,' growled Pollard.

'Because she'd have to admit to being on deck, against company rules, drinking purloined champagne,' Jemima reminded him. 'Olive had much to lose.'

'A job as a chambermaid?'

'All is relative, Detective Inspector. Would you like to lose your career in one stroke?'

'It's a crime, a witness concealing a murder.'

'Probably,' Jemima agreed. 'But Olive reported it when she reached Southampton, and you ignored her. That's incompetence.'

Pollard growled something ungentlemanly, which Jemima chose not to hear.

DC Rose, who had been studying the hand-coloured photographs in the Muirhaven book, said suddenly, 'They've got blue eyes. Father and son.' He jerked his chin at Cecil Cleeve. 'His eyes are grey. Eyes don't change.'

He gets there in the end, Jemima thought. He'll go far. To DI Pollard she said, 'I hope you feel you have been spared unnecessary investigation, Detective Inspector.'

Cecil Cleeve shouted, 'Nobody can prove any of this.' He jabbed a finger at Olive. 'Who's going to believe a woman who lives on a boat and daubs incomprehensible paintings? A boat she set fire to through wilful stupidity.'

Mrs Beddoe had sat listening all this time, with a revulsion she'd taken no pains to hide. She said, 'You might get away with your crime, my man, but what about Mairwen?'

What about Mairwen indeed. That wasn't going to be brushed off as misadventure, Jemima vowed as she slipped out of the library. One more trip upstairs, she promised herself, one last revelation.

Chapter Fifty-Seven

In the dining room, Jemima retrieved Honor's suitcase, which she'd earlier slid beneath the sideboard. She also took out the wrench wrapped in her stocking.

Returning to the library, she found that in her absence Sergeant Maddox and the detective from Mold had concluded their inspection of Mrs van Doorn's body and her rooms. A conversation was taking place in Welsh, which Mrs Beddoe translated for Jemima.

'They're deciding whether Mrs van Doorn can be removed tomorrow morning, and if she can go by train to the mortuary at Mold.'

'They'll need to find a sturdy cart to get the body to the station.'

'Beddoe will do so at first light,' the housekeeper said.

Only Mrs Beddoe saw Jemima place the suitcase on the table, and a cotton stocking, which clunked oddly when she laid it down. When she loudly cleared her throat, however, the talking stopped. She spoke in a carrying voice, so nobody could say later that they hadn't heard.

'Mairwen's death requires your attention,' she informed the Welsh police officers, 'and you will want to go to it once I show you this.' She took out the scissors she always carried in her handbag and cut the stocking lengthways, revealing the murder weapon.

All five policemen crowded round the table and perceiving the blood on the implement's head, their interest sharpened.

Jemima forestalled the obvious question. 'It's a wrench,' she said.

'It's a windlass,' Olive corrected. 'For opening lock gates. It's the one I keep – kept – in the cabin of my boat.'

'A windlass,' Jemima acknowledged. She drew attention to the dark strands of hair stuck to the bent end. 'I assumed they were Olive's, but clearly they cannot be. Nobody realised Mairwen went to the canal to see her friend.'

'I wasn't there when she arrived, I was out for a walk.' Olive had so far hidden her grief, but now it poured out. 'My head was full, I was so angry.'

'And afraid?' Jemima prompted.

'No.' Olive seemed puzzled by the question. 'Should I have been?'

'Yes, of Cecil Cleeve. You sent him a postcard. A diagram. That line: *"The Captain shouts, 'Turn the ship around!'"* You were baiting him, letting him know you knew. Demanding money. Didn't it occur to you that eventually, he'd strike back?'

'Nothing was ever found of my half-brother,' Olive said. 'The current sweeps a body away in minutes, and the sharks – always hungry. Only the moon and stars saw it all.'

'You saw enough to make you dangerous. Coming to live in this part of Wales, on the canal so close. Why? In itself it's a provocation. But I think you wanted the Cleeves to see you. A cryptic message or two, a ghostly presence at nightfall, runes scrawled in the dust.'

Maybe, said the set of Olive's jaw.

'You sent a postcard on Friday which should have arrived on Monday morning. By then, you, your boat and Honor van Doorn would be safely away, down the canal. Fate had other plans. The post-girl made an unscheduled trip, bringing the postcard early. For Cleeve, it was too much. He had no more money. Nowhere to run. The police would soon be humming like bees around Castle Gloaming. You played your hand too soon and, sadly for Mairwen, his temper fractured.'

'You're saying it was my fault Mairwen died?' Olive faltered.

'Not your fault, but you were part of the cause. You were blackmailing Cleeve over his murder of Hildebrand Woolton, and he was paying because he thought he had no choice.'

Jemima addressed the detectives, who were listening intently, though none were taking notes. 'Miss Nettle will explain her motives for choosing her mode of life but having reported the murder in Southampton at the end of her round-Africa voyage and being ignored, she can be forgiven for setting off in pursuit of justice on her own terms.'

Olive spoke as if remembering a bad dream. 'I couldn't face another circle of the clock face. Sleeping in a tiny cabin, mopping floors, changing beds for tips and being called "girl" though I'm past forty. I jumped ship.'

'What else could you do but follow Cleeve to his castle and extract what you could?' Jemima again addressed the officers. 'Olive acquired a boat, fuel, art materials and a dear friend in the person of Mairwen, a maid here at Castle Gloaming.'

'We loved each other,' Olive said, holding her ground despite the murmurs. 'And this lady hasn't told you that I sell my work. I'm not reliant on anyone.'

'You are good,' agreed Jemima, 'but dazzling as your talent is, your work is unlikely to find favour with tourists, tea-shop galleries or the general population. You need extra.'

'I sell to a dealer, with contacts in London.'

'And he pays you handsomely?'

Olive gave her one-sided laugh. 'Let's say he pays me.'

'My point is made. Since coming to Britain, Cleeve has been your last resort. You have no steady job, nor citizenship.'

'I've a right to be in this land,' Olive burst out. 'My father was the Honourable Leopold Woolton. Why are you interrogating me, and not him?' She levelled a finger at Cecil Cleeve. 'And her too.' She swung her anger at Elaine.

'I'm saving the detectives the trouble,' Jemima answered. 'Your life story will come out, Olive. Truth is the surest armour, and I say that not from a moral perspective, but as a constant and avid reader of *The Weekend Sleuth*. Lies are a trap.'

At the mention of Jemima's favourite reading matter, DI Pollard sneered.

'I recommended it,' Jemima hit back, 'if only for the advertisements at the back, for deerstalker hats. Where was I... yes, Olive sent a postcard to Cecil Cleeve, a nudge for more money. Cleeve reckoned he had paid his dues and what she was asking was impossible.'

'I needed fuel,' Olive said bleakly. 'I'd run out.'

'Your boat was stacked with dry wood,' Jemima pointed out.

'Oil for my lamps. I can't paint in the dark. I can't cook on a steam boiler. I needed domestic oil, and it's expensive. Life's hard on the water.'

'When your postcard arrived a day early, Cleeve decided to put a stop to the demands once and for all. You were taking a walk, your boat should have been empty, but it was not.'

Olive lowered her head. 'We'd planned, Mairwen and I, that when this was all over, we'd live together on the boat. On the Shropshire Union where nobody knew us. She wasn't meant to come today.'

Jemima pointed to the windlass. 'Cleeve found Mairwen in the cabin and guessed she knew of his past. He hadn't expected the confrontation but even so, he had to kill her.'

'I didn't.' Cleeve tried to get to his feet, but was pushed back down. 'That's not how it was.'

'You were there,' Jemima said. 'I saw you come to the canal and followed you on board the *Miss Nettle*. I heard you telling someone you'd been "covering up long enough, letting her come and go". I assumed you were threatening Honor but it was Mairwen who couldn't have the life she craved. "The world won't allow it," you said.'

'It's true,' Cleeve said. 'Two women? It's not natural.'

'I live with my sister Vicky. Nobody questions us.'

'That's different.'

'Not really. It's all a matter of interpretation. The point is, Mr Cleeve, you had shown your true colours coming to the boat, and Mairwen could not be allowed to leave.'

'I was going to talk to her – to Olive. That's all.'

'Talk to a person you had already insisted didn't exist? *Garn* with you, Mr Cleeve. Having mercilessly struck your victim, you conducted a one-sided conversation with her, then set the cabin alight. You got out, leaving her.'

Mrs Beddoe moaned. 'Don't tell me you left her to burn, you devil!' She beat her fists together. 'I hope you burn too, in Hell.'

'She was already—' Cleeve caught himself. This time too late.

'Dead,' Jemima finished. 'I overheard you talking to a body, Cecil. A deplorable habit, but not a murderous one. Mairwen was killed about ten minutes before I reached the canal, twenty minutes before you did. Someone got there first.'

'Who, Mrs Flowerday?' This was Sergeant Maddox, and he, Jemima realised, had been writing in his notebook all along.

She spoke slowly so he could write down what she said. 'I believed I'd followed a single set of footprints along the river's edge. Smallish feet, definitely a woman's. Only today did I realise I'd been following two sets.' Jemima went to stand in front of Honor van Doorn. 'The first set was yours.'

Honor shook her head, but she did not meet Jemima's eye.

'There was mud on your shoes when Sergeant Maddox brought you back from Chirk earlier. You took the river path to the canal and went to the boat. Not to get on board, but because you'd decided to make your own way to London, by train. You no longer needed Olive's help, but you did need something from her boat.'

Jemima opened the suitcase she'd placed on the table and took a quantity of paintings and drawings from it, arranging them on the congested table. 'Gentlemen, come and enjoy an art exhibition.'

After some grumbling, once again the men crowded round.

'Not my kind of thing,' said a Welsh voice. 'I like a landscape, where you can see what things are.'

'Art is subjective,' Jemima commented. 'Look at the signature on the drawings.'

'HON.' Sergeant Maddox sounded the 'H'. 'Honor van Doorn's work?'

'That's the idea,' Jemima said.

'They're mine.' Olive pushed to the table. 'It's my work.'

Jemima had never doubted it. 'You tried to teach her, to lift her mind above the trite and prosaic, but nobody could as, the truth is, you cannot teach talent. For all Honor van Doorn's passion to set the art world alight, she hasn't got what it takes.'

'But she got into art school,' Elaine Cleeve said in a ferocious voice. 'They offered her a place on the spot, which they never do ordinarily. You said so.'

'They offered her a place based on the work she showed them – this woman's work.' Jemima touched Olive on the arm. 'Did you agree to that?'

Olive admitted that she had, at first. 'I was paid to build a portfolio for her, and coach her into saying the right things at the interview. No more than that.'

'How was it going to work once she stood at an easel in the company of other students – and daubed primroses?'

313

Olive shook her head, and Jemima took from the gesture that, by that time, Olive had planned to be on the Shropshire Union Canal with Mairwen and didn't care.

'I didn't know she'd stolen these.' Olive picked up one of the paintings. 'They're my work in progress. My income for this summer.'

'Stealing is what Honor does,' Jemima said. 'She needed a body of work to get started at the Slade. You sign your paintings "O", "N", one letter on top of the other. Honor, who used to sign hers "H. van D." realised she could simply add the letter "H". What she didn't plan was for poor Mairwen to interrupt her bundling them into her suitcase.'

Olive's eyes filled with tears. 'Mairwen interrupted Honor taking my work.'

'I suspect Honor was amidships, doctoring your pictures, and Mairwen stumbled on her. We imagine Honor to be guileless because she looks it. She'll have talked Mairwen into joining her in the cabin. "A cup of tea, let's be friends." Something like that. At some point – well, Honor,' Jemima invited the girl, 'you tell us.'

Honor shook her head. No comment.

'Fortunately, for justice, there'll be fingerprints on the windlass, unless you thought to wear gloves?' The dismay that crossed Honor's face told Jemima everything. 'Honor van Doorn is ruthless. She clears her path of anything that gets in her way, people included. What she lacks is an understanding of how the world really works.' Jemima held Honor's eyes, ignoring the glimmer of unshed tears.

'You killed Mairwen, left her for Olive to find, and changed clothes. You crossed the aqueduct to Trevor, a stolen cheque in your pocket. If I'd had the courage to keep going along the aqueduct, I'd have found you at the railway station, dreaming of your new life. You are still taking notes, Sergeant Maddox?'

'I am, madam.'

'There it is, gentlemen. Mr Cleeve did not kill Mairwen, but he did set fire to the boat, thereby depriving her loved ones of a last goodbye. Cornelia van Doorn was poisoned with the root of hemlock water-dropwort, inserted at the base of a tea kettle. The killing of Mairwen... I don't know her surname...' Chambermaids were only ever known by their given names. Jemima turned to Mrs Beddoe.

'Williams. Mairwen Williams,' said Mrs Beddoe. 'And I knew who she loved.'

'Mairwen Williams was clubbed with a windlass and left to burn,' Jemima said flatly to the detectives. 'I came here to make clothes and almost forfeited my life. Saved only by this woman,' she indicated Olive, 'who flew like an angel on silent wings and made me drink a potion. All I want now is a night's sleep and to go home.'

With a single nod that said everything else, Jemima walked out of the library.

Chapter Fifty-Eight

Monday, 4 June

The following morning, a farm cart took Mrs van Doorn's body to the railway station to begin its journey, under escort, for a delayed autopsy. Honor van Doorn and the Cleeves, husband and wife, were taken separately to Chirk police station, there to await formal charges.

Breakfast at Castle Gloaming was eaten in the kitchen. Jemima and Olive sat at the table, Mrs Beddoe stood at the range. Ifor and Gwen had gone in the pony cart to deliver Jemima's suitcases to the railway station. Mr Beddoe had ridden with the farm cart, to help lift Mrs van Doorn's body at the station.

Jemima was astonished to find she had an appetite, but perhaps tying up loose ends stimulated the system. Going to Mrs Beddoe, who was turning rashers in a pan, she asked about the poppet. Mairwen's charm, now a memory of ashes.

'What was its purpose? Mairwen said it was "for love, not hate". Love of whom? Not the man calling himself Lord Muirhaven, though it resembled him. Nor Ifor.'

'No. Ifor's for Gwen,' said Mrs Beddoe.

Olive, who had been listening, said, 'Mairwen had us make the poppet together. Of course it wasn't a love token. It was to bind the spirit of the man in the gatehouse. To keep him here, away from us and our boat.'

'I see,' said Jemima, conscious that there was a large gap in her education. 'Then Mairwen knew that the man passing himself off as Lord Muirhaven was Cecil Cleeve. You would have confided as much.'

'Of course she knew,' Olive said. 'Mairwen could keep a secret better than anyone I've ever met. *Our* secret.'

'The pair of you bound him,' Mrs Beddoe said, turfing bacon out onto an oval plate and dropping mushrooms into the sizzling fat. 'Putting that godless thing in the chimney breast, you kept Cleeve and his wife here. They'd have given up and gone without that.'

'That wasn't the intent,' Olive insisted.

'No, but those things are more powerful than you know.'

'You burned the poppet, Mrs Beddoe,' Jemima pointed out. 'And no time afterwards, Cleeve was aboard the *Miss Nettle*.'

'May I be forgiven. I thought it was for the best.'

'Be at peace,' sighed Olive. 'You are not to blame.' She had slept in Mairwen's room and looked bruised around the eyes.

Jemima, coming downstairs shortly after dawn, had found her in the kitchen, pounding something with a pestle and mortar. She'd chosen not to ask what, but now she said, 'You will be careful?'

Breakfast was ready, yesterday's bread revived to freshness in the oven. Before sitting down again, Jemima took the gloves Honor had used to protect her hands against deadly poison. She had wrapped them in newspaper with utmost care and now cast them into the firebox of the range. They caught light at once.

'My children gave them to me at Christmas.'

Mrs Beddoe offered advice. 'Buy another pair the same and tell nobody.'

'I'll have to ask my sister where they were bought,' Jemima said, 'but I'll tell her I left them on the train.' Some stories were too unsettling to pass on.

'I think I'll walk to Trevor,' she decided out loud as coffee was poured. She'd intended to wait for Ifor to return with the trap, but the sun was shining, a sparkling day in prospect. 'It's a long trip to London so I ought to stretch my limbs before I start.'

Olive offered to walk with her.

At just past nine that morning, they set out. Jemima wore her coat, which she'd sat up late to mend, her cloche hat and town shoes. All she carried was her handbag containing her purse and journal, and the edition of *The Weekend Sleuth* that Mrs van Doorn had found on the Wrexham train, folded small.

As the castle gate clashed behind them, Olive suggested they take the drier route across the bridge, but Jemima said she'd like to walk once more by the river and see the aqueduct.

'We'll have to go across it,' Olive reminded her. 'I thought it scared you.'

'I'm terrified,' Jemima admitted. 'That's why I need to do it.'

With Olive walking between her and the rail, Jemima got halfway along with no more than a mild shudder. But when her companion stopped to tie a boot lace, Jemima felt the familiar sensation rising up her legs, settling in her belly.

'I think I'm going to pass out.'

'You can't.' Olive straightened up. 'I won't carry you.' A boat was approaching, the horse pulling it only fifty feet away. In half a minute, Jemima would either have to press herself against the rail or become an unpassable obstacle.

'Think about it,' Olive continued. 'How many tens of thousands of times have narrowboats crossed this channel? How many tens of thousands of horses have walked it? Nobody has yet fallen over the edge.' She offered her hand. 'Face your fear.'

Eyes firmly shut and one hand on the crown of her hat, Jemima allowed Olive to manoeuvre her to the rail. She felt it pressing her breastbone. She heard the rhythmic clop of hooves and the breath of the horse, smelled its warm flanks and the odour of churned-up water as the boat passed by.

She opened her eyes. 'I think I'm all right if I don't look down.'

'Then don't.'

She stared over the trees where Castell Glan yr Afon shimmered as if newly varnished. She remembered the moment she'd thought Honor had plunged to the ground, and how she had gone back to fetch her hat, carrying a lantern with her.

'Was it lamplight that brought you to the castle when I was so ill?' she asked.

At first, Olive denied it, but Jemima needed to know. 'You saw a lantern flashing, and thought Honor was signalling.'

Finally, Olive admitted it. 'I assumed she was running away again, a change of plan, but she didn't come.'

'You were the stranger who came to the castle, and you found me.'

Olive nodded. 'I found Mrs van Doorn first, but it was too late. I went to look for Honor and accidentally walked into your room. You were writhing on the bathroom floor. I guessed what it was, because you'd been so curious about that bucket of dropwort. Calling it by the wrong name.'

'Fool's parsley.'

'I thought you might have taken some—' Olive gave herself a shake. Sending a vile memory on its way.

'You had no idea that Honor had smuggled a root of it from your boat?'

'I'd have got it off her if I had! I made you drink an emetic.' Olive took a stoppered bottle from her jacket. 'Mustard and ransom root in oil, which I mixed in a tooth mug with some of your soap.'

'It tasted hideous, but afterwards I thought I'd done it to myself and dreamed you. You saved my life, Olive.'

'They called me "Nettle" here when I first arrived.'

'Because they couldn't pronounce your name.'

'That, and because I was sharp and used words to sting. But I had so much to hide.'

Jemima looked again at Castle Gloaming. Castell Glan yr Afon, set above the reach of the river. 'Who will get that place now, I wonder?'

'I expect they'll follow the Muirhaven lineage,' Olive said, 'and find an heir or heiress.' She gave her odd-cornered smile. 'Or I might get it.'

'You?'

'Why not? My father was Leopold Woolton and, in his will, he left instructions that should he die childless, the property not entailed to the earldom should come to my mother.'

Jemima blew out a breath. 'You'll need a good lawyer.'

'I can do better than that. I put another poppet in the fireplace. This one is my likeness, filled with sage, bay and hawthorn to bind me to the place.'

'Mrs Beddoe won't approve. And would you want to live there, all that space, all those rooms?'

'I'm staying for a while, anyway. Mrs Beddoe will find work for me for the time being and I like to lay my head where Mairwen's lay. We Chirk painters need a new headquarters. Our gallery is falling down. The Chirk School will do very well here.'

At the station, Jemima claimed her luggage. On the platform, she gave Olive one of her Fleur du Jour business cards.

Olive read it and smiled. 'Fleur du Jour, Flowerday. Very clever.'

'You speak French?'

'I worked on a ship. I speak five languages and understand more. Good luck, Jemima.'

'And you. If you come to London, look me up and I'll make you a new suit of clothes.'

'That's a deal.'

They hugged, after which Jemima consulted the station clock. She fancied she could hear the tracks singing. Steam rose like a giant ice-cream cornet above the trees. Her train was coming. A man in uniform blew a whistle. Jemima turned to say another goodbye, but Olive Nettle had gone.

Minutes later, Jemima Flowerday was sitting alone in a compartment, her luggage stowed above her head. After taking off her coat, she turned to the window and watched the countryside move past. She then took out her journal, turned to a clean page and wrote a heading:

Notes on a murder

I arrived at Castle Gloaming on the last morning of May, thinking I was to be designing new clothes for two socially aspirant ladies. I soon discovered I'd been hired to bring home a vulnerable runaway. My heart was touched and I agreed.

That was the first of many mistakes.

Acknowledgements

Thank you to my editor at No Exit Press, Carolyn Mays, and to my agent, Sophie Gorell Barnes, whose support and input make these books a pleasure to write.

About the Author

Kay Blythe, who also writes as Natalie Meg Evans, is an award-winning historical author on both sides of the Atlantic, having reached the New York Times top 100 list with her debut novel, *The Dress Thief.* Writing crime as Kay Blythe fulfils a long-held ambition. Her dressmaker-sleuth, Jemima Flowerday, follows in the tradition of clever women set free by the social upheaval of the years after the First World War. Jemima combines her skills as a dressmaker and sleuth to solve crime in the crumbling stately homes of Britain.

NO EXIT PRESS

More than just the usual suspects

— CWA DAGGER —
AWARDED BEST CRIME &
MYSTERY PUBLISHER

'A very smart, independent publisher delivering the finest literary crime fiction' *Big Issue*

MEET NO EXIT PRESS, an award-winning crime imprint bringing you the best in crime and suspense fiction. From classic detective novels, to page-turning spy thrillers and literary writing that grabs the attention. Our books are carefully crafted by some of the world's finest writers and delivered to you by a small, but passionate, team.

In over 30 years of business, we have published award-winning fiction and non-fiction including the work of a Pulitzer Prize winner, the British Crime Book of the Year, numerous CWA Dagger Awards, a British million-copy bestselling author, the winner of the Canadian Governor General's Award for Fiction and the Scotiabank Giller Prize, to name but a few. We are the home of many crime and noir legends from the USA whose work includes iconic film adaptations and TV sensations. We pride ourselves in uncovering the most exciting new or undiscovered talents. New and not so new – you know who you are!

We are a proactive team committed to delivering the very best, both for our authors and our readers.

Want to join the conversation and find out more about what we do?

Catch us on social media or sign up to our newsletter for all the latest news from No Exit Press.

f fb.me/noexitpress   X @noexitpress

noexit.co.uk